Did you enjoy yourself today?"

"Yes," she said slowly. "I guess so. No one made any ugly remarks within my hearing. But it's hard. Women I've known all my life won't look at me, won't acknowledge me. I suppose in time things will get better."

Jess put down his book and startled her by curling around her body. The shock was abrupt. Stiffening, Annie stared at the wall next to the bed, unable to breathe and unsure how to respond. . . . His hard callused hand slipped around her waist and stroked her with a long sensuous touch.

An explosion of conflicting emotions scattered her thoughts. She wanted to shove his hand back and roll away from him. But the solid strength of his body wrapped around her felt protective and so good, so comforting. His breath on her cheek made her wonder crazily what it would be like if he ever kissed her on the mouth, really kissed her. And his hand on her waist seemed the most intimate moment she had ever experienced. It would be so easy to turn and face him. And then what would happen?

By Maggie Osborne

PRAIRIE MOON
THE BRIDE OF WILLOW CREEK
I DO, I DO, I DO
SILVER LINING
SHOTGUN WEDDING

SHOTGUN WEDDING

MAGGIE OSBORNE

IVY BOOKS • NEW YORK

An Ivy Book
Published by The Random House Publishing Group
Copyright © 2003 by Maggie Osborne

All rights reserved under International and Pan-American Copyright Conventions. Published in the United States by The Random House Publishing Group, a division of Random House, Inc., New York, and simultaneously in Canada by Random House of Canada Limited, Toronto.

Ivy Books and colophon are trademarks of Random House, Inc.

Shotgun Wedding is a work of fiction. Names, places, and incidents are either a product of the author's imagination or are used fictitiously.

www.ballantinebooks.com

Library of Congress Catalog Card Number: 2003094377

ISBN 0-8041-1991-0

Manufactured in the United States of America

First Edition: November 2003

OPM   10   9   8   7   6   5   4   3   2   1

To Meg Ruley
With love and gratitude

CHAPTER 1

~~~~~~~~~~~~~~

M ARRY me."

"Before I'd marry an outlaw, I'd throw myself in front of a runaway team and leave instructions that my remains be fed to the chickens."

Ordinarily Annie Malloy would have smiled as she recalled the teasing marry-me exchange between herself and Bodie Miller. But not today.

Today, the worst disaster that could happen to an unmarried woman had happened to her. She was pregnant. A cold shock of fear skittered down her spine and she gripped the windowsill to steady herself.

Pregnant. The word reverberated in her mind like an executioner's sentence.

At first she had desperately denied the possibility. Such a nightmare simply could not happen; she and Bodie had been careful. There had to be an innocent reason why the curse had not come at the expected time. But a tiny voice of reality whispered that she was indulging in wishful thinking since she was regular enough to set her calendar by the onset of her menses.

At the start of the third week, disbelief had given way to an urgent bargaining session with God. *Let this be a mistake and I'll never go to bed with a man again. If*

I'm not pregnant, I'll never again do anything wrong for the rest of my life; I promise. Please, God, help me now and I'll never ask for another thing.

But apparently God was not in a bargaining mood. After weeks of fervent prayer, Annie was still pregnant. In fact, she had progressed from a few days pregnant to five weeks pregnant.

Turning from her bedroom window, she pushed the heels of her palms against her eyes, pressing back tears before she glanced at the little clock on the mantelpiece. She had wasted twenty minutes frozen in worry and now she would have to rush.

Avoiding any thought about what would eventually happen to her waistline, she peered into the mirror above her vanity and wished she had used these twenty minutes to do something with her hair. Long ago Annie had decided that Medusa must have had hair like hers, unruly red curls with a life of their own and determined to slither free of pins and combs. If she were truly the New Modern Woman that she strove so mightily to be, she would simply accept her rebellious hair as part of her whole and sail forth unperturbed that she always seemed to look as if she'd been interrupted in the midst of arranging her coiffure. But Annie didn't possess that degree of confidence and self-assurance. Especially not now.

Pregnant. The shock and horror of applying the word to herself stopped her heart in her chest. When she could breathe again, she reminded herself that she was a New Modern Woman. And if she had to—oh God, please don't let it happen, please, please, please— she could do as others had done and manage alone. But please don't let that happen.

Throughout the last week she had scanned all her back issues of the *Modern Woman's Manifesto*, rereading every article about bearing children out of wedlock. When she'd first read the articles, she remembered feeling enormous admiration for the women. A New Modern Woman did not need a husband. She could raise a child herself and happily. The New Modern Woman felt no shame about her sexuality or about bearing children with or without a Mrs. in front of her name. She walked proudly in the world wrapped in a cloak of independence and self-reliance.

But the pregnant New Modern Woman lived in a big city in the East, Annie had finally noticed. None of the articles about unwed mothers were penned by a New Modern Woman living in a town as small and provincial as Marshall, Kansas.

"Will you be late tonight, dear?" her mother inquired as Annie came down the staircase and headed toward the foyer mirror to adjust her hat.

The day had been warm for mid-March, so despite the evening chill she had chosen a spring hat to improve her mood, as if anything could. Leaning to the glass, she inspected the circles under her eyes. "The *Manifesto* came today. There'll be a lot to discuss. I'll probably be late."

Ellen Malloy glanced over her shoulder, then leaned to her daughter's ear. "Stop by the parlor and tell your father good night."

"You know he doesn't approve of the New Modern Woman's Association." She bit her lip. Lately everything seemed to irritate and provoke a sharp response. "But I'll say good night," she added in a softer tone.

"He doesn't forbid you from going."

The statement made Annie smile. From the time she had first curled her hand around Harry Malloy's finger, she'd been her father's Buttercup. If he had ever denied her anything, she didn't remember what it might have been. "Mother, I'm twenty-five years old."

"And far too independent, if you ask me," Ellen said tartly. "But your father sets the rules."

"Which is fortunate for me," Annie said, winking at her mother in the mirror. Annie knew women her age who enjoyed no more freedoms than they had been permitted as adolescents. She, on the other hand, had a small allowance and the independence to spend it as she wished. She came and went as she pleased, a privilege she had used to deceive her parents. Her smile vanished.

Her mother brushed a speck of lint off of Annie's shoulder. "I ran into Sheriff Jesse Harden down by the stables this morning. He asked to be remembered to you."

"That's nice," she said, her mother's comment not registering. Her parents would be devastated when they learned what she had done. Hurting them was the worst of it, the part she dreaded most.

"With a little encouragement . . ."

That remark caught her attention. As little as a month ago, she would have answered with a rousing response, listing the reasons that she had chosen never to marry. Tonight she didn't have the energy. And everything had changed. Shaking her head, she turned her steps toward the parlor.

"Papa?" Pausing in the doorway, she reached deep and summoned a smile. "I'm going to my meeting. I won't be home until late." The words stuck in her throat. She wasn't lying, not exactly, but she wasn't telling the whole truth, either.

Annie always knew when they made butter at the creamery because the good creamy scent clung to her father like perfume. She inhaled the buttery fragrance when she bent over his chair to kiss the thinning spot on top of his head.

Harry Malloy lowered his newspaper and raised an eyebrow in an expression that was partly a tease, partly disapproval. "Is it your book club tonight or the New Modern Woman's meeting?"

Her father had become a bit portly over the years as befit a prosperous business owner and a man who was considering a run for mayor. Annie thought the weight added substance and dignity.

"The New Modern Woman's meeting. This week we're going to discuss addressing our parents by their given names." For a moment she was not pregnant; her world was not shattered. For one instant all was as it always had been. She and her papa, bantering back and forth.

He frowned. "Not in this house, Buttercup. You can be as modern as you like as long as your newfangled ideas don't inconvenience or annoy anyone. So, we'll stay with 'Mother' and 'Papa'."

She had to trust that Bodie would make everything right. Of course he would. He had to. She'd die if her actions brought shame on her parents. She'd just die.

"Then I guess I won't have much to say at this meeting," she said, holding her smile steady.

When she glanced back from the doorway, her father was watching with pride, admiring her spring hat and tiered winter cape, noting the length of her blue serge walking skirt and the gleam of polish on her boots. Usually it amused her to know that he would already have examined her for hints of lip rouge and cheeks brighter than nature provided. No daughter of his, no matter how modern she might think herself, would ever leave Harry Malloy's house wearing paint. As far as Annie knew, her father didn't suspect that she occasionally added rouge after she left the house.

Her mother was waiting in the foyer. A mother's examination was more thorough and of a different kind than a father's.

"Are you feeling well?" Frowning, her mother peered into Annie's eyes, then tucked an errant tendril behind her ear. "You look tired and pale. I've heard you moving around when you should be sleeping."

"I've been a little crampy lately," Annie admitted carefully, pulling on her gloves. And headachy and worried sick.

"Cook says you hardly touch your breakfast anymore."

Annie pressed her mother's hands, then edged toward the door. "Don't worry; I'm fine." *Please, God, let it be true. Please give me a happy ending.*

Once outside, she turned at the end of the stepping-stones and looked back at the house, the second largest on the block. Ellen smiled through the glass window on the front door and Annie waved, regretting her mother's concern.

Something would have to be decided tonight, she told herself, feeling a nervous tightening in her stomach. But first, she had to attend the New Modern Woman's meeting.

The others were gathered and waiting by the time she arrived at the back entrance to Morrison's Apothecary.

"We wondered if you were coming," Helen Morrison said, looking up from the meeting table. Helen claimed the chair at the head of the table since it was her father who allowed them to use his back room for their meetings.

"I apologize for being late." Annie slid into her usual chair.

"Janie and I just got here ourselves," Ida Mae Blue said.

Janie Henderson gave them a sweeping glance. "Frankly, we might as well dispense with tonight's topic. We all know that none of our parents will permit us to call them by their given names. No amount of discussion is going to change that."

"I agree," Ida Mae said with a sigh.

Apparently they all had a touch of spring fever. None of the women had been able to resist wearing a lightweight cape or mesh gloves or a light-colored purse. A longing for spring was not all they shared in common.

Although they never spoke the word aloud, they were all spinsters beyond the age of twenty. Each lived with her parents. And each preferred to think of herself as modern and independent rather than passed over or on the shelf.

Annie also suspected they all had secrets, just as she did. Like her, the others didn't always turn toward home when they left Morrison's meeting room.

"Where do you go after these meetings?" Immediately she was horrified by the blurted question. "I don't always go straight home," she explained reluctantly, feeling a wave of heat color her cheeks. "I assume you don't, either."

An uncomfortable silence opened and Annie became aware of the strong odor of chemicals emanating from the boxes on the shelves along the storeroom walls. Ordinarily, she was interested enough in the evening's topic that she didn't notice the odors. Given a choice, she decided she would rather have a father who smelled like fresh butter than like medications.

"If you must know, every now and then I visit . . . someone." Ida Mae pulled her gloves through her hands.

Relief dropped Annie's shoulders. "Thank heaven," she whispered. "I've felt so guilty and upset about using these meetings to cover up seeing . . ." She paused. "Someone."

Janie looked around the table. "Well . . . I meet Miss Grogan at the schoolhouse after our meeting. She's teaching me to speak French." Her face turned red and her chin came up. "I don't care what anyone says; someday I'm going to go to Paris, France."

"I visit my grandmother," Ida Mae admitted. "My mother would skin me alive if she knew. She hasn't spoken to Nana Blue in three years. That's her choice and that's fine, but I don't think it's right to forbid me to see my grandmother."

"I don't believe what I'm hearing." Helen Morrison stared. "I wouldn't dream of using our meetings to deceive my parents." She focused on Annie. "Who do you see? A man?"

Annie's heart sank. "Why would you guess that?"

"You don't have any grandparents, and you've never expressed a desire to learn a foreign language."

The true New Modern Woman would feel no qualms about admitting to seeing a man of her choosing. The New Modern Woman went her way without apology. For an instant Annie was tempted to tell them about Bodie Miller. She'd wanted to talk about him for so long. But it wasn't just that she was seeing a man; it was who that man was. And if she talked to anyone, it shouldn't be Helen Morrison, who wasn't known for keeping secrets. From the looks on Janie's and Ida Mae's faces, they had also remembered Helen's fondness for gossip.

Janie gave Annie a long look, then leaned forward and changed the subject. "If we're not going to discuss how we address our parents, I think we should talk about ways to make extra money. I only have eight dollars saved toward a trip to Paris. At this rate, I'll never get there."

Ida Mae tapped her fingernails on the tabletop. "And we should discuss setting up a New Modern Woman's table at the Summer Crafts Fair again this year. It's not too soon to think about it."

From where she sat, Annie could see the storeroom clock. Bodie would be waiting for her at the old Miller homestead a quarter mile east of town. Most people assumed the cabin was vacant, and much of the time it was. Sometimes Bodie stayed a few days; sometimes he stayed a few weeks. It occurred to her now to wonder if someone in town kept the place clean and provisioned for him. She'd never thought to ask.

Tapping her foot under the table, twisting her gloves in her lap, she listened to the others discuss selling embroidery work, raising chickens, or forming a scribe service. Listened to plans for the Summer Crafts Fair. All she could think was: The minutes are flowing by and I'm getting more pregnant with every tick of the clock. I need to get out of here. I need to see Bodie; I need to feel his arms around me, need to hear him say the right words.

Finally, the meeting concluded and the women stood, pulling on gloves and buttoning cloaks. Thank heaven.

Helen gave them a stern glance. "I shall have to ponder your deceits and decide if you have made an accomplice of me by using my father's storeroom to cover your deceptions. I will inform you of how I choose to proceed."

Janie and Ida Mae gave Annie dark looks before they waved good-bye. Helen waited on the storeroom steps to see which direction Annie took. "Shall I walk you home?" she asked sweetly.

"I wouldn't think of inconveniencing you," Annie said firmly. Angry, she headed toward home, turned a corner, then looked back to see if Helen was bold enough to follow. That would have been a disaster. She had to see Bodie tonight.

In fact, no one observing her would think her direction odd, as she walked as far as the old Miller homestead several times a week. She did this partly to diffuse curiosity but mostly to check the tin box hidden in the willows where she and Bodie left messages for each other.

When she felt safe, she pressed her lips together and walked briskly toward the edge of town, her nervousness increasing with every step.

How would she tell him? What would he say? She wet her lips as she left town behind and followed a rutted lane that wound down an embankment and out of sight through a copse of willows and old cottonwoods. In summer, leaves and brush hid the cabin from the county road. Even now the low cabin would have been easy to overlook if not for the light shining from the windows and the smell of wood smoke that grew stronger as she approached the door.

Usually meeting Bodie infused Annie with a sense of empowerment. She came here with a spring of eagerness in her step, feeling proud that she had made an independent decision and acted upon it. She had claimed her sexuality and had spit in the eye of convention. She had made of herself a whole New Modern Woman.

But tonight she arrived in fear and uncertainty, praying that Bodie would forget everything she had ever said about New Modern Women and offer the conventional solution of marriage and save her.

Trembling, Annie drew a deep breath and smoothed her skirts. This was Bodie. He hadn't actually said the words, but surely he wouldn't take her to bed if he didn't love her. Or was she putting her feelings on him? Swallowing hard, she lifted a shaking hand and rapped once on the door.

"Well, aren't you a sight for sore eyes," he said, filling the doorway. "As pretty as a picture."

Everything about Bodie Miller was big, his tall frame, his shoulders, his hands, his smile.

Annie had planned to greet him as she usually did, with a kiss and some light conversation before she eased into the matter at hand. But the solid bigness of him undid her. She burst into tears and collapsed against his chest.

"Annie?" His hands waved like he didn't know what to do; then he pulled her inside and shut the door. "Annie? You're cold and shaking. What's wrong, sweetheart?" He leaned down, trying to see her face. "Annie? Come over by the fire."

"I'm sorry." She accepted the handkerchief he pushed into her hand. "I've been so weepy lately. I just . . . It's been so awful. I thought tonight would never come, I've needed you so much. Oh, Bodie." The tears wouldn't stop. This wasn't at all what she had planned.

"Sit here while I get you something. I have coffee, or whiskey if you'd rather."

As a New Modern Woman, she had sampled whiskey, but she didn't like the taste. Moreover, she worried that her parents would be awake when she got home and would smell liquor on her breath. She didn't want coffee, either, but the cup would give her something to do with her hands.

After bringing her coffee and forgetting that she liked cream, Bodie knelt in front of her. "Now what's this all about?"

The firelight made his hair shine like a cap of gold. That's what Annie had noticed first when she met him at last year's Summer Crafts Fair, that shock of white-gold hair. Then she'd seen eyes as blue as berries twinkling back at her from a boyish face and her heart had done a somersault in her chest.

"I don't know how to tell you."

Usually by this time she would have removed her hat and cape and be sitting in his lap. And later . . . From the corner of her eye she glimpsed the bed next to a log wall. The quilt was turned back and the pillows plumped, waiting for them. They had been so careful. That's what she didn't understand. How could this have happened?

"Move closer to the fire; you're still shaking." He peered at the tears swimming in her eyes. "Now, tell me why you're so upset."

"I'm pregnant."

His eyes widened and his mouth rounded. She watched his shoulders tighten, and his fingers gripped the arms of her chair. "Pregnant?" he asked after a minute. "Are you sure?"

She pressed the handkerchief against her eyes so she wouldn't have to watch him work out his response. "I'm sure."

"Maybe I'll have some of that whiskey."

She wanted him to take her in his arms and tell her that he was glad, that they would be married immediately. But she understood he needed time to grasp the enormity of their situation.

While she waited for him to return from the sideboard, she removed her hat, gloves, and cloak and dropped them beside the chair. A sip of coffee would have eased the dryness in her mouth, but she didn't think she could get the cup to her mouth without spilling. She set the coffee on the floor.

When she looked up, he had taken the rocking chair and was leaning forward, cradling a glass of whiskey between his big hands. "I can't say I don't have mixed feelings about this because I do. But I also know what's expected when a respectable woman gets in a family way."

Her head snapped up and she stared expectantly, willing him to say the words.

"I guess we have to get married."

The air ran out of her body, leaving her limp and trembling. "Oh, Bodie." Jumping up, she ran to him and fell into his lap, covering his face with kisses.

He set aside the whiskey and caught her hands. "Did you think I wouldn't stand by you?"

"I knew you would." But there had been a tiny fear, barely acknowledged, that maybe he wouldn't. Maybe asking her to marry him had never been more than the tease she'd always believed it was.

Annie buried her face in his collar, breathing the male scent of him. He didn't smell buttery like her father. Bodie smelled of pomade and bay rum. At the end of their evenings together he usually smelled like whiskey and man-sweat, scents she ordinarily found exciting. Tonight, however, the smell of his whiskey seemed exceptionally strong and unpleasant. Recently, and oddly, she seemed to be acutely aware of odors that ordinarily she didn't even notice.

He stroked her back, patting her awkwardly. "Have you told your parents?"

"I haven't told anyone but you. But we should tell my parents soon."

"You want me there," he said, not sounding happy about it.

Annie sat up so she could see his face. "We can't delay the wedding, Bodie. It should happen quickly."

She had never imagined herself discussing a wedding, since she had decided long ago that she would never surrender herself to marriage. She had watched her mother swallow opinions and bow to her father's wishes. She had heard her father berate her mother for bungling household accounts as if she were a dim-witted child. Everything she said or did was directed toward pleasing Annie's father. And Annie's parents had a good marriage.

Bodie nodded, his arms around her, his gaze on the fire. "I guess I should think about the questions your father will ask. Like where we'll live, things like that."

Annie doubted those questions would arise immediately. First, there would be a terrible scene about the pregnancy; awful things would be said, which she hoped could be forgiven in time. She wet her lips and tried to swallow. There would be plenty of time to fret about telling her parents. Right now, there were things they had to decide.

"I'd like a house of our own," she said, feeling shy about stating opinions she hadn't quite known she held. "It doesn't have to be as large as Papa's, of course, but it would be nice if it had a yard."

He kissed her nose. "You've had more time to plan than I have." He stood her on her feet and went to the sideboard to refill his whiskey glass. "We'll have a house, but we'll have to choose the location carefully. It can't be in town. I need a place away from nosy neighbors, where no one will notice when I come and go."

Her smile faltered and a silent alarm sounded in her head. "Bodie . . . you can't continue to be an outlaw."

"Why not? That's what I do. I rob banks and trains."

Raising a hand, she touched her forehead, then tried again. "But everything's different now. You need an honest job." She tried to make the demand sound more like a logical assumption. "You'll be a husband and a father. It's time to," she almost said "grow up" but amended it to, "settle down. It's time for a legitimate profession."

"Sweetheart, we've talked about this. You can't expect me to change my life. I like what I do and I'm good at it. You won't want for a thing, married to me."

"Bodie, please. We're going to have a baby. We can't live a dishonest life."

"I had a job at my uncle's carriage factory in Kansas City. I hated it." He took a long swallow of whiskey, watching her over the rim of the glass. "The hours were long; the pay was small; the place stank of lacquer and axle grease."

"You don't have to work in a factory," she said, trying not to sound desperate. "I'm sure my father would make a place for you at the creamery."

Bodie's mouth twisted in distaste. "I'm no butter maker or egg sorter. No thank you. I like my present job."

For a long moment, Annie held his gaze, finding no yield in his blue eyes. Slowly, she sat down and clasped her hands in her lap. The first time he had raised the subject of marriage, months ago, she had suspected it was in the nature of a compliment that he'd spoken to others before her, a comment he didn't intend to be taken seriously. Nonetheless, she'd carefully examined her feelings.

As much as she believed she loved Bodie, she didn't want to be a wife. A wife had to give up too much of herself. But if she ever changed her mind, she certainly didn't want to be the wife of an outlaw. She couldn't possibly live on stolen money, didn't want to worry every time he left the house that he might get shot or arrested. She didn't want to be frightened by a late-night knock at the door or by a posse in her yard. Now she saw another reason. She didn't want to live isolated from family and friends.

"There must be a way to work this out," she said, looking up. Surely they could find an acceptable compromise.

"The men I ride with—they both have wives and families."

"And their wives don't mind that they're married to outlaws? Living on stolen money that someone else worked for?"

He shrugged, but the boyish expression faded and his eyes narrowed at the sharpness of her tone. "Their wives seem happy enough when I've been around them. Seems like you should be, too."

This raised another issue. Their friends would be outlaws. The thought appalled her. "Bodie, do you at least foresee a time when you'll retire from . . . stealing and take up another profession?"

He grinned and tossed back the whiskey. "Sure. If I get shot or caught." When she didn't smile, he cleared his throat. "Annie, you have to take me as I am."

"I thought robbing banks and trains was just something you did occasionally, like a prank almost." That's what she'd told herself. He was the same age as she, twenty-five. She'd been able to sell herself the idea that being an outlaw was an adventure for him, nothing really serious, a youthful holdover from boyhood. Since discovering that she was pregnant, she'd tried to persuade herself that once he knew about the baby, he'd be willing to settle down and adopt an honest vocation.

Instead, irritation flickered in his eyes. "If what I do

is such a moral problem, then why have you kept coming here? You can sleep with an outlaw, but you're too all-fired high-and-mighty to marry one?"

His bluntness shocked her and made her cringe. This was a side of him that she didn't know. "I was amazed that I agreed to see you at all. You made me feel daring and modern." Discovering that he was an outlaw had added an additional thrill of excitement, which she no longer understood. "It seems stupid now, but I didn't think about how this might end."

"I'm willing to do right. But I'm not willing to change my whole life just because you say so."

There was a warning in his tone, but she didn't acknowledge it. "How can we teach our children to be honest if their daddy steals other people's money? What would happen to me and the baby if you went to prison?"

Annoyance flickered in his gaze, and it occurred to Annie that if they were married he very likely would not tolerate this conversation or her tone of criticism and censure. Another alarm rang in her mind.

"I imagine my parents would help out, and your parents likely would, too."

"Does that sound responsible to you? It's not our parents' duty to take care of your family."

Sudden anger flashed in his berry-blue eyes. "Look, I didn't ask for this."

"Neither did I." Despair thinned her voice. Everything was turning sour. After blinking back tears, she came at the problem from a different direction. "What does your family think about you being an outlaw?"

"That's neither here nor there."

"Are your parents still alive?" No Millers had lived

in Marshall since Bodie's grandfather had abandoned the old homestead. "Where do they live? Do you have brothers or sisters?"

"My parents are alive, and I have two sisters. We won't be seeing them, so it doesn't matter."

"So they don't approve of what you're doing." They wouldn't have any contact with his family, and their relationship with her family would be difficult at best. Annie's heart sank to her toes. "Where do you live when you aren't here?"

His mouth smiled, but his eyes were harder than she had seen them. "You're starting to sound like a deputy. I think it's wise, now and in the future, if there are things you don't know."

Like where he went and what he did. Like which bank he robbed and where it was located.

They both glanced toward the bed, aware that time was passing and the evening wouldn't end as it usually did. Abruptly Annie stood and held her hands to the fire, watching her fingers shake.

If she married Bodie Miller, she would have to compromise everything she believed in. She would have to accept an isolated life. She couldn't keep old friends, couldn't make new ones, because she'd worry herself half to death about saying something careless that would betray the secret of Bodie's livelihood. Her only social contacts would come from Bodie's friends, other outlaws and their wives. Would that make her an outlaw, too? She wouldn't know where Bodie went when he rode out of the yard or when or if he would come home again. She could easily spend years of her life alone while he was in prison. Certainly she would worry about that.

Tears swam in her eyes. "I can't live that life. Bodie, I just can't."

She didn't know he'd come up behind her until his big hands closed on her shoulders. "You don't have a choice, Annie."

She thought about the New Modern Women raising children alone back east. "I do have a choice."

The life he offered would be solitary and lonely, filled with anxiety and the knowledge that everything they owned came from stolen money.

He turned her to face an angry expression. "I don't want any child of mine to be raised as a bastard. Have you thought about this, Annie? You'll be ruined. Right now you have friends; you're respected in the community. If you don't marry me, you'll be shunned. There won't be a house in town where you'll be welcome."

Silent tears ran down her cheeks. She couldn't let herself think about what he was saying.

"Damn it, why are you being difficult? You should be grateful to have a man willing to marry you in this circumstance."

"I am. It's just . . ." They had never spoken about love. He'd joshed about marriage, but neither of them had said the word *love*. "I told you all along that I couldn't marry an outlaw."

"I won't let anyone tell me what to do or how to live," he said slowly. "Don't try to change me."

She stiffened and pulled back. "I'm not trying to manipulate you into doing what I want."

"That's exactly what you're doing." His hands fell to his sides. "And it's not going to work. I don't believe for a minute that you'd choose a life of shame and disgrace, or that you'd make a bastard out of your child rather than marry me. So let's not waste any more time on foolishness."

"It's my life, too. And I won't live with an outlaw for a husband." The words hung between them, stark and final. Until Annie heard herself speak she hadn't realized that she'd committed to a decision.

He stared down at her. "When I was sixteen my daddy told me never to sleep with a woman I wasn't willing to marry, because I might have to. Didn't it ever occur to you that you might get pregnant?"

Of course she had thought about it, but not often. She'd praised herself for knowing how and when conception occurred and had believed that knowledge was armor against disaster. And if the worst happened, she had naively told herself that she was a New Modern Woman and she could handle whatever life threw in her path.

The bewildering thing was that she'd come here with a prayer on her lips, praying that he would be willing to marry her. But it was she who was unwilling to marry him.

"You're not going to stop robbing trains and banks, are you?" she whispered.

"No, I'm not. That's final, Annie."

She shook her head and moved backward a step. "I can't live an outlaw's life. I won't do that to myself or to my child. I'm sorry. I wish to heaven that I could accept your life, but I just can't do it."

Bodie clenched his teeth and visibly summoned patience. "Now, you know you don't mean that."

A wave of dizziness passed across her vision and she feared she might faint. "I do mean it."

"Annie, that's crazy," he said, narrowing his eyes.

"I have to go." He caught her arm, but she shook him off and retrieved her cape, gloves, and hat.

The cabin seemed stifling. The air was hot, suffocating. Annie pulled on her hat without looking into the mirror that Bodie had bought for her. She didn't care that she'd buttoned her cape incorrectly. Pushing past him, she rushed to the door and threw it open, gulping deep breaths of cold air as she hurried up the path toward the county road.

He caught up to her, pulling on his coat. "Damn it."

She wiped her gloves across her eyes, willing the tears to stop before she reached the lights at the edge of town. Then, stopping abruptly, she covered her face with her gloves. "Oh, God." When she peeked into the future, she felt sick inside, afraid and overwhelmed. "I don't want to face this alone."

"You don't have to." Frustration rolled off him in waves. "I'm willing to—"

"Stop." Shaking her head, she stepped away from him. "You're *not* willing to do what's necessary!"

"Neither are you, unless you get your own way."

"That's it then," she said, staring at him in the shadowy light. How did she say good-bye to a man she would have married if not for the impasse they'd reached? Should they embrace? Shake hands like polite strangers?

Annie wet her lips and lifted her head. To hide the pain, she held her expression as steady as she could. "It'll be easier if we don't see each other again." The words sounded frozen, so brittle they could crack and break in the chill night air.

"You're behaving like an idiot. I don't like that." Bodie scowled ahead at the silhouettes of trees and houses. "Meet me tomorrow. We'll talk some more."

She couldn't think. Her mind had stopped when she understood she couldn't marry him. That thought froze like a plug that blocked any other thoughts.

"There's nothing more to say." All she wanted was to crawl into bed, curl into a tight ball, and sob into her pillow. She hoped Mary had put a warm brick at the bottom of her sheets. Right now she didn't think she would ever be warm again.

Bodie caught her wrist and this time she couldn't jerk away. "Think about how selfish and foolish you're being." His eyes turned narrow and hard. There was nothing boyish about him now. "Then come here tomorrow, and we'll figure out the next step."

"No," she said in a low, despairing tone.

The image she held of herself was that of an honest and honorable person. Keeping secrets, deceiving her parents, and having an affair had been harder on her than she had admitted until now when she was faced with living dishonestly for the rest of her days. Accepting Bodie's life would compromise everything she had always believed in.

Blinded by tears, she lifted her skirts and ran home. She was ruined. Utterly, irredeemably ruined.

CHAPTER 2

ANNIE didn't know what to do.

Suicide seemed the swiftest answer to her problems, since she felt as if she were dying anyway. Stomach churning, she sat on the floor beside her bed, holding the chamber pot on her lap while waiting to see if she would throw up again.

This morning she hadn't tasted a bite. Merely the smell of fried eggs and bacon had caused her stomach to rebel. Certain odors could make her feel queasy at any time of day, but she'd noticed that breakfast smells were the worst.

When she could stand without saliva flooding her mouth or her head spinning, Annie peeked out her door, then took the chamber pot to the water closet, where she cleaned it, not her favorite job. Back in her room, she seated herself before her vanity mirror and stared into the glass.

What was she going to do?

Suicide was far and away the best solution. If Annie died, she would never have to face the consequences of her mistake. Her parents would never know that she had been pregnant. Everyone would be sad and talk about what a wonderful person Annie had been. Everyone would wonder what secret sorrow had driven such a fine young lady to take her life, but no one would ever learn the truth.

A sigh lifted her bosom. The insurmountable problem with killing herself was pain. Dying had to hurt. Plus, she couldn't think of any way to do it that wouldn't be messy. The true horror would occur if she botched the job and ended up not dead but maimed, crippled, or disfigured. And still pregnant.

Another possibility was to medicate herself with an abortifacient. Everyone knew the advertisements offering cures for "female problems" or sometimes more specifically for "blocked menses" were actually promising a remedy for unwanted pregnancy.

The difficulty with this course of action was twofold. First, no one Annie knew had admitted to using one of these elixirs, so she didn't know if the potions were actually effective. One could hardly complain if they weren't. And second, Annie would rather throw herself in front of a train than march into the pharmacy and ask Helen Morrison's father to sell her an abortifacient.

Annie pulled the hairbrush through an explosion of loose curls, watching electricity tease the strands into a red halo around her face. What was she going to do?

She might not be pregnant at all. Possibly she had some hideous foreign disease that happened to mimic the symptoms of pregnancy. She thought she'd heard about such a thing. Or maybe she would miscarry. Her mother had a history of miscarriages; possibly Annie had inherited the same trait. And finally, in the long odds category, maybe it was remotely possible that Bodie would give up thieving and robbing and offer her an honest life.

Annie stared at the young woman in the mirror, thinking she had never seen anyone who looked less like a New Modern Woman. Her face was so pale and worried that her freckles stood out like painted dots. Her lips had no color; her eyes were glassy green and red-rimmed from crying. The girl in the glass didn't look as if she had ever entertained an independent idea or a daring thought. The modest nightgown wrapping her from throat to toes did not suggest a woman with the boldness to engage in a thrilling love affair with a handsome outlaw.

No one she knew would think her capable of sneaking off to meet a man alone in his cabin. She could hardly believe it herself.

Biting her lip and turning her head away from her image, she thought about her parents. The necessity to tell them what she had done made her feel ill again, but she had to confess, and soon. Her mind rushed back to the search for a tidy, painless suicide.

Time was passing. Now when Annie asked herself what she was going to do, the answer was: You have to tell them. Right now. Today.

Panic welled in her heart, her hands shook, and she could not make herself face her parents and say the words.

"I'll tell them tomorrow."

She wanted a little more normalcy before the earth spun on its axis and threw her into a different place. Just a few more days and then she would give up the closely held hope that a miracle would intervene to save her.

Picking up her skirts, she crossed Main Street, dodging puddles left from last night's rain, feeling the thin spring sunshine on the shoulders of her walking suit.

There would never be another spring like this one, Annie realized, strolling along the boardwalk and peering into shop windows. Henceforth, her life would divide into the time before this spring and the time after. The time when she had been herself and the time when she would be someone else. Her mind froze when she thought about it, refusing to imagine the person she would be next spring.

So far, the changes that had come with pregnancy could be explained by other causes. Flashes of temper weren't unusual; folks often got cranky in the spring. A heightened sense of smell could happen to anyone. As for the cessation of her menses, a visit to the medical shelves at the library had revealed a multitude of exotic, often fatal, diseases that caused the menses to cease.

Annie stopped before a display window and lifted a gloved hand to her forehead. Why was she doing this to herself? Hoping the pregnancy wasn't real only lifted her up, then dropped her lower than she had been before.

"The park."

Startled, she lifted her head and recognized Bodie's reflection in the glass.

"Meet me near the bandstand."

Blinking hard, Annie watched his image turn and stride away. Oh Lord. His appearance surely meant something positive. Hastily she smoothed her skirts and straightened her collar.

Her shoulders lifted and the strange fatigue she'd been experiencing for weeks dropped away as she hurried toward the park. There could only be one reason that he had sought her out.

Bodie waited on one of the two back-to-back benches, wearing a brown suit and vest and a narrow-brimmed hat. At the last moment, Annie decided against sitting beside him and sat on the second bench with her back to him but close enough that she could inhale the scent of expensive pomade and bay rum.

She had missed him so much. She had been struggling to cope not only with the disaster of pregnancy but also with the pain of losing him.

A frown touched her brow. Usually she loved the fragrance of bay rum, but today was one of those days when her sense of smell seemed to run amok. A gagging sweetness wafted toward her every time Bodie moved.

From there, things got worse. The first thing he said was, "Are you finally ready to see things the right way?"

The fatigue returned and Annie's shoulders slumped. For one fleeting moment rescue had dangled before her like a bright gift from heaven. "I told you how I feel. Nothing has changed."

"You're doing wrong, Annie. You're making a dishonest man out of me, and that isn't fair."

There was no hint that he recognized the irony of what he'd said, and she was too weary to point it out.

"What if he looks like me? Have you thought about that? People would think I fathered a child on you but didn't do right. That's wrong, to make me look bad when I don't deserve it."

"The baby could be a girl. She could look like me."

She scanned the traffic to see if anyone watched and she thanked heaven that she hadn't seated herself beside him. "Besides, no one knows who you are."

"The cabin is one of my safe places. I've been coming here for several years and I've been in town on many occasions. There are people in Marshall who don't know what I do but who recognize me and there might be some who have noticed you walking out to my place." She could hear him cracking his knuckles, a habit she deplored.

"This is pointless." And painful. "I wish you hadn't come here today," Annie said softly. Talking to him when she knew they couldn't work out their problems just made it harder.

"I don't know what to make of you. I thought all that New Modern Woman nonsense was just talk. No woman walks away from a genuine offer of marriage."

"You liked the New Modern Woman philosophy well enough when it brought me to your bed." Her voice was as sharp as she could make it. She could be blunt and a bit vulgar, too.

"Well, I don't like it now. Have you considered how you're going to support this child? How you'll raise it? Where will the money come from? Or do you plan to drop this problem in your parents' laps and expect them to handle your mistake? If so, I'll remind you of what you said to me. It's not your parents' responsibility to raise your family."

"I haven't thought about any of that," Annie admitted finally. When she tried to plan ahead, her first thought was: Let's wait and see if this pregnancy is real. It was as if she moved within a bubble insulated from practical matters that she'd never dreamed she would have to cope with. Occasionally a panicked thought penetrated her shield and the devastation of the situation overwhelmed her. She rubbed her arms trying to warm herself. "I will, though. Soon."

"I have a couple of things to say." He shifted on the bench and she felt his shoulders flex, brushing hers. Not that long ago, an accidental touch would have made her tingle inside. But she was too tired, too numb, too scared to tingle.

"If you change your mind about taking me as I am, I'll marry you. But you've got to decide soon. Whatever you decide, I'll be responsible financially for you and the baby. I don't want no one ever saying that Bodie Miller shirked his duty or his debts."

"What a strange man you are," she said with a sigh. After a minute she lifted her head and stiffened her shoulders. "You don't listen, Bodie. I didn't want dishonest money firsthand and I don't want it secondhand."

The problem between them wasn't only what he did for a living. If they had truly cared for each other, they would have found a compromise. They would have been willing to bend toward each other's happiness. They would have listened and they would have heard. "This was such a mistake, you and me," she whispered, hurting inside. How could she have been so stupid? "It will be easiest if we make a clean break."

For an instant she felt as if she floated upward, looking down as Annie Malloy isolated herself in every way possible. Refusing marriage, refusing financial assistance, refusing rescue.

Even if Bodie had agreed to a job in Harry Malloy's

creamery, Annie suddenly understood that a marriage between them would never have been solid and happy. "I'm sorry," she said. This was one of the times when she felt about thirty years older than he was. "I can't live your life, and I don't want your money."

A terrible thought gripped her heart and squeezed. Was she thinking clearly enough to make the right decisions? Was there a tiny possibility that Bodie could be right? That a child with an outlaw father and a miserable mother was better off than a child of an unmarried mother? The New Modern Woman's Association certainly didn't see it that way.

But Bodie was gone. Feeling a vacancy behind her, she twisted on the bench and saw him striding rapidly toward the bandstand. She didn't understand his abrupt departure until she turned back toward the street and spotted Sheriff Jesse Harden driving a wagon toward the park.

For one stricken instant she felt guilty and trapped. Her heart raced beneath her bodice. Then she reminded herself that she had done nothing wrong and the sheriff had no reason to guess that she knew or associated with a criminal.

But she'd had a panicky glimpse into one kind of future, and she didn't want it.

"Good morning, Miss Malloy."

Jess Harden reined up in front of her and set the brake; then he tipped his hat and smiled. If Helen Morrison had been sitting beside Annie, Helen would have swooned. During the three years that Jess Harden had been enforcing the law in Marshall, the New Woman's Association had spent many hours discussing the sheriff's attributes.

The consensus was that the sheriff was too hard-edged and intense to be classically handsome unless one liked the rugged, craggy type. Helen and Ida Mae did, but Janie and Annie weren't sure. They guessed him to be in his early to mid-thirties, and since he hadn't walked out with any Marshall belle, they speculated that a woman in his past had broken his heart. They knew from listening to their fathers that Harden had done some scouting for the army before he went into law enforcement. He'd come to Marshall because his mother had moved here.

Today he wore a pale Stetson that had seen some use and a white shirt and waistcoat without a jacket. His boots weren't fancy with intricate tooling like the boots Bodie wore, and they weren't polished. Men who worked for a living didn't have time for everyday polish, Annie thought, then bit her lip. She had liked Bodie's polished boots well enough not too long ago.

"Are you all right, Miss Malloy?"

She looked up and forced a courteous smile to her lips. "I'm fine, Sheriff. Thank you for asking." But she didn't think it was a polite inquiry. Resisting the urge to pinch some color in her cheeks, she clasped her hands in her lap.

As always, he invited her to call him Jess, then paused, waiting for her to invite him to call her Anne or Annie. And as always, she said nothing, but she wondered how on earth Helen, Janie, and Ida Mae could refer to him as aloof when he seemed so forward with her.

And it irritated her the way he looked at the carroty frizz escaping her hat and didn't even try to hide a smile. In her opinion, Sheriff Jesse Harden was a disturbing man, one of those men who stayed in one's mind long after thoughts should have moved to something else.

"It's a beautiful morning," he said, still looking at her. "I'm taking a load of provisions out to my mother's place, about a mile outside of town. Would you like to ride along? It's a pretty drive. A few wildflowers are blooming along the creek."

"Mr. Harden!" Shock brought her to her feet. "What would people say if they saw you and me heading out of town together?"

He thumbed back the Stetson. "They might say, 'There go two adults, the sheriff and a New Modern Woman. I hope they enjoy this fine day.' "

For a moment she was speechless. "What do you know about New Modern Women?"

"I picked up a couple of the *Manifestos* that you ladies handed out at the Summer Crafts Fair last year." He gave her a short nod of what looked to be approval. "I took them to my mother, but I read them first."

"You gave them to your mother?"

He smiled. "Ione was a New Modern Woman before there was such a thing."

"You call your mother by her first name?" Ione Harden didn't come to town often and Annie didn't know anyone who knew her. But she must be remarkable if she permitted her son to call her Ione.

Jesse Harden glanced at the sky, judging the time. "Would you like to ride along?"

Too late she recognized his cleverness. He had reminded her that she was a New Modern Woman and New Modern Women went their independent way without regard for the opinion of others.

"Usually I don't care what people think," she said

defensively. And, based on recent thoughts, untruth-fully. "But today I'm not in the mood to tempt gossip. And there would be gossip, Mr. Harden. Before we returned, half the town would be saying we're courting." As he surely must be aware.

His dark eyes caught a sparkle from the sun and he swept her with a long look. "Would that be objectionable, Miss Malloy?"

Good Lord. When she realized how stupid she must appear with her mouth dropped open and the rest of her frozen in the act of turning away, she closed her lips and reminded herself to breathe.

"Are you requesting permission to court me?" she asked after the second wave of shock passed and she could again speak.

"I apologize for going about it so clumsily. I'm not good at this sort of thing." He frowned down the street, then glanced back at her. "I'd like to know you better."

"I don't know what to say." This was an enormous understatement. Biting her lip, she gazed down at the tips of her boots. How could she possibly explain all the reasons that he was making a mistake?

"It's simple. Just say yes."

After a minute she lifted her head, feeling as if her cheeks were on fire. "I can't. The reasons are complicated, but I can say that none have anything to do with you."

Even if he hadn't approached her at the worst time in her life, she would have refused him. Annie's courting days had ended at age nineteen when a serious beau had chastised her for expressing an opinion contrary to his. Shortly afterward, she had committed herself to never marrying. Since then, she had turned away all overtures toward a conventional courtship. She hadn't allowed any man close enough to tempt her.

And Jess Harden would have tempted her. She didn't know exactly why, which irritated her. There was an odd tension between them, a wariness that made her think of him as interesting and a little dangerous. In fact, before Bodie erupted into her life she'd been looking at Jess Harden in a way that embarrassed her to remember now.

Mrs. Genesse drove by in her fancy little gig and waved at them, and it suddenly penetrated Annie's mind that others had done the same. Mr. Homer, the barber, leaned in the doorway of his shop, enjoying the sunshine and observing them from across the street. Dozens of people had noticed her in private conversation with Jesse Harden.

"Oh my God," she whispered, horrified. When news of her pregnancy hit the gossip circuit, some would remember her having a lengthy and earnest conversation with Sheriff Harden. And since her name was not linked to that of any other man, they might conclude that Jess Harden was . . .

Annie covered her eyes with a shaking hand. "I should never have spoken to you."

He looked behind him, seeking the source of her distress. When he started to climb down from the wagon, Annie threw out her hands. "No! I just . . . I'm so sorry." Panicked, she turned and fled.

CHAPTER 3

❧❧❧ ❧❧❧ ❧❧❧

ARE you paying attention?" Hoss Baylor narrowed his eyes and stared across the table through a haze of cigar smoke.

Bodie let the front legs of his chair hit the cabin floor. "I'm paying attention."

Jimmy Baylor rubbed his forehead, then set down a glass of whiskey. "It sure don't seem like it."

Bodie had been listening with half his mind, a lapse that was stupid, possibly dangerous. The success of any job lay in the planning and preparation, and the Baylor brothers were superstitious. They accepted that anything could happen when they walked into a bank or rode up to a train, but the planning process had to be exactly the same every time. Bad luck was sure to follow if the routine deviated from the usual.

"We've been sitting here for two hours," Bodie said, pushing back his chair. "Let's take a break." And to hell with the look that Hoss and Jimmy exchanged as he strode outside.

Automatically his gaze swung up the lane toward the county road. After a minute he swore and kicked the boot scraper. What did it take to get it through his head that Annie meant the lunacy she was spouting? She wasn't going to come here and capitulate on her outrageous demands. She was going to persist in being selfish and shortsighted.

"Damn her!"

He would have wagered every penny he owned that a woman would gush gratitude and marry a grave digger if she found herself unmarried and pregnant and about to lose her family, friends, and respectability. A woman facing such disaster ought to kiss the feet of a man willing to make her an honest woman, and then spend the rest of her life showing her appreciation.

That Annie had refused him was a shock and an insult. She'd carved a pond-sized hole in his self-esteem. He couldn't get over it. Every woman he'd ever been interested in would have been proud and happy to marry him.

He lit a cigar and gave the boot scraper another kick. All right, she'd refused him when he'd asked her to marry him after he made love to her. But she had refused in an amusing manner and he'd known she was teasing, just as he assumed she knew he was teasing when he made the offer. So her argument that she'd been refusing him all along didn't hold water.

What astonished him was that she'd refused him when the offer was genuine and her situation was dire. The selfishness of it infuriated him. Because *she* was so high-and-mighty and judgmental *he* should change his whole life to accommodate her opinions. God forbid that *she* should be inconvenienced by a life that provided *him* a lucrative living. Well, it would be a cold day in hell when Bodie Miller allowed a woman to dictate how he would live his life. No skirt was going to tell him what to do.

Stepping off the stoop, he paced through the weeds making a tangle out of the yard. Most men would have taken her refusal with a sigh of relief and walked away. In the throes of anger, he'd actually considered that. If she was too morally superior to marry him, then to hell with her. There were more where she came from, and they'd be happy, thrilled in fact, to marry a man like him.

He plain hated everything about this situation. In all the months that he'd been seeing Annie, he hadn't spent half the time thinking about her as he had recently. Not once had he wondered if he really cared about her. But he was wondering now. How else could he explain not walking away?

To begin with, he liked the look of her. He'd always had a weakness for red hair and sea-green eyes. Such women usually had smooth lightly freckled skin and Annie was no exception. A naked Annie standing before the fire was a sight to behold. With an explosion of red hair capping a lush hourglass figure, she'd reminded him of stories he'd read about Greek goddesses and how he had pictured the goddesses in his mind. And she'd been coming along in bed, still inhibited but showing promise. Finally, unlike some women he'd known, Annie was a spirited conversationalist, entertaining even when they weren't making love.

On the negative side, Annie Malloy had opinions and wasn't shy about expressing them even when she knew he disagreed. She would be a difficult woman to control and he blamed her parents for that. They'd given her too much independence, which had resulted in her interest in the New Modern Woman nonsense. Consequently, she believed women should be given the vote, should be encouraged to run for city and county offices, and he didn't know what all else, but nothing he'd heard yet sounded plausible or reasonable.

He also didn't like the qualities he'd seen in her recently. The stubbornness and selfishness. Her shortsightedness and unwillingness to bend. The bossiness that made her think she could decide their future and his life. Such attitudes pissed him off.

"Miller? We ain't getting any younger sitting here waiting for you."

"I'll be there in a minute," he called toward the door.

There was another thing. Could he trust her? When he'd spotted the sheriff and walked away from her two days ago, he'd stopped between the bandstand and a bank of lilacs and parted the branches to look back. To his surprise, Annie and the sheriff had a lengthy conversation. And Jess Harden had spent most of it looking at Annie like a man did when he favored a woman. Watching irritated Bodie and he didn't like it that Annie had never mentioned that she and the sheriff were on friendly terms. He'd spent several hours pondering whether this might be significant and trying to judge Annie's character in regard to whether she would inform the sheriff that he could make a name for himself simply by leading a posse out to the Miller place.

Shading his eyes against the sun, he glanced again toward the county road. If she had told the sheriff about him, the sheriff would have come before now. He had to trust that her morality was too damned refined to marry him but not so stringent that she would put the father of her baby in prison.

Jimmy Baylor came to the door. "If you have objections or reservations about the Missouri jobs, then say so right now. We got the right to hear about them."

For a moment he wondered if he had an obligation to tell them that Annie Malloy knew enough to put them all in jail. But he was almost certain that he'd never referred to the brothers by name.

"I don't have any reservations," he said, walking toward the cabin. "The Missouri plans look good."

As for Annie, that particular frustration wasn't going to vanish. He'd have plenty of time to infuriate himself again and again. He didn't like losing.

Jess Harden was nearly certain that he had just seen Annie Malloy duck through the door of Henderson's Saddle Shop. Since she didn't own a horse and he'd never seen her ride, he could think of no reason that she would enter a saddle shop except to avoid encountering him.

Cursing under his breath, he reversed direction and headed back to his office. He had badly bungled his conversation with her. The impulse of inviting Annie to ride with him out to Ione's place had turned everything sour. It simply hadn't occurred to him that people their ages required a chaperone or that his suggestion would offend Annie. But he should have thought of it. Marshall was a small town where gossip served as the primary source of entertainment and pleasure.

If that wasn't enough to upset her, he had compounded his error by seizing what had seemed like a heaven-sent opportunity to request permission to court her.

He cursed again, opened his office door, and dropped

into an old cracked-leather chair. After a few minutes of looking through wanted posters, he tilted back and stared at the ceiling.

What kind of idiot was he? Annie Malloy had never given him so much as a flirtatious glance. She'd never encouraged his attentions in any way. She had never addressed him by his first name although he'd invited her to do so on at least three occasions, and certainly she had never offered permission to address her in a familiar manner. There were ladies in this town who invited him to dinner and to socials, who clung to his arm if he stood anywhere near. Ladies who left no doubt they would welcome his favor. But who was he interested in? A prim and proper woman who was offended by any mention of a drive or courtship and who was definitely not interested in him.

Still, he couldn't stop thinking about her. She was not a simple woman but impressed him as intriguingly complex. For instance, her anxiety about propriety didn't mesh with her membership in the New Modern Woman Association. And although he'd reviewed their conversation a dozen times, he had no idea what had upset her so greatly that she all but ran away from him.

The question was: Should he apologize? And for what, exactly? Inviting her for a ride on a bright April morning didn't seem to merit an apology. Nor did a request to court her. But clearly he had said something that did require an apology. Even silly women didn't turn pale as death and run away for no reason, and Annie was not a silly or frivolous woman.

Glaring at the people passing his office window, he tried to imagine himself apologizing for an unknown offense. He would only make a fool of himself. Besides which, if she was intent on avoiding him, the most considerate course was to honor her wishes and not force an encounter.

But he kept thinking about that curly red hair and her full, rosy mouth. About the sprinkle of freckles across her nose and cheeks. He'd never before seen eyes the color of tender new grass. Last year at the Summer Crafts Fair, he'd said something that made her laugh. She had a wonderful laugh, warm, generous, and unself-conscious, and it made him feel good inside. Made him want to make her laugh again.

He rifled through the posters, frowning at the faces of men who had committed a variety of crimes. Some looked dangerous; others looked like they'd been photographed sitting in a Sunday pew. Some even looked vaguely familiar. None had red hair or green eyes.

Occasionally, one of the desperadoes in the wanted posters passed through Marshall. A quiet little town with only two saloons and no dance hall or brothels, Marshall didn't have much to offer a man on the run, few places where he might spend ill-gotten gains to amuse himself. But Marshall straddled the road that eventually led to Kansas City, and not all outlaws were smart enough to take a time-consuming detour.

Shortly after the first of the year, Jess had caught one of the thugs he'd spotted in a wanted poster. He planned to catch a few more.

After thumbing through the posters a final time, he decided enough time had passed that Annie could have completed whatever errand had brought her to Main Street. Standing, he stretched, then stepped outside into the spring sunshine and settled his hat at the angle he preferred.

In a bad mood for no particular reason, he found himself wishing a brawl would erupt at the saloon. A fight would do him good. But then he'd show up at the bimonthly meeting of the book club with bruises and scraped knuckles. It probably didn't matter. Since Annie seemed to be avoiding him, very likely she wouldn't attend tonight.

"Are you going out?" Ellen looked up from her desk as Annie passed the door of her small study. "Is it the New Modern Women again?"

Annie paused, then returned to the door. "No, it's the book club tonight." In the past it had never bothered her that her mother was interested in where she went and what she did. But recently it had begun to annoy her greatly that she was expected to account for every minute of her time. Her sudden new irritations were the result of the pregnancy, she was sure of it, but knowing the reason didn't increase her patience. "You're not coming?"

"Actually, I forgot the meeting was tonight. I didn't finish the assignment anyway," Ellen said absently, gazing at Annie's bodice.

Immediately Annie adjusted her cape to cover her breasts. It seemed too soon, but recently she had begun to think her breasts were growing larger. Judging from her mother's puzzled expression, perhaps Annie wasn't imagining things. Certainly the uncomfortable tenderness was real. And she wasn't imagining the frequent and inconvenient urge to pee.

Just thinking the word instigated a sense of urgency. Frowning, she glanced down the hall toward the door of the water closet. "I should be going."

Ellen stood. "It seems you never have time to talk anymore."

Guilt stabbed down to her toes. "I'm late," she called, dashing for the water closet.

Mr. Waters was waiting when she dashed out of the house. He opened the door of the dark blue phaeton that Annie's father had bought for her mother, and handed her inside.

"To the library, miss?"

"Please."

Already Annie knew that she would be bone-weary by the end of tonight's meeting. On Thursday she had returned from paying calls too exhausted to eat. She'd excused herself from supper and been in bed asleep before darkness. Even if Annie had been happily married and had wanted a baby, she was discovering that pregnancy changed a woman's body in ways she had never imagined. She saw now that she hadn't been nearly sympathetic enough to married friends in this condition.

But she also knew that her life would soon change drastically, and she wanted to cling to normalcy as long as she could. There was comfort in following her usual routines.

"I'll wait here," Mr. Waters said after he handed her to the ground. "Ready to leave when you are."

The library was new and fitted with gas globes. Light blazed from every brick-framed window. Because of the good light, there was scarcely a night that the library didn't play host to a club or society or meeting.

Lifting her skirts, Annie climbed the stairs. She wondered if Jesse Harden would be present tonight.

He was the first person she saw when she entered the meeting room. His dark hair was neatly combed and he wore a crisp high-collared white shirt beneath his jacket, but he had a cut near his lip and a bruise high on his cheek. This wasn't the first time that Annie had seen him looking like he'd been in a fight. Tomorrow she'd hear that he'd arrested an outlaw or broken up a bar fight. He and Bodie saw the world in such different terms.

When she realized Jess was looking at her, Annie felt herself go red to the roots of her hair. Should she apologize for acting peculiar and running off the last time she had seen him? But if she spoke privately to him he might say something more about courting her.

Every time she recalled Jess Harden asking permission to court her, she felt a fresh jolt of surprise. She'd had no idea that he might have a personal interest in her. She peeked at him through her lashes, scanning the craggy lines of his face and a set of broad squared shoulders. He was handsome enough to make Annie shift uncomfortably in her chair.

Frowning down at her notes, she wished she didn't know that for a brief while at least he had wanted to come courting.

As usual, the meeting started late. Jess didn't have anywhere to go after the meeting, but it still annoyed him that Mr. Duchane never began the discussion on time. And lately Jess hadn't cared for the book selections. He understood that everyone should be allowed to select an assignment in turn, but still—*Duchess Barstow's Dilemma?*

That was Miss Hillingham's choice. Jess preferred Annie Malloy's choices. Usually she selected something by Mark Twain or a historical biography. When it was Jess's turn, he intended to suggest something by the Russian author Leo Tolstoy.

He glanced across the long, wide table. Tonight Annie looked particularly fetching. High color brightened her milky cheeks and throat; red curls escaped her hat and floated around her face. Though she was studiously avoiding any eye contact, he caught a flash of green.

"Well, Miss Hillingham, was *Duchess Barstow's Dilemma* as interesting as you hoped when you chose it?" Mr. Duchane urged Miss Hillingham to give the group the benefit of her opinion.

"Oh yes," Miss Hillingham sighed. "It's a thrilling novel, don't you all agree?"

A farmer from south of town glared. "This is the stupidest book I've read. It was a total waste of time."

"Miss Malloy," Mr. Duchane said, a mischievous glint in his eye. "Which of our two readers will you side with?"

Jess leaned back in his chair and smiled. He could guess what Annie would say. She was smooth as honey to look at and as tonic as vinegar to hear.

"I have to agree with Mr. Knox," Annie said, casting Miss Hillingham an apologetic glance. "This silly book propagates the nonsense that women need to be protected from reality. Or that mention of a body part will send a female crashing to the floor in a faint. How can anyone take this seriously?"

Jess wanted to applaud as he watched heads nodding around the table. If Annie would have left it there, most of the group would have been in agreement. But she didn't, of course.

"When is someone going to publish a book depicting women as they really are?" Annie frowned at the groans coming from the far end of the table. She lifted her hands. "I'll spare you a tirade about women's issues." A smile curved lips made for kissing. "But only because I recall making that speech at our last meeting." The groans softened to chuckles.

That was one of the many things Jess liked about Annie Malloy. She was an independent thinker and wasn't shy about voicing opinions that went against the majority. But she also sensed when the group would be receptive and when it wasn't, and she had the sense to follow her instinct.

Also, he liked it that she read across a broad spectrum. She seemed to have a light side that enjoyed humor, and a studious side that gravitated to history, and a side that didn't shy from the challenging themes of the serious authors that Mr. Duchane invariably chose.

There were many sides to Annie Malloy, undoubtedly several he hadn't seen. What he did see he admired. She didn't pretend to be empty-headed like some women inexplicably did. Unlike Miss Hillingham, she didn't look vaporish and fan her face if the discussion strayed into indelicate areas. Annie didn't refuse to read a selection because it targeted a male audience and might contain vulgarity. She didn't flirt, didn't make fluttery gestures.

In Jess's opinion, she was the most desirable woman in town. Beautiful, intelligent, curious, sensible. And at the moment, very uncomfortable being in the same room with him.

During the break for refreshments, she managed to keep the table between herself and Jess, and although he sensed her looking at him occasionally, he never caught her at it, so he couldn't be certain.

But now he did have an idea why she'd gotten so upset that day in the park. Between leaving his office this morning and getting involved in a property line dispute between two farmers, a few discreet questions had turned up the information that Annie Malloy didn't welcome any man's attention. It seemed that every male in town except Jess knew it was hopeless to set one's cap for Annie Malloy.

For whatever reason, Annie had decided against a husband and marriage. That was a decision she had made several years ago and held to with no apparent regrets.

Jess ate an oatmeal cookie and sipped a cup of overly sweet punch. Leaning against the doorjamb, he watched Annie Malloy exchange a word or two with every member of the book club but him. Her deliberate avoidance told him that she was as aware of him as he was of her. Not in the same way, of course, but it was a beginning.

He decided her position against marriage was an interesting obstacle but not insurmountable. He'd let some time elapse, then begin his courtship. Subtly this time. Patience was one of his virtues, and he liked a challenge.

The instant the meeting ended, Annie grabbed her cloak and rushed outside. Tilting her head back, she drew a long breath of chilly night air. It must have been a thousand degrees in there. And she hardly remembered a word of the discussion. She didn't even recall Jess Harden's comments about Miss Hillingham's dumb reading choice, and she usually looked forward to his assessment of the book assignments.

But he was the cause of her agitation. When it occurred to her that he would be stepping out of the library door any moment, she hurried down the steps and out to the phaeton where Mr. Waters waited. Once safely inside the carriage, Annie let her head fall back and she closed her eyes.

Jess Harden was a closed chapter. He'd asked to court her and she had said no thank you. End of story. She had refused overtures before and felt no discomfort encountering the gentleman afterward. Why should this time be different?

But it was. There was something about Jess Harden that made her secretly wonder how she would have responded if she wasn't pregnant, if there had never been a Bodie.

A long sigh escaped her lips and she pressed her fingertips to her eyes. If she could speculate about Jess Harden while in her condition, then she couldn't have loved Bodie Miller very much. That was a hard truth to face.

CHAPTER 4

~~~~ ~~~~ ~~~~

*F*OR the first time, the New Modern Woman's meeting didn't interest Annie. Helen's, Ida Mae's, and Janie's excitement about the plans for their table at the Summer Crafts Fair impressed Annie as unbearably trivial. Did it matter one whit whether they offered passersby a mint or a piece of hard candy? Did the number of giveaway *Manifestos* or the wording of new membership application forms really merit endless discussion?

"Annie?" Helen asked sharply. She was piqued and had let it be known, because no effusions of gratitude had been forthcoming in appreciation for her decision not to betray their secrets to their parents. "What do you plan to contribute this year?"

"We have weeks and weeks before the fair," Annie answered listlessly.

Janie touched Annie's wrist. "You could bring a cloth for the table, or a decorative vase." She didn't ask why Annie was so quiet tonight, but the question lingered in her gaze.

"I'll think about it."

Helen threw up her hands. "We've had a table at the fair for three years. We've been discussing this year's event for the last hour. What is there to think about?"

"The fair isn't until the end of June. Besides, I may not attend this year," Annie admitted finally, testing the words on her lips. She didn't know exactly when her pregnancy would become obvious, but the prospect loomed. To her dismay, her waists had already begun to fit snugly. She suspected that by the time the fair opened her condition would be painfully evident.

Suddenly she felt as if she were traveling down a tunnel with ever-narrowing walls and eventually the walls would crush her.

"Are you going somewhere?" Ida Mae inquired. She sighed. "I'd love to go somewhere as badly as Janie would."

"Look at the time." Annie stood so abruptly that she almost toppled her chair. "I really must rush."

"I do hope you're going straight home," Helen said, narrowing her gaze.

"Don't worry; you'll have no cause to tattle." It was not to her credit that Annie took pleasure in the spark of anger behind Helen Morrison's glare.

Proceeding down Second Street, Annie pushed Helen out of her mind and concentrated on the profusion of plants springing up around foundations and porches. Peonies were out of the ground. Here and there she spotted the distinctive yellow blossoms of spreading forsythia. In a few more days the buds on the trees would unfurl into tender new leaves. Drawing a breath, she inhaled the fertile scent of spring.

With all her heart she wished she could halt the clock. Wished she could hold on to this time before her world exploded.

When she looked up, she spotted Jesse Harden riding down the street, and her step faltered. She had managed to avoid the sheriff, even at the book club meeting, but she supposed that sooner or later it was inevitable that she'd run into him. Looking around, she felt a burst of relief that no adults were outside, just a few children chasing across yards in the last rays of a golden sunset.

"Good evening, Miss Malloy." He raised his hat above a smile.

But it wasn't the full, attentive smile he usually gave her. This was the tight professional smile that irritated Ida Mae and Janie and that seemed to challenge the town's marriageable young ladies.

When it appeared that Sheriff Harden intended to ride past her, Annie stopped and cleared her throat.

"I owe you an apology," she said as his horse came abreast. "I behaved badly when we last met."

"I'm sure you had your reasons," he said politely, reining in beside her.

"I was upset about . . . something else . . . and then you surprised me. I just . . ." She gripped her purse and felt the color rise in her cheeks. Unfortunately, red hair and easy blushing seemed to go hand in hand. At moments like this, she wished she were brunette.

"Miss Malloy, it's me who owes you an apology."

The setting sun bathed his face in shades of bronze, sharpening the angles and making his tan seem darker. He really was a good-looking man, Annie decided, irritated that she noticed this every time they met.

He rested his forearm on the pommel and squinted into the sun, looking down at her. "It's no wonder you were surprised. You've given me no reason to think an invitation would be welcome. I apologize for any distress or offense I may have caused."

"I wasn't offended, Mr. Harden." Every woman knew

a man's pursuit had to be rebuffed gently. Annie wasn't certain why women had to shelter a man's feelings when it seemed that men felt no such compunction. At least that was her impression.

Tilting her head, she gazed up at the sheriff. Unlike Bodie's smooth features, Jesse Harden's face showed the weather and wear of a life lived largely outdoors. Sun and wind had etched lines around his eyes and framed the corners of his mouth. And there was a whiff of aloofness and danger about him, as there was about all men who wore a badge. Her gaze dropped to the guns on his hips and she wondered if he'd ever killed anyone. Someone like Bodie who lived a life that this man despised.

The thought startled her and her spine stiffened. It would be someone like Jesse Harden who one day brought Bodie Miller to justice.

"I have to be getting home," she said quickly, stepping forward.

He touched his fingertips to his hat and gave her another of the tight smiles. Oddly, she found herself wanting one of his more personal smiles. "It was a pleasure to see you again, Miss Malloy. Give my regards to your parents."

She was almost home before it occurred to her to wonder if their meeting had been accidental. It was Sheriff Harden's job to know what went on in Marshall. Was he aware that the New Modern Woman's group met every other Thursday in the back room of Mr. Morrison's pharmacy? That she would walk home along Second Street?

Her steps slowed as a new thought occurred. Did Jesse Harden know where she usually went after a New

Modern Woman's meeting? No, she decided finally, it was only recently that the sheriff seemed to appear wherever she did.

"Annie? Is that you?" Her mother peered toward the gate in the deepening shadows. "You're home early."

Guilt tightened her forehead. Her parents believed the New Modern Woman's meetings lasted at least two hours longer than they did.

She latched the gate behind her, then walked toward the house, listening to the pleasant squeak of the porch swing. "It was a short meeting."

"Sit for a minute." Ellen patted the seat beside her on the swing. "We haven't seen much of you lately," she said lightly.

Annie told herself firmly that she absolutely did not have to pee, then sat beside her mother. It felt like she had to pee. But it always felt like she had to pee. "I haven't been in the mood for company. And I haven't been good company, either."

"I'm worried about you," Ellen said, taking Annie's hand.

"I know."

After that, there didn't seem to be anything to say. Annie suppressed a sigh. She and her mother were such different types of women. Ellen moved easily in the world, whereas Annie did not. Annie resented the way women were relegated to second-class status, but Ellen didn't appear to notice or care. Annie's idea of independence made it imperative that she know how to do things, the chores that Ellen assigned to Mary and Cook. Annie liked to read, which Ellen usually felt was a waste of time. The list of differences went on.

"Are you paying calls tomorrow?"

They had that in common. They both enjoyed calling and receiving. "I haven't decided yet."

Someone nearby had cooked cabbage for supper, and the odor hung in the evening air. Suddenly Annie craved the taste of cabbage, wanted cabbage as badly as she wanted air in her lungs. Saliva poured into her mouth as she imagined eating a head of raw cabbage, with salt liberally sprinkled on the leaves. Closing her eyes, she pressed her fingertips to her lips, swallowing several times. Pregnancy made a woman's body go crazy. Never in her life had she wanted to eat raw cabbage.

"Mother . . . how far along were you when you had your miscarriages?" The gathering darkness concealed Annie's expression and she was glad. This wasn't a question she could have asked if Ellen were able to study her face.

"What on earth prompted that question?"

Annie's mind raced. "I ran into Mrs. Payton recently."

Her mother sighed. "It's a disgrace that the young women today go out wearing loose clothes. In my day, when a woman moved into loose clothes, she no longer showed herself in public."

"Surely some women did."

"Not people like us. Not the better classes."

It was really too early in the season to stay outside much past darkness. As soon as the sun dropped beneath the horizon, the temperature also sank. Any moment, Ellen would stand and suggest they go inside.

"Did you know before it happened? That you were going to miscarry?"

"Is Mrs. Payton having difficulties?" Annie heard the frown in her mother's voice.

"No one talks to someone like me about such things. I'm just curious."

Her mother settled back in the swing. "Those pregnancies never felt right," she said softly. "I think I knew from the beginning they wouldn't go to term." She sighed and turned her head toward the distant glow of the Main Street lamps. "I was so happy when I knew I'd carry you all the way. I just knew in my heart that all was well. Even so, you came a month early. But you thrived just like a full-term baby."

Frustrated, Annie lowered her head. She knew the story of her birth, had heard it a dozen times. What she wanted to know now was if miscarriages ran in the family and, if so, when a miscarriage might happen and what it felt like.

She blinked hard and her feet pushed against the porch floor, stopping the motion of the swing. What in the name of God was she thinking? Or hoping. Leaning forward, she covered her face in her hands and shuddered.

Even after she extinguished her lamp and crawled into bed, she was still trying to sort out her feelings. Eventually she understood that she could think about a miscarriage because the baby wasn't real to her. Craving raw cabbage was real. The urgency to pee was real, and the lack of energy. But the baby had no true reality, was nothing more than a gauzy idea. If Annie had a miscarriage, it wouldn't be like losing a real baby. So maybe it wasn't so horrible that part of her wished for a second chance.

The next morning, tired and red-eyed, she asked her mother when Mary's next evening off would be.

Ellen looked up from her writing desk and the menu she was reviewing. "Mary has Sunday off as usual."

"Do you and Papa have plans for Sunday evening?"

"Nothing out of the ordinary." Frowning, she gazed down at the week's menus. "If I've told Cook once, I've told her a dozen times. No one in this house likes cabbage." She lined out an item with an irritated gesture.

Annie cleared her throat. "I requested slaw."

"What?" Ellen stared, then laughed. "Well, now I've heard everything."

Lifting the skirt of her morning gown, Annie continued down the staircase and carried her coffee through the house to the back porch. The yard smelled of recently turned earth and dew, a combination of good scents that usually calmed turbulent thoughts.

But this morning she sipped her coffee and inhaled the morning air and thought: Sunday.

Bodie wasn't going to save her. She wasn't going to have a miscarriage. And this morning, she'd had to move the button on her waistband. She would tell them on Sunday.

After a minute, she let her head fall backward and she gazed up at the morning sky. "I'm a New Modern Woman," she whispered. "I'm brave and independent. I'm strong and unafraid."

It was odd that she could be so capable and fearless and still have tears leaking down her cheeks.

Ellen Malloy sank to her knees slowly, as if her legs were melting. She stared at Annie with stunned eyes and her hands flew to her bosom. She made small gasping sounds.

Annie's father stepped toward the sofa, his face flushing a dangerous red. "Who is the man?"

"I can't tell you," Annie said again. Silent tears streamed down her face, choking her. Telling them was a thousand times worse than she had imagined.

Harry Malloy backhanded her across the face. "His name!"

An instant of utter shock and disbelief passed before Annie felt the pain of the blow. Never in her life had her father struck her. She blinked up at him, struggling to grasp what had just happened.

"Stop protecting him, and give me his name!"

He struck her again and she slid off the sofa to the floor, sobbing and covering her face. Her shock was so great that she couldn't think, couldn't function. Only dimly did she hear her mother scream, climb to her feet, and grab her father's arm. "Harry, for the love of God!"

Ellen pulled him to the hearth, where he propped his elbows on the mantelpiece and dropped his head in his hands. White-faced and shaking, Ellen watched Annie slowly lift herself back to the sofa.

"Your father is right. We have to know the man's name, Anne. We'll arrange a hasty marriage and try to salvage what we can from this disaster."

"I can't marry him," she said, speaking into the folds of her handkerchief. Her cheeks burned but not as hotly or as painfully as her heart. She couldn't breathe, couldn't think. Her father had struck her. It was unimaginable. She wished the floor would open and swallow her. Life would never again be the same in this house. Her father had struck her.

"You can spread your legs for him, but you can't marry him?"

"Harry!"

It was the first vulgar comment Annie had ever heard from her father. Tonight, everything in their lives was changing. She would never again be the apple of his eye, never again be his Buttercup. And he'd never again be her gentle, permissive father. She would look at him and see his hand swinging toward her face. A knifing loss carved an ache in her heart and she wept into her handkerchief.

Her father turned and focused an icy look that Annie had also never seen before. Squeezing her lashes shut, she pressed the handkerchief against her eyes and lowered her head. "Is he married? Is that why you won't name the bastard?"

"I just . . . I can't." She didn't dare state that it was her choice not to marry Bodie. From the first she had grasped that they would never understand. They would have insisted the shame of pregnancy be dealt with first in the belief that a solution could be found later for marrying Annie to an outlaw.

Ellen sank into a chair and pressed shaking fingers to her lips. "I never ever once imagined that you . . . not you . . . We trusted you!"

"Do you have any idea what you've done? To us? To yourself?" Her father's shout made Annie cringe, but he remained beside the hearth as if he feared striking her again if he came closer. "I was going to run for mayor. Christ." He thrust a hand through his thinning hair. When he could speak again, his mouth twisted. "Your mother won't be welcome in respectable homes."

"I'll resign from my clubs, of course," Ellen said in a faraway voice. Her eyes swam.

"I'm sorry," Annie whispered. "I'm so sorry." Right now, she hated Bodie. She hated herself. It seemed inconceivable that she had placed herself in a position where this might happen.

"Who in the hell could that be?" Her father's head jerked and he peered at the windows even though the front door was not visible from the parlor. In the abrupt silence, Annie heard another knock at the door, more insistent this time.

Harry Malloy tugged down his jacket and ran his hands over his hair, then strode out of the parlor and down the short hallway.

"Oh, Annie," Ellen whispered, her voice trembling with accusation and a wrenching sadness. Then she fell silent and they listened to the voices in the foyer.

"Sorry to trouble you, Mr. Malloy, but the Jenkins boy came to my office to say there's a disturbance here."

Oh, God. It was Jess Harden. Annie shrank in on herself. Please, please, make him go away.

"Everything is fine. We are not in need of assistance."

There was a sound as if Annie's father had tried to shut the door, but Jess Harden had stopped him. "I'm sure you won't mind if I have a quick look around."

Jess's voice was smooth and experienced and most of all firm, Annie thought, wanting to die. She listened to Jess brush over her father's angry objections. Heard his boots strike oaken floor, then the carpet. She and Ellen exchanged stricken glances before they frantically attempted to straighten their clothing and hair and mop their eyes.

But there was no way to disguise that both had been crying. Moreover, Annie knew her cheeks were flaming and long tendrils had escaped the twist on her neck. She balled her soggy handkerchief in her fist, and in some recess of her mind she recognized this would be but the first in a long line of humiliating encounters. But Jess Harden. She hated it that of all people, it was Jess Harden who was about to see her at the lowest point of her life. Some small kernel of pride had drawn comfort from knowing that Jess Harden admired her.

Neither she nor her mother looked up when Jess paused in the parlor doorway, with Harry Malloy sputtering in outrage just behind him.

"Good evening, ladies."

Annie felt the weight of his gaze noting her disheveled appearance, the marks on her cheeks, and the handkerchief gripped in her fist.

"Is everything all right here?"

Ellen rose to the occasion as she always did. She stood from her chair and managed a thin smile. "We're fine; thank you for inquiring. We're merely discussing an upsetting matter. Certainly nothing you need concern yourself with."

"Miss Malloy?"

Finally, Annie forced herself to look up, her eyes pleading with him to leave. There was nothing soft in his expression. He wore a hard look of professionalism. She had an impression that he was aware of every detail of the room and the people in it. That he could see inside her and know her shame.

She told herself that was impossible, then lowered her head and twisted her handkerchief between shaking hands. "I'm fine, Mr. Harden," she said, struggling to steady her voice. He knew that none of them were fine. "We just . . ." Her voice trailed and she felt tears filling her eyes again.

A period of silence seemed to go on forever. The tick of the clock sounded like a gong. Annie heard a carriage pass in the street. Heard a child's shout and an answering call. A scream built in her throat, and she swallowed hard.

"Have you seen enough?" Harry Malloy's voice emerged as a low, furious growl.

"Ladies?"

Something in Jess's voice told Annie that he was giving her an opportunity to request assistance if she needed it. Turning her head away, she bit her lower lip and prayed that he would just leave.

"All right, then," he said after a minute.

"The front door is this way." Stiff and icy, her father showed the sheriff out and slammed the front door. When he returned, his face was ashen. "See what you've done?" he hissed.

Ellen fell into a chair. "Oh, my stars. The neighbors complained of us. I shall die of mortification." She stared at the ceiling and silent tears slipped down her cheeks. "By this time tomorrow, everyone in town will know the sheriff had to come here. And the sheriff. Now he'll think we're the kind of people who have family fights." She pressed her knuckles against her lips.

"The sheriff is the least of our problems." Knots ran up Harry Malloy's jawline as he turned to Annie. "One last time. Who did this? What's his name?"

Annie hadn't believed it would be this hard, this terrible. For one crazy moment she wanted the relief of telling them about Bodie. Maybe her father could persuade Bodie to adopt a normal, honest life. But she didn't believe that. If Bodie's own father had no influence, then her father wouldn't, either. And if she told her parents Bodie's name, she placed them in a dilemma. The right thing for them to do would be to turn Bodie over to the sheriff. But self-interest would urge them toward a marriage between Annie and Bodie. And then they would hate themselves for giving her to an outlaw and for compromising principles they had lived by.

"I can't," she whispered, choking on a fresh onslaught of tears.

"Get out of my sight," her father ordered in a low, shaking voice. "It makes me sick to look at you."

Dying by inches, Annie slowly pushed to her feet. Her father had struck her. He could not stand the sight of her. Her mother was ashen and devastated. Her father would never know if he could have been the mayor of Marshall, Kansas. Her mother would resign from her position as president of the garden club.

This was how she had repaid them for all the years of loving her.

CHAPTER 5

〜〜〜 〜〜〜 〜〜〜

*H*OW far along are you?" Ellen asked in a listless voice.

"Toward the end of the third month."

After Annie's father left for the creamery, Ellen had sent word by Mary that they would breakfast on the back porch. This morning Annie had been given juice, tea, and toast. The aroma didn't make her so queasy and she guessed she would be able to keep the toast down, but she pushed the plate away.

"Your appetite will improve in the next week or so," Ellen commented, watching Annie pull her napkin through her hands. She touched the bow at the throat of her morning gown and turned her gaze toward her prizewinning gardens, letting the sun warm her face. Her eyes were as puffy as Annie's and she looked equally as exhausted. No one in the Malloy household had slept last night.

"I'm so sorry," Annie whispered, forcing her hands to be still.

Ellen didn't look at her. "My friends said we were wrong to give you so much independence, said we would live to regret it." She blinked hard. "I thought we'd taught you morality and about men and women. I guess the lessons made no impression. We should have kept you in Bible school. We should have kept a closer eye on what you were reading and doing all these years."

"It's not your fault."

"Of course it's our fault," Ellen said sharply. "The acorn doesn't fall far from the tree." She paused and her eyes filled with tears. "I keep asking myself, What did we do wrong? And I can't get past realizing that we don't know you at all. We didn't know you were a liar and a deceiver. I never dreamed that you could do something like this. I thought you were honest and decent."

Each word was like a dagger thrust to the heart. And Annie could say nothing, could do nothing but bow her head and bleed inside. She raised a shaking hand to her forehead to blot out the morning sunshine. The sun shouldn't be shining on a day like this. Not on a day when her mother was in pain and while Annie still felt the sting of her father's hand across her face.

"Do you love this man?"

"I thought I did," Annie said finally, speaking in a low voice. "Maybe I just needed to believe that." Some days losing Bodie was a dull ache. Other days, like this morning, she hated him for making her face this alone.

Ellen lifted her hands, then watched them fall back into her lap. "If you can't say that you love him, then what in the name of heaven made you turn your back on everything right and do something that you had to know was immoral and dangerous to you?"

The same questions had been spinning through her mind since the terrible moment when she had finally admitted that she was pregnant. The sad truth was, the answers no longer made sense.

"Was it the New Woman's Association? Have you

deceived yourself into believing that modern women fornicate and bear children out of wedlock? Is that where we went wrong? By allowing you to become a member of that damnable organization?"

Her mother had said "fornicate." Her father had struck her. She, Annie, had caused this to happen. She watched with flat eyes as a butterfly floated among the early blossoms. The lilacs were thick with fragrance, and the trees were in full leaf. When had this happened?

"Annie?"

"Do you resent having to ask Papa about every decision you want to make? Do you ever long to do something impulsive, something you wouldn't ever do except this one time?"

"Is that your idea of a new modern woman? An impulsive, selfish woman free to make disastrous decisions no matter who those decisions hurt? Does the modern woman run roughshod over her family? Is decency and respectability an affront to her?"

She couldn't explain something that her mother had no basis to understand. After a length of silence, she said, "I didn't lie to you or Papa. I deceived you, yes, but I didn't lie. And I hated deceiving you."

"But you did it anyway." Ellen shoved at a wave of hair, then swallowed a sip of tea. "Why won't you tell us his name?"

"He's not someone you know. And I swear to you, he is not married," Annie said slowly.

"He should be tarred and feathered for refusing to do the right thing! He's not worth protecting, Annie."

Standing, Annie carried her tea to the edge of the steps and inhaled the morning scents of dewy grass and motes of dust from the fields outside of town and the crisp odors of other people's breakfasts. It amazed her that the rest of the world was going about its business as if the universe had not changed forever.

"If you knew his name, you and Papa would force me to marry him. If I did, I'd be throwing my life away."

"Have you lost your mind?" Ellen reached Annie in three steps and spun her around, waving a hand in front of her stomach. "Look at yourself! You have already thrown away your life! Your shame and disgrace will follow you all of your days, no matter where you go or what you do in hopes of redeeming your reputation. And your child will bear the stigma of being a bastard! He'll never be accepted, because he's the offspring of an immoral mother."

Her mother's words stung as hotly as her father's blows.

"And your father and I . . . From now on this town will judge us for your shame, and we'll share your disgrace. For God's sake, Annie. There is more at stake than your happiness and your life! Don't you care at least a little for your father and me? For that baby you're carrying? If there is the smallest chance that the man who seduced you will do right by you, in the name of heaven, tell us his name and let your father arrange an elopement."

Finally the wall between Annie and reality crashed. Everything her mother was saying was true, and now the horror of it penetrated Annie's defenses.

She had been thinking only of herself. For weeks, she had dream-walked through a strange period of calm, shielded from the hard truth that her pregnancy and her decisions would cause deep pain to those she loved.

Since the baby wasn't yet real, she hadn't considered the effects of bastardy. She'd admitted her pregnancy would cause her parents pain and grief, but she hadn't imagined her mother resigning from her clubs or her father being judged for her actions. She hadn't allowed herself to accept the unthinkable, that her mistake would result in her parents' becoming pariahs, too.

"Annie, I beg of you." Ellen's fingers dug into her arms. "If it's your decision not to marry this man, then you are a fool beyond imagining. If there is any possibility that the man will accept you, you must seize the chance and marry him."

She made one final attempt, pleading for understanding. "People can count. They would still know I was pregnant when we married."

"They would also know the two of you did the right thing. And because you did, people will pretend to believe the baby arrived early. Your child will have a name. Annie . . . for God's sake. You have already thrown your life away. Now salvage what you can!"

Would her mother urge this advice if she knew that Bodie was a criminal? That Annie could end up alone, with a husband in prison? Was it better to be the wife of an outlaw than an unwed mother?

"He won't marry me." Not on her terms. And selfish as it might be, she could not believe that a child would fare better with a thief for a father. Confusion made her head ache.

Turning aside, she rubbed her temples, and that's when she spotted a gleam of sunlight shining on something pushed amid the cluster of potted plants in a corner of the porch. A breath caught in her throat as she recognized the tin box from the willows near the creek at

Bodie's cabin. She darted a glance at Ellen, wondering if she saw it, too.

"I can't talk about this anymore right now," Ellen said, tears swimming in her eyes. She stepped off the porch and walked toward her gardens, her hands opening and closing at her sides.

When Ellen bent at the edge of the flower bed and blindly reached to pull a weed, Annie scooped up the tin box and concealed it in the folds of her wrapper.

"I'm going to my room," she called, unable to bear the sight of her mother's tears.

After locking her door, Annie sat on the side of the bed and drew a deep breath. Bodie had come into the backyard and onto the porch. He could have been seen. Or Ellen could have found the tin box instead of Annie. He'd taken a foolish and reckless risk, and thinking about it made her angry.

But maybe he'd reconsidered. God help her, right now she was ready to marry him even if he continued as an outlaw. She wasn't strong enough to stand up to her parents' pain.

Finally, her breath steadied and she eased off the lid. Inside were eighty dollars in bills and a twenty-dollar gold piece. She closed her fist around the gold coin and ground her teeth. This was what her life would be like. She'd told Bodie that she didn't want his stolen money, but her opinion didn't matter.

She dropped the coin back into the tin box and withdrew a folded sheet of paper.

Dear Annie,
  I'll be gone for a few weeks. If your folks send you away, leave your new address in the tin box in the

usual place. Some day you will regret your stupid de-cision. By then it will be too late. I will be with some-one else. Use this money however you see fit.

Sincerely,
B.

She dropped the note to her lap and tilted her head back to blink at the ceiling. Was he attempting to ma-nipulate her by making her jealous? Did he already have another woman in mind?

Carefully she examined her feelings as she thought about Bodie making love to another woman. She wasn't sure how she felt. Was she really indifferent, or did she just want to be? Bodie had been exciting and in-teresting and a big part of her life for many months. But everything had altered when he refused to end a dishonorable life so they could have a marriage and a home.

Now he was planning his next conquest. Never again would she secretly praise herself for being a smart woman.

Annie read his letter a second time, studying his cramped, nearly illegible penmanship. Then her gaze settled on the phrase "if your folks send you away." Her heart skipped a beat.

Hastily she stuffed the note and the money back into the tin box and thrust the box under her bed before she ran downstairs.

"Mother!" Dropping to her knees in the grass beside Ellen's pile of weeds, she grabbed her mother's hand. "I could go away. Then no one would have to know. You wouldn't have to resign from your clubs or stop receiv-ing calls, and Papa could still run for mayor!"

"And where would you go?" Ellen blotted her forehead with her handkerchief. "I won't send you to my aunt. I'd rather die than involve her in your disgrace. It wouldn't be seemly to have you stay with my brother. There's no one else. As for one of those awful places that take in unwed mothers, your father is going to look into it, but he suspects the decent places are terribly expensive."

A chill ran down Annie's spine. Her parents were discussing sending her away without having spoken to her. More than ten years had passed since they had made decisions for her without soliciting her opinion.

Annie reminded herself that going away had seemed a solution a minute ago. Because her parents had glimpsed the possibility first didn't make it less of a good idea.

Leaning forward, Ellen wrenched a weed out of the ground with an angry yank. "I don't know much about it, but I've heard those places only accept a woman if she agrees to put the baby out for adoption. If the man won't marry you, is that what you intend to do?"

The questions her mother asked seemed sensible and reasonable. Every question addressed an issue that Annie should have considered but hadn't. The shock of her condition and then her embarrassing hope that Bodie would rescue her, followed by a drugged-like sense of drifting—these things had kept at bay decisions she didn't want to make.

"I didn't think about going away until now. And I didn't realize it could mean adoption."

Ellen rocked back on her ankles and stared at Annie with a flushed face. "When do you plan to start thinking beyond today? You haven't said a word about loose clothes, but you'll be needing them next month. Apparently, you haven't given a moment's thought to the baby. If you keep it, how will you raise it and provide for it? How will you spend your days when you aren't welcome in respectable homes?" She threw out her hands. "If you plan to keep the baby, there's a lot to be done. You'll need bottles, a cradle, swaddling, diapers, on and on. If you intend to place the baby for adoption, arrangements need to be made."

"I . . ." Annie's voice sank to a whisper and she pressed her fingertips to her lips. All she wanted at this moment was to sleep for ten years. "The baby doesn't seem real. Maybe I hoped if I didn't plan anything, then the pregnancy wouldn't be real."

"I'm so angry, Annie." The admission wasn't necessary. Annie saw the fury in her mother's expression, in her thin mouth, in her clenched fists. "We had a wonderful life, and now you've ruined it. You had no right!" Furious tears glittered in her eyes. "First you decided you would never marry. You didn't care that I'd been planning your wedding since you were a toddler. And you rebuffed every effort I made to introduce you to a suitable man. Then, after I finally reconciled myself to your idiotic decision and decided to take comfort in knowing I'd have you as a companion in my old age, what do you do? You reveal yourself as someone I can't understand, someone who doesn't care at all about her family. If there is any decency left in you, then marry the baby's father! It's the least you can do."

Standing, Annie brushed at the grass stains on her morning gown. Silently she turned in a slow circle, looking at the back of the house, then down the neighborhood across the green yards of neighbors. Mrs. Colburn was hanging wash on the line. Already Mrs. Hogan was working in her garden. Annie's gaze settled on the Malloy carriage house and she thought about the shiny blue phaeton within, purchased by her father so her mother could pay calls in style, as befit the wife of a man considering a run for mayor. And it occurred to Annie that Ellen Malloy wanted to be the wife of the mayor as strongly as she had wanted to be president of her garden club.

There was nothing wrong with that ambition. Her father would be a dedicated and good mayor, and Ellen Malloy would be a gracious and accomplished mayor's wife. Rather, they would have been before Annie crushed those dreams.

"If I married," she said in a low voice, looking down at the back of Ellen's neck, "would you still have to resign from your clubs and stop receiving? Would Papa still have to give up his campaign?"

Ellen sat very still. "The situation would be . . . awkward. Rumors would circulate, but no one would know anything for certain." She rubbed her shoulders and stared at the buds on the gladiolus. "Marriage would be a thousand times better than no marriage. If you marry, rumor will stain our name, but only a few doors will close. Life won't be as socially comfortable as it is now, but the Malloy name won't be ruined."

Bodie had called Annie selfish, and to her shame, she saw how correct he was. She had believed she had a right to choose an independent life that gave her the least chance of compromise or hurt. And she had known that choosing not to marry in her current circumstances would result in embarrassment and pain for her parents, but she hadn't understood that the long-range loss of respectability would be theirs as well. In her persistent state of denial, it had not occurred to her that bastardy would be a heavy weight for a child to carry. She simply had not thought things through.

And she had been wrong. She did not have the right to ask Bodie to change his life. She did not have the right to devastate her parents' lives. She did not have the right to place an intolerable label on a child because she didn't want to marry the outlaw she had slept with, because she couldn't see happiness in the life he offered.

Blinded by tears, feeling herself grow smaller, she closed her eyes. "He's gone," she whispered to her mother. "He won't be back for weeks. But I'll try to contact him. And if he's willing . . ." The words choked her.

"The sooner, the better."

That night, she sat dry-eyed in the darkness, watching a square of moonlight climb the wallpaper and clutching her pillow close to her body.

If someone had to pay a price, then it had to be her. How important were love, security, pride, and contentment? Others lived with a few or none of those things. And it wouldn't be all bad. Bodie had his charming moments. It was also true that she had turned a blind eye to his livelihood while sharing his bed. As his wife, she could continue trying to pretend that he held a normal honest job. She could tell that lie to her parents and to her child.

Silent tears slid down her cheeks.

None of the *Manifesto* articles about pregnant New Modern Women had mentioned their families or the men who had fathered the babies. Why was that? Annie wondered, knowing the answer.

Near dawn, she wiped her eyes on the hem of the pillowcase and tortured herself with new anxieties.

What if Bodie was gone for several months? What if there really was another woman in his life and he was no longer amenable to marrying Annie? What if he returned when it was too late, when she was already heavy and showing and the whole town knew the truth? Would her parents still insist that she marry him?

"I beg your pardon?" Jess Harden stared at the mayor in disbelief.

"All I'm saying is, there's talk." The mayor put his beer down on the saloon counter and frowned. "If you're courting Miss Malloy, that's your business. But if you got her pregnant and won't marry her, then it's my business. The man who upholds the law in my town has to be above reproach."

Jess felt like he'd stepped into the middle of a brawl without knowing what the fight was about or who had started it. "Hold it," he said sharply. "I don't know what the hell you're talking about." He narrowed his gaze on the mayor's round face. "But I'll tell you this. You'd better be able to back up those slanders against Miss Malloy—and I don't think you can—or you and me are going to have trouble."

"Miss Malloy ain't no better than she ought to be, something I suspect you already know." The mayor signaled the bartender for another round.

"Not for me," Jess said. He wasn't in the habit of drinking his breakfast.

"Bill Jenkins's kid was playing between his yard and

the Malloys' yard, and he overheard a hell of a row going on in the Malloys' parlor. He heard Miss Malloy tell Harry and Ellen that she was pregnant. I don't know why I'm telling you this. You know it already."

There weren't many things in Jess Harden's life that had genuinely shocked him. But this news did. Annie Malloy, unwed and pregnant? The woman who wouldn't go for a drive without a chaperone? Pregnant? Could the mayor possibly be talking about that Annie Malloy? And suggesting that he had gotten her pregnant?

Jess changed his mind about another drink and signaled the bartender. "Make it a whiskey." He shifted on the stool, struggling to grasp that Annie Malloy, *Miss* Annie Malloy, *his* Annie Malloy, was carrying some bastard's child.

The mayor downed a long swallow of beer and wiped foam off his lips. "Harry demanded to know who the man was, and then he sent the Jenkins kid to fetch you. Now it doesn't take a genius to put two and two together."

"The hell," Jess said angrily. "Harry Malloy didn't send the Jenkins kid to fetch me. Bill Jenkins sent his kid because he'd never heard shouting from the Malloys' place before and he thought it needed looking into. Bill Jenkins thought something was wrong over there."

"That's not how I heard it."

"Well, you heard wrong."

"Not too many people know about this yet, but you know this town. They will. And they'll start wondering who knocked up the Malloy girl. My wife says you're the only man anyone's seen her speak privately with. The barber says you had a one-on-one conversation with Miss Malloy a few weeks back and, whatever you two were arguing about, what you said sent her running off looking as pale as a potato."

The implication was that they had argued about Annie's pregnancy and she had run off when he refused to marry her. "I don't believe this. First, there was no argument. Second, our conversation was hardly private. There were people in the park, people driving past in the street."

The mayor studied him with a raised eyebrow. "You have to admit this looks suspicious."

"For God's sake, Hiram. I admire the woman, yes. I would have courted her if she'd been interested, but she wasn't." Now he understood why, and he was angry about it. She could have told him that she was seeing someone else instead of leaving him to wonder if he'd offended her.

"You know everything that goes on in this town. Who's doing what and who's sleeping in whose bed. So, just for the sake of argument, say, if the man isn't you, then who is it?"

"I don't have a fricking idea."

"Which brings us back to you, doesn't it?"

"If you want this badge, you can have it."

The mayor looked away from what he saw in Jess's eyes. "All I'm saying is, if you're the man, then do right and marry that girl."

"I'm not the man."

Angry, he strode out into the sunshine and scowled up and down Main Street. Mr. Bolander was sweeping the boardwalk in front of his store. Mrs. Hope's boy washed the windows fronting her notions shop. There was nothing else of any interest. No strange vehicles or horses.

Annie Malloy. Jess could scarcely believe it. And he was surprised by the sharp sense of betrayal he felt.

CHAPTER 6

W**HERE** are you going?" Ellen asked as Annie passed her mother's morning room dressed to go out. The question was not a polite inquiry but a demand for accountability.

"I'm going for a walk." Unconsciously she squeezed the drawstring purse looped over her wrist, checking to make sure the gold coin didn't clink against the sides of the tin box.

Ellen's steady gaze was long and searching. "And when will you return?"

"In an hour or so." She was suffocating, choking on silence, solitude, and shame. If she didn't get out of the house, she thought she would go crazy.

"Very well," Ellen decided after a minute. "You may go."

Annie's eyebrows soared. It hadn't occurred to her that she needed permission. "Oh my heavens," she whispered. Apparently, from now on she would require Ellen's consent to leave the house. Shocked and humiliated, she half stumbled down the stairs and out of the house, pausing near the gate to collect herself before she set off for the old Miller cabin.

Treating her like an adolescent was something her

mother and father must have discussed and agreed upon. Therefore, it was futile to appeal to her father. First, he was unlikely to change his mind, and second, she couldn't beg him to reconsider because he refused to see her.

Harry Malloy departed for the creamery before Annie got up and he had begun taking his noon meal at the Marshall Businessmen's Club. In the evenings, Ellen sent an early supper tray to Annie's room. Annie had thought this a temporary measure, but she'd eaten supper alone in her room for a week now. Her isolation was deliberate.

In an attempt to raise her sinking spirits, Annie made herself lift her head and walk with purpose. She told herself, as she did several times a day, that she was strong. She could bear whatever she had to. She could. But her heart ached with the pain of knowing her father couldn't endure the sight of her. And lately she didn't feel strong; she felt tired and helpless.

Her steps slowed as she turned off the county road and onto the driveway leading to the cabin. Earlier this morning, she would have given all she owned if Bodie had opened the door as she arrived. Then she could tell him at once that she would marry him, and the ugliness in the Malloy household would disappear. They could all pretend that the baby was conceived in wedlock. Her father would surely speak to her and her mother wouldn't be so angry. They would love her again.

Bending, she pushed the tin box beneath the willows in the usual place and piled grass up around it. When would Bodie discover the money and her message? Did someone check the tin box and know where he was? Or would her note remain unread for several weeks?

Surely he'd return soon. He just had to. A delay of several weeks would present worrisome difficulties, as she had already let out her skirt waists twice. In another week, two at the most, she would need loose clothing. But she was borrowing trouble. He'd said a couple of weeks in his note, and one week had already passed.

Annie blinked hard and gazed at the cabin with a feeling of sadness. The cabin wasn't grand or lovely or even romantic. The old place had settled on one side. A few bricks had fallen from the blackened chimney and some of the chinking was missing. It looked so small.

She wandered down the weed-choked path and sat on the stoop, remembering Bodie filling the doorway and the compliments he always paid when he saw her there. He'd made her feel pretty and interesting. At least she'd had that. She wouldn't go to her grave not knowing about sex. She had that, too.

Opening her purse, she withdrew a cabbage leaf and a twist of paper filled with salt. Tears swam in her eyes as she salted the leaf and rolled it into a tube. Nothing made sense anymore. Here she sat, missing a man whom she had allowed to ruin her life, and she was eating cabbage, which ordinarily she couldn't stand.

"Miss Malloy."

Her head jerked up and she stared at Jess Harden, riding down the path toward her. Oh Lord. She had prayed that she would never see him again, but if she did see him that she would never ever see him alone. Hastily she dabbed at her eyes and shoved loose tendrils beneath her hat.

"Did you follow me?" The blurted question embarrassed her, but why else would he ride out to the old Miller cabin?

"This is my job." Harden thumbed back his hat and gave her a pained look as he reined his horse near the stoop. "There are five vacant properties in the county. Vacant houses are attractive temptations for vagrants and outlaws. My deputies and I regularly check these places."

Did Bodie know the cabin was subject to random checks? Annie placed a hand over her racing heart. After the sheriff departed, she'd add this information to her note in the tin box.

"Believe me, Miss Malloy, you are the last person I want to see."

The words skimmed past, not registering. "Are you looking for a particular outlaw?" She hoped she didn't sound as anxious as she felt.

Jess Harden narrowed his gaze on the cabbage roll still in her hand; then he studied her face for a beat longer than was comfortable. "No one in particular," he said finally, swinging down from his horse. After a minute he added, "But someone has been here since I checked last."

"How do you know?" Annie followed him to the corner of the cabin, watching his gaze sharpen and his shoulders tense. Lord, he was a good-looking man. Lean and hard and bronzed by the sun.

"See the boot tracks in the dirt? And the horse droppings aren't more than a week old." Talking over his shoulder, he walked toward a small corral built against a storage shed. "One person in residence. Probably two visitors who tied their horses in the yard." Hands on hips, he slowly surveyed the corral area. "Looks like someone stayed here a couple of weeks."

Annie swallowed. "Maybe they just used the place to keep their horses?"

Jess tested the locked door of the shed. "When I last saw the stoop, it was furry with dust and would have shown any footprints. Someone took pains to sweep it clean. And the woodpile is lower." He examined the padlock. "This appears new."

He didn't miss much. Annie hadn't noticed him looking at the stoop or woodpile. He'd taken them in with a glance. When she added a note to Bodie's message, she'd warn him that the sheriff possessed impressive powers of observation.

"And what would you be doing out here, Miss Malloy?"

He hadn't smiled as he usually did. In fact, Jess Harden's tight expression and the way he moved suggested that he was angry. Maybe he was thinking about the last time he'd seen her, after the horrible scene with her parents. But would that make him angry?

He stopped several yards from her and ran a long look up and down her body, making no effort to disguise a rude examination.

Shock stiffened Annie's spine. Until now, she had not considered Jess Harden vulgar or offensively bold. Face flaming, she clutched the ends of her shawl near her throat and spun toward the stoop to collect her purse. How dare he look at her like that? She regretted having felt a spark of admiration for him.

"Miss Malloy?"

"I've come here before," she snapped, twisting her purse strings around her wrist. "It's a pleasant walk. Good day, sir."

"I've been told that you're pregnant."

"What?"

The blood left her face and head so rapidly that she

might have fainted if she hadn't sat hard on the top step. He couldn't possibly have said what . . . But how could he know? Only a week had passed since she'd told her parents. They certainly wouldn't have told anyone. Disbelief and horror tightened her throat.

White-faced, she stared with dry, burning eyes. "Who told you that?"

"The mayor."

"Mayor Meadows?" Confusion made her gasp. The mayor knew? But, oh God, if the mayor knew, then his wife also knew, and Vera Meadows was the biggest gossip in town. Any options had just disappeared. Tiny dots speckled Annie's vision and her mind froze as the day turned into a nightmare. Eventually, when the buzzing in her ears diminished, she realized Jess was swearing.

"It's true, then," he said, slapping his hat against his thigh.

In the silence Annie heard bees droning around a hive in one of the old cottonwoods. She imagined the tick of a clock inside the cabin. Tilting her head back, humiliated and struggling not to cry, she watched a puff of cloud thin and pull into two misshapen forms.

"How did the mayor find out? How is that possible?" Annie whispered when her voice was steady enough to speak. It devastated her that Jess Harden knew she was unwed and pregnant. She hadn't realized how much it meant that he thought well of her. Biting her lip, she looked away, unwilling to meet his eyes. She wished she'd never been born.

"The Jenkins boy," she repeated dully after Jess told her where the story originated. The Jenkinses had never been comfortable neighbors. Mrs. Jenkins was not one of the ladies whom Ellen's set called on or received. The Jenkins boy had a propensity for causing trouble. Annie didn't know Mr. Jenkins except to nod to, but he wore a sour expression that suggested he was someone who took pleasure in the misfortunes of others.

"I need to go," she said, standing abruptly. Very soon the implications of the Jenkins boy's eavesdropping would hit her hard, and she wanted to be alone when she fell apart.

"There's something else," Jess said uncomfortably. He turned away from her and dropped his hands to the butts of his guns. Knots ran along his jaw. "I've figured out why you ran off that day we talked beside the park. I suspect you suddenly got worried that folks would remember us talking and when your condition became known folks might think I was the bastard who did it. Is that right?"

Annie cleared her throat and blinked down at her boot tips. *Yes.* No sound emerged. "Yes," she said louder. Unreality clouded her thinking. She was standing here discussing her pregnancy with a man who had wanted to court her. What did he think of her now?

"That seems to be what's happened. The mayor thinks I was your lover and now he believes I've refused to marry you."

"Oh, my God." She sat down again and covered her face with her hands. "I'm so sorry."

Her fall from grace was sweeping others into the quagmire. First her parents and now Jesse Harden. It was bewildering and unjust. She had never intended others to be injured by her actions.

"When I said earlier that you were the last person I

wanted to see, that wasn't exactly true. There are a couple of questions I need to ask."

She could guess one of them. "I can't tell you who the father is. I won't tell anyone." Lowering her hands, she turned her face toward the wall of the cabin, wishing she were a million miles from here.

"From that answer, is it fair to infer that the man is unwilling to do the right thing?"

"At the moment, there are no plans for a wedding," she said carefully. "But the matter isn't settled. There might be a wedding." She forced herself not to scan the willows where she had hidden the tin box. First Bodie had to receive her message, and that wouldn't be for at least another week. Then he still had to be willing to marry her, and based on his note, that wasn't a certainty. Maybe he was already involved with someone else. "I don't know yet."

"When will you know?" When she didn't answer, Jess cleared his throat and glanced her way. "I don't mean to sound insensitive to your situation, but I have a selfish interest in whether or not you marry and how soon."

"Because the town blames you." What a mess she had made of things. "I wish I could explain more fully, but I can't." She twisted her hands in her lap. "He doesn't live in Marshall." She didn't know where Bodie lived; with his parents, she guessed. But she didn't know where his parents lived.

"Have you written to him?"

"Yes," she said, distracted. "Who owns this cabin?"

An eyebrow rose. "Someone named Charles Miller. Miss Malloy, do you expect your," he paused, searching for a word, "your gentleman friend to respond soon? And do you expect an offer of marriage?"

"Truly, I don't know. Where does Mr. Miller live?"

"There's no record of a current address. There are no assessments or liens on the property." His lips tightened. "I apologize if these questions upset you, but like it or not, I have an interest in what happens to you. The sooner you marry the father of your child, the sooner this town stops looking at me like I should be tarred and feathered."

For an instant Annie wished she could tell him the whole story. If Jess was going to be blamed for her misfortune, he deserved to know what had happened. And oddly, their conversation was becoming easier the longer it continued. To her relief and gratitude, there was no trace of judgment in his voice or expression. But on the other side of the coin was Bodie. She couldn't bring herself to inform the sheriff that Bodie robbed banks and trains and then add that she hoped he wouldn't arrest Bodie because she had decided to marry him anyway if he would still have her.

"I don't know what to tell you," she said finally. "I hope I hear from my . . . gentleman friend . . . soon, but it might be another week." She lowered her head and her voice sank. "And he might not answer the way I hope he does. I think he will, but . . ."

"Tell me his name, Miss Malloy." Jess spoke in a voice that could have cracked rocks. "I'll guarantee that the bastard does the right thing."

If she and Bodie actually wed, the marriage would be a disaster. They would be together for absolutely the wrong reasons. The way things were now, they wouldn't even be trying to keep a secret and they could hardly pretend the baby had arrived early. Everyone, including Bodie and herself, would know their marriage was merely a nod toward convention and respectability. They didn't stand a chance at happiness.

Annie closed her eyes and shook her head. "Would you think me hopelessly immoral if I told you that some days I don't want to marry him?"

Jess Harden's fingers gripped her shoulders and pulled her upright. He leaned over her, his face as hard as a mask. "Marry him!"

Stunned, Annie's mouth dropped open. She stared up at him, reading pain and fury in his dark eyes. "You're hurting me," she whispered.

Instantly he dropped his hands and apologized. "You have no idea what it's like for a child with no father and no name. You made this bed, Annie; now you have to lie in it whether or not it still suits you. Now there's someone else to consider. If the son of a bitch won't marry you, that's one thing. But if he offers, then you owe it to your child to marry the man. That's all I have to say about it."

"Well, good," she snapped, recovering her wits. "Because whether I marry or not is really none of your business."

A red stain spread beneath his tan. "It's my business if I get fired because the whole town thinks I'm the man who's not marrying you. I don't care about getting fired. But it should be for a reason that's a damned sight better than this. If I get fired, it should be because I didn't do right, not because some nameless bastard didn't do right."

"You and my parents want me to marry, but none of you know anything about the man. And you don't even know *me*. But you all think you know best, and do you know why?" She jabbed her finger on his chest. "Because if I marry, it's the best solution for you. No one cares what is the best solution for me!" In fact, she no longer knew what her best solution might be.

"I care about what's best for the child you're carrying. Maybe that's your parents' concern, too."

Annie wasn't sure. She suspected the baby was no more real to her parents than it was to her. But losing the bid for mayor was real. Resigning the presidency of the garden club was real. Getting fired from a job was real.

"Get out of my way," she said, speaking between her teeth. "I have to go."

She felt his eyes on her back as she hurried up the path toward the county road. When she reached the willows, she darted a glance to the left, relieved that no flash of sun or gleam of metal betrayed the presence of the tin box. If only Bodie found her message soon. As for warning him about Jess Harden and the cabin, maybe she'd come here again tomorrow and add that message. Or maybe she wouldn't. Her emotions were swinging like a pendulum.

If only she hadn't been impulsive the day she met Bodie, and if only she had said no when he asked her to walk with him. If only she hadn't agreed to see him again. If only she hadn't agreed to meet him at the cabin. If only she hadn't let his kisses and embraces sweep her away. If only the man had been someone like Jess Harden instead of Bodie Miller.

If only. The saddest two words in any language.

*   *   *

The conversation with Annie Malloy was the frankest Jess had ever had with a woman. From the moment he'd realized he'd have to speak to her about the pregnancy he'd dreaded it. No matter what direction he came at the subject, there was no tactful way to ask a lady, "Is it true that you're pregnant?"

He knew that he'd shocked the hell out of her. Clearly she had believed her condition was a secret. Thank God she hadn't burst into tears. He'd never known what to say to a crying woman. Once or twice her eyes had turned moist, but she'd held herself in check, and it couldn't have been easy.

Cupping his hands near his eyes, he peered into the side window of the Miller cabin. If he'd needed additional proof that the cabin had been in use recently, he had it now. The last time he'd looked inside, the bed had been unmade and the rocking chair placed nearer the hearth. Now there was a deck of cards, an overflowing ashtray, and an empty whiskey bottle on the table.

He hated it that some other man had slept with Annie Malloy. Hated it that he kept seeing them together in his mind.

The fact that someone was using the cabin didn't mean anything was necessarily amiss. The person who had been here might be the owner or have permission from the owner. Whoever it was obviously had a key, and he hadn't damaged anything.

Who the hell was Annie's man? And what was so damned special about him that she had chosen to risk her reputation and her future for his sake?

Before Jess rode back to town, he spent a minute

studying the old Miller place. Of all the vacant properties in the county, this was the one he would have chosen as a hideout if he were an outlaw. The place was isolated and well screened from the road. There was a front and back door. A person could come and go without being observed. Still, whoever used the cabin needed provisions. Someone must know who he was. Jess wasn't going to feel comfortable about this place until his curiosity was appeased.

As for Annie, he thought, swinging back on his horse, he hadn't been entirely truthful with her. He didn't care if every gossip in town believed that he had fathered her child. And he didn't care if the mayor fired him. It irritated him that apparently folks believed him capable of refusing to do the right thing, but at bottom that issue was a small one.

What he cared about, damn his hide, was Annie Malloy. He cared what happened to her. He cared that she was suffering and that her situation could only get worse.

Shaking his head, he grimaced, then laughed out loud. Of all the women in the whole fricking world, he had to fix on one who had gotten herself pregnant by some son of a bitch. This had to be the ultimate example of stubborn hardheadedness.

But he'd never wanted to hold a woman as much as he'd wanted to hold Annie when she lifted big green eyes swimming in tears and looked at him as if her world had turned dark and hopeless.

Back in town he checked on the two drunks in the holding cell, then summoned his deputies to assist the fire brigade in extinguishing an outhouse fire. Probably started by kids. There was a late afternoon free-for-all at the Tree Stump Saloon followed by a shooting incident involving two feuding farmers. All in all, a routine day.

"Would you like to grab a bite of supper?" John Anderson asked, smothering a yawn. "The special at the hotel is meat loaf and mashed potatoes."

Jess looked up from his desk in surprise. Apparently Anderson, who was new on the job, hadn't yet heard that the sheriff was a loner who didn't socialize.

An automatic refusal sprang to his lips, but this time he checked it. He wasn't a lonely man, but like all outsiders, he was alone. His conversation with Annie had been necessarily intimate, the kind of conversation he imagined friends might have. That unusual period of closeness had touched something inside that he hadn't felt in years, a restlessness that wondered about the bonds between people.

Reaching, he picked up the wood carving at the top of his desk and ran his thumb along the smooth line between the small horse's neck and tail. He'd carved this horse years ago and wasn't sure why he kept it. The proportions were wrong and the details were not skillfully executed.

He glanced at Anderson, then cleared his throat, put the horse back in place, and closed the file on his paperwork. "Meat loaf sounds good," he said, curious to discover if he and Anderson could find something to talk about. The job, of course. The weather. Horses. Vacant houses. Nothing intimate in any of that, but intimacy required trust and time. And Jess didn't know if he truly wanted to move in that direction.

It wasn't until he was riding out to Ione's place, enjoying moonlit shadows drifting across the fields, that it occurred to him that he and Annie had moved from Miss Malloy and Mr. Harden to an intimate discussion without much time involved or any discussion of trust. But the circumstances were unusual.

He wished he knew the name of the bastard who had ruined her life. There'd be no holding his temper after he discovered the man's name. And he would. Marshall wasn't a town that kept secrets well. Once he knew the name, he thought, his gaze going cold and hard, that man would pay for humiliating and shaming Annie Malloy. He would pay for wrecking Jess's courtship plans.

"Damn!" Hoss Baylor slid off his horse and slumped to the ground, staring at his bloody shirt. "I knew this was going to go bad; I just knew it!"

Bodie squinted through the trees behind them and listened hard. All he heard was the horses' heavy breathing and the Baylor boys' swearing. He swung to the ground to have a look at Hoss's side.

The wound was bad. Bleeding profusely. Worse, the bullet hadn't passed through; it was still inside.

"We can't stay here long," he warned. "We've got a good start, but we're leaving a trail a mile wide." Unfortunately, Hoss was in no condition for a hard, fast ride. Damn it.

"My brother's hurt." Jimmy elbowed him aside. "I think we should stay here." There was a challenge in his tone, but he didn't look at Bodie.

"If you boys want to go to prison, fine. You can stay here." He waved his hands. "Hell, build a fire. Break out the harmonica. Enjoy yourselves. But I'm heading out."

"All we got out of that bank was a fricking bullet." Hoss pinched his lips as Jimmy stripped off his belt and used it to bind his bandanna over Hoss's wound. "Jesus. Does it have to be so tight? I can't breathe."

"Shut up." Jimmy gave the belt a yank. "You know why they're after us. You shot the teller. If you hadn't shot the teller, that idiot in the glasses wouldn't have shot you."

"I told you, damn it. I didn't shoot at the teller, I shot a warning round, but the bullet ricocheted. It wasn't my fault."

"Yeah, well, it was your fault that you called me by name," Bodie said, kicking a rock. He figured descriptions existed for all three of them, but without a name the descriptions didn't go far. Now the law had a name.

Hoss looked down at his bloody side, then wiped sweat off his brow. "There must be a hundred Bodies in Missouri."

"How many of them are blond-haired, blue-eyed, and six feet tall?" Jimmy demanded. "Bodie's got a right to be pissed."

"I'd just got shot, for Christ's sake. I wasn't thinking too clearly."

Jimmy took a long pull from his canteen before he handed it to Hoss. "How far behind do you figure they are?"

Bodie shrugged, straining to hear through the woods. "Can't be more than about thirty minutes."

"Do you think that teller died?" Hoss looked at his brother. "Murder's a hanging offense." He swore. "I just knew this was going to go bad! Didn't I tell you?"

"I think we should split up." Grabbing the saddle horn, Bodie remounted. "We'll meet up at the Nook."

"I don't know." Jimmy's frown cut a line through the dust on his forehead. "I'd feel safer if we headed back to Kansas."

"They're too close behind us. It's not smart to lead them right to the border. Then they'll notify the authorities in Kansas and we'll be wanted in two states."

"You don't think we're wanted for the Kansas robberies?"

He gave them both an impatient look. "They don't have a name in Kansas and I'd just as soon keep it that way. You boys do what you want, but I'd suggest you split up, too." His gaze lingered on Hoss. "Be careful. I'll see you in a few hours."

The Baylor boys weren't stupid; he knew that. But they didn't think quickly on their feet. Plus, Hoss had been muttering about the job going bad ever since the planning session. The way things turned out, he'd been proven right. The question was: Exactly how bad had it gone?

Bodie crossed three creeks, following the water upstream and exiting on shale deposits. Then he headed back to Blevens, Missouri. Even if the posse followed him this far, which he doubted they could, they would never believe that he'd double back to Blevens. They'd figure they were tracking the wrong man.

Two hours later he entered the saloon nearest the bank and took a stool at the bar. He'd pulled his hat down to his ears and hunched over a tankard of beer, trying to look shorter.

"Heard you had some excitement earlier today," he said when the bartender extended a pitcher to refill his tankard.

With help from the man sitting on Bodie's right, the

bartender told the story. Both men's eyes shone with anger and excitement. "A murder in Blevens," the bartender said. "We haven't had a murder in two years."

"A murder?" His heart sank.

"One of the killers shot Mr. Harvey right in the heart. The poor bastard was dead before he hit the floor."

That was it, then. Now they were wanted for murder. Struggling to keep his expression bland, Bodie unleashed a torrent of swearing in his mind. That goddamned Hoss.

"How much did the robbers get away with?"

"Didn't get a nickel. Dumb as fish, all of 'em." The bartender laughed. "Serves 'em right."

Son of a bitch. "Well, that part's good," Bodie said. "Did anyone get a description of the robbers?"

"Oh, yeah." The man on his left nodded. "And a name, too. Jodie. They won't get far. The sheriff is on their trail right now."

Bodie hunched down farther. Hoss was shot bad and they didn't have a dollar to show for it. The teller was dead. The worst of it was if they got caught the law would hang all three of them. Only a week ago he'd read about a similar situation. The sheriff didn't know which of four robbers pulled the trigger, so the judge tried each man separately, convicted them each of the murder, and the sheriff hanged them all.

Twenty minutes later, he left the saloon and rode for the Nook. When he arrived, smoke was coming out of the chimney and he recognized the Baylor boys' horses tied near the water barrel.

He took a quick look around, satisfying himself that the Nook was as deserted as it usually was. Whoever owned the small house had put its name on a wooden gate and had built the property at the base of a low hill. Trees and thick brush surrounded the house and a small barn. Long ago weeds and underbrush had taken over the field to the east. There had never been so much as a hint that anyone except Bodie had used the place in years.

"Where the hell have you been?" Jimmy demanded when Bodie walked into the house. Blood on the floor led to a cot where Hoss was staring at the ceiling and muttering. He clutched a whiskey bottle. "I need your help," Jimmy said. "If we don't get that bullet out of him, he's going to die."

Bodie dropped his saddlebags and removed his hat and duster before he rolled up his sleeves. Most of the whiskey in Hoss's bottle was gone. "No sense putting it off," he said, feeling squeamish. He'd never been good at this kind of thing. The sight and smell of blood made his stomach squeeze and roll over. "I'll hold him down and assist, but you'll have to do the cutting, probing, and stitching."

Jimmy swore. "It'd go easier on me if you did it. That's my brother, for Christ's sake."

"You'll be gentler and more thorough. What have you got for tools?"

After Hoss passed out, the process was less difficult and proceeded more quickly. Still, it was the longest hour Bodie had endured for years. At the finish, Hoss, the bed, Jimmy's shirt, and Bodie's sleeves were all wet with blood.

Once they'd cleaned up the mess, Jimmy fell into a chair and stared at the bullet in a dish on the table. "I don't know," he said in a tired voice. "There's no way to guess if it nicked something vital or if he's bleeding inside."

"We'll just have to wait it out and see." Bodie had already figured they were going to be stuck here for a while. He'd stand lookout while Jimmy tended to Hoss, and tomorrow he'd ride to the nearest town to fetch provisions. Maybe there was some kind of poultice that he could buy for Hoss's wound and something to help with the pain and the fever that were sure to come.

"You think that posse is still looking for us?"

Bodie shrugged. "Like I told you, the teller's dead. They aren't going to give up easily. But they won't find us." The Baylor boys had used the creeks and the shale.

"I don't know, Bodie. I got to think about all this. And it looks like we'll have plenty of time to do it. We could be here for a couple of weeks at least," Jimmy said, frowning toward the cot. "Maybe I should write Dot a note and tell her not to worry. She could let Hoss's wife know. I don't think I should mention Hoss getting shot, though, do you?"

"It's not smart to post a letter." He pulled to his feet, feeling the effects of a long day, and rummaged for another bottle of whiskey.

"If we're going to be here awhile, Dot's going to get anxious and imagine the worst. So's Alice. Me and Hoss have responsibilities to our families."

Bodie heard the stubbornness in Jimmy's voice and knew there'd be trouble if he didn't agree. Angry, he slammed down a whiskey bottle and two cloudy glasses. "Why don't you just drop the sheriff a note while you're at it and tell him where we are."

"I'm going to write Dot." Jimmy lifted his gaze. "If

she don't get my letter, I'll find out and you and me are through. Hoss, too. I know he don't want Alice getting frazzled, either."

After a quick supper of half-cooked beans and scorched biscuits, Bodie stepped outside for a breath of air that didn't smell like piss, vomit, or blood.

He'd accepted what he couldn't change. He'd post the damned letter that Jimmy was writing to his wife. In fact, part of him envied the boys for having someone waiting for them, someone who would notice they were late and worry about them.

Right now he was thinking that Annie Malloy could have been that someone for him. When he'd offered to marry her, he had taken the view that he was making a large sacrifice to do right. But occasionally he glimpsed that marriage had hidden benefits.

It would have felt good to know that someone was waiting for him to come home.

He smoked, looked at the night sky, and wondered if Annie thought of him, wondered how she'd spent the money he had left for her. With Hoss in such a bad way, it would be several weeks before he got back to Marshall, Kansas. By then, her parents would have sent her out of town. He hoped she'd left her new address in the box in the willows, but he couldn't predict what Annie Malloy would do. That was one of her virtues and one of her flaws.

On the positive side, he was slowly realizing that she belonged to him. Starting to wrap his mind around that idea and like it. He'd been her first and only man. He'd planted his seed.

It wasn't just that she'd rejected him. That wasn't why he thought about her so often. She was his, by God.

CHAPTER 7

Mrs. Morton's maid opened the front door and Annie's and Ellen's smiles faded as the maid's expression faltered while she turned crimson from her chin to her cap. Fixing her gaze on a point above their heads, she spoke to the air between them.

"Mrs. Morton is not receiving today."

"I beg your pardon. That's not true," Ellen began, gesturing toward the carriages parked along the street. Then her fingers dug into Annie's arm.

Female chatter rose and fell, the noise drifting from Mrs. Morton's parlor, and they could smell the aroma of Mrs. Morton's famously strong coffee.

"Do you wish to leave a card?" the maid asked, ignoring the conversation and laughter behind her.

The shock of being turned away froze Annie. Struggling to breathe, she blinked at Mrs. Morton's maid and desperately commanded her feet to turn and flee. Only when she heard a carriage roll to a stop behind them, followed by the squeal of a brake, did she grasp Ellen's wrist and hasten down the path. The slam of Mrs. Morton's door shutting seemed as loud as a rifle shot fired at her back.

"Keep your head high," Ellen whispered as they saw

Mrs. Payton being assisted from her phaeton. "Smile as if we've had a lovely time in Mrs. Morton's parlor." Her face was ashen, her lips bloodless. "Good morning, Mrs. Payton. Your mother isn't with you today?"

Mrs. Payton hesitated on the path and frowned uncertainly. Then she lifted her head, settled her parasol on her shoulder, and marched past without a glance or a word.

Anger and humiliation choked Annie. Everyone in town knew and condemned her. She felt as if she might be ill on Mrs. Morton's lawn.

"How dare she?" Ellen seethed. "How dare that crude little social climber cut us when she's out paying calls wearing loose clothing! I don't know why anyone receives her." She stormed toward the shiny blue phaeton, ignoring Mr. Waters's surprise when he saw them return so soon. "Put the top up," she snapped, waving aside his assistance. "Then drive us home."

"Begging your pardon, ma'am, but it's hotter'n a cat on a griddle. You'll be more comfortable with the top down, so's you can catch a breeze."

Ellen slid across the seat to make room for Annie. "Do as I say, Waters. Put up the top."

"Yes, ma'am." He glanced at Annie's flaming face, but she wouldn't meet his eyes. She didn't know if he'd heard about her yet, but he would. Despair made her stomach cramp.

Once the top was up, Ellen leaned across Annie to pull the shades. "I didn't believe you." She moaned softly. "I didn't believe Hiram Meadows would listen to that nasty Jenkins boy." She struck her knee with a gloved fist. "I imagine Vera Meadows is loving this! I'll wager she couldn't spread the tale fast enough. Now she doesn't have to worry that your father will beat Hiram at the polls and I'll step into her shoes."

Annie stared straight ahead. Nothing she had feared or imagined had come even close to the paralyzing horror of being turned away at Mrs. Morton's door. It was the absolute worst moment of her life. Her hands trembled against the lap of the only dress she'd found that still fit. Her breath emerged in small gasps.

"You said a friend told you about the Jenkins boy telling the mayor. Who was it?"

"Does it matter?"

"It was undoubtedly one of those women from your New Modern Women Society. Mark my words, Anne, I hold them partly responsible. All those newfangled, immoral ideas! Well, wait until the same thing happens to them and we'll see if they sing the same tune! Wait until they're ruined and doors are slamming in their faces!"

Mr. Waters was right. They were protected from curious eyes, but it was sweltering inside the phaeton. The hot, dusty days of summer had arrived in force. In an attempt to conceal her waist, Annie had worn her spring shawl, which added to the heat and her discomfort. She pressed a handkerchief to her damp forehead.

"Dear God." Ellen let her head fall back on the seat cushion. This was the first time Annie had seen her mother crush a hat brim and not care. "Nothing like that has ever happened to me, not in my whole life." The anger ran out of her, leaving her white and limp. "By now everyone in Mrs. Morton's parlor knows we were turned away. By supper time, everyone in town will know. I can't stand it. And no one has even bothered to ask if the gossip is true." She covered her face, then drew a breath and called to Mr. Waters, "I've changed my mind, Waters. Take us to the creamery.

"I have to talk to your father," she said to Annie, avoiding her gaze.

When they arrived, Ellen let Mr. Waters hand her down; then she leaned back inside. "You wait here."

Annie folded her hands and closed her eyes. She was hot, sick at heart, and she had to pee. Her mind had slipped to a dull place where few thoughts could intrude on her misery. But as the minutes ticked by, she discovered her defenses weren't strong enough to block the pain of what had just happened.

None of the articles about pregnant New Modern Women had mentioned the nightmare of arriving at a doorstep believing you were welcome and then discovering the hostess sees you as something too dirty and offensive to be permitted into her home. Not a single *Manifesto* article had mentioned the humiliation and disgrace that extended to those one loved or suggested how to cope with the crushing guilt of causing one's family pain.

Before Ellen returned, it occurred to Annie that a true New Modern Woman would appreciate the irony of pregnant Mrs. Payton being the next guest to be admitted after Annie and her mother had been turned away. But the memory of Mrs. Payton's contemptuous glance and the superior lift of her chin made it impossible for Annie to find anything bearable about that moment.

Tears swam close to the surface, but she swallowed them. Since learning of her pregnancy, she had cried a lifetime's worth of tears. Tears of anger, frustration, helplessness, and self-pity. And the only thing her tears had accomplished was to give her a raging headache.

In the end, Jess Harden had called it correctly. She had made this bed. Now she had to find the strength to lie in it. If only Bodie would return. And if only he meant it when he said he would marry her if she changed her mind.

"This place is turning into a pigsty," Bodie complained, frowning at the front parlor of the Nook house.

"I can't do everything." Jimmy scowled, looking up from a game of solitaire. "I don't know how often I've washed Hoss's sheets. I'm cooking, playing nursemaid, and trying to keep an eye on the road out there. Which you were supposed to do."

Hoss was still on a cot in the parlor. Jimmy hadn't moved him into one of the two bedrooms. Bodie could feel the heat rolling off of Hoss before he reached the side of the cot. "What are you giving him for the fever?"

"I sliced onions and strapped 'em to the soles of his feet. Our mother used to do that. And every few hours I mix up vinegar, honey, and water. Sometimes he keeps it down." Jimmy leaned back and closed his eyes. "I don't know if he's going to make it. He's been out of his head since you left yesterday."

Hoss looked terrible. Sweat soaked his undershirt and the sheet beneath his body. His eyes had rolled back in his head; his mouth was open and dry; his skin looked like a fire burned beneath the surface.

"Is he eating anything?" Bodie asked, heading for the kitchen. It looked to him like Hoss had lost twenty pounds in the last ten days.

The kitchen, he discovered, had nearly disappeared

beneath an onslaught of dirty dishes, laundry in various stages, and food and cleaning supplies. The place needed a woman.

An odd memory came to him as he set two cups of coffee on the parlor table. The last two times he'd served Annie, he had forgotten to put cream in her coffee. Hadn't thought of it until this minute. But she would have noticed, and being a woman she would have read the omission as a sign of neglect, insincerity, selfishness, or some other negative. Was it possible that she refused to marry him because he'd forgotten to pour cream into her coffee? He'd heard of crazier things.

Jimmy had told him that Dot refused to marry him until he promised her a wheelbarrow of her own with her name painted on the side. She didn't want a fancy ring, didn't care about a big house, wouldn't budge even when Jimmy promised her household help. She didn't agree to marry him until she saw that wheelbarrow with her name on it.

"So, what did you find out?" Jimmy asked.

"The bank in Rawlee looks good," Bodie said after a minute. "Rawlee is a hub point for three railroads. The word is the Rawlee bank is where all of the lines do business. The way I see it, that bank has got to be crammed to the rafters with gold and paper. If the bank doesn't work out, we can hit the train. There are two daily stops."

"If Hoss recovers, we're both going to need a bankroll. If he don't recover and I got to take on his family, I sure as hell am going to need money." Jimmy turned a brooding glance toward his cup.

When Bodie got tired of hearing Hoss tossing and raving, he stepped outside where it was cooler and lit a cigar. His gaze wandered to the overgrown fields east of the house. Thick drifts of dandelions cut yellow swaths through the weeds, a shame really. Idly he wondered who had originally cleared the field and farmed it. Who had built this house, named it the Nook, then walked away from it all? He didn't blame the man. Farming was a damned hard life.

He walked out to the field to have a closer look, thinking that Annie Malloy wouldn't mind if he quit the outlaw business and became a farmer. Then he laughed out loud. Forgetting to add cream to her coffee didn't have diddly to do with anything. Annie would have told him straight out if it mattered.

She had told him clear as daylight why she wouldn't marry him. She didn't want something easy like a fricking wheelbarrow, no, not Annie. She wanted him to change his whole life to suit her.

Squinting, he tried to see rows in the field, but time and weeds had obscured whatever order had once existed. An enormous amount of work would be required to restore the field to something productive. The house also showed the effects of weather and neglect.

The odd thing was, during those hours after the botched robbery in Blevens, when he was riding back to find out if the teller had died, Bodie had thought about farming and it hadn't seemed all that bad. He could imagine himself and Annie laying low for a year or two, operating a farm.

Now he took a hard look around him and admitted he was no sod buster. Hell, he wouldn't know where to start on a place like this. Did a man plow the weeds under or dig them out by hand? Was there a machine that planted the seeds, or was it stoop labor? Was there any real money in farming? He didn't know the answers and decided he didn't want to know.

In fact, he wasn't the type of man to quit after a setback. The teller's demise was to be regretted, but he'd always known the time might come when someone got shot or killed. And hell, the law thought his name was Jodie. The Blevens debacle wouldn't bounce back on him.

Spirits lifted, he walked toward the house, sniffing Jimmy's stew on the evening air. As for the nice image of Annie waiting for him to come in from the fields, that was a pipe dream. She was no more a farmer's wife than he was a farmer.

Women things were mysteries to Bodie, so he didn't know if her pregnancy would be showing by now; therefore he didn't know how to visualize her. He hoped she had left a message telling him where her parents had sent her. He'd find her and persuade her to be sensible.

Mary knocked, then popped her head inside Annie's bedroom door. "You're wanted downstairs, miss." A flicker of disappointment furrowed her brow when she saw that Annie was seated before the vanity, brushing her hair and already in her nightgown. Mary had yet to catch a telling view of Annie's pregnancy.

Annie lowered her hairbrush. "Downstairs?" Flustered, she stared at her hair, then began to pin it up again. "Tell them I'll be along shortly."

The house had been as quiet as a tomb for days. Lacking the courage to venture out, Annie had stayed in her room. She had napped, read, sewed, and written weepy apologetic letters to everyone she knew, knowing even as she dipped her pen in the ink that she would never post the letters.

One evening, despite the summer heat, she had built a fire in her bedroom hearth and fueled it with the pages from her diary. The life she'd recorded was destroyed and most of it had been dull and uneventful anyway, so why keep the diary? The other nights, she'd picked up her sewing and bent beside the lamp altering summer waists and gowns to accommodate her burgeoning stomach.

One positive thing, she thought, leaning to the mirror. Pregnancy had made her hair more manageable. For once, there weren't a dozen crazed tendrils pulling out of the twist on her neck less than a minute after she'd finished pinning.

Should she get dressed? Instinct told her that was not a good idea. Most of her clothing was too tight now and would only call attention to her condition. She pulled a wrapper out of the armoire and tied it loosely before she examined herself critically in the mirror. A sigh eased past her lips. Well, it was the best she could do.

Not until she paused outside the parlor door did she draw a deep breath and command herself to be strong. Her racing pulse told her this wouldn't be pleasant.

Her gaze flew first to her father, whom she had not seen in three weeks. Before he finished closing the windows, Annie noticed that his shoulders seemed more rounded than the last time she'd seen him. And he looked tired and distant when he turned. There was no spark in his eyes. His skin was pale, as if he'd spent as much time inside as she had.

What saddened her to the soul was that he seemed a stranger. He had struck her, and those two blows would always stand between them.

"We'll miss any breeze, but at least that Jenkins brat won't be able to eavesdrop." Still without looking at her, Harry Malloy sank into his chair and closed his eyes.

Annie glanced at her mother, then folded her hands and lowered her head. There was so much history among the three of them. She remembered fragrant summer nights when her father had taken her into the backyard to point out the constellations. And Ellen, seated beside her at the piano, nodding encouragement. She remembered the trip to Kansas City after her grandparents had died, and drives to the cemetery to place flowers on the graves of the brothers and sisters who had not lived. The checker games with her father before a winter fire. Helping Ellen in the kitchen on receiving days and when it was Ellen's turn to host one of her clubs. The Christmases in this room.

"We never thought we'd ever be ashamed of you," Ellen said quietly. "Never dreamed we'd hide in our home like prisoners."

"You've ruined our good name," her father said. "You've thrown away the respect and goodwill that your grandfather and I worked two generations to build. You've defiled your reputation and thrown away whatever future you might have had. You have disgraced your mother and me and blighted our future, too."

Each word lacerated her heart. She couldn't speak.

"Your mother tells me there is a possibility that the

man responsible may yet marry you. She says you wrote an appeal nearly three weeks ago. Have you had a reply?"

"No," Annie whispered.

"One last time . . . what is his name?"

"Please . . ."

"If he had agreed to marry you, you would have revealed his name. Why are you protecting a man too dishonorable to do the right thing?"

Half cringing, she glanced up to see if he would bound out of his chair and strike her. When he saw her expression, pain darkened his eyes and he turned his face away. He gripped the arms of his chair, but he didn't rise.

"If I told who he is, it would just make things worse."

"I don't see how things could be worse," Ellen snapped. She drew a breath. "Is the sheriff the man who's responsible?"

Annie's head jerked up. "No!"

In the silence, she hoped to heaven they didn't guess other names.

"The question is what to do now," her mother prompted, looking at Annie's father.

"We've considered every possibility. Before your fall was exposed, we had decided to send you away. That is no longer reasonable." Anger roughened her father's tone. "If your mother and I must stay in Marshall and face the censure of this town, it seems just that you share our disgrace."

Oh, God. Annie thought about Mrs. Morton's door slamming and shriveled inside. Staring at nothing, she tried to imagine herself walking down Main Street wearing loose clothes. The stares, the whispers behind her. She covered her hot face in her hands.

"None of our lives can be the same," her father continued, his voice flat and cold. "Already some of the creamery's accounts have moved their business to Greentown. Your mother's social life is all but destroyed. But this is our home. Three generations of Malloys have lived in Marshall and this is where we will stay. We will not live like shut-ins. We will go about our business as we have always done, and we will participate in community events as we have always done."

The implications of her father's words settled on Annie like a nightmare. She moistened her lips. "You want me to go out in public?" she whispered.

"I expect you to run errands for your mother, to go to the library and the post office, to attend the crafts fair and the Fourth of July celebration, and to perform any other chores that would ordinarily take you out of the house. I have instructed your mother not to do these things for you. That is your punishment, Anne. You live with your shame and face the judgment of the community you have offended."

Ellen studied the handkerchief she twisted around her hands. "Even if the man changes his mind and marries you . . . your reputation won't survive this. But the disaster would be cut in half. At least the town would know that the two of you did the right thing. That's the best we can hope for now."

Annie tried to swallow the dryness in her throat. "I'm not optimistic. Every day that goes by without word . . ." Bodie should have returned by now. She was beginning to accept that silence was his answer. Marriage was not in her future.

"Finally." Her father's stare bored into her. "You must decide the disposition of the baby. You have two options. You keep the child, or you place it out for adoption. If you keep the baby, you will not keep it here. I'll not have your mother taken advantage of or turned into a nursemaid. We will not appear to condone what you've done by raising your bastard."

Stunned, Annie could not speak or move.

"If you keep the child, I'll rent you a small house and give you an allowance. You will be on your own."

Annie tried to rise, but her knees would not support her. She fell back on the sofa.

Ellen leaned forward, white with misery. "We love you, Annie. I know it doesn't seem that way to you right now. We must seem selfish and coldhearted. Your father and I are very angry and resentful. We've been swept into a situation we never dreamed could happen and we've lost a way of life that was comfortable and satisfying to us. We will suffer the consequences of your downfall for the rest of our lives. But we do love you."

This time Annie was able to stand and leave the room on wooden legs. For the next minute her only thought was to reach the water closet before she threw up.

CHAPTER 8

※ ※ ※

OVER here. I found them."

Frowning, Jess swatted at the netting draped over his hat. He couldn't see through the damned thing. Eventually he spotted Ione and took the swarm box over to her, set it on the ground, then opened the lid and stepped back. Years ago his mother had dispensed with netting, swearing that bee stings prevented rheumatism and arthritis, but in fact she seldom got stung.

"They usually stop near the hive to get their bearings before they fly off someplace where I might never find them again."

As she spoke, she worked a long-handled net, settling it around what looked to Jess like a thick oblong ball of bees. With the efficiency of long experience she scooped the swarm into the box as gently as possible and eased the lid shut. "There we are." She straightened with a wide smile of satisfaction.

Enough bees hadn't made it into the box that Jess didn't yet raise the netting that fell to his shoulders. "Do you need help returning them to the hive?"

She shook her head. "Put the swarm box beside Lady Jane's hive. They need some time to settle down and I need some time to install another framer. I've got some lemonade and fresh corn bread up at the house."

"Isn't it late in the season for bees to swarm?"

"It is, actually." She stopped at the bee shed to put away her net and Jess's netting and gloves before they continued to the house. "If they're going to make a run for it, they usually go in May. What is today? The fifth of June?"

Even as a boy, Jess had enjoyed spinning honey out of the combs. He'd liked pasting labels on the jars and filling them. He had a weakness for the taste of honey and could distinguish between honey based on the nectar from apple blossoms or dandelions and honey that resulted from a mix of wildflower pollens. He liked everything about the honey business except the bees themselves.

"It's because you stand in their flight path," Ione said, reading his mind. She tied on an apron, then set out plates and a pan of corn bread before she took a pitcher of lemonade from the icebox. "I've been telling you since you were this high not to block the entrance to a hive."

"After we finish the lemonade, I'll build the new framer and install it."

"No need."

"Damn it, Ione." Frowning, he slid a slab of corn bread onto his plate and dusted crumbs off his hands. "We agreed you wouldn't do anything strenuous."

"And I didn't," she said, offering him pots of butter and honey. "I ordered ready-made combs from a place in Kansas City. I also sent dimensions for new framers and I have several sets in the shed." She raised both hands. "Now don't go asking how I feel. I feel fine. So tell me about Miss Anne Malloy, the creamery man's daughter."

Ione Harden was stubborn, cantankerous, and she'd never lost the capacity to surprise him. "Why would you ask about Miss Malloy?"

"Aside from the fact that you talk about her every time we sit down?" Her eyes sparkled. "I saw her, you know." When Jess stared, she smiled. "She was sitting in a fancy rig outside the creamery, all by herself. She's a handsome young woman, smaller than I pictured. I liked the look of her, all that magnificent orangy-red hair springing out of her hat. Except that girl was about as miserable as misery can be."

He talked about Annie Malloy enough that Ione had taken note? That was a sobering thought. He'd had no idea.

"Is it true that she's pregnant and half the town believes you're responsible?"

Jess almost dropped his glass. "Where did you hear that?"

"I heard people talking when I was in town replenishing my accounts, so I asked Mr. Charlie about her."

"Charlie Hare is as much a gossip as the mayor's wife!"

"It's one of the things I like about him. I'd keep him on as a driver even if he didn't know which end of a horse to harness. So. Is it true about Miss Malloy?"

"Yes." He'd lost his appetite. Pushing aside his corn bread, he frowned, then explained why Hiram Meadows and his gossipy wife believed that Jess Harden was the bastard refusing to marry Annie. "She won't say the man's name. I'm guessing he must be married or prominent."

Shortly after he'd spoken to Annie at the old Miller cabin, he'd started wondering if she'd been entirely truthful. It seemed feasible that she'd invented the possibility of her lover deciding to marry her as a nod to pride. If the man was willing, it seemed to Jess that he would have wed Annie long before any chance that she would be shamed and humiliated. At this point, marrying her would be akin to locking the house after a thief had already made off with the goods.

"Oh, I don't know," Ione said, catching a dollop of honey on the twizzler and letting it spin out over her corn bread. "There are lots of reasons why she might not want to reveal the man's name."

"Like what?"

Ione shrugged. "Maybe he's someone her family wouldn't approve of, someone beneath them financially or socially. Maybe she loves him and is loyal to him even though he won't marry her. Or maybe it's she who doesn't want to marry him."

"That's ridiculous," Jess stated flatly. "She'd have to be crazy not to marry in her circumstances."

"Really?" Ione gave him a long look over a hint of a smile. "Isn't this the same young lady who gave you the *Manifestos* you brought home for me to read?"

"You don't know her," Jess said, irritated by this discussion. "Annie may read the literature, but she doesn't strike me as a genuine New Modern Woman."

"Look a little harder, Son. This young lady turned her back on society's rules and had a love affair. If she isn't a modern woman, she certainly has the makings." Leaning back in her seat, Ione let Jess refill their lemonade glasses. "The question is . . . Miss Malloy's silence about the man responsible has swept you into her troubles. So. Do you see a way out of this pickle? Or do I need to worry about the good citizens riding you out of town on a rail?"

"I have a couple of ideas," he said finally. "I'm mulling over the problem."

"Be careful, Jesse John. Don't go doing something rash." Shrewd eyes judged his expression, lingering on the black eye he'd gotten as a result of a turbulent arrest. "You think hard about consequences."

"Do you suppose we could talk about something else?"

"Actually, there is something else," she said, her voice softening. "Isn't it time you moved back to town? You can see that I'm fine. I don't need a nursemaid anymore."

"The doctor said this bout of pneumonia damned near killed you. What if you get sick again?"

"If I get sick it'll happen whether you're near at hand or living back in town." Reaching across the table, she stroked his fingers. "I love having you here, Jess; you know that. But it's also true that you being my nursemaid must cramp your style."

Now he smiled. "If you think my style is some mad social whirl, you're wrong. When I'm in town I work twelve or fourteen hours, fall into bed, then get up and do it again. My style is being the meanest and hardest-working son of a gun in Marshall. You only think I've been taking care of you. Actually, I've been slacking off on the job, enjoying a vacation."

"All right, then you're cramping my style," she said, laughing. "So pack up your shaving things and whatever else you brought out here. To make it up to you that you'll be doing your own laundry again, I've put together a supper basket that you can share with your

new deputy, that Anderson fellow. Bring him out for
Sunday dinner if you like."

When he looked back from the road, she was standing on the porch waving and he knew she wouldn't go
inside until he was out of sight. Jess waved his hat, then
kicked the palomino into a trot.

If he didn't hurry, he'd be late for his meeting with
the mayor. It didn't take much thought to guess what
Hiram wanted to discuss.

When the door knocker sounded, Annie licked her
lips nervously and ran a glance over the tea cart. This
morning she'd baked a lemon cake and two sheets of
carrot cookies; then she'd tried three cloths on the cart
before she settled on white linen embroidered with
cheerful yellow daisies.

Her own attire had been more difficult to decide. The
only items that fit were those she had altered, and they
did little to disguise her condition. Worse, in the last
week her stomach had bumped out. Now she could no
longer tell herself that the pregnancy still might be a mistake.

Finally she'd chosen a sprigged summer poplin, but
she wore no jewelry and no hair adornments. Her idea
had been that any jewelry she wore would call attention to the jewelry she was not wearing on her left
hand. Now, when it was too late, she wished that she
had at least worn earrings.

Mary showed the New Modern Women into the parlor, looked them up and down, then withdrew. For a
moment no one spoke; otherwise Annie had guessed
their reactions correctly. Helen Morrison pursed her
lips and held herself stiff with disapproval. Ida Mae

was bright with curiosity, and tears brimmed in Janie Henderson's eyes.

"Please sit down," Annie said. She wouldn't offer tea immediately, as her hands shook too much to pour. "It was good of you to come. I've missed you."

Very likely they didn't realize that they sat aligned in a row, like a jury facing the condemned.

To begin, there was the usual straightening of summer hats and the removal of gloves. The glances to examine one another's ensembles. Then Ida Mae placed a basket on the low table before the sofa.

"I brought you some strawberries. Mama had a good patch this year."

"Thank you."

When no one else spoke, Ida Mae drew a breath and babbled on. "We're making jam almost every day. Is anyone else?"

"We came to see if the rumors were true," Helen stated flatly, coming to the point. She stared at Annie's stomach with a grimace of distaste. "Frankly, I don't know what to say."

"That surprises me," Annie said quietly. It occurred to her that Helen had never really been a friend.

Janie blew her nose. "The three of us have been arguing. Ida Mae and I want to support you in every way we can, but Helen insists that is impossible."

Helen nodded. "I'm sure you understand, Annie. If we align ourselves with you, it will appear that we condone your behavior or even that the New Modern Woman's Association advocates illicit rendezvous and unwed motherhood. We'd never get another new member. Parents wouldn't allow their daughters to join."

"What I can't make Helen understand," Janie said in

exasperation, "is that the New Modern Woman's Association certainly doesn't recommend unwed pregnancy, but the association doesn't condemn it, either." She ducked her head to look at Helen past Ida Mae. "If we turn our back on Annie, we're betraying the association and being untrue to its principles."

Unperturbed, Helen folded her hands in her lap. "What would your parents say if they knew where you were right now?" Janie and Ida Mae didn't answer. "Do you think they will allow you to come again? Even if it made sense for Annie to continue her membership with the Marshall branch of the association, our parents will never permit us to attend another meeting with her."

Annie was intended to notice—and she did—that Helen expected her to resign from the New Woman's Association. She had dreaded that this might happen but had dared a small hope that an organization that spoke of unwed pregnancy as entering a brave new world would continue to accept her. Resigning from her book club and sewing circle had hurt, but losing the New Modern Woman's Association was anguish.

"I understand completely," she whispered. A rush of crimson burned her cheeks. "You'll have my resignation effective immediately." She glanced down at her trembling fingers. "Janie, will you pour the tea, please?"

"Are you upset?"

Annie refused to give Helen the satisfaction of knowing how devastated she felt, so she pretended to misunderstand. "Actually I feel better physically than I have—" She paused, drew a breath, and made herself go on. "Since I learned I was pregnant."

Ida Mae smothered a soft gasp. "You don't mind talking about it?"

She minded with all her heart. She wished she would wake up and discover everything that had happened since she met Bodie Miller was only a nightmare. "I don't mind."

Immediately Janie and Ida Mae peppered her with questions. How far along was she? Had she felt the baby move? Had she been terribly sick? Was her bosom larger? Tender? Was she eating more, or less?

"Have you had cravings?" Ida Mae told a story about her cousin craving oranges and her husband sending all the way to California and then the oranges were spoiled when they finally arrived. The word *husband* caused an abrupt silence.

"I doubt we'll be seeing each other much in the future," Annie said slowly, the words choking her. "And I understand. But there is something you could do to help me. . . ."

"You know we will," Janie said earnestly. "What can we do?"

The words came hard. "If you hear anyone accuse Jesse Harden of . . . Well, please tell them that you heard it directly from me that Mr. Harden is not the man responsible."

"You could stop the innuendo and accusations yourself," Helen said tartly. She tasted her tea but shook her head when Janie offered cake and cookies. "All you have to do is reveal the name of the true father."

"I won't do that," Annie said quietly.

"Why not? Everyone wants to know."

Annie raised her head. "It's no one's business but mine, that's why not."

"Well!" Helen set her cup down with a rattle. "I don't have to sit here and be insulted."

"And neither do I," Annie said, standing. She thrust her shaking hands behind her, but there was no hiding her flaming face.

"I could have predicted that you'd come to no good." Helen stood and motioned Janie and Ida Mae to their feet. "And it serves you right for deceiving people and sneaking off to your . . . your love nest!"

"Love nest?" Annie almost laughed. "At least I know what it means and how it feels to be a whole woman."

A shudder rippled Helen's shoulders. "I'd rather not know if it means having doors slammed in my face and being the target of salacious gossip. I'll never be labeled promiscuous or destroy my family's good name because I'm not stupid enough to let some man manipulate me into bed and then abandon me." She turned on her heels and marched out of the parlor, beckoning Janie and Ida Mae to follow.

"I'm so sorry," Ida Mae said, giving Annie a quick embrace.

"Helen's right about our parents," Janie said, tears brimming. "They won't let us see you again." She folded Annie in a hug.

Then they were gone, and Annie was left standing alone in the parlor, blinking at the beautifully arranged plates of cookies and cake squares.

Ellen materialized at her side. Annie hadn't heard her enter the parlor. "Was it terrible?" she asked gently, looking at the bright cloth and untouched treats.

"Yes." Annie sank into her chair, gripped the arms, and closed her eyes. She hated it that she had lashed out at Helen. "I truly wanted to believe that we were modern thinkers and we could help shape a freer, more independent future for women. But we were just fooling ourselves. We're prisoners of convention, just like everyone else."

"Except you," Ellen said dryly, pouring herself a cup of tea.

"Even me," Annie whispered. "For a while I tried to be a New Modern Woman, but right now I would give anything in the world to take it all back. I'd give ten years of my life if . . . a certain man . . . would return and marry me and save me." Silent tears slipped down her face.

Ellen sat on the arm of the chair and stroked Annie's hot forehead. "Do you think that will happen?"

"For a while I deceived myself . . . but he's never been gone this long before." Her voice caught on a hitch of hopelessness. "He isn't coming back."

Ellen stood and sighed. "Well, that's that, then. It was too much to hope for." Moving around the room, she picked up cups and saucers, banging them together with an angry, careless sound. "Have you given any thought to adoption?"

"How soon must I decide?"

"I'd think within the next month. Arrangements will have to be made."

"What if the baby has curly red hair and freckles and no one wants to adopt him?"

"You think it's a boy, then?"

"Is there some way to tell?"

They spent the next few minutes discussing old wives' tales about predicting a baby's gender. It wasn't until Annie was brushing out her hair for bed that she realized Ellen hadn't told her what happened to children no one wanted to adopt. No, she wouldn't think about that. Not now.

Lowering her hairbrush, she stared at herself in the mirror, taking stock. She was a twenty-five-year-old unwed mother-to-be. Her parents were justifiably furious at her. No respectable woman would receive her. Her friends had abandoned her. Since resigning from her clubs she had nowhere to go, nothing to fill the long summer days. Bodie had now been absent long enough to have taken up with someone else. And Jess Harden . . .

She blinked. Why had she suddenly thought about Jesse Harden? He had nothing to do with anything. Except . . . she wished he had been her mysterious lover as half the town seemed to think he was. Things would have gone so much differently.

Oh, Lord. She covered her hot face with her hands. Too soon foolish and too late smart.

Jess and Deputy Anderson tossed aside the men on the fringes and waded into the middle of the brawl. Jess took some punches and gave a few, but all in all breaking up the fight went smoothly. Standing back-to-back he and Anderson got between the main agitators and started backing them off. The more Jess saw of Anderson and the better acquainted they became, the more he respected and liked the man.

He hauled Abe Cotton to one side of the room, and Anderson took Pete Flowers to the other side.

"All right," Jess said, one hand on his holster, "what's this all about?"

"It's about you," Abe said, spitting blood. He wiped his sleeve across his mouth and nose. "Flowers says there's no proof you and the Malloy girl were doing the dance. I say where there's smoke, there's fire." He stared at Jess through rapidly blackening eyes. "So which is it?"

His arm flashed out and he backhanded Abe Cotton, watching impassively as Cotton spun around, then dropped to his knees. Someone cheered as Jess pulled Cotton to his feet, then pushed his face close. He stared into Cotton's bruised eyes. "I'm going to let you go with a warning. No more brawls, Abe. Next time you start a fight in a public place, you're going to jail, you hear me?"

Abe swore at him and spit blood, but the fight was over.

He and Anderson tossed Cotton and Flowers outside, then sat at the bar until they were confident tempers had cooled and the saloon had settled down. But Jess was in a bad mood when he and his deputy left and headed for Rocker's Chophouse for a bite of pie and a decent cup of coffee. "All right," he snapped, stopping in the doorway. "Where do you stand in this?"

Anderson rocked back on his boot heels. "I don't see you walking away from your duty," he said finally. "So if you say you aren't the man, then I believe you. What I don't grasp is why Miss Malloy doesn't step up and name the real father."

"I guess she has her reasons," Jess said, pushing through the door. He wished to hell he knew what those reasons were.

In any case, he'd made up his mind how to solve the situation she'd put him in. Since she hadn't responded to his notes asking permission to call, he'd decided to turn the tables and put her in a situation of his making.

Brooding, he stared out the window of the chophouse and thought that he hadn't seen Annie in a while. When she came to Main Street he heard about it from someone, but he hadn't run into her himself. He hoped she would attend the Summer Crafts Fair. That was the opportunity he was looking for. He didn't like it, but he'd have to force her to talk to him.

Before they continued on to the Summer Crafts Fair, Mr. Waters drove them to the north edge of town and parked in front of a small clapboard house situated in a row of homes owned by farm laborers, clerks, city employees.

"Take a look, Anne."

The sun was hot and heavy. Even so, Annie's father had insisted that Waters lower the top of the phaeton. Because, he said, he was damned well not going to hide from the citizens of the town where he'd grown up. He and Ellen sat grim-lipped, faces forward, looking to neither the left nor the right, while Annie kept her head lowered, hoping the close brim of her bonnet shielded her misery from view.

"The yellow house is the one I'll buy if you're foolish enough to keep your bastard."

The first thing she noticed was the lack of trees and cooling vegetation. Either the soil was poor in this area or the residents didn't care or didn't intend to stay long enough to make the commitment that trees required.

Waves of heat shimmered along the rooflines and plain chimney stacks. A few residents had made a half-hearted attempt at a vegetable garden, but most of the yards were given over to sun-browned weeds and prairie grass. Annie could smell the privies behind the houses.

"It's smaller than I expected," Ellen said at length. She glanced at Annie's father, then straightened her shoulders. "The windows need washing. Perhaps some paint." Her voice trailed.

Gripping her hands in her lap, Annie tried to imagine living in a space that was less than the size of the Malloy carriage house. There couldn't be more than three rooms, a tiny parlor, a bedroom, and a kitchen. Was this the modern, independent living she had daydreamed about? A shudder rippled down her spine.

Harry Malloy nodded to Mr. Waters, and the phaeton turned in the street. "Think about it. I'll expect your decision next week, at the end of the month."

Annie couldn't speak, didn't look at him. Biting her lip, she watched her hands twisting in her lap and told herself that she'd been spoiled. Most people didn't live in a large, airy home with a maid and cook and weekly cleaning woman. The people Annie knew did, but most did not. She darted a quick glance back at the house and felt her heart plummet. The rooms would be hot and smothering. If she paced eight steps, she would run into a wall. Where would she store her winter coats and boots? For that matter, where would she keep the baby?

The baby. Closing her eyes, she opened a hand on her swelling stomach. Damn Bodie Miller. Damn the New Modern Woman's Association.

"Please don't make me do this," she whispered when Mr. Waters drew up before the entrance arch to the

Summer Crafts Fair. The thought of facing the whole town made her feel ill. "I beg you. Please let me go home. Please, Papa."

The day was too hot for the concealing folds of a shawl. Now that she was ending her fourth month, nothing she tried on had hidden her condition. In the end, Annie had chosen a cream-colored cotton with a summery rose pattern. From the front she could fool herself that she looked much as she always had. But a side view revealed a woman in the mid-stages of pregnancy.

Moreover, her palms had turned red and itchy and she had a pimple on her chin. She, who had passed through adolescence with a minimum of skin eruptions, now had regular breakouts.

"Everyone will stare at me."

"You should have thought of that before you took a lover," her father said flatly, extending his arm to hand her down.

Despair gripped Annie's heart. "Will you and Mother ever forgive me?"

Her father held her gaze, then turned aside and offered his arm to Ellen. "We'll inspect the creamery's booth first, then wander among the other exhibits. We'll leave after the fireworks."

He could have forgiven her almost anything except a secret lover, Annie thought dully. There was something of a feudal lord in Harry Malloy, and his household was the kingdom he ruled. He had expected to choose the man for his daughter and had expected that man to beg his permission to wed Annie. When Annie bypassed convention and made her own independent choice, she had unwittingly wrested control from the lord of the manor and she had made his kingdom seem trivial. No, her father wouldn't soon forgive her.

In the past, Annie hadn't minded taking responsibility for the picnic basket. She had decided on the picnic menu and had usually decorated the basket and handle with ribbons and fresh flowers. This year Ellen had packed the basket and had left the wicker plain, without adornment. Before they reached the creamery's booth, the weight of the basket and contents had raised an ache in Annie's back.

"Good afternoon, Mr. Malloy, Mrs. Malloy." Mr. Haskell, the creamery's floor manager, slid an uncomfortable glance toward Annie but didn't acknowledge her. He moved behind the display table, straightening and rearranging cartons of brown and white eggs, tubs of melting butter, and jugs of milk and cream that were beginning to curdle in the sun. "The ice cream was gone before ten this morning." Mr. Haskell showed Annie's father a sign that advertised free quarter-pint samples to the first forty people who visited the booth.

Saliva poured into Annie's mouth. Once during each of the summer months, her father ordered the big butter churn scrubbed out and used to make vanilla ice cream. From the time she was a child, Annie had looked forward to the evenings he came home with a gallon of fresh ice cream for "his girls." She turned aside, wondering if he'd brought ice cream yesterday or if that summer ritual had ended.

"When folks stop by," Mr. Haskell said, laying the FREE ICE CREAM sign facedown on the ground, "I tell 'em to look for Malloy's Marvelous Ice Cream at the grocer's."

But Annie heard a sharp voice behind her instead of Mr. Haskell: "Turn your face away. Don't look at that woman and don't speak!" And then the Windell girl's question: "But why, Mama? I like Miss Malloy." Annie held her breath and closed her eyes, waiting. "If I catch you speaking to that low hussy, I'll paddle you good."

It was the beginning of a seemingly endless nightmarish afternoon. No one met her gaze during those rare moments when Annie managed to lift her head. She knew she was seen and recognized, but expressions stiffened and cold eyes looked past her or through her. Remarks were made that she was intended to overhear: "Sinner!" "The nerve of her, coming out in public among decent people." "Go home!" "For shame!"

In an agony of humiliation, Annie stumbled along behind her parents, traveling up and down the grassy aisles between the tables and booths, bowed with hot shame and the weight of the picnic basket. When she flicked a glance upward, she saw the crimson flush on the back of her parents' necks and knew they also heard the comments.

"I'll take the basket," Ellen said at one point, but Annie refused to give it up. The basket gave her something to do with her hands and a place to look.

She would have surrendered ten years of her life to go home. But Harry and Ellen Malloy ignored her whispered pleas. They stopped at this booth or that and forced those behind the tables to speak to them. While Annie lingered to one side in abject misery, they chatted about the heat and the number of booths this year and the embroidery work and handmade furniture and dried flowers and paintings. Her mother bought more fresh produce than they would ever eat, and Annie's father purchased a raffle ticket for a quilt that none of them wanted. Annie bought nothing. She tried not to hear the voices around her. She endured.

Twice they wandered past the table where Helen, Ida Mae, and Janie sat behind a stack of *Manifestos* and membership applications. The second time, a trim young woman stood at the table leafing through the material. Annie's throat closed, and she hurried past them.

"Are you going to say hello?" Ellen asked, pressing a handkerchief to her brow.

"No," Annie said. That part of her life had ended.

Ellen put a hand on Annie's arm. "I know it doesn't seem so now, but you'll make new friends. Better friends."

The unexpected sympathy brought tears to her eyes. She shifted the basket to her other hand and resisted an urge to rub the small of her back. "Do you think so?"

Ellen sighed. "Honestly? I don't know. I've never paid attention to what happens to girls like . . . to girls who make this kind of mistake. But surely they find others like themselves. They must make new lives and new friends."

Aeons elapsed before the sun began to drift toward the horizon. Then finally a boy with a megaphone strode through the crowds announcing that the box supper auction would begin in twenty minutes. "Arrive early for a good seat," he bellowed.

"Thank heaven," Ellen said quietly. "I can't bear any more of this. Please, Harry, let's stay for the auction, then leave. We can eat our picnic at home. You don't really care about the fireworks and whatever else is planned for this evening, do you?"

A lifetime ago, when they had arrived at the fair, Annie's father had insisted they would stay until the last of the Chinese rockets had exploded against the night sky. Now, narrow-eyed and thin-lipped, he nodded his consent to Ellen's suggestion.

Sick with relief, Annie slipped into the stream of people flowing toward the rows of seats inside an open-sided striped tent. An hour, perhaps two at the most, and then she could escape the icy stares and the hissed comments and condemnation.

She looked up, not wanting to lose her parents in the crush, and that's when she spotted Jesse Harden. He leaned against one of the tent poles, arms crossed over his chest, watching the crowd narrow at the official entrance to the tent.

Annie's stomach tightened, and her scalp tingled. Annoyed, she told herself the reaction was an expression of guilt for not responding to his requests for permission to call. But surely he understood that she couldn't agree. If Mary admitted Jess Harden to the Malloy house, the gossips would take it as proof that he was the father of Annie's baby.

Jess straightened when he spotted her, as if he'd been waiting for her. Annie steadied herself for the moment when he stared at her stomach, but he didn't. His lips twitched as he scanned the damp red tendrils sticking to her cheeks; then his dark eyes locked on her gaze. An electric charge flashed through Annie's body and she caught a surprised breath.

She was no longer an ignorant maiden. Annie recognized that jolt of sudden intense connection for what it was. And what it was shocked, embarrassed, and confused her.

But what did the heat in their eyes feel like to Jess? If he felt anything, that is. Annie couldn't guess. But she understood her burst of gratitude when he smiled, the sole smile directed at her today. Blinking hard, she silently mouthed the words, *Thank you,* then hurried inside the tent to catch up to Harry and Ellen Malloy. When she found them, she cast a quick glance over her shoulder, but she didn't see Jess's tall frame and decided he must have left or he'd taken a seat.

Confusion and a tiny shiver of alarm spun her mind as she settled herself on a seat beside her parents. She had a strong sense that Jess had been searching for her in the crowd. But why would he?

CHAPTER 9

~~~~~~~~~~~~~~~~~~~~~~~~~~~~~

*T*HE auction of box suppers provided by Marshall's unmarried young ladies was the town's favorite charity event and the most anticipated moment of the fair. To keep things interesting, the baskets and boxes were not auctioned by name but by number. In consequence, the ladies covered their boxes and baskets with elaborate decorations in an effort to alert their beaux as to which number to bid on. Hilarious mistakes occurred every year, and the audience eagerly anticipated that this year would be no exception.

Once the auction got under way, Annie let herself relax in the relief of knowing that finally no one paid any attention to her. Slumping against the back of the wooden chair, she tried to find a comfortable position. There was no such thing.

"Four dollars!" If the young man won the bid, he would receive the basket and the lady who prepared it would join him to enjoy the contents.

A second anxious-looking fellow sprang to his feet and shouted, "Four-fifty!" The crowd urged the bidding higher with laughter and encouragement.

The first time Annie had entered a box supper in the auction, she'd been fifteen. Bill Krutzer had bought her basket for five dollars and they had spent the next two hours in the throes of embarrassed silence, trying not to dribble food on themselves and struggling desperately to think of something to say to each other. The memory made her smile. When last she'd heard, Bill Krutzer was married, the father of four children, and shoeing horses in Kansas City.

The next item came up for auction, a box heavily pasted with red paper hearts topped by a spray of violets. A boyish young man jumped to his feet with a bid of four dollars and a fierce glare to discourage competitors. The crowd roared with laughter when Miss Almond, the town librarian, came to the stage. The young man's jaw dropped and his face turned crimson. Miss Almond was Annie's age and clearly not the lady he had expected to spend the evening with.

Annie scratched her palms and touched a fingertip to the pimple on her chin to see if it had grown larger. She let her mind drift to this and that, settling eventually on the last time she had participated in the auction. Shortly after the fair that year she had made the decision never to marry. Had she ever regretted her commitment? Once or twice. But by and large she had been comfortable with the independence of going her own way.

That is, until last year when she'd met Bodie Miller. This time last year she had started thinking crazy things like wanting to have her cake and eat it, too. She had rejected marriage, but she longed to experience the mysteries between men and women. Dying an old maid didn't trouble her, but dying an incomplete woman did. Those had been her thoughts when Bodie Miller dazzled her with his boyish grin and asked if he might buy her a cherry ice.

"I'm glad that's over," Ellen sighed. "I don't enjoy this event as much as I used to." Bending, she reached for the picnic basket near Annie's feet. Voices filled the tent as everyone gathered their things and chattered about where to have their picnic and enjoy the promised fireworks.

"Wait." A commanding voice lifted above the din. "I want to bid on a basket."

Falling silent, most of the crowd sank back to their chairs, craning their necks to see who was speaking. But Annie recognized Jess Harden's voice and her heart sank in a spasm of foreboding. *Please don't do anything foolish,* she prayed.

The auctioneer grinned from the stage. "Sorry, Sheriff, you missed your chance. All the boxes and baskets are spoken for."

"I bid twenty dollars for Annie Malloy's box supper."

A collective gasp buzzed across the tent and Annie squeezed her eyes shut as hundreds of stares swung in her direction. Damn him. Tears scalded the backs of her eyelids. How could he do this to her? Dimly she felt Ellen's fingers dig into her arm, heard her father's blustering.

"Twenty dollars is a very generous bid, sir. If the lady is willing, I know the Marshall Benevolent Society would be happy to receive that twenty dollars." The auctioneer scanned the crowd. "Is Miss Annie Malloy here?" He was the only outsider present and the only person who didn't know exactly where Annie sat.

Desperately trying to hide behind the wings of her bonnet, Annie shook her head and whispered, "No. Papa, tell him no."

"You can't refuse," Ellen hissed in her ear. "If you do, everyone will believe the sheriff is trying to do the right thing, trying to be with you, and it's you who are refusing him!"

Annie's father grasped the implications at the same moment. Standing, he nodded to the auctioneer, then took the basket from Ellen and raised it for show before he leaned to place the picnic on Annie's lap.

"The sheriff is very clever," Ellen said, betraying both irritation and admiration.

"We're leaving now." Annie's father settled his hat firmly, then turned his head to scrutinize Jess Harden with a long, expressionless look. "I'll send Waters back for you. He'll be waiting outside the arch whenever you're ready."

The day had gone from bad to worse to unthinkable. Head bowed and face flaming, Annie waited in her seat as the tent slowly emptied. If any comments were tossed in her direction, she didn't hear them, but the gossips would be busy tonight.

"Annie?" Jess waited until everyone had departed before he sat in the seat her father had vacated, leaving Ellen's seat empty between them. "Are you angry?"

"Yes." Eyes blazing, she raised her head. "If there was anyone in town who doubted that you fathered my baby, you just squashed that doubt. What in the world were you thinking?"

Though she saw him and could smell his scent of soap and starch and the faint odor of the oil he used to clean his guns, she couldn't believe he was beside her and this was happening. Tears of embarrassed anger stung the backs of her eyes.

He shrugged and placed his hat on the seat between them, then raked his fingers through curly dark hair that looked freshly barbered. "You wouldn't see me, and I need to speak to you."

"Nothing has changed, Mr. Harden. I haven't heard from . . . my friend. No wedding is planned." A note of bitterness entered her voice; she couldn't help it.

"Not much of a friend if you ask me."

"I didn't," she snapped. Instantly she regretted her sharpness. None of her troubles were Jess Harden's fault. But she was to blame for at least one of his problems. "I'm sorry," she said in a softer tone. "It's been a terrible day and I just want to go home." She touched her fingertips to her chin, checking the pimple and trying not to be obvious about it. "Look . . . if it would help, I . . ." Annie swallowed hard. "I'd be willing to speak to Mayor Meadows and tell him you're not responsible for my error."

"Is there anything to drink in that basket?"

"Lemonade," she said reluctantly. "It won't be cold."

The jug was beneath the checkered cloth and he found it immediately, along with two glasses. Annie sighed. It appeared she wouldn't be leaving at once. She tasted the glass he handed her and decided that warm, sugary lemonade wasn't as bad as she had expected.

Jess tugged on the bandanna around his neck and cleared his throat. "Thank you for offering to speak to the mayor, but after tonight he wouldn't believe you. I doubt he would have before. I'm sorry, Annie, but after tonight the gossips are going to conclude that I'm not refusing you; you're refusing me. They'll figure out that

I bid on your basket because that's the only way I could think of to get you to talk to me. The blame will shift to you."

"Oh, I'm getting plenty of blame, thank you." But the condemnation would swing away from him; he was right about that.

"People won't understand why a woman in your situation would refuse to marry the man responsible, but that's what they will conclude."

The anger went out of her in a rush. "That's fair," she said finally. "But they'll still think you're that man."

"I've figured that out, too. Unless you marry the man responsible—which you say won't happen—then this town is going to go right on believing that you and I were lovers." He watched her turn her face away. "That realization led me to the next thing, and that's what I want to talk to you about. Annie, look at me."

She didn't want to meet his eyes. Jess Harden had a way of studying her as if he saw more than other people did, as if he looked inside her and saw everything she had been and everything she might or might not be. Reluctantly she raised her head, not liking him much right now.

"I want you to marry me."

"What?" Shock stopped her heart. Lemonade spilled over her skirt, but she hardly noticed. "Have you lost your senses?"

"You need a husband. I'm ready to settle down. We can let the child believe what everyone else does, that I'm his or her father. That child," he nodded at her stomach, "needs a name and a father. I believe I can be a good father to your child and a good husband to you."

There wasn't enough air in the tent. She could hardly

breathe, let alone speak. "I . . . don't know what to say. I can't marry you, Mr. Harden."

"Why not?"

"For one, and there are many reasons, we're practically strangers."

"I've thought about you enough that I feel like I know you."

"But you only know the surface, and that's all I know about you." She spread her hands, spilling more lemonade. "Marriage is a very serious matter."

"So is having a baby. Children need two parents."

"We don't love each other!"

"Couples have made successful marriages without love. Respect and friendship can be enough."

Her mind reeled and she felt so dizzy that she worried about sliding off the chair. "You can offer respect and friendship knowing what I've done?"

"What have you done, Annie?" He stared at her so intently that she noticed green flecks in his intense dark eyes. "Except something couples have been doing since we lived in caves. Should you be condemned forever because you're human?"

"A lot of people seem to think so," she whispered, looking at him as if she'd never seen him before.

There was nothing boyish in Jesse Harden's expression or in his gaze. This was a man. A man who knew his mind and was seasoned and set in his ways. He had thought his offer through, and she sensed he wouldn't back away.

"There are two things I need to know." He took the empty lemonade glass from her hand and set it on the chair beside his hat. "Is the man who's responsible someone I'm going to run into every day?"

"No," she said, surprised that she answered. She couldn't stop staring at him. Couldn't focus her mind on what was happening here.

"Do you love him? Could this man show up sometime in the future and take my family away?"

What had she said in the note she left for Bodie in the box in the willows? Had she written that she would marry him? No, she had said they needed to talk because things had changed. By now she felt certain that she would never see Bodie Miller again.

"If I hadn't believed I loved him, I could never have . . ." She bit her lip and turned to watch the crew of men folding the chairs and stacking them to one side. "But that part is confusing." Annie flicked a glance at him, then drew a deep breath. "The fact is, Mr. Harden, I don't know if I loved him or just believed that I ought to. Maybe I did. I don't know anymore. But the truth is, he offered to marry me and I refused him."

"I'll be damned," he said softly. "You refused him. You chose a hard road for yourself. Can you tell me why?"

She had to be careful with her reply. "We didn't want the same things for the future," she said at length. "Compromise was not possible. I hoped he would reconsider when he learned about the baby, but he didn't."

"And you didn't, either."

She couldn't read his expression. "No."

"Then you're prepared to see this through alone," he said, frowning.

Tilting her head back, Annie gazed at the top of the

tent and thought about the dismal yellow house at the edge of town. "I wasn't prepared at all. I was so naive. I never dreamed it would be this humiliating or this hard. But the damage is done, Mr. Harden. I'm learning that words can wound and shame me, but they won't kill me, although sometimes it feels like they will." Oddly, she could say things to this man that she couldn't say to anyone else. "So, yes. I guess I can see it through alone."

The thought frightened her and she couldn't yet bring herself to think about all her decision entailed. The best she could manage was to take each day as it came. Every morning she awoke and pulled herself together with the promise that all she had to do was get through this one day.

Jess glanced at the men advancing down the steadily disappearing rows of chairs. "Shall we find a place to eat your picnic?"

Her palms itched, her back ached, and her head was spinning. "I think I'd just like to go home." When he offered to escort her, she shook her head. "Mr. Waters is waiting."

They stood at the same time and Annie looked up at him, abruptly aware of his height and broad shoulders. He wasn't big in the rawboned way that Bodie was big, but he was equally as tall and imposing. Standing next to him, she was aware of hard muscle, sinew, and tendon. In a fight he would be agile, fast, and dangerous.

"Why are you willing to marry a woman you hardly know who is disgraced and whose reputation is ruined?"

"I'm not good at soft talk," he said, looking uncomfortable. "You're very pretty, and I've admired you for a long time. What I do know about you I like. As for the rest, I can live with it."

It wasn't a complete answer and she sensed there was more as strongly as she sensed that she would not learn the full truth tonight.

"One thing," she said, her face flaming. "I assume you're talking about a marriage in name only . . . ?"

"No. If you accept my offer, I expect our marriage to be like any other."

The color burned on her cheeks. "Oh."

He picked up the basket, then offered her his arm. After a brief hesitation, Annie sighed, then wrapped her arm around his sleeve. Let the gossips make of it what they would.

Outside the tent, darkness had fallen. The fireworks would begin soon, not that she cared. They followed a line of torches to the arch, and she spotted the phaeton waiting for her.

Before he handed her inside, Jess looked down into her face. "Take your time deciding."

"You should also do some thinking, Mr. Harden. The reason I decided never to marry is because I'm not good wife material." She met his gaze full on and felt an unexpected tingle in her stomach. This man wanted to marry her, a marriage complete in every way. She would never look at him the same way again. "I'm opinionated, accustomed to independence, and if you think I'll obey an order because you issue it, I can tell you that won't happen. I don't want you or any man making decisions for me, and I come and go as I please without asking permission. I'm grateful for your offer, though I don't understand it, but I won't hold you to it."

His laughter surprised her. "Ah, Annie. I hope you accept. We'll have some interesting times, and Ione will love you."

His reaction was so far from what she had expected that she didn't know what to say. And she'd forgotten about his mother. Frowning, she glanced at the carriage, then turned back to him, aware of his height and warmth. "Does your mother . . . ?"

"If we marry, we'll live out at Ione's place, at least until after the baby is born. Then we'll decide about a house and if we want to stay in Marshall."

We'll decide. If he meant what he said, then Jess Harden was unlike any other man she knew.

"You've told me what to expect from you. Here's what you can expect from me." His dark gaze held her fast. "I have some money put by, and I can give you a comfortable life. I'm a solitary man, but I'll be your friend and I'll learn to say the things a woman likes to hear. I'm opinionated and independent, too, and we'll bump against each other on occasion. Frankly, I don't know how well I'll adjust to having a wife, but I'm willing to try and to make compromises if you are. The one thing I ask of you is truth. No secrets."

Three-quarters of the people in Marshall would not believe Sheriff Jesse Harden capable of the speech he had just made. Annie stared at him, not certain that she could trust what he was saying. On the other hand, she knew her father was a stern and demanding taskmaster at the creamery, while at home he generally permitted her and Ellen to have their way unless he was inconvenienced or aggravated. Was that what Jess was promising?

Annie stepped toward the carriage, then came back.

"I guess I should tell you this. I haven't decided yet, but I'm considering putting the baby out for adoption."

"No," he said simply. Lifting his hand, he smoothed a tendril off her cheek, leaving a burning sensation where his fingers brushed her skin. "Adoption isn't acceptable."

"It's not your decision." Frowning, she scrubbed her knuckles across the hot place on her cheek.

"Don't throw away a child because you made a mistake."

There was no answer to that statement, so she went to the phaeton and allowed Jess to hand her inside. When she leaned to the window, the light was behind him and she couldn't see his expression. A whistling noise signaled the starburst that showered sparks of red and green across the black sky, and in the brief explosion of light she saw his face. Hard, handsome, intense. She looked at his tall, lean silhouette until the carriage turned and rolled into the darkness.

The day had been long and emotional. Exhaustion swept her the instant she settled into the soft leather cushions, but Annie doubted she would sleep much tonight. Jess Harden had given her another, totally unexpected option to consider.

Jess dipped water from the barrel behind the jail, then stuck his head in the bucket, washing four days of sweat and grime from his hair and neck. Tossing his shirt aside, he used his bandanna to wash his chest before donning the fresh shirt he kept in his office.

Most of the posse had gone home, but a few men and his four deputies had parked themselves on the benches facing the street, swapping stories of the chase. Jess scrutinized Main, satisfying himself that all was quiet; then he leaned against the wall of the office to enjoy the tales that grew with each telling.

"Maybe I should remind you boys," he said, still smiling after an hour of tall talk, "that we didn't get those sons a bitches."

"We were this close," Josh Mercer swore. "I tell you, they were headed for Missouri. We should have just ridden on to the border."

"Wasn't our call," Anderson reminded him.

Three men had robbed a train out of Atchison, and the Atchison sheriff had telegraphed for assistance. Jess and his men had responded, but the trail was cold.

After the others left, Jess, Anderson, and Mercer went to the saloon for a whiskey. "Tell me again about your cousin in Blevens," Jess said to Josh Mercer.

Mercer shrugged thin shoulders and scratched his whiskers. "There's nothing much to tell except the three train robbers match the descriptions of three men who robbed the bank in Blevens."

"Blevens is in Missouri?" Anderson asked.

"Yeah. They killed a teller but didn't get any money. Then, almost a month later they went back, robbed the same bank again, and that time they got about two thousand dollars."

"That's all the bank had? Two thousand dollars?"

"I don't know. But that's all they got. One of them is named Jodie. He appears to be the leader."

"If you're right, now they're operating out of Kansas," Anderson commented, signaling for another round.

"I'm thinking they may be working both sides of the border," Jess said after a minute, recalling the wanted posters he regularly read. "And if it's the same three who keep showing up in the posters, they've been at this for a few years."

The descriptions of the men varied, but a few items remained constant: Three men working together. The tallest and biggest was the leader. There was speculation that the other two might be brothers, although Jess didn't know what that guess was based on. The tall one was blond; the other two were dark. They weren't the most successful outlaws that the area had seen. This gang ran into bad luck about half the time. And, if it was the same gang, they hadn't killed anyone until the bank job in Blevens and the train robbery. Now the search would intensify.

"They'll surface again," he said, tossing back the whiskey and stepping down from the bar stool. "If Missouri doesn't catch them, someone on our side of the border will."

Mercer puffed out his chest and grinned. "The word must be out about us. Banks in two bordering counties have been hit, but not ours. We're too tough. Those Atchison boys might let outlaws slip through their fingers, but not us."

Jess smiled. But the comments were interesting. Maybe the outlaws weren't hitting local banks because these banks were too close to home. He was too tired to examine the thought closely.

However, he wasn't too tired to take a short detour on the way to his boardinghouse. Leaning against a tree across the street from the Malloy house, he took a thin cigar from the box in his pocket, lit it, and waved out the match, his gaze on the upper-story curtains. If he had a daughter, he wouldn't put her in a room fronting the street, so he doubted he would catch a glimpse of Annie passing a window. But at this time of evening she was probably inside the house.

She hadn't refused him outright, and that was a good sign. But she hadn't given him any reason to think she would accept him, either. Still, given that he'd never offered marriage before, he thought the proposal had gone pretty well.

What he wanted was to knock on her door and demand an answer. But acting on impulse wasn't his way. That was a good thing considering he hadn't bathed or shaved in four days. No, he'd wait for his answer until she came to him.

"I told you before, I don't know what to do next. I'm thinking about it." Scowling, Bodie laid out a game of solitaire. The way his luck was running he'd lose again.

Hoss carried a glass of whiskey to the door and leaned heavily against the jamb. "We've been hitting the border towns for three fricking months, and we don't have crap to show for it. We might as well go home, since things aren't working out. We've been gone too long anyway. Alice is going to skin me alive."

"You shouldn't have shot that idiot on the train," Jimmy said, frowning at Bodie.

"You may recall that he was shooting at me." He was sick to damned death of talking about everything that had gone wrong with the attempted train robbery. "Besides, after Hoss killed the teller in Blevens, what does it matter if we kill one man or ten?"

But it did matter. Riding around the countryside

robbing a bank here and there was no longer a lark that Bodie could walk away from. The minute he killed that man on the train, everything changed. He couldn't walk away from being a killer. He couldn't claim that he wasn't really hurting anyone.

He had watched a man die by his hand, and had silently shouted, *No.* But he couldn't bring the bullet back. Couldn't make a different decision.

"Yeah, well before you and Hoss got careless, if the worst happened, we went to prison. Now, it's a rope."

Hoss swore and moved out of the doorway. "Someone's riding down the driveway."

"Stay in the house. Cover me."

Jumping up, Bodie stepped out on the porch and partially closed the door behind him. The man riding toward him didn't look dangerous; he looked like a farmer. But you never could tell.

"Hello there. I'm Ben Caddish." Caddish waved toward the east. "I've got eighty acres butting up against yours."

"Is that right?" Bodie said pleasantly, wondering where this was going.

"Saw your lights last night and decided to stop by and say welcome to the area. We didn't expect you until next week."

"Ah, I came earlier than I'd originally planned."

"The missus is planning to drop in later with a cake and some rolls. There hasn't been another woman in this house for a long time."

Bodie's mind raced. "Tell your missus to wait a week until the family gets here. I came early to make the place livable."

Caddish nodded. "Yeah, the house has been vacant so long that squatters use it occasionally. Can't be in too good shape."

They visited a few more minutes; then Bodie said he needed to get back to work and Caddish rode away with a promise to lend a hand if Bodie needed help.

"Well, ain't that just the way our luck is going?" Jimmy said when Caddish was beyond hearing. "Now we're going to lose the Nook."

"I say we go home," Hoss said, tossing back his whiskey. "Spend the rest of the summer getting our farms in shape. We can get back together in the fall. Maybe our luck will have changed by then."

Jimmy agreed. "There should be plenty of time to make some money before the snow falls."

Misfortune had plagued them since they left Marshall. It had all started with Annie Malloy demanding that he change his life to suit her ideas. Bodie poured a glass of whiskey and returned to the porch. Now, three and a half months later, he had a string of failed bank robberies behind him and the disastrous attempt to rob the Atchison train. Now he and the Baylor boys were wanted for murder and they'd just lost the Nook. The string of bad luck was unbelievable.

He had told himself that he wouldn't return to Marshall until he had enough money to build a big house in Greensboro near the Baylors. Greensboro was thirty miles west of Marshall, near enough that Annie could see her parents on occasion. But all he had to show for his trouble was about two thousand dollars. Gambling and women had taken a chunk of his paltry proceeds, and he'd had to buy a new saddle and some clothes. In the end, he didn't have enough to buy the land he wanted and build a house bigger than Harry Malloy's. Not nearly enough.

By now, he thought, casting a brooding glance toward the west and Kansas, Annie was languishing in some unwed mothers' home feeling lonely, missing him, and finally ready to see things his way. The long delay in returning to Marshall would work to his advantage.

Realistically, Greensboro probably wasn't a wise settling-down place anymore. Now that he was wanted for murder, he'd need to put some space between himself and the border area, and Annie wasn't going to like that.

Every time he thought about it, he could hardly believe that he'd killed a man. No question, killing had changed him inside. He felt harder, meaner, tougher, a man with no limits, and sometimes he liked that. But other times he understood that he'd turned down a path leading to nowhere. All the choices that were possible a few weeks ago were now gone. There was only one direction to follow.

And that direction pointed to a fresh start somewhere else. There were banks in all parts of the country. He could make a living anywhere. Right now, though, it was time to cut his losses and return to Marshall. He didn't doubt that Annie had left him a message in the tin box under the willows telling him where to find her. He knew she loved him.

"All right, boys," he said, striding inside. "We're going home tomorrow."

CHAPTER 10

Now that Annie had learned Jess Harden regularly checked on the old Miller place, she didn't go to the cabin anymore. But she made an exception today. Nothing had changed except dust had thickened on the stoop and weeds had taken over the small yard and corral.

Keeping an anxious eye on the road, she located the tin box beneath the willows and retrieved her note. Scanning her words, she winced and thanked heaven that Bodie would never read of her desperation. She sounded pathetic, willing to throw away principle and an honest life. Angry that she'd nearly let herself be persuaded to do something that every instinct said was wrong, she ripped the note into tiny pieces and dropped the bits of paper into the creek.

Leaving nothing but the money behind, she returned to the county road, then walked along the backstreets of Marshall to the other side of town. Her steps slowed as she approached the yellow house, and her spirits sank. It was as small and discouraging as she remembered from five days ago. She had hoped that her initial shock had colored her perception and the house wouldn't be as bad as she'd originally thought.

Nothing stirred in the neighborhood. The air was still and hot. Swallowing hard, Annie stiffened her resolve and followed a dirt path to the front door of the house. To her surprise, the door opened when she tried the knob.

Inside it was stifling, the baking air stale and noisy with the buzz of flies batting against the windows. A series of footprints disturbed the dust on the floor, leading to the doors opening off the front room. Probably her father's. Annie peeked into a tiny windowless bedroom, sighed, then inspected a minuscule closet. The kitchen was the largest room in the house, but she examined it with dismay.

The windows had been painted shut; not a breath of air moved in the thick heat. The pump handle was rusty and the stove crusted with use. The sagging wooden floor slanted toward a wall with a door leading outside to the privy.

Choking in the heat and the dust disturbed by her steps, Annie returned to the front room. The house would take an enormous amount of work to clean and make livable.

But she supposed it could be done. And at the finish, she would have a small nest of her own. Squinting, she tried to visualize her favorite chair beside the window and could almost see herself idling away a long winter day with a book in her lap and only steps away from a teakettle on her freshly cleaned stove.

Her bedroom furniture would never fit into the tiny bedroom; she'd have to have a smaller bed and bureau. And lamps. She could store out-of-season clothing at her parents' home. Geraniums on the sill would brighten the kitchen, and perhaps some wallpaper. A lawn and a flower bed.

Oh, Lord. She'd forgotten the baby. Where would she put the baby and all the things a baby needed? She turned in a slow circle. Where had the previous residents stored their laundry tub and bathtub? Gardening utensils? There wasn't space in the front room to hold three chairs for the times her parents came to visit, not if she wanted a bookcase and a lamp table. The place was dismal.

Her brief forced spurt of optimism evaporated and she leaned against the wall and closed her eyes, lifting a hand to her forehead.

The house was horrible. But what was the alternative? Giving her baby to strangers because she was accustomed to comfort? Because a baby was an embarrassment to her parents and a shameful burden to her?

Feeling the walls closing in on her, Annie remembered what Jess had said about throwing away a child because she had made an error. His words rang true in her heart.

Absently she checked on a new pimple, this one near her nose, and pressed at the frown between her eyes. How genuine an alternative was Jess's offer? Jess scared her. He wasn't like Bodie, who she had always known wasn't suitable and wasn't someone who could make her heart ache for long. But she didn't understand Jess Harden's offer, and that made her uneasy, afraid to trust. Afraid to surrender herself into the hands of a stranger when she'd never wanted to marry in the first place.

Then something happened, something so momentous that it changed everything.

She felt a fluttery movement, like a butterfly brushing a wing against the inside of her stomach. At first puzzled, then astonished, Annie placed a hand against the swell of her cotton skirt. After a moment, she felt the slight movement again and tears sprang into her eyes.

Good God. There was a baby inside her! Wide-eyed with amazement, she slowly slid down the wall and sat in the dust on the floor, staring down at her hands pressed to her stomach. For the first time she didn't have to struggle to convince herself that the baby was real. She felt him or her. He was alive and very real. Good heavens. She was going to have a baby.

She, Anne Malloy, was going to be a mother. She would be responsible for another life. Blinking hard, she stared at her stomach, silently willing her baby to reach out to her again. When the tiny nudge came, a thrill of goose bumps rose on her skin and tears spilled over her lashes.

She was going to have a baby. The world tilted and forever changed. Suddenly the life inside her was very, very real. And her decisions were no longer just her own.

"Hey, Sheriff. You've got a visitor."

Stepping back from the mirror at the end of the row of cells, Jess tossed his comb on the shelf and settled his hat. "Tell him to come back later. I'm due in court to testify against Murdock." Amos Murdock was a nasty piece of work and Jess would be glad to see him hang. He looked forward to the next hour.

"It's not a he; it's a she," Anderson said with a grin.

Annie? He studied his testifying suit in the mirror, thinking this was a good time if it was her. "Do I know the lady?"

Anderson's grin widened. "Some say you know her better'n you ought."

Already Jess had learned that friends took liberties. It was part of the package. But she was in his office. Would she meet him face-to-face if she meant to refuse him? He thought about that. If he knew her character the way he hoped he did, then yes, she wouldn't refuse him in a cowardly note. She'd march in here and tell him her decision whatever it was.

He'd told Ione that he didn't care one way or another what Annie decided, but Ione had watched him start remodeling her bunkhouse into a real house and she'd seen through him. She had smiled and said she hoped Annie Malloy had the sense that Jess thought she did. Well, he was about to find out.

"Take a walk, Anderson," he said when he entered his office. Then he couldn't say another word.

Today Annie Malloy was as beautiful as he'd ever seen her. Tendrils of curly red hair escaped from her bonnet; a few strands stuck to her moist cheek. She wore a loose pale yellow dress covered with dust. He guessed she must have been outside awhile, because there were fascinating damp circles beneath her arms and breasts.

He noted these things without dwelling on them, his mind focused on her radiance. Her cheeks glowed and her eyes flashed like a green sea in sunlight. She looked dazzled, her lips parted in an expression of wonder.

This was how she would look in bed, he thought, the image vivid before him. Irritated, he lowered his hat to cover himself and silently swore. Even if she accepted him, they were months from actually sharing a bed. Maybe she'd refuse altogether.

He cleared his throat. "Good afternoon, Annie. You look lovely today." Soft talk wasn't his strong suit, but with her the words came naturally.

"Thank you." Her cheek twitched and she appeared to notice his testifying suit. For some reason, she kept her hand on her cheek and nose. "You look very nice, too."

"Thank you." That was the problem with small talk; you didn't know what to say afterward or how to get from the trivial to a topic of consequence. Jess bit down on his back teeth and told himself that he absolutely would not ask if she'd made a decision. The next words that fell out of his mouth were, "Have you decided?" Damn it anyway.

A tide of pink intensified the color in her cheeks. She looked down and fumbled with the strings on her purse. "If you haven't changed your mind . . ."

"I haven't."

"Well, I'm definitely in need of a husband and you've said you're willing. You may speak to my father."

Good God. She had decided to marry him. He was the luckiest man on earth. But now what? Did he embrace her? Shake her hand? Lord knew he wanted to touch her. A rush of color tinted his own jaw; then he cleared his throat and ran his fingers over the brim of his hat. "How soon may I speak to Mr. Malloy?"

"Tonight perhaps?" Her eyes widened and sparkled. "Mr. Harden . . . I'm going to have a baby!" She smiled and his heart stopped. If she'd smiled at him like this before, he would damn sure have remembered. She was incandescent. "Think of it . . . I'm going to have a baby!"

Her amazement and joy made him smile. "You're just realizing that?"

She shook her head as if she couldn't believe it, either. "I think I am."

Of all the times to have to appear in court, this was the worst. More appropriately, they should have gone somewhere private to make plans and be alone together.

"That's all right," she said after he'd explained about Amos Murdock and being required to testify. She backed toward the door, one hand on her stomach and the other hand covering her nose. "Then I'll see you tonight?"

"Right after supper."

There were lists to be made, things to do. The instant he finished in court, he'd hire every man in the Tree Stump Saloon to ride out to Ione's place and work ten hours a day until the bunkhouse was finished and transformed into a home that a woman like Annie would approve of for the short term. The bunkhouse would have to serve until they decided on a permanent home after the baby was born.

Three hours later he galloped out to Ione's, skidding to a halt near the lumberyard's delivery wagon. The sound of hammers rang in the air. "Make sure not to close up the kitchen area until the stove is delivered," he said, walking through the chaos and shouting orders. The men had only been working an hour, but he could see progress already. It was satisfying to observe what eight men could do as opposed to just himself.

"I take it she said yes," Ione said, smiling when he went to the house. Stretching up on tiptoe, she kissed his cheek. "Congratulations." Then she leaned back and gazed into his eyes. "You're sure about this?"

"Are you sure about having us in such close proximity?"

She led him inside and poured glasses of the wine she saved for special occasions. "To you and your bride." Then her face sobered. "We need some rules, Jesse John."

"What sort of rules?" His mind raced with everything that needed to be done in a very short while.

"I'll never visit the bunkhouse without an invitation."

"You don't need an invitation," he objected, his eyebrows rising. "This is your place after all."

"Which you're fixing up for me, and for which you insist on paying rent." She shook her head and her long gray-and-brown braid slid from her shoulder to her back. "I won't offer advice unless I'm asked. I'll consider the baby as much my grandchild as if you truly were the father. Here's the most important rule of all. . . . If ever there is a dispute between your Annie and me, you are to side with your wife, you hear me, Jesse John? And if there's ever a dispute between any of your children and Annie, you side with her then, too. Always put your wife first."

"What are you talking about? There aren't going to be any disputes between you and Annie."

"I don't think so, either. Certainly I'm going to try like thunder to be a good mother-in-law, but we're all entering new territory. So you remember what I told you. Your wife always comes first. If I raised you right, you already know that."

He grinned at her and pushed a piece of paper across

the table before he refilled their wineglasses. "Check this list, will you please? Have I forgotten anything?"

"Where are my glasses? Let's see, now. When is the wedding?"

"I'll settle that tonight with her father, but I'd guess within the next three or four days."

"Will the bunkhouse be finished?"

"I think so. The furnishings will be sparse, but Annie should handle that anyway, get what she wants."

Ione fetched paper and ink and began a list of her own. "I'll need to provision the kitchen. Does she have a trousseau?"

He had no idea.

"All right, I'll buy some starter linens, too." They talked about the necessities required immediately; then she pushed his list back across the table and handed him her pen. "Add haircut and a new suit, new boots if you need them. And did you plan to give the bride a ring?"

"A ring!" He swore and wrote "ring" on his list before he returned to the bunkhouse. Some good hard manual labor would keep his mind off things until it was time to ride into town and speak to Annie's father.

He'd been alone all of his life, but he was about to be a married man. And a father. The wonder and the absurdity of it made him laugh out loud.

Annie waited on the porch for the farce to play out in the parlor. There could be no doubt that her father would grant Jess Harden's request for her hand. The real question was if she had made the right decision in accepting him. Her opinion changed from minute to minute but usually ended in much the same way. She was breaking her vow not to marry and doing so for the wrong reasons.

Now that she'd felt the baby quicken, adoption had become unthinkable. And she refused to take her baby to that awful little yellow house. Her parents would be happy about her marriage and the town would approve. Once she and Jess had "done the right thing" in the eyes of the community, attitudes toward them would relax. Marshall wouldn't forget her history—she would always be remembered as having been no better than she ought to be. But, if Ellen was right, the worst of the scandal would fade quickly the minute she and Jess said their I dos.

Annie waved her best fan before her face, stirring the warm evening air. The strongest motivation for marrying Jesse Harden was to give her baby a name and a father. And Jesse was right. No one in town would ever doubt that Jesse was her baby's real father, so her child wouldn't doubt it, either. He'd never know about Bodie Miller.

She pressed her lips together and looked down at the hand cupped over her stomach. Where was Bodie? In his note he had said he would be gone for a couple of weeks, but he'd been gone for three months. Had something terrible happened? Had he been captured and jailed? Something worse? This was what her life would have been like with him. Not knowing. Worrying herself sick.

Or, she thought after a few minutes, maybe this was a case of out of sight, out of mind. Perhaps he'd ridden away and forgotten about her. She believed that he'd meant his offer of marriage when he made it, but Bodie could change his mind as quick as lightning. Maybe he'd decided never to return to Marshall. A small pang of regret constricted her chest as the door opened. Bodie was an unfinished chapter in her life. She wasn't sure why she felt that way, but she did.

Jess emerged, followed by her mother carrying a tray. Ellen set the tray on the wrought-iron table in front of the porch swing. "I brought you coffee and spice cake with Cook's special icing." Her voice was bright and a little shrill. "Is there anything else you need? Annie? Sheriff?" They both said no, and Ellen twisted her hands together. "Well, then. I'll just . . ." The door shut softly behind her.

The swing sagged lower as Jess sat beside her and placed his hat on the porch floor. For his interview with her father Annie noticed that he'd worn a crisp white shirt and dark jacket with his badge prominently displayed. He'd gone through the motions of asking for Annie's hand, but he'd presented himself as Harry Malloy's equal.

"The wedding will be the day after tomorrow," Jess announced as Annie poured coffee. "We'll be married in Greensboro at five o'clock, followed by supper at the hotel."

"Do you take cream or sugar?" How odd to marry someone and not know how he preferred his coffee.

"Just black."

"I take cream in mine. Will your mother attend the ceremony?"

"It won't be much of a ceremony, but yes. Ione will be there. Everyone will stay the night at the hotel and return to Marshall the next day."

Annie's hand jerked and drops of coffee landed on a slice of cake. In two days her life would veer down a path she had never expected to choose. From now on, she would go to bed with a man and wake up with his head on the pillow next to her. It was unimaginable. Particularly as right this minute she couldn't have stated that man's eye color if her life had depended on it.

Suddenly frantic, she turned and studied him. His eyes were a warm saddle-colored brown capped by feathery dark eyebrows. His narrow face settled naturally into stubborn, authoritative lines. Annie liked it that he was clean-shaven. All in all, it was no wonder that half the ladies in town watched with a hungry look as he passed. Finally, tentatively, she let herself examine his mouth. Full, well-shaped lips met her gaze and she caught a glimpse of white even teeth. She stared at his mouth a beat too long and a skitter of heat rippled down her spine.

"I'm sorry, what did you say?" She hoped the evening shadows were deep enough that he couldn't see the new pimple. She must have looked like an idiot at his office, holding her hand over the pimple the entire time they talked.

He glanced at her. "I said your parents will make all the arrangements, and I'd started to tell you where we'll live."

When he finished speaking, Annie nodded slowly. She liked the idea of not living in town, of not having people watching them all the time. Getting acquainted in their circumstances would be difficult enough without a gossipy audience. "Tell me about your mother," she requested after she'd heard about the intensive remodeling he was doing on the old bunkhouse.

"I think you'll like each other."

That's all he intended to say? Waiting for more, Annie let a silence spin out, then sighed. "What happened to your father? Did he die?"

"That's Ione's story to tell if she chooses to."

Another fruitless wait convinced her that he'd revealed all he intended to about his parents. "All right, do you have any brothers or sisters?"

"No."

"This is like prying up nails, a lot of work for little reward."

He laughed, and she liked the deep, rich sound of his amusement. "I'm sorry. I'm not used to sharing personal information. But I do want us to get acquainted," he added quickly. "What else do you want to know?"

"Where did you grow up?"

"I was born in a small town north of Chicago. We moved around a lot while I was growing up. Wherever Ione is, that's the place I think of as home."

A twinge of envy tightened Annie's throat. Jess spoke of his mother in a matter-of-fact manner, but Annie heard the closeness behind his words. A year ago she would have characterized her relationship with Ellen as close, but in truth they lived in different worlds.

"I heard you were an army scout at one time," Annie said, prompting him to continue.

He tugged his collar as if he'd tired of talking about himself. "I went west after the war; I was sixteen or seventeen." A shrug lifted his shoulders. "I tried every job you can think of, some not very pleasant. But I enjoyed scouting."

"And then what? How did you get from scouting to wearing a badge?"

"I saw a lot of things while I was drifting around the

frontier," he said after a lengthy silence. "Things not fit
for a lady's ears. I made a lot of mistakes, almost went
to jail for a few of them. Finally I grew up and got on
the right side of the law. I served as a deputy in a few
towns." A smile touched his lips. "It didn't take long to
notice that I was better at giving orders than taking
them. I make a better sheriff than a deputy."

"Just as long as you don't issue orders to me," Annie
said lightly.

"Does your father burden you with unreasonable orders?" he asked curiously.

His shoulder brushed hers as he leaned forward to
replace his cup on the tray, and Annie drew in a soft
breath at the sensation of heat and strength and the
soapy scent of him. She wasn't sure if she wanted to be
aware of these disturbing things.

"Don't judge him by that one awful night," she said
softly. "He's not a tyrant." As long as the house ran
smoothly her father didn't feel it necessary to issue orders. Only when things ran counter to his liking did he
raise his voice and use such words as *forbid, refuse,
you must.*

She explained this to Jess as best she could. "I suppose you could say my father has been lenient. I know
he thinks so." Her expression tightened and her chin
came up. "But fathers and husbands are not the same
thing. While I would most likely try to follow an order
from Papa, I won't take orders from a husband."

"I'm not asking you to give up your independence,
and I'm not asking you to change anything about yourself. I don't want you to ask me to change, either."

An unpleasant echo of her conversations with Bodie
rang in her ears.

"I'm good at law enforcement and that's what I do for a living. If you have any qualms, now is the time to say so."

The irony made her head ache. "How often do you get shot at?" she inquired after a moment.

"Not as often as people think. Most of my job is putting down domestic disturbances, hauling drunks off to the cells, dealing with kids' mischief, discovering who took what from whom, that kind of thing. About once a week something more serious occurs. But I've been shot at. That's part of the job."

A part of the job that would worry her. "Have you had to kill anyone?"

"Yes."

"If the worst happened . . . ?"

"You'll be taken care of," he said hastily. "You'll always have a home with Ione if you want it. But you'll also have the wherewithal to live on your own if that's your preference." He stroked her hand lightly, a brief touch, then gone. "I don't mean to minimize what I do, Annie. It's a dangerous job that generally deals with the lowest element of society. I could get wounded or killed. But it's a job I care about and do well. It isn't a job where I can promise to be home for supper at the same time every night; some nights I'll be detained. Some nights I'll have to work. If you want to hear what happens on a daily basis, I'll tell you. If you'd rather not know, we'll talk about other things."

Annie stared, hearing Bodie's voice saying much the same things. But Jess defended an honorable profession.

She gazed at him unblinking, experiencing a small flush of pride that the people of Marshall, Kansas, slept more soundly knowing a man such as Jess Harden looked after their safety. It was a far cry from what she had felt when Bodie had spoken the same sentiments about what he did for a living.

"I have a lot to do to get our home ready and not much time to do it." Standing, he gazed down at her through the warm darkness. "Unless you object, I won't see you again until the wedding."

Annie pushed to her feet, feeling bulky and awkward. When she realized they stood close, she stepped backward, suddenly embarrassed by her awareness of his solid height and warmth and scent. "I have much to do, too." She dusted her hands together. "Well then . . ."

They studied each other, uncertain how to part. Finally Jess walked to the steps. "Good night."

"Good night." They hadn't touched the cake or finished their coffee.

At the gate, he turned and called through the darkness, "Annie? I'm glad everything worked out the way it did."

She wished she could feel as certain as he sounded. "Thank you, Mr. Harden. I'm grateful."

She also wished she better understood why he wanted to marry a disgraced woman in her condition. After all the rhetoric, she supposed her reason for marrying him was simple: she was too much of a coward to face the town and raise a child alone.

What a hypocrite she was. For five years she had taken great pride in belonging to the New Modern Woman's Association. All she had done was deceive herself. She'd never been a New Modern Woman at all.

*　　*　　*

"Have you killed anyone?"

"No, Ma," Bodie lied. Reaching across the Stafford Hotel's dining-room table, he gave her hand a reassuring pat.

In fact, if he were the type of outlaw to cut notches in his holster, he'd now have two. Raising a hand, he rubbed his forehead, wishing he could smooth out the knot of craziness behind his brow.

His mother, frowning at the expensive lunch he'd bought for her, pushed at a spear of asparagus. "I don't believe you. There's something different. You're harder and wilder in the eyes."

He knew it. But he hadn't known it showed.

"I guess you're still robbing trains."

"Mostly banks." Trains were a complicated venture, and he needed more men than just the Baylor brothers to be assured of success. Banks, on the other hand, sat there ripe for the plucking. Easy to study, a quick in-and-out operation.

"You're getting too old for this." His mother looked at him with his own eyes. "It's time you grew up and settled down before you get caught and disgrace us more than you have already."

Scowling, he gazed across the gilt and mirrored dining room. "You sound like Pa." Bodie hadn't seen his father in years. Meeting his ma required an inconvenient set of relayed messages to prevent his pa from learning that she met with him, and she always made sure he knew that she came reluctantly.

"From the time you were born, me and your pa had such expectations for you."

Bodie put down his fork. "There's more to life than sweating in a smithy. I don't want to spend my days pounding out fancy fences for rich people or putting an edge on the butcher's knives."

"Your father has made a good living. It's honest work."

"It's dirty, hot, sweaty work." He touched the lapels of his new suit, which had cost more than his father earned in a month.

"No one wants to put your father in prison. He'd never take a penny of stolen money. Your father can hold himself with pride."

Those were the kind of words that made him feel crazy inside, made him realize how much things had changed. If all he'd done was rob banks, maybe his pa could have forgiven him in time. But his pa wasn't the kind to forgive killing.

"If I'd known you were going to harp on this subject, I would have bypassed Kansas City and ridden straight to Marshall."

"I'm tired of worrying all the time. Tired of searching the newspapers for word of your arrest or hanging." She pressed her fingers to her forehead. "I have a son whose name is forbidden in my house. Months go by and I don't know if you're alive or wounded or dead. I want a son I can be proud of. Not a thief, a liar, and a murderer."

She knew how to put a knife between his ribs. Yet he continued to make the effort to see her a couple of times a year, hoping she'd notice his expensive hats and boots and feel a little of that pride she always talked about.

Leaning back in his chair, he examined the same bonnet she'd worn forever and a summer suit that she had refashioned a half-dozen times. His father might have his damned pride and the blacksmith shop, but his family lived on the edge of poverty. That wasn't good enough for Bodie.

"Actually," he said eventually, "I'm thinking about going farther west. I'm planning to get married and settle down."

"I've heard this before," she said, her eyes sad.

"This time I mean it. All we have to do is set the wedding date. Her name's Annie and I want her to meet you."

"Don't bother. No respectable woman would marry an outlaw, and I'm not interested in meeting the other kind."

It was odd to think that Annie was probably waiting out her confinement here in Kansas City, possibly not far from where they now sat. A day's ride to Marshall to get Annie's message out of the tin box, a day at the cabin, then a day's ride back to Kansas City to find her and settle their future together, that's all it would take.

"What would you think about a grandchild, Ma? Would that make you happy?"

"If having a child convinced you to live decently, I'd be relieved." But she didn't believe he would change his life. She never believed half of what he said.

"I'll show you. I promise."

His bad luck had begun when he'd let Annie walk away. His good luck would return once he had her again.

"You'll see, Ma." He'd make her proud, damn it. All he needed was Annie.

CHAPTER 11

⬧⬧⬧⬧⬧ ⬧⬧⬧⬧⬧ ⬧⬧⬧⬧⬧

*T*HE Malloys departed for Greensboro at mid-
morning, traveling with the top up on the phaeton to
protect them from a steady, warm rain. Annie fixed her
gaze on the low, wet hills and rolling fields and tried to
make sense out of what she was doing.

Marriage had never been part of her life plan. Yet
here she was, traveling to her wedding. Pregnant. And
about to marry not the father of her baby but a man
she hardly knew. How on earth had this happened?
Confusion and bewilderment tightened her throat.

She wasn't the only person on the edge of tears.
Every few miles Ellen's grim expression collapsed and
she wept into her handkerchief. Annie's parents might
have been traveling to a funeral instead of a wedding.

But their attitude was easier for Annie to bear and
more honest than if they had pretended this was a
happy occasion. Certainly it wasn't the elaborate and
happy wedding her mother had dreamed of when Annie was an adolescent. There would be no rejoicing today, just relief and a profound hope that now the
scandal would begin to ebb. She had disappointed her
mother in so many ways.

Whenever lengthy silences demanded a scrap of conversation, Annie's father mentioned that the farmers needed the moisture or spoke of the Fourth of July celebration following so close on the heels of the Summer Crafts Fair or her mother wondered how much longer the journey would take. Twice her mother mentioned that if Jesse Harden had planned to offer marriage she wished he'd done so months earlier. Neither of her parents offered advice about marriage.

The sky remained low and leaden as Mr. Waters braked the carriage before Greensboro county's boxy brick courthouse, but the rain had finally stopped. Biting her lip, Annie began what seemed an endless walk toward the courthouse steps, lifting her skirts to avoid glistening puddles. The pulse drumming in her ears sounded so loud that she wondered if her parents could hear it, too.

To her relief, Jess came forward as they approached the courthouse, and Annie released a small breath. She had half feared he wouldn't be here and half feared that he would. He nodded to Ellen and extended his hand to Annie's father before he turned his attention to her, scanning her newly trimmed hat, a summer shawl, and a blue silk dress that she'd altered to fit. She knew she looked dismayingly pregnant, but his gaze softened and nothing in his fine brown eyes suggested that he thought she was anything but beautiful.

Suddenly she felt like crying.

Her throat closed when Jess straightened his shoulders, then leaned forward and kissed her lightly on the forehead by way of greeting. Surprise widened her eyes, but he'd already turned to her father. In silence she listened to Jess assure her father that Annie's belongings had arrived at his mother's place, and her father mentioned a box of last-minute items they had brought with them.

"Our wagon is just down the street." Taking a pocket watch from his waistcoat, Jess consulted the time. "We're early. We have time to put Annie's box in the wagon."

Expressionless, Annie's father signaled for Mr. Waters, and the men returned to the vehicles. "We may as well go in," Ellen suggested irritably. "They should have escorted us inside before dashing off."

At the top of the steps, Annie spotted a tall, handsome woman striding toward them and guessed it must be Jess's mother. Etiquette required that Mrs. Harden wait until her son returned to introduce her to his bride, but on first impression Mrs. Harden didn't impress Annie as a woman who ranked etiquette high among her priorities.

"You must be Annie," she said, smiling and taking Annie's gloved hands. "Welcome to our family." For a long moment she gazed into Annie's eyes, taking her measure before turning to Ellen. "I am Ione Harden, and you would be Mrs. Malloy. I'm pleased to make your acquaintance."

"Likewise, I'm sure," Ellen murmured, her raised eyebrows giving her a startled look.

The mothers were as different as pie and cheese. Ellen had chosen a shimmery green silk suit, heavily draped and trimmed, cut in the latest fashion. Her hat was tilted at a modish angle, and square-cut emeralds sparkled in her ears. Mrs. Harden wore a well-tailored grosgrain walking suit that was almost severe in its lack of flounces and frippery. A single silk rose adorned her hat, nothing else, and she wore small pearl earrings.

To Annie's surprise, when she watched the two women eyeing each other, Ellen appeared unfinished somehow, as if she required the accessory of a man at her side to look complete, whereas Ione Harden seemed whole unto herself. Frowning, Annie watched through her lashes.

Mrs. Harden regarded Ellen Malloy with frank curiosity, but Ellen gazed around the courthouse foyer, obviously having made up her mind that Mrs. Harden was not her sort. Ione Harden, with her disregard for etiquette and her direct gaze, was too forward by half. Mrs. Harden was smartly turned out and the clean lines of her ensemble suited her, but she was not fashionable and the sunny tan on her cheeks and forehead was far removed from Ellen's ladylike milky complexion.

Relief brightened the ladies' expressions as the men returned. When Harry Malloy offered his arm, Ellen clutched it with an audible sigh. Amusement danced in Ione's gaze as she took her son's arm on one side and Annie accepted his right arm. Listening to the click of their heels on a marble floor, they proceeded in silence to the antechamber where a judge waited.

This was going to happen. Annie swallowed hard. She was going to marry and her husband-to-be was essentially a stranger. Jess looked down at her as a wave of dizziness caused her to stumble and she gripped his arm for balance.

"Are you all right?" Jess asked, covering her hand with his.

"Yes." Then she noticed the judge staring at her

stomach with a scowl of disapproval and scarlet flooded her cheeks. The ceremony would be brief, she reminded herself, and then she would never see the man again.

Ione walked straight to a vase of yellow yarrow and blue delphinium. "I brought these in earlier," she said, removing the blossoms from the vase. With an economy of effort and fuss she twisted her handkerchief around the damp stems and handed the hasty bouquet to Annie with a smile. "These are for you."

They all looked at Ellen when she gasped. "I forgot the flowers!" An appalled rush of color lit her cheeks. "I left them on the back porch."

"There's no harm done," Ione said pleasantly.

The judge beckoned everyone forward. "If you please," he said, glancing at the wall clock.

"I'm so sorry, Annie." Ellen shot a venomous glance at Ione. She would never forgive Ione Harden for remembering flowers when she had forgotten. "I didn't think about the bouquet until this minute."

"It's fine, really." Annie's voice was high and wispy. Her mouth was dry, the pimple was still there, and her palms itched like blue blazes. And if she didn't pee in the next two minutes there was going to be a hideous accident. She would never recover from the embarrassment. She would have to swallow rat poison.

Turning from the judge, she cast a desperate glance at Ellen and Ione. "I'm sorry. I have to . . . this minute. I can't . . ."

Once again Ione came to the rescue. "The facility is down the hallway to your left."

Annie fled.

She couldn't go through with the wedding. It was morally wrong to marry Jess Harden when the baby's real father had been willing to wed her. Maybe he still was. There were a thousand possible reasons why Bodie had not returned to Marshall. Had she given up on him too soon? And yet . . . to her knowledge, nothing had changed. Bodie was a thief and she didn't want his life for herself or her baby. Confusion made her head ache.

When she left the water closet, Jess was leaning against the opposite wall, ankles crossed, his arms folded across his chest. "Having second thoughts?"

"I don't know what to do," she whispered. He was so handsome today. Tall and lean, wearing a dark suit and waistcoat, his boots polished to a high gleam. Jess wasn't the kind of man to wear pomade in his hair, but he'd tamed his dark curls somehow. When he moved forward and offered his arm, she smelled lemon and starch.

"Let's take a walk."

Annie looked behind her. "The others . . ."

"Let them wait."

Outside, thin sunlight pushed at the clouds and the air smelled of wet grass. Using his handkerchief, Jess dried one of the courthouse benches, and they sat down. "You don't have to do this, Annie."

"You don't understand. I do have to." Annie twisted her hankie between her hands. "On the way here, Ellen dropped off an announcement at the *Marshall Gazette.*"

Jess shrugged. "The announcement can be retracted." He cupped her chin and gently turned her to face him.

"We don't 'have' to get married unless that's what you want. If you've changed your mind, it's all right. We'll all go home, and that's that."

His hand on her skin was as warm as his eyes and Annie had the disconcerting feeling that she looked into the gaze of a friend. The words poured out of her in a torrent. She spoke of being a pariah and doubting if she had the courage to face down the town and raise a child alone. She told him about the awful yellow house and how much she hated the idea of living there. She told him about her friends abandoning her. Marrying him would save her from the yellow house and, in time, might remove some of the tarnish from her reputation.

Yet marrying Jess presented a moral dilemma that was driving her crazy. "I don't know what's right," she said at the finish, blinking back tears of frustration. "Is it right to give my baby one father when his real father would have married me?"

"You've said you don't believe you would be comfortable or happy in a marriage with this man," Jess said finally, ticking down one finger. "For whatever reason, you don't believe he would be a good example for your child." Another finger ticked down. "And it appears the man has vanished."

"But he might return and he might still be willing to marry me. Is it right to keep my child and his real father apart?" She stared into his dark eyes, hoping for an answer she could believe.

"He *might* return, and he *might* marry you. Let me ask you something. If there were no baby, would you marry this man?"

"No." She didn't have to think twice.

Jess let the word hang between them. "Do you think it's fair or right to marry when the only person who is presumably happy with that situation is the man? Not you and not your child?"

"No," she admitted slowly.

"Whether or not you marry me, if you want my opinion, you're doing the right thing not to marry the other man."

It was what she needed to hear. "But I don't understand why you're willing to marry me."

"I care about you," he said softly, "and I believe we can build a good life together."

After pressing her gloves to her eyes, she sighed. "You're a good man, Jesse Harden."

"Maybe. Maybe not as good as you think." He spread his arms along the back of the bench and narrowed his eyes at the patches of blue sky appearing overhead. "I've killed several men. Most of them deserved it. A couple probably didn't. I've put two innocent men in jail and let a couple of guilty ones go." He turned his head to meet her eyes. "When I was thirteen years old, I killed my father."

Annie's hand flew to her lips and she stared at him. "Good heavens. I don't know what to say." She didn't know him at all. "Why?"

"Someday we'll talk about it." His gaze examined her face. "The only thing I have to say now is that I've never regretted killing the son of a bitch." He looked at his pocket watch. "You need to make a decision."

Ironically, though Jess admitted to killing his father and several other men, Annie didn't doubt that he was an honest, decent man. Whereas Bodie had never killed anyone, at least not that she knew about, but he readily admitted that he made his living through dishonest means. If it was true that a woman could judge a man's husband potential by observing how he treated his mother, then Jesse would be a good husband. But Bodie had indicated he was not on speaking terms with his parents. Yet Jesse had killed his father. Her head ached, trying to work it out.

"Oh!" Startled, Annie pressed her hands on her stomach. "This baby is kicking up a storm." After casting a quick look around and discovering that no one paid them any attention, she impulsively caught Jess's hand and placed it on her stomach.

His eyebrows soared and he stared at her. "My God," he said softly. His hesitation vanished and he flattened his hand, laughing when the baby kicked again. "It's a miracle."

"Jesse?" They were head-to-head, close enough that she could smell lemon drops on his breath. "Will you throw this pregnancy up to me every time we're angry with each other?"

He looked deep into her eyes. "I promise never to think of this child as anything but my own."

"And I promise to be the best wife that I can be. But you'll have to be patient."

He took her hand. "I'll never run out on you, Annie. I'll be there when you need me. You can count on that."

"Don't lie to me. No matter how hard the truth is, don't lie to me."

"I won't lie to you, strike you, abuse you in any way. And I trust you not to lie or deceive me. We're going to be friends and eventually lovers." His fingertips strayed to her cheek, warm and light. "I'm going to make you love me."

She drew a sharp breath. Was that possible? His eyes turned almost black and a thrill skittered down Annie's spine. No one had ever said such a thing to her. Nervous, she wet her lips and eased away from him.

"I can't promise love," she murmured in an odd voice that didn't sound like her own. "But I think my decision has been made." In fact, she suspected they'd just exchanged their wedding vows.

The ceremony performed by the judge went swiftly and well, then came to an abrupt halt when he asked, "Do you, Anne Margaret Malloy, promise to love, honor, and obey . . . ?"

Her New Modern Woman thinking blazed to the forefront and Annie fidgeted, tightening her fingers around the bouquet. "No," she said finally, causing a gasp from her mother. She glanced at the amusement sparkling in Jess's eyes. "But I promise to honor you all the days of my life."

"That's good enough."

The judge had started to close his book and turn away, the service canceled when Annie refused to promise what she was supposed to. At Jess's response, he turned toward them again, rolled his eyes, then completed the marriage with an expression of disgust.

"You may kiss the bride," he said, slapping his book shut before he strode toward the whiskey bottle on his desk.

Jess tilted her head up, looked into her eyes, then brushed his lips lightly across her mouth. Annie's knees trembled and her hands shook. His kiss felt like a brand. She was married. For better or worse. Until death parted them. She placed a hand on her stomach, then stared down at the gold band on her finger.

No one offered congratulations.

The wedding supper was held in the gilt and mirrored dining room of the Wheat Land Hotel. Ellen might have forgotten to bring the flowers, but she had overlooked nothing when deciding the wedding menu.

They began with littleneck clams, followed by consommé au Parmesan accompanied by crystal glasses of sherry. The entrée was larded fillet of beef with horseradish sauce, served with flutes of champagne and Delmonico potatoes, string beans, and artichokes in béchamel sauce. Fruit and cheese officially ended the meal, followed by ladyfingers and bonbons served with coffee.

"Shall we retire to the club room for brandy and cigars?" Harry Malloy sounded eager to leave the silence of the table. Jess glanced at Annie, then nodded.

The women watched them leave before Ellen signaled for more coffee, looking resigned.

"That was a lovely meal," Ione said, moving to Jess's vacant seat next to Annie. "I'm always surprised by the quality of fare in small-town hotels."

"The asparagus was a bit underdone," Ellen said, toying with her spoon. "Have you sampled the fare in many large-town hotels?" she added, almost as an afterthought.

"We lived in the Chicago area for several years," Ione said pleasantly. "The hotels there are magnificent.

They employ some of the best chefs in the world. Or so they claim," she finished with a smile.

Annie lowered her head, knowing that her mother had dismissed Ione Harden as being provincial and was surprised to learn that Mrs. Harden had ventured beyond small-town conventions. Annie also knew her mother was pained by Mrs. Harden's next direct question.

"When are you due, Annie?"

"I should deliver around the middle of November."

"Then you've felt movement." Ione smiled. "That's a thrilling moment, isn't it?"

Annie looked up, startled.

"My dear," Ione said, taking Annie's hand. "My son has decided to accept this baby and raise it as his own. I will do no less. Babies are happy events. Miracles, really. Have you considered names?"

"I . . . no. Not yet."

"This baby is not a happy event!" Ellen objected in a low, horrified voice. "This baby has caused a scandal, has destroyed my daughter's reputation, and has brought shame and disgrace on our family."

"With apologies, Mrs. Malloy, I beg to differ. Your daughter did those things. Not this baby."

Annie stiffened and then slumped. Ione was painfully blunt, but she was also correct.

"I'm sure you'll agree," Ione continued, "that the baby is innocent of any wrongdoing." She turned a smile on Annie. "You don't blame the baby, do you?"

"No," Annie said in a low voice. "The wrongdoing is all mine."

Ione squeezed her hand. "You made a mistake that

others have made before you and many will commit after you. But a new beginning was made here today. We go on from here." Her eyes sparkled. "I was sad that you couldn't vow to love our Jesse, but to tell the truth, I wanted to cheer when you refused the promise to obey."

Ellen glared. "That was disgraceful, Annie. Did you see the judge? He was ready to cancel the service."

The tension between her mother and new mother-in-law was escalating alarmingly. Already it was apparent there would be few points of commonality between them. Annie struggled to smile. "Shall we inspect the grounds before the sun sets? A walk might do us all good."

Ione looked from mother to daughter. "I think I'll forgo a walk and go directly to my room. I brought the book I'm reading. . . ." Standing, she thanked Ellen again for a lovely supper, then pressed Annie's shoulder. "I look forward to deepening our acquaintance. Good night, my dear."

In silence, Annie and Ellen watched her tall figure stride across the dining room, out the door, and into the lobby.

"What a dreadful woman!"

"She's direct but kind," Annie said slowly. It occurred to her that Ione Harden appeared to live by many of the New Modern Woman's tenets. In fact, it seemed possible that Ione Harden was more of a New Modern Woman than Annie herself. That surprised and chagrined her.

Ellen threw down her napkin and rose with studied grace. "She hasn't the least concept of etiquette or polite conversation. I was speechless when she asked your due date."

Annie didn't bend in the middle as she once had. Rising from a seated position had become something of a struggle. Feeling awkward and clumsy, she pushed upright, then checked the progress of the pimple before she put on her gloves. It seemed the pimple was fading, and that raised her spirits a little.

The hotel gardens were at their best, lush with bloom. The mingled perfume of roses and primrose and dianthus scented the evening air. "I must plant more dianthus," Ellen commented after inspecting the gardens. She took Annie's arm. "I suppose you think we've been terribly hard on you."

"No more than I've deserved." Pausing on the path, she smiled down at a riot of Johnny-jump-ups. Ellen considered them no better than weeds, but Annie had always loved them.

"We had such dreams for you. For a time I fancied you might marry the Brownwood boy and live in the mansion on Elm Street. But you decided never to marry."

This was where her mother usually said that Annie's decision had been an affront like a slap in the face. But tonight she didn't.

"I never imagined that you'd ever do anything to cause us shame or disgrace. It's been very hard to bear, Annie. A terrible shock."

There was nothing to say. She had already said she was sorry a hundred times.

Ellen turned away from the blaze of sunset and squared her shoulders. "You did the right thing today. Everyone will believe you married the baby's father and the gossip will die out. Your name and ours will always be tainted, but not nearly to the degree it would have been if you hadn't married Mr. Harden."

"Perhaps we should go inside now." The urgency of Annie's desire to escape this conversation was matched by her dread of going upstairs to the bridal suite with Jess.

"First, let me say that we support your marriage and wish you well. If we can do anything more to help out, please let us know."

"Thank you."

They met Jess and Annie's father in the lobby, smelling of cigars but appearing more relaxed than either had during supper. "Would you ladies care for more coffee?" Annie's father gave her shoulder an awkward pat.

"Thank you, no." Remembering that she had to consider someone else now, she threw Jess a quick glance. "It's been a long day, and I'm very tired. Unless you're craving coffee, I'd like to go to the room." She couldn't bring herself to say "our" room.

Jess tucked her hand around his arm. "We'll order coffee upstairs. Good night, Harry. Mrs. Malloy."

For a moment her father hesitated; then he briefly embraced her, and her mother kissed her temple. "Good Lord, I forgot to give the toast," Harry said, as if he'd just noticed. "Well. Good luck to you both."

"Oh dear, I'm getting teary again." Ellen fumbled in her bag for her handkerchief.

Annie couldn't stand another minute. Tugging on Jess's sleeve, she tilted her head toward the staircase. They didn't speak until they had climbed three flights and entered Bridal Suite A.

"It's lovely," Annie said, examining polished antiques and colorful carpets that picked up the dusty blue of a sweep of velvet draperies. "You shouldn't have gone to this expense."

Jess threw open the drapes, then unlatched French doors leading to a small wrought-iron balcony. The cool air smelled as if it might rain again. "You only have one wedding night, Annie. It's worth doing right."

Unless she was mistaken, he'd purchased new boots for today. He'd been to the barber, bought her a heavy gold ring, and arranged for the bridal suite. He'd gone to this trouble and expense for a woman who didn't love him and who was carrying another man's child.

Turning aside, Annie inspected the water closet and then checked the bedroom. The bellman had placed their overnight bags side by side. There was only one bed. Her heart sank.

"Jesse?" She wet her lips and tried to speak above a whisper. "Jesse?"

"In a minute," he said, heading toward the knock at the door. "That will be the coffee."

Her eyebrows lifted. "When did you order coffee?"

"After your father and I had brandy. I noticed you hardly ate a bite at supper. I thought you might be hungry later, so I ordered sandwiches, dessert, and coffee."

After their order had been arranged on the balcony table and Jess had seated her, Annie drew a deep breath. He was trying so hard. "Thank you. I didn't think I was hungry, but I am."

"Your father gave us two hundred dollars. A wedding gift."

"He did?" She lowered her sandwich. A hundred dollars for each time he'd struck her. The thought leapt into her mind, shaming her.

"I put the envelope on top of your overnight case. Use the money however you like."

"It's generous of your mother to let you remake her bunkhouse and let us live on her property."

"We'll pay rent, but only a fraction of what the place is worth."

"I like your mother, Jess." It was true. Ione Harden was an interesting woman.

"I'm glad. She likes you, too."

After that, there didn't seem much to say. They finished the sandwiches in the lowering darkness.

"What did you start to ask me earlier?"

"Oh. Well, I was just wondering." And she wished she wasn't. "Do you have any disgusting habits?"

"Probably." He laughed. "It's my understanding that women believe all men have disgusting habits. Did you have any particular disgusting habit in mind?"

Embarrassed, she frowned down at her hands. She knew he had good table manners; there was no need to worry on that account. "Do you drop your clothes on the floor at night?" Bodie had done that. "Do you chew tobacco?" Bodie had done that, too, and she'd hated it. "Do you crack your knuckles?"

"I smoke a cigar occasionally, but I don't chew. I'll put the dirty clothes wherever you want me to. And no, I don't crack my knuckles."

"Do you play poker all night with your friends?"

"No. Do you?"

"Me?" Her eyebrows soared. "I don't know how to play poker."

"I'll teach you."

She studied his smile. "You're making fun of me, aren't you?"

"We'll discover these things as we go along. Are you

warm enough?" Once the sun sank, the air had cooled rapidly.

"Yes, but I'm very tired." The darkness concealed a fiery blush. "You do know that we can't . . . Well, maybe we can, I don't know, I didn't ask anyone, but . . ."

"I know. But I would like to watch you brush your hair."

"What?" Her head snapped up.

"I've pictured you a hundred times, sitting before the mirror in your nightgown, brushing out your hair."

She stared at him. All this time, she had believed he was secretly laughing at her unmanageable hair, but he'd smiled at her hair because for some unfathomable reason he liked it.

The idea of Jess Harden seeing her in her nightgown deepened the color in her cheeks. Brushing her hair while he watched would feel indecent.

But he had rescued her. And he'd tried to lend some normalcy and dignity to their wedding. And he was her husband.

"I'll call you when I'm ready." Face flaming, she left the table.

Jess stayed on the balcony and smoked a cigar while he waited, blowing smoke rings into the night. Somewhere out there was the man she had lain with. And one day that man was going to come; Jess knew this as surely as he knew the weight of a gun in his hand.

When he heard the door to the bedroom click open, he put out his cigar and kicked his boots off. He didn't look at her until he'd mounded the pillows and stretched out on top of the bed.

She was as lovely as he'd imagined, clad in a white nightgown with lace at a slightly scooped neck and trailing from her sleeves. After a quick glance at him, she bit her lips, then returned her gaze to the mirror and removed her hairpins. Long coils of red tumbled down her back, almost auburn in the lamplight and shadow. When she raised the brush, her sleeve fell away revealing the white curve of her arm.

The first stroke freed the tightly curled tendrils and her wonderful wild hair sprang every which way, rising in an electric nimbus that reminded him of red mist framing her face. His eyes narrowed and he wondered if she had any idea how beautiful she was.

After another quick glance at him in the mirror, she braided her hair more swiftly than he would have believed possible, then stood and came slowly toward the bed.

"Is that the side you usually sleep on?" she asked, quickly looking away.

"Yes." There were some changes he was not willing to make.

"Fine." Stretching, she covered an exaggerated yawn. "I think I'll be asleep the instant my head hits the pillow."

"Annie. I'm not going to touch you." Standing, he unbuckled his belt, then pushed down his trousers. She gasped and from the corners of his eyes he watched her hands fly to cover her face and she turned away. His trousers went into the armoire beside tomorrow's shirt and he packed his dirty shirt and underwear in his traveling case. He placed his boots neatly beside the chair.

"Don't you have a nightshirt?" she asked as he slid into bed.

Ah, so she'd peeked. "I don't wear one."

"You sleep naked?" Her voice emerged high and wispy.

"Yes."

He was almost asleep when she spoke into the darkness. "Would you wear a nightshirt if I bought you one?"

"No." It appeared that he had a few disgusting habits after all. Smiling, he turned his back to her, resisting an urge to slide a foot into forbidden territory and reassure himself that she was really in his bed.

CHAPTER 12

HUNDREDS *of candles scented the air in a cavernous bedroom. Flickering shadows stretched into distant recesses. In the strange way of dreams, Annie was both participant and observer, watching herself and a lover through a golden haze of light.*

The man was tall and muscled, wearing trousers, his torso bare and gleaming with the damp heat generated by the kisses Annie trailed up from his throat to his mouth. Even as she watched from somewhere above, she felt his lips claim hers with the fiery possession of desire.

An electric shock flashed through her body and her nightgown vanished, leaving her naked and trembling against him. His skin felt smooth and firm, rippling beneath her fingertips as she stroked his shoulders, his chest, his stomach. His breath bathed her cheek and he spoke to her, but she couldn't understand his fevered whisper.

Grasping her hair, he pulled her head back and kissed her deeply; then his hands cupped her naked buttocks, pulling her tightly against the heat and power of his erection. From above, she saw that he, too, was now naked, his male hardness an exciting contrast to the milky softness of Annie's femininity.

While he kissed her with growing passion, his hands moved up her waist and opened across her back. She felt the calluses on his palms, felt each finger as a brand on her skin, marking her as his. Her own hands flew over his shoulders, explored his jawline and the corners of his mouth. She moved against him to experience the heat and tension on his skin, feeling a frenzy of need building inside her.

Golden shadows shimmered and the musky scent of the candles dizzied every breath. They were on the bed now, an enormous bed with sheets of glowing satin. Clasped in an embrace they rolled together, drinking deep kisses from gasping mouths, hands stroking, teasing, chasing, bodies pressing against each other as if seeking to melt and become one with the other.

He rose above her and she felt his weight on her thighs and stomach, spread her fingers on his chest, touched the pulse at the base of his throat. A great weakness shuddered through her body, followed by a surge of wild urgency. She thrashed beneath him, her hair flying across the satin pillows like strands of flame leaping in the candlelight. Perspiration glistened on her throat and breasts, and she felt the lower dampness of desire.

She cried his name, but Annie the observer couldn't hear.

And she couldn't see his face.

The long ride from Greensboro to Ione's property outside Marshall exhausted Annie. The seat of the wagon was lightly padded, but she felt each rut and pothole. Her back ached, the sun scorched through her bonnet, and she couldn't get enough to drink, which was embarrassing because the water sped through her system and necessitated frequent roadside stops near large bushes or trees. Jess and Ione took the stops in stride, but Annie was in a state of tired humiliation by the time Jess guided the horses into Ione's yard.

The main house was a shuttered two-story clapboard, much like the other farmhouses that dotted the landscape. A covered porch shaded the front door, and silver maples caught the heat on the west side. A half-dozen outbuildings could be glimpsed among the trees and flowering shrubs that ran riot across the rolling land. It cooled a person just to look at the different shades and textures of green.

"Don't worry about supper," Ione said, climbing out of the wagon. "Rest if you can, and come up to the house about six. We'll have something light." She smiled at Jess, then lifted her skirts and walked toward the house.

"That's our place," he said, directing Annie's attention to a low rectangular house about a hundred yards south.

Annie hadn't known what to expect when he'd told her that he was remodeling a bunkhouse. But the result charmed her. He'd added a wide front porch, and shutters painted crisp green framed the row of windows. A room had been added at the end, turning the rectangle into an L, and the roof extended to cover the porch.

"I also added a kitchen on the back," Jess explained, drawing up the wagon before the door. He handed her to the ground and squinted, running his eye along the new porch railing. "It's not finished yet. We'll have workmen here off and on for another two weeks. But we're close."

Before Annie could protest, he scooped her into his arms as effortlessly as if she didn't weigh more than she'd ever weighed in her life. "What are you doing?" she asked, clutching him around the neck.

"I'm going to carry you across the threshold."

"Jess, you don't have to do that."

"It's bad luck not to," he said, smiling into her eyes.

He carried her up two steps and across the porch; then, as generations of grooms had done before him, he fumbled the door open and set his bride on her feet inside her new home.

"Well, what do you think?"

"Give me a minute," Annie said, smoothing her skirts and removing her bonnet and gloves.

The front door opened directly into a large parlor. She would have preferred a foyer, but she supposed most farmhouses didn't waste space on foyers. The first thing she noticed was the pile of trunks and boxes, hatboxes, shoe boxes, dress boxes that her father had sent to her new home. It would take several days to sort and put everything away.

But the room was bright and airy; sunshine gleamed on a polished floor. A bookcase ran along half of the end wall, offering enough space for books and collectibles, and she could picture a cheery fire in the fireplace come winter.

"There's not much furniture," Jess said, watching her expression. "I thought you'd want a hand in picking out everything. Rugs, lamps, chairs, pictures for the walls."

"Thank you." Forgetting that she was exhausted, Annie moved down a central hallway, peering into doors. There was a water closet furnished with all the necessities, a linen closet, a clothes closet. "There's plenty of storage," she noticed, her spirits lifting.

He hadn't waited for her to furnish the bedroom. He'd chosen curved mahogany for the head- and foot-board, and matching armoires, bureau, and vanity. Etched-glass lamps sat on the side tables.

"There's space for a couple of chairs if you want them," he pointed out.

There wasn't a stick of furniture in the room he had added across from their bedroom, and for an instant Annie couldn't guess its use.

"It's the baby's room," Jess said, tugging his collar. "I didn't know what ought to go in here. Ione said you would definitely want to do this room yourself."

"Of course." It was the nursery. It hadn't occurred to her that Jess would build a room for the baby. For a moment she couldn't breathe. He really was going to accept this child as his own. The process had begun. And the baby would have a room of his own, which Annie could furnish and decorate however she chose.

Sudden tears of gratitude sparkled in her eyes, and impulsively she rose on tiptoe and brushed a hasty kiss across his cheek. "Thank you, Jesse."

He wasn't perfect. He'd killed his father, which she didn't understand, and slept naked, which she refused to think about. But he had built a room for her baby.

Turning quickly so he wouldn't see the moisture in her eyes, she returned to the parlor, then entered a dining room. This was another unexpected surprise.

"In case your parents come to supper," Jess explained, seeing her startled expression.

The first jolt of being married had occurred last night when she had shared a bed for the first time in her life, and with a man. The second jolt came when she realized that she could have a dinner party of her own. She would choose the date and the guests, and she would compose the menu.

Refusing to remember that she no longer had friends to invite, she continued into a bright, roomy kitchen. "That's a new stove!" There wasn't a woman alive who didn't dream of being the first to cook on a new stove.

"It's a Windsor," Jess explained. He showed her the enamel-lined reservoir and a feature Annie hadn't seen before. "This long narrow door beneath the oven is a place to dry fruit or store irons and pokers."

"I've never seen a more beautiful stove!" Annie ran her fingertips over the clean shining surface.

Jess looked relieved. "You do know how to cook then?"

"Well . . . I love to bake. My everyday cooking skills are adequate, I suppose." Her chin came up. "Don't worry; we won't starve. And I'll improve as I practice." Another marriage reality jolted her. She would do all the cooking. "You take your noon dinner in town, is that correct?" Surely she could manage two meals a day. But it would behoove her to search her belongings immediately to find her cookery books.

Jess tested the pump handle and gave a satisfied nod when water splashed into the sink. "So. What do you think?"

Annie stared at the pull of his shirt across his broad shoulders, ran her eye to his waist and then to the curve of his buttocks. Something in the way he stood reminded her of the man in her dream. A violent blush set fire to her skin and she hastily turned away, pressing her palms to her cheeks.

The dream had shocked her. Never before had she dreamed of making love, nor had she ever imagined that she would. It seemed particularly indecent to have such a dream when she was pregnant. Still, to her shame, she secretly hoped the dream would return.

"Someday we'll have a real house with space for live-in help," Jess said when Annie didn't answer. "For the present, this will have to do."

"You've done a wonderful job. Truly, Jess, I like it." An image of the tiny yellow house at the edge of town rose in her mind. Living in that house would have slowly crushed her. But this, with the sunshine flooding every room and the fresh scent of newly sawed wood. And the closets and the new stove. This was so much better than anything she had imagined.

Jess shrugged. "Do whatever you want. Wallpaper, carpets, whatever. When you run out of your father's wedding money, tell me. All I ask," he said with a grin, "is that you don't put too many ruffles and pink foo fas in our bedroom."

Our bedroom. Would she ever get used to that phrase? Would a time come when it would feel natural and normal to share a room and a bed with a man?

Summoning a smile, Annie promised. In fact, she had often wondered what her father thought of all the ruffles and bows and the flowered paper in her parents' bedroom.

"You look tired, Annie."

Suddenly she was. "I think I'll take your mother's suggestion and lie down until supper." At the door she looked back at the sunshine streaming through the kitchen windows, finding red highlights in his hair. "What will you do?"

"There's plenty of work around here. I'll try not to disturb you."

"Will you go back to town tomorrow?"

He nodded. "Do you mind being left alone out here?"

She'd had her fill of people for a while. The stares and whispers. "I'll be fine. Don't concern yourself."

As tired as she was, Annie expected to fall asleep at once, but her mind jumped from one thing to another. The house was hers to do with as she wished. That was a nice benefit of marriage that she hadn't considered. What colors did she prefer? If she had to order furniture and curtains, how long would it be until the items arrived? And how should she decorate the baby's room?

Would it be pleasant or awkward living in close proximity to Jesse's mother?

They hadn't had a honeymoon. Well, of course not. Rolling onto her side, she squeezed her eyes shut.

Was Jess the man in her dream? Or had it been Bodie?

He couldn't believe it. Annie Malloy had gone and married the fricking sheriff. Reaching for the bottle, Bodie poured another whiskey and reread the newspaper announcement although he could have quoted every word from memory. She had taken his baby and married the sheriff. It was the worst betrayal he'd ever heard of. What the hell kind of a woman did such a thing?

Swinging his arm, he knocked the tin box off the table and cursed at the gold coin as it rolled across the cabin floor. She hadn't written a word about what she was thinking; she'd just spit on his money. His money wasn't good enough for her any more than he was. And she'd made a liar out of him with his mother, damn her. He didn't think he could forgive that.

Hunching down on his elbows, he stared into his glass. A man couldn't have been more optimistic than he'd been, riding to Marshall. Such plans he'd had. He was going to charm her into marrying him, then take her back to Kansas City to meet his mother, by God. Show his mother that this time he wasn't throwing words into the wind. He'd meant it about a wife and a baby and settling down. The way he had it figured, he could make a fine living robbing banks and trains during the summer and take the winter off to spend time with his family. But Annie had up and complicated everything.

When he heard steps on the stoop and then a knock, he thought it was her, come to apologize and beg his forgiveness like she ought to. But when he threw open the door it was the sheriff standing in front of him, a shiny badge prominently displayed on his vest. "Well, isn't this a surprise." He was drunk enough that he snarled.

"I'm Sheriff Jess Harden. And you are . . . ?"

"Bodie Miller, not that it's any of your business."

The sheriff's eyes narrowed and he dropped his hand to the butt of his gun. "Do you have a right to occupy this cabin?"

"My grandpa built the place, my pa owns it, and one day it will be mine. That good enough for you?"

For a long minute the sheriff studied him. They were about the same height, but Bodie outweighed Harden. That didn't mean Bodie could take him in a fight. There was no give in Jess Harden, no yield. Fair wouldn't mean much in a fight with this man; he'd do what he had to do to win. But fair didn't count for much with Bodie, either.

"We've had some incidents of vagrants using vacant properties. This cabin has been vacant for a long time."

"I come here every few months." This was her husband standing here in front of him, the man she'd chosen over him, the man she crawled into bed with every night. This man could touch her, kiss her, fondle her anytime he wanted to. Hatred set his blood on fire.

"How come I've never seen you in town?"

Bodie clenched his teeth and stared into Harden's cold gaze. "I go in for provisions, stop by the saloon. Last year I went to the fair. I didn't know I was supposed to check in with the law whenever I went to town. Is that a new ordinance?"

The sheriff was squaring off, not liking his attitude; he could see that and it pleased him. The urge to beat the living hell out of Jess Harden almost overwhelmed him. He hadn't forgotten the way Harden had smiled at Annie that day in the park, and it was for damned sure certain that Annie hadn't proposed to the sheriff. The sheriff had gone poaching in Bodie's territory.

Harden moved off the stoop and walked to his horse, a big palomino. "How long are you staying?" he called as he swung into his saddle.

"As long as I fricking well want to." They stared at each other across the weed-choked yard. "I read in the paper that you got married." He hadn't meant to say anything but didn't regret it once he had.

"About a week ago." Harden's gaze narrowed to slits. "It's no concern of yours."

An hour later, Bodie was still swearing and berating himself for not shooting the son of a bitch when he'd had the chance. He'd also figured out that Jess Harden didn't know who he was. There had been no flicker of recognition when he gave his name. That meant that the killings hadn't caught up to him, and it also meant that Annie had kept her mouth shut. Which had to mean that she still loved him.

Knowing that settled his thinking somewhat. But damn it all, why couldn't she for once do things the easy way?

"Is the mattress too hard?" Jess lowered the files of reports and wanted posters he was reviewing and turned his head on the pillow to look at her. Every night, she squirmed and tossed, trying to find a comfortable position.

"No, it's my back. It aches like blazes." Making a face and sighing, she pushed up to rest on the pillows mounded against the headboard. "It's been a busy week. I don't think I've worked this hard in years." A smile touched her lips, but she didn't look at him. She never looked at him when they were in bed, and she kept so far to the side that it seemed a wonder that she didn't roll off onto the floor. "I'm not complaining, mind. I guess I just didn't realize how spoiled I was." Hastily she added, "I'll get used to being a wife."

This was the time of day Jess most enjoyed, when they were side by side in bed together. Conversation seemed to come easier when she was relaxed and preparing for sleep, and he liked the look of her. The side lamp shone almost directly on her face and he could see the tiny freckles that sprayed her white skin. Those freckles fascinated him. They began across her nose and ran down her throat to disappear into the frothy lace of her nightgown. He'd spent many recent hours speculating about where those freckles ended, if they did.

One of the things he liked best was her hair. Even before she'd completed braiding it for sleeping, red strands had pulled loose to float around her face. Last night, when she was asleep, he'd lifted the end of her braid and been surprised to discover that her hair was fine and silky. For some reason, he'd half expected such vibrant tendrils would be slightly coarse.

She made a sound and pushed both hands beneath her waist to press the small of her back.

"Would you like me to rub your back?"

Every night he offered, and every night she firmly refused. To his astonishment, she hesitated. And her pause concerned him. The ache must be bad tonight.

"Would you put on your trousers first?" she asked, pulling out her hands and examining her fingernails.

"If you like."

When he returned to bed, she'd rolled on her side, presenting her back to him. "I don't think I should lie on my stomach," she explained, her voice muffled.

What he wore or didn't wear was of no concern since she couldn't see him, but if his wearing trousers made her more comfortable, then all right. Ione kept reminding him that pregnant women occasionally got peculiar ideas. And Annie had a few. She ate raw cabbage, got upset if the chairs weren't pushed under the table when not in use, and there was her continued refusal to look at him when they were in bed.

Kneeling on the mattress, he contemplated the current challenge, trying to figure how to massage her back from the side. "Could you roll more into a three-quarters position?"

"Maybe this isn't . . ."

"We can manage. That's better." This was the first time she had invited him to touch her, and he was not going to let the opportunity slip past.

Feeling awkward and clumsy, he placed his hands just above the small of her back. Instantly she tensed and he swore she held her breath, waiting to see what he would do. Which would not be what he wanted to do.

"Tell me if I rub too hard."

He started gingerly, far too aware of the warmth he felt through the thin folds of her summer nightgown. Beneath this flimsy layer of cotton she was naked. He stared down at the curve of her buttocks and swallowed.

"I stopped by the Miller place today," he said, desperately seeking a distraction. "The owner's son was there." The ridges of muscle framing her spine stiffened like iron and her whole body twitched. "Too hard?" He lifted his hands.

"No," she said in an odd-sounding voice. "It feels good."

He began again. "He's a surly bastard. Half-drunk, and the noon whistle hadn't yet blown. Something's not right there."

During the afternoon, he'd found an hour to ask around, but only the barman at the Tree Stump Saloon remembered Bodie Miller. The Goodmans at the grocery didn't recall him. Morrison at the pharmacy didn't know anyone named Miller. Bodowski at the general store thought maybe he sort of remembered a man fitting Miller's description who came in a few times a year to buy liquor and cigars. Everett at the Tree Stump said Miller kept to himself when he came in and didn't mix with the locals. Played it close to the vest.

Jess's gut told him that Miller was treating the old cabin more like a hideout than a home. It would be interesting to know where Miller went and what he did when he wasn't in Marshall.

"What else did you do today?"

She shifted slightly and the heels of his hands brushed the cotton covering her buttocks. Lord. Apologize? No, that would call more attention. He ran his hands up her spine, kneading gently. Trying not to think about buttocks or if the freckles extended that far.

"This was my day to ride over to Plains." Glascon County was small; there were only two towns under his jurisdiction. "Nothing much going on; there never is. Anderson and I talked to the volunteer fire brigade about their Fourth of July plans. Came back to Marshall in time to finish the week's paperwork and lock up a couple of drunk-and-disorderlies."

"Are people still talking about us?"

He moved her braid and massaged her shoulders, pleased by a small sound of pleasure. "Several folks have offered congratulations or best wishes." Which had surprised him.

"Thank you." Shifting position, she signaled the massage had ended. "That helped a lot," she said, sitting up again. Pink bloomed on her cheeks, overwhelming the freckles. She didn't look at him of course.

"Better cover your eyes; I'm going to take off my trousers and get back into bed." He'd intended the comment as a tease, but she did as he'd suggested, placing her hands over her face.

Smiling, he lifted his files for another perusal of the wanted posters. What he was looking for he couldn't have said, but he thought about Bodie Miller as he read the descriptions of the outlaws working the east end of the state and the Missouri border. One or two could have been Miller, but the details were not specific enough to warrant any follow-up.

Annie glanced at what he was reading, then leaned back against her pillows. "I haven't seen anything of your mother this week." Absently he reminded her that Ione wouldn't intrude without an invitation. "Do I need to wait for an invitation from her to visit the main house?"

"No," he said, looking up. "She'd be delighted to see you."

"Do you think so?" Forgetting herself, she glanced at him, saw his naked chest, and quickly looked away, biting her lip. "Maybe I'll bake a pie and take it to her tomorrow."

"She'd like that. So would I if you're inclined to bake two."

After a moment, Annie blew out her lamp, murmured good night, and slid down beneath the sheets. Jess studied her braid, a column of red against her white nightgown. Then, beginning what he intended to be a habit, he leaned over and kissed her on the back of the neck. "Good night, Annie."

She stiffened slightly, but she didn't say anything. He

waited, and when no protest sounded he nodded, pleased, then turned his attention back to the files.

Miller prodded his instincts. Men didn't generally provoke a man with a badge unless they had something to fear or something to hide. Which was it with Bodie Miller?

CHAPTER 13

⧫⧫⧫ ⧫⧫⧫ ⧫⧫⧫

I BROUGHT you a pie," Annie said uncertainly, hoping
she'd be as welcome as Jess had promised. "I found
wild strawberries and rhubarb growing along the path
to the old privy."

"That's one of my favorite pies," Ione said warmly,
taking the dish. "Come in, come in. And look at this
fancy crust. I suspect you're a wonderful cook."

Smiling, Annie followed into the sun-bright kitchen.
"I love to bake; it's everyday meals I find hard."

"We all dislike everyday cooking. I'm so pleased that
you came to visit. Would you like tea? Coffee? It's hot
enough for lemonade, but I didn't make any because
the iceman doesn't come until tomorrow. I'll send him
to your door, too."

"Tea would be nice, if it's not too much trouble." Annie sat at the table, admiring a cheerful yellow cloth. A
vase of white daisies made a centerpiece, flanked by a
half-dozen small carved animals. It said something ad-
mirable that although Ione lived and ate alone, she
dressed her kitchen table in more than a spill-proof oil-
cloth and salt and pepper shakers.

"These carvings are marvelous. May I?" Annie
asked, picking up a sow and one of three piglets. "Do

you collect these carvings? The workmanship is astonishing."

"I suppose you could say I collect them. Jesse gives me one every Christmas and for my birthday. He makes them."

"Jess made these?" Startled, Annie took a closer look, scarcely believing her eyes. Every detail was executed to perfection. She ran her thumb along the smooth polished wood of the little piglet's spine. "This is amazing." Replacing the sow and piglet, she examined a squirrel. Jess had managed to give the lifelike squirrel a sly and mischievous expression. "There's so much I don't know about your son." She looked toward the dry sink where Ione was setting out a teapot and cups. "Or you."

"One of the things you wish you knew," Ione said, pouring water into the teapot, "is why Jesse John is so accepting of another man's child."

Annie stared. During the past week, she'd wondered if she had imagined Ione's blunt directness the day of the wedding. Apparently not. "Well . . . yes."

"Do you use cream or lemon in your tea? Just sugar? Try honey instead." Seating herself, Ione poured, then handed Annie a honey pot. "I use honey in everything. This is a fresh batch. It's clover honey, mild but sweet." When Annie tilted her head, Ione laughed. "Didn't Jess tell you? I'm a beekeeper."

"I don't know any beekeepers." Fascinated, Annie looked from Ione's smile to the small carved animals. If she departed right now, she had already learned enough to occupy her thoughts for several days.

"After tea, I'll show you my hives. That is, if you're interested."

"I'd love to see them."

"Most people first ask if the bees will sting them." A look of approval crinkled Ione's eyes. "I like it that you didn't."

The comment pleased her. But she didn't entirely deserve the praise. The minute Ione mentioned stinging, her enthusiasm diminished. Still, it would be interesting and she trusted that Ione would not place her at risk. "I like the honey in the tea."

"Before we get into old history . . . how are you feeling?"

Annie sighed. "Some days I feel a burst of energy and no task is too great. The next day I'm so flattened, I can hardly get out of bed. My back aches, my stomach itches, and I'd swear my feet are getting larger."

Ione's ready smile curved her lips. "They probably are. When I was pregnant with Jesse John, I had to buy shoes a full size larger. Don't stand when you can sit, and when you sit, put your feet up." She looked into her teacup and her expression sobered. "Which brings us to that old history which Jesse tells me he didn't relate since it's mostly my story."

"You don't have to—"

"Yes, I do." Ione drew a breath and pushed a loose pin into the bun on her neck. "You see, Annie, you and I have more in common than you probably think."

In the following silence Annie suddenly guessed what Ione was about to reveal. A feeling of sadness stole over her, but now she understood why she had sensed no condemnation from her new mother-in-law.

"I grew up on a dairy farm outside Chicago. I had a loving family and a good life, but my heart was set on the big city. So, when I was sixteen my cousin Silla and I ran off to make our way in Chicago." She shook her head, smiling at the foolishness of a sixteen-year-old's dreams. "We found employment at Kestler's Emporium. Silla sold ready-made ladies' hats, and I worked up to managing the beauty products counter. Back in those days beauty products mattered to me."

Rising, Ione carried her teacup to the windows and stood looking out at the sunflowers running riot across the summer fields. "We told ourselves that we were sophisticated city women. Independent. Self-reliant." She shook her head. "We really didn't know how innocent we were, or how ignorant."

Ione spoke to the light, warm breeze meandering through the window, almost as if she had forgotten that Annie listened.

"One day a man came by my counter to buy perfume. For his mother, he said. His name was Edward Everett Hobarten. A fancy name for a fancy man. I'd never seen such a man before. I remember his walking stick had a gold knob, which says it all. He invited me to have tea after work at the tearoom in the new Aldorf Hotel. I was sophisticated, independent, dazzled, and didn't recognize that I was green as new grass. I said yes. I suspect you know where this is leading. We began seeing each other. We became intimate."

"I don't know what to say." A flush of embarrassment and discomfort spread from Annie's throat. It wasn't easy to listen to another woman's secrets.

"I wasn't pregnant yet the first time he struck me. I should have walked out the door and never returned. But he apologized, bought me a pretty bauble, seemed genuinely appalled and contrite. But it kept happening. The night I told him I was pregnant, he broke my arm."

Annie gasped and her fingers flew to her mouth. She had never been beaten and could not imagine the horror of it. But she would never forget the profound shock she had felt when her father struck her. That moment would be with her until the end of her days. "I'm so sorry," she whispered.

"He was married, you see. It was something I could easily have checked, as his family was prominent, but it didn't occur to me not to trust him. I didn't know about his wife until the night I told him I was carrying his child."

"What did you do?"

Ione shrugged. "I was in despair. I couldn't go home. I'd already broken my parents' hearts by leaving. I couldn't break their hearts again by returning in shame." She turned back to the window. "I tried to break it off with Edward Everett Hobarten. He couldn't marry me—by that time I didn't want to marry him—but he wouldn't let me go, either. Silla and I moved several times to escape his attentions, but he always found me. And he was angry for the trouble." Her fingers fluttered over her collarbone, her ribs, her arms. "I moved north. Jesse was born in a little town on the Illinois border. He was six months old when Edward found us the first time. I'd put out the usual story about being a young pregnant widow. I doubt anyone believed it. Anyway, the pattern was established. I'd move; Edward eventually found us. He'd beat me half to death, then apologize, drink, and brood. At some point, he had to return to his business interests in Chicago and I'd relocate. That's how it went for years."

"Oh, Ione."

"There was no point making friends or getting involved with a new community. I knew I'd be moving on. But somehow they always knew. Even before Edward showed up." Lowering her head, she touched her fingertips to her forehead. "There was gossip and it followed me. Ugly whispers I was intended to overhear. The worst part was Jesse. People can be cruel. Other children weren't allowed to come to our house or to play with him. He grew up alone, a solitary child, amusing himself in solitary ways." Her gaze swung to the carved animals on the table. "The saddest thing was that he was shunned not because of anything he did but because of what I did. I don't know why he didn't blame me and hate me, but he never did."

Annie placed her elbow on the table and dropped her head in her hand. "That's why he was so concerned with what was right for the baby. From the very first."

"Jesse never complained, but it was hard on him. He'd come home from school with bruises and scrapes and I'd know he'd been fighting. He'd walk away if someone called him a bastard, but he'd fight if they made a remark about me."

Staring past Ione, Annie thought about Jess's childhood. That Jess would marry a stranger to protect another man's child from suffering the childhood he had experienced told her how painful his childhood had been. "He married me to save my child from loneliness and from being ostracized."

Ione returned to the table and poured fresh tea. "I

suspect that's part of it. But Jesse John has encountered unwed mothers before and he didn't rush to put a ring on their finger." She patted Annie's hand. "Jesse's been carrying a soft spot for you for a long time."

Annie nodded slowly, remembering the times Jess had stopped to talk to her, the way he'd looked at her. Another of the damnable blushes heated her face. "There were moments when I . . . but I'd decided never to marry. And then . . . there was someone else."

"Those moments are something to build on."

It occurred to her that Ione had shared her story and might now expect Annie to do the same. Flustered and upset, she bit her lip, struggling to think of a graceful way to say nothing.

Then she heard a shout from the front yard and her dilemma became moot.

"Annie Malloy? Are you in there?"

Ione's brow lifted. "Are you expecting company?"

"Oh, God." The blood drained from her face, then flooded back in a rush that made her dizzy. How could Bodie do this to her? What was he thinking?

Staring, Ione fell back in her chair. "I see," she said quietly. "Jess said the man wasn't local. But he's returned."

"Annie Malloy. I'm not leaving until you come out here."

"What should I do?" Annie whispered. She gripped the edge of the table so hard that her knuckles turned white.

"If you don't talk to him, he'll just come back," Ione said grimly. "He might anyway. Is he likely to be belligerent?"

"No. I don't know. Maybe. I just . . . I don't know."

Her heart was beating so rapidly, she could hardly breathe. But she struggled to her feet, sensing that Ione was right. She had to speak to him.

Together they went to the door, and Annie stepped onto the porch, hiding shaking hands in the folds of her loose housedress.

Bodie sat on top of his horse, dressed like a man come courting. He wore an expensive dark suit and waistcoat and one of the fashionable new narrow-brimmed hats. But he didn't look like the Bodie Miller that Annie had known. Something hard had replaced the boyish look that she'd always associated with him, something angry and defensive and turned inward.

"I've come to get you." He didn't smile, didn't say "how are you?" or acknowledge Ione standing in the doorway. "Get up behind me. We're leaving."

Seeing him here shocked her so badly that she couldn't think. Didn't he see that she was heavily pregnant? She couldn't possibly hoist herself up behind him on a horse. Clasping the porch post to steady herself, she gave her head a shake.

"I'm married now." But he had to know that if he knew where to find her.

"It's not a legal marriage. You're my woman, and that's my baby you're carrying. Now do as I say, Annie."

"I can't. You know that. It never would have worked for us." She sounded shrill and pleading, but she had the sense not to say his name, knew she couldn't speak in specifics, not with Ione overhearing everything they said. "Whatever was between us is finished. We both knew that when we parted."

"Damn it, I didn't come here to argue. I'm warning

you. You married the wrong man, and I won't stand for it. If you're going to marry anyone, it'll be me."

Angry color pulsed in his face and his fists closed on the saddle horn. Annie saw the man he was beneath the charm he'd always shown her, and the glimpse both frightened her and gave her strength. She was glad he didn't know how close she had come to agreeing to marry him.

"Things happened. I couldn't get back here as quick as I said I would, but that's no excuse for what you did." His stare burned on her face. "You did wrong, Annie. Not marrying at all is one thing, but marrying someone else? That's dead wrong, and you know it."

Was he saying that he would have been happier if she'd remained a pariah and raised their child as a bastard? Surely he wasn't that possessive. But he was.

"Please. There's nothing for you here."

"I'm not leaving without you." He started to dismount, but Ione's sharp voice stopped him.

She stepped up beside Annie and leveled a shotgun. "You set one foot in my yard, mister, and we'll be picking up pieces of you for a week. You heard what she said; now git."

Bodie shoved back his jacket and put a hand on the pistol at his waist. Annie gasped. "For God's sake!"

Ione didn't waver. "If you're the kind of man to shoot a pregnant woman and an old lady, go ahead and try. The question is: Are you fast enough to get that gun out and up before I can pull this trigger?"

For an instant Bodie appeared to think it over, and Annie felt like weeping. This simply was not the man she had believed she knew. The man who had swept her off her feet had made robbing banks sound almost like a prank or an adventure. But the man she watched ease his jacket over the butt of the pistol was not a boyish prankster. This man was a thief and a killer. Things had taken a bad turn over the summer. Or she had been the most naive of women. Maybe she had seen only what she'd wanted to see and not what had been right before her.

Bodie looked from Ione to Annie; then he swept off his hat, letting the hot sun polish his hair into a golden cap. A wide smile transformed his face. "I apologize to you both. I don't know what came over me, ma'am. I saw the shotgun and just reacted. I'm real sorry if I frightened you."

"Please," Annie said, struggling to put some force behind her voice. "Just go." She sagged against the porch post. "And don't come back." There was something sad and wild in his eyes.

For a long moment she thought he would refuse to leave. "This isn't over," he said finally. "I need you to turn my luck around. You owe me." Then he wheeled his horse toward the road.

Ione kept the shotgun at eye level until Bodie was only a dot in the distance; then she swore under her breath and half collapsed against the doorjamb. "I haven't had that much excitement in an age." She waved a hand in front of her face. "I'd trade this whole place for a block of ice," she said, looking down at the sweat stains beneath her arms. "But I'll settle for a glass of whiskey."

"I'm sorry," Annie apologized when they were back at the kitchen table. Her dress stuck to the frightened sweat on her skin, and her heart still raced. "He wasn't like that when . . ."

"I know." Tilting her head, Ione took a swallow of whiskey, shuddered, then swallowed again. She leveled a look at Annie. "You made the right decision not to marry that one."

"I've never been so grateful for Jess." The minute she spoke his name, a heavy silence fell between them. "I can't tell him about this," she said in a low voice.

"If you don't, that puts me in an awkward position," Ione said slowly. She picked up one of the small carved animals and closed her fingers around it. "Jesse and I don't keep secrets from each other."

"It would only cause trouble." Annie pushed a hand through her wild hair. And she thanked heaven that she'd maintained the presence of mind not to call Bodie by name. At least Ione couldn't tell Jess his name. Miserable, she fanned her face with her napkin. "I promised Jess that he'd never run into the man who . . . you know . . . and at the time I believed it."

Ione gazed into space for several minutes before she slowly nodded. "I'll agree to this. I won't say anything to Jesse, because you're right. Trouble would follow. But if that man shows up here again, I won't hold my silence."

"Thank you." She drew a breath and stiffened her backbone. "I've thought about it until my head aches, and I still don't fully understand why it happened. Impulse. Loneliness. Infatuation." She spread her hands and let them fall. "I don't know. He did offer to do right by me. He offered marriage. Until then I hadn't really looked at the life he represented or the kind of husband he would make. I was so shortsighted and stupid. When I finally saw him and the life he led, I couldn't accept either for myself or my child."

"I suspected it might be something like that."

"In retrospect, the decision not to marry him was as impulsive as the decision to be with him. I thought I was a New Modern Woman. I really believed I could survive the censure and rejection from the community I grew up in. But when it happened the shame crushed me. I couldn't endure my parents' pain. And finally, the idea of raising a child on my own terrified me. I don't have your strength. I discovered I'm a coward."

"My dear, stop stirring that tea. You're driving me crazy."

"What?" She looked up to find Ione smiling. "Oh. I'm sorry." Putting the spoon aside, she folded her hands in her lap. "So, when your Jesse made his offer, I took it and blessed him for rescuing me."

"Don't sell yourself short. I didn't raise a child alone because I was strong. I had no choice. And they were terrible years, Annie. Years of poverty, loneliness, and guilt. Years of feeling a dagger in my heart every time I looked out the window and watched my boy playing by himself." She shook her head as if to dislodge the memories. "Well. Now that we're thoroughly depressed . . . shall we go visit the bees? The bees will set things right again."

Any enthusiasm for examining the hives had vanished long ago, but Annie heaved herself to her feet and tried to look agreeable.

"We'll stop by the shed and pick up some netting for you," Ione said, leading the way.

The colonies were a short walk from the house, placed between two fields of clover and alfalfa, near flowering shrubs and riotous wildflowers. A spreading cottonwood offered shade.

"The hives look like small houses!" Each had a peaked roof and they were painted in bright pastels. Annie hadn't expected to find beehives charming, but they were. The golden afternoon light, the small houses, the lazy soothing buzz of the bees thick in the air. Squinting through the netting, she puzzled over the names printed above the platforms and doors of each hive. "Katherine A., Anne B., Lady Jane, Anne C., Catherine H., Catherine P." When the answer came, she laughed in delight. "You've named them after the wives of Henry the Eighth!"

Ione turned full around to smile. "What a clever woman. Are you interested in history?"

"Yes. And Henry's daughter Elizabeth is practically the patron saint of the New Modern Women. She was intelligent and independent, went her own way, and she never married rather than subjugate herself to a husband's rule."

"I predict we'll have many happy hours gossiping about Henry and his family."

"But who is Zelma?" That hive's name was a puzzle.

"Zelma was my mother, God bless her. If I were in charge of bestowing crowns, she would have been a queen like the others." Ione beckoned Annie forward with a caution not to wander into the path of bees returning to the platforms and doorways. "Come have a peek at Queen Anne B.'s brood."

Hesitant at first, Annie quickly got caught up in Ione's talk of bee lore and forgot any stirrings of apprehension. Ione lifted the roof of Anne B.'s hive and showed Annie the frames of honey inside. The little houses were stacked boxes and Ione explained the purpose of each box. The honey was stored here; the queen resided there; the nursery was here. There were worker bees, guards, nurses, attendants.

"Oh my," Ione said, glancing at the sun. "Look at the time. Charlie Hare is coming at noon to drive me into town to service my honey accounts. I'll have to rush."

"Do you mind if I stay a bit longer?" Annie loved the idea that each hive was a unit unto itself, functioning busily and smoothly. The look and sound of the bees in the air around her was a delight that she couldn't have anticipated. "I'll put the netting back in the bee shed."

Ione rubbed Annie's shoulder. "We may have the makings of a beekeeper here. Which isn't a bad idea at all. Every woman should have a skill or a trade that can earn money." Before she turned up the path to the house, she called back, "There's an old tradition among beekeepers that says if we give our troubles to the bees, our troubles will be less."

Annie stayed with the bees for another hour, watching, learning. Discussing her troubles with bees wasn't something she felt comfortable doing, but oddly, she could foresee a time when she might.

What a strange up-and-down day it had been.

Jess found his wife, a word that continued to surprise and please him, in the kitchen, and a fresh pie waited on the windowsill. A lovely woman and a pie went a long way toward chasing the irritations of an eventful day in town.

"I brought these for you," he said, extending a bouquet of sunflowers. Do we own a vase?"

The heat was high in the kitchen, and she shoved at a damp tendril clinging to her cheek. She was hot,

flushed, and wearing a loose dress that didn't hide the
swell of her belly. To Jess, she was the most beautiful
woman he'd ever seen. Women without carroty red
hair and green eyes seemed pale and colorless now that
Annie was his.

"In fact, we do." After wiping her hands on her
apron, she opened a cabinet and produced a cut-glass
vase. "It belonged to my Grandmother Malloy." In the
way that women had, she added water to the vase, then
dropped the flowers inside, made a few adjustments,
and they looked wonderful. "Thank you."

"Hold still a minute." He brushed a kiss across her
forehead even though she frowned. Most of his new
habits involved kissing her. It was his intention to kiss
her every time an occasion appeared to merit kissing.
Arriving home impressed him as such an occasion. "Do
you love me yet?"

Startled, she blurted, "No."

"It's nothing to apologize for," he said, hiding a smile
by hanging his hat, vest, and gun belt on the kitchen
hooks. "It's only been a week."

"I wasn't apologizing. Now move out of the way; I
need to take the potatoes off the burner."

The way she banged the pot around caught his attention. Men had an inbred alarm that recognized signs of
woman trouble. "Did something happen today?"

She whirled from the stove and planted fists where
her hips used to be. "Why didn't you tell me that your
mother is a beekeeper and that you carve wonderful little animals? Why did I have to learn these things from
Ione and not from you?"

Jess blinked. The green eyes he'd been admiring were
now flashing fiery sparks. "Neither thing is a secret,"

he said slowly. "They just didn't come up in a conversation. Do we have any beer?"

"It's in the icebox, except there won't be ice until tomorrow, so you'll have to drink it warm. What else hasn't come up in a conversation that I should know about?"

"I have no idea." Warm beer on a hot night wasn't appealing, but he opened the bottle anyway. "Is that why you're riled up? Because I haven't talked about beekeeping or carving?"

"It seems like you should have."

Reading expressions was a skill Jess had cultivated over the years, and he thought that he saw a flash of guilt before she turned to the stove. He doubted his impression, because he couldn't think of anything she possibly could have done to feel guilty about.

Taking a seat at the kitchen table, he watched her slamming and sliding pots around the stove top. "Did you order furniture and rugs and curtains?" Had she spent more money than she thought he would approve?

"Not yet. I'm still looking through the catalogs. Before I place an order, I want to stop by Bannon's in town and see what's on hand and how the prices compare."

"Did you take a pie to Ione?" Had she said something to his mother that she regretted?

But her shoulders appeared to relax at the mention of Ione's name. "Your mother is truly a remarkable woman, Jess. I don't think I've met anyone like her." Pushing his arm out of the way, she set a plate and silverware before him. "We decided to combine our laundry and do the work together, and we agreed to have at least one meal a week together."

He'd never doubted that Ione and Annie would develop a warm relationship. They shared a similar philosophy, admired many of the same traits. There were significant differences between the two women, but their commonality would allow them to value each other.

Midway through supper, Annie suddenly put down her fork and stared across the table. "Do you think I'm using you?"

"What?"

"Do you feel like I took advantage by agreeing to marry you? That I've been selfish at your expense, by marrying you without loving you?"

"Where on earth did this come from? Did Ione say something that—"

"No, she didn't. It's just that I've been thinking about the choices I've made. I know how those choices look and feel to me, but I was also thinking about how marrying you might look to you."

"It looks fine to me."

"Because if you think I'm using you to save myself, you're right. I'm not proud of that, but the alternatives were so horrible. You came along and threw me a lifeline and I grabbed it, Jess. But our marriage isn't much of a bargain for you, and you deserve better."

So that's what she was feeling guilty about. She had decided that he didn't have the sense to know who he wanted to marry.

"Do you have someone better in mind?"

"Well, no," she said after a minute, frowning. "But I'd say anyone who isn't pregnant and someone who could promise to love and obey."

"Annie, I was teasing when I asked if you loved me yet."

"Well, I know that," she said, waving her napkin. "At least I do now. I'm just upset because . . . because . . ." Throwing down her napkin, she struggled to her feet and rushed out of the kitchen.

After he finished his pie, Jess took his carving knife and a small block of apple wood out to the porch. There was a mouse in the block. All he had to do was carve away the extra wood and find it.

What he knew about pregnant women wouldn't fill a measuring spoon. So he had to take care in attributing Annie's behavior to her pregnancy. Her agitation might not be related to pregnancy at all. But he couldn't think of anything else to explain the flashes of anger and guilt or the suggestion of tears before she'd fled.

Thirty minutes passed before he became aware that she was standing behind him in the doorway, watching him search for the mouse inside the apple wood.

"Your carvings are marvelous."

"It passes the time," he said, uncomfortable with compliments.

"Do you know anything about England's Queen Elizabeth?"

"Some," he said carefully, having no idea where she was heading with this.

"Elizabeth was an intelligent and curious woman, unafraid to try new inventions, sample new foods, try new things. She was passionate about everything she did," Annie said from behind him. "I can understand why she didn't want to marry and subjugate herself and her royal power, but I cannot believe that she didn't yearn to know and experience the physical side of love. I believe her curiosity and her desire to know herself fully led her to surrender to her love for Robert Dudley. I think they became lovers for a brief time."

Jess didn't move, didn't turn to glance at her for fear she would regret coming to him. But he understood that she was telling him about Annie Malloy.

"I suspect she cherished the knowledge of herself as a complete woman and did not regret the experience. But the risk for her would have been great. Fortunately, she possessed the discipline and self-control to break off any physical liaison before disaster struck. That's what I believe anyway."

Now he understood. Annie's pregnancy was not the result of a grand passion as he had worried that it might be. Nor had some slick-tongued bastard seduced her against her will.

He also understood why the man she had chosen was not local and why she would choose a man whose life choices were not acceptable to her and whom she would not consider as a husband. She'd simply been curious about her sexuality.

After a lengthy silence, Jess cautiously looked over his shoulder. Annie was gone. For several minutes he sat unmoving, watching the sun slip toward the horizon. Then in the last of the evening light he applied himself to carving out the broad shape of his mouse, turning the block of wood this way and that.

When he thought enough time had passed that Annie would have calmed down, he returned to the kitchen, where he found her finishing the supper dishes.

"I think I'd better tell you this," he said, standing by the cool evening air wafting in the opened back door.

"My deputies and I captured an outlaw passing through Marshall today. There was a gunfight."

She stiffened, her spine going as rigid as a tree trunk. "Was anyone injured?"

"Alfred Eckles, the outlaw, was shot in the shoulder and the thigh. No one else was hit."

She relaxed, which he took as a good sign regarding her feelings for him. Perhaps he was making progress.

Turning from the sink, she shoved back a wave of hair on her forehead, then wiped her soapy hands on her apron. "You were right to tell me, Jess. If I'd heard about the gunfight from Ione, I would have been angry at you. That isn't fair and I know it." She bit her lip and turned away from him.

"It sounds fair to me." He decided not to press when she didn't explain. "Do you want to go to the Fourth of July celebrations?"

Wandering to the window, she focused on the dying sunset. "I know I have to go to town eventually, but I'm dreading it."

"I'll be with you. If anyone says anything offensive, they'll have to deal with me."

"If my mother is correct, the scandal should begin to die out now that we're married." She thought a minute. "We could invite Ione and my parents to join us. Take a picnic."

Later, when she'd turned over in bed, prepared to sleep, she said in a low voice, "I'm sorry I was in a bad mood when you came home. There are reasons, but . . ."

"It's all right," he said, lowering the book he was reading to enjoy the look of her braid and the shape of her shoulders. When she said nothing more, he smiled.

Even with the awkward moments of their first week, he'd discovered he liked being a married man.

Leaning, he kissed the back of her neck. Sometimes it alarmed him to recognize how much he could love her. Being alone was ground he understood, but loving someone took him into unknown territory. There were traps in that territory. A man could get hurt.

CHAPTER 14

Y OU really shouldn't be out in public now that you're wearing loose clothes," Ellen remarked as she chose a seat at the back of the audience gathered to hear Mayor Meadows's Fourth of July address. Bunting draped the podium, and a pair of flags hung limp in the still, hot air. Ellen waved a palmetto fan in front of her face. "It's like an oven today."

"That wouldn't be practical, not to go out, Mother." The sun pounded the top of Annie's straw hat. A wide brim provided some shade but not enough to offer an illusion of coolness. She felt like she was slowly baking. "There's no one but me to do the shopping and town errands."

"Mr. Harden should hire some help. I'll ask your father to speak to him."

"Please don't." The last thing she wanted was to have her mother taking charge of her life. Since her marriage, Annie had already received one visit and four letters from Ellen filled with household instructions, suggestions for furnishings, and a timetable of tasks Annie needed to accomplish before the baby's arrival. "We don't have space for a live-in, and I'm managing well. It will do me good to get out occasionally." Much as she dreaded it. "Besides, look around. I see several pregnant women. In today's day and age, women don't hide pregnancies."

"If you ask me they should. It's indecent."

Annie loved her mother, but she and Ellen would always see the world and women's roles differently. They couldn't grasp each other's viewpoints. There had been times in the past when Annie had enjoyed their ongoing debate, other times when she found it depressing that they agreed on so little.

It was a relief to notice Jess, Ione, and her father returning with cones of shaved ice. Her father looked hot and tired, but Jess and Ione were laughing.

"I didn't know what flavor you'd prefer," Jess said, handing Annie and Ellen a cone. "Ione claims that whenever there's a choice of color, always choose red. So you two get cherry cones."

"Anything red is always the best," Ione agreed, smiling. She sat on the other side of Jess. "Does anyone really enjoy Fourth of July speeches? The mayor could give the same speech he gave last year and I wouldn't know the difference. When the speech is over, hours or days from now, I'd like to examine the booths over by the carnival. Maybe they have a fortune-teller."

Ellen leaned forward to stare past Annie and Jess. "Surely you don't believe in fortune-tellers!"

"Not at all. But I love hearing someone promise that I'm going to live forever and come into a fortune." Even Annie's father laughed, everyone but Ellen.

They fell silent when Mayor Meadows mounted the red, white, and blue platform, but they sat too far back in the audience to hear clearly. Annie tired of trying to imagine his speech by interpreting his gestures and let herself think about running into Janie Henderson and Ida Mae Blue.

Both had rushed up to her shortly after she arrived. They grasped her hands and congratulated her on her marriage; then Janie had confided that she thought her mother was weakening and would allow her to call on Annie in a year or so, but Janie was pressing to call after the baby was born. Annie hugged the good news close to her. No matter what happened the rest of today, nothing could spoil her good mood now that she knew the community would eventually accept her again. It would just take time.

She was wrong to think nothing could depress her spirits.

After the mayor's interminable speech, Ellen, Ione, and Annie stopped by the ladies' facilities to refresh themselves, then again emerged into the hot sun prepared to inspect the carnival and the booths surrounding it.

The first person Annie saw was Bodie Miller leaning against the men's facilities, staring at her.

Her heart lurched in shock, then raced, and she felt dizzy. His arms were tightly crossed against his chest. His lips had thinned as if he clenched his teeth. Despite the heat his blue eyes were icy and angry.

"Annie?" Jess appeared beside her and tucked her hand around his arm. "Are you all right? You look as if you've seen a ghost."

Her ghost intended to haunt her today. During Mayor Meadows's speech, she'd experienced an uncomfortable feeling that someone was staring at her, but she'd credited the sensation to her anxiety about appearing in public for the first time as Mrs. Harden.

And people did stare, and some muttered under their breath, but by and large she'd begun to grasp that she wasn't as interesting to the gossips as she had been. Yet during the mayor's address she'd felt as if someone were staring a hole in the back of her neck.

And now that same someone followed as they wandered among the carnival rides, listening to the children whoop and shout. And followed again as they inspected the booths and games where Jess and Annie's father vied to win prizes for the ladies by entering the ringtoss and then trying their hand at the shooting gallery. Jess easily won tiny dolls with painted faces for Annie, Ione, and Ellen but lost to Harry Malloy at guessing how many ducks fit into a rain barrel.

Annie said little then or later as they visited several of the booths to examine the summer produce and quilts and trinkets for sale. Every time she glanced around to discover if Bodie was still watching, she spotted him nearby. Once he smiled at her. Another time he blew her a kiss, which caused her to choke and feel as if she were strangling. She hoped to heaven that no one had noticed.

By the time Ellen insisted they should select a spot for their supper picnic, Annie's hands were shaking, she had a painful headache, and she felt frantic inside.

"Before we settle down to eat, there's something I want to take care of," Jess said, bending beside Annie's ear.

Before she could inquire, his gaze had hardened and he'd walked away from her, straight toward Bodie. Gasping, she gripped Ione's arm. "Yes, I noticed him, too," Ione said in a low voice.

Jess planted himself in front of Bodie. "You seem to

turn up wherever I do, Miller. You got something you want to say?"

Bodie straightened and closed his eyes to slits. "I have as much right to be here as anyone else."

"I don't dispute it. But it strikes me as more than co-incidental that every time I turn around there you are staring at me and my family."

Annie recognized Deputy Anderson as he stepped up beside Jess. "You having a problem, Sheriff?"

"Are we having a problem, Miller?"

"Not at the moment." But Bodie's snarl promised an-other time and another place.

"Something's not right about you," Jess said, un-blinking. "Eventually I'll figure it out."

"All I want is what's mine," Bodie said, loud enough for Annie to hear.

"Look for it somewhere else," Jess said flatly. "The next time I turn around I don't want to see you. Under-stand?"

"Annie, for heaven's sake." Ellen tugged at her sleeve. "I don't think you've heard a word I said."

"I'm sorry, Mother." When she looked back Bodie was striding toward the exit gate and Jess and Deputy Anderson had paused to talk. Then Deputy Anderson tipped his hat to Annie and followed Bodie.

"That was the man I mentioned," Jess said to Annie. "The one who's staying at the old Miller cabin." Frowning, he swung to face the exit gate. "I have a gut feeling about that one, but so far I can't prove any-thing."

She had promised that Jess would never meet the man who had fathered her baby, but it had happened in a little more than two weeks. Annie lifted a hand to the headache throbbing against her temples. She ought to tell him, but if she did then Jess would do his duty and arrest Bodie, and Bodie would go to prison because of Annie. That he belonged in prison was a fact she could no longer ignore. But she didn't want to be the cause of it.

Throughout supper, the following fireworks, and the moonlit ride home, all she could think about was what bad choices she had made.

Once they were in bed, Annie waited for Jess's kiss on the back on her neck. As confusing as it was, she'd discovered she couldn't go to sleep until he'd kissed her.

"Jess?"

"Is my reading light keeping you awake?"

"I truly want to do the right thing, but I don't always know what the right thing is."

"I'm not sure any of us do," he said after a minute. "The important thing is to keep trying. Do you want to tell me what this is about?" When she didn't answer, he changed the subject. "Did you enjoy yourself today?"

"Yes," she said slowly. "I guess so. No one made ugly remarks within my hearing. But it's hard. Women I've known all my life won't look at me, won't acknowledge me. I suppose in time things will get better." She told him about Janie and Ida Mae. "They give me hope that eventually attitudes will relax and the town will pretend to forget."

Jess put down his book and startled her by curling around her body. The shock was abrupt and as great as that of seeing Bodie at the fairground. Stiffening, Annie stared at the wall next to the bed, unable to breathe and unsure how to respond.

"This town is going to forget about the scandal, and

sooner than you think. I'll see to it," he said next to her ear, his warm breath stirring the tendrils that had squirmed out of her braid. "In the meantime, if anyone says anything offensive to you or behaves in a manner that causes you distress, you tell me and I'll make sure it doesn't happen again."

She didn't move, hardly dared to take a breath. God help her, he was naked and molded around her, pressed up against her thin nightgown. "Jess," she blurted, "I'm pregnant."

"And so beautiful. There wasn't another woman at the celebration who could hold a candle to you." His hard callused hand slipped around her waist and stroked the curve of her stomach with a long sensuous touch.

An explosion of conflicting emotions scattered her thoughts. She wanted to shove his hand back and roll away from him. But the solid strength of his body wrapped around her felt protective and so good, so comforting. His breath on her cheek made her wonder crazily what it would be like if he ever kissed her on the mouth, really kissed her. And his hand on her stomach seemed the most intimate moment she had ever experienced. It would be so easy to turn and face him. And then what would happen?

"The baby must be asleep," he said, removing his hand with a display of reluctance. "Good night, Annie."

When he returned to his side of the bed, she felt the void where his body had been and her emotions spun wildly.

"Sometimes life is so confusing," she whispered.

"That it is," he agreed.

He was so handsome, her husband. Tall and lean and as hard as iron with everyone but her and Ione. And he was courting her; she understood that. Every day he brought her flowers, or a treat from Mrs. Adam's Bakery or a penny he'd found or a rock with interesting markings. He praised her cooking, which didn't always deserve praise, and even when she felt hot and tired and sweaty he paid her lavish compliments. He bent over backward to be accommodating and considerate.

Wiggling, seeking a comfortable position, she pressed her face into the pillow.

It was too hot to make love. She was days from being six months pregnant. They weren't strangers any longer, but there was still much to learn about each other. The time wasn't right. Yet.

Good heavens, what was she thinking? But she couldn't push the thoughts away. She continued to sense his nakedness only a hand's reach away. Remembered the slow erotic stroke of his palm curving over her belly. Annie swallowed hard and stared at the wall.

As had become her habit, she visited the bees after she'd done up the breakfast dishes and straightened the house. Today Ione had harvested several frames and she showed Annie what happened next. They sat in the bee shed, wearing leather aprons to protect their dresses, each resting a frame on her lap and each holding a large-bladed knife.

"You dip the knife in the hot water," Ione explained, "then pull the knife down the frame, scraping off the wax." It looked easy when Ione demonstrated. "Catch the wax in the bucket. Candle makers pay good money for beeswax, but not if it's got dirt in it. And hold the frame so the honey doesn't leak out of the comb, which it will once the protective coating of wax is removed, unless you hold it at the right angle."

Annie's apron was sticky with honey before she got the hang of it and could scrape off the wax without spilling honey out of the cells. On her last frame she managed almost as efficiently as Ione.

"You see? I knew you'd learn fast."

"Now what do we do?"

"The frames go into the extractor."

The extractor reminded Annie of a potbellied stove. Once the frames were secured inside, Ione replaced the lid and cranked a handle that spun the frames inside the device.

"It spins the honey out of the combs. The honey collects at the bottom." She pointed to a spigot. "We'll collect it, filter it, let it ripen a bit, and then put it in jars. Once I paste labels on the jars, they're ready to be sold."

"What a wonderful business."

"Isn't it? Beekeeping was the perfect thing for me," Ione said, sitting and letting Annie have a turn at the crank. "I wasn't tied to one place. I could move and easily set up my business again. It's only time-consuming at harvest, and there's a good profit. I sell the honey for thirty cents a jar, and my cost is approximately five cents. That's for the jars themselves and the labels, and I pay Charlie Hare to drive me and do the heavy lifting. I bought the equipment years ago, so there's no cost there."

"My heavens, you're rich!"

Ione laughed. "Not rich, but comfortable certainly. I haven't worried about money for years. Believe me, that's a good thing." She watched Annie turning the crank and her expression sobered. "He isn't going to disappear, you know."

"I know," Annie said softly, concentrating on spinning the frames at an even pace. For a week she'd been startled by every noise in the yard, rushing to the window and half expecting to see Bodie's horse in front of her porch.

"What do you want to do, Annie?"

It was an odd question from her husband's mother, but not so odd from a friend. And they had become friends in the short time they had known each other.

"Most of the time the answer seems clear. Other times," she said, thinking aloud, "I feel like I'm denying a father his child, and denying my child the right to know his real father." Raising her head, she gave Ione a stricken look. "That feels wrong."

Ione nodded, then took the crank out of Annie's hands. "When we were in town yesterday . . . the grocer gave you too much change. Without thinking about it, you returned the extra three cents." She smiled. "I don't think you would have made a good outlaw's wife."

Annie's head snapped up. "I never said he was an outlaw."

"It's clear that Jesse thinks he is, and I trust Jesse's instincts. Trust your instincts, Annie, and you'll do what's right even if it doesn't always feel good to you. Now go have your morning nap. I think we wore you out with bee work."

Annie enjoyed smart, independent-thinking women. But women such as Ione could be unnerving, too. Rattled, she cleaned her leather apron and hung it on a row of hooks before she returned to her house, letting herself in the kitchen door.

She was halfway to the stove before she saw Bodie seated at her kitchen table. He sat sideways, an ankle on his knee, a cup of coffee near his hand. He'd draped his jacket over the chair back and set his hat on the table.

Annie clapped a hand on her chest and sagged against the sink front. "You frightened me half to death!" Anger surged with the color that flooded her face. "How dare you come into my house uninvited and make yourself at home as if you belonged here!" The image of Bodie rummaging in her cabinets for a cup and then pouring himself coffee made her head reel.

"Would you have invited me in?" he asked with a lazy smile, running his gaze over the swell where her waist had been.

"Bodie, you can't just walk into my house. It isn't right."

"Let's talk about that. What's right."

If Jess walked in the door now, how would she explain Bodie's presence? In a flash she realized she wouldn't have to explain. Jess would know. And then what would happen? The two men already hated each other.

Fighting to collect herself, Annie stared at him. Even with the new ruthlessness she saw in Bodie, she also recognized why she'd been attracted to him. Bodie Miller didn't accept rules, and she had met him at a time when she had chafed under the restrictions of the world she lived in. Bodie had offered a slice of life where limits didn't apply. Where rules didn't exist. In

Bodie's world a person did whatever felt good at the moment and the devil take the consequences. It was an audacious, utterly selfish world.

For a while Annie had found that type of self-indulgent existence exciting and freeing and exhilarating. But it was a world to visit, not to live in. Now his world appalled her.

"Sit down. Can't two lovers sit at the same table?" He cracked his knuckles, going about it methodically, one finger at a time.

The color burned deeper on her cheeks, and she struggled to keep her voice level. "We aren't lovers and never will be again. Why are you here, Bodie? What do you want?"

"You know what I want. I want my woman and my child."

"I'm not your woman. I married Jess Harden."

A shrug moved his big shoulders. "A mistake. I forgive you. I know now that I need you, Annie. You're my luck. All you have to do is walk out the door and ride away with me."

To him, marriage was a rule to be recognized if convenient, to be ignored if not. Her vows meant nothing to him; therefore, they were not binding.

"Even if I weren't married, I wouldn't leave with you." Slowly she approached the table and seated herself across from him. "You must know that. Nothing has changed."

"I should have quit when you asked me to. Things went bad after that. What if I gave up robbing banks?"

"I don't believe you really want to do that."

"Things didn't go well this last time out." He was silent so long that she thought he'd said all he intended to until he seemed to reach a decision and spoke again. "One of my men accidentally killed a teller and got shot himself. Damned fool almost died." He glanced at her and then away. "I had to shoot two men myself. Since then, there's been a craziness in my head."

"Oh, Bodie." Her guess had been correct. Now he was a killer and it couldn't be undone.

"One was a bank teller. The other was a train guard." He turned the full force of those blue eyes on her. "You see, Annie? I'm telling you the whole truth. No sugarcoating."

"If you get caught, they'll hang you."

"That's the point." He reached across the table for her hand, but Annie pulled away. Swearing softly, he leaned back in his chair. "I'm telling you this so you'll believe me when I say I'm considering a different line of work."

Considering. Even the threat of hanging hadn't moved him to a commitment.

"It depends on you, Annie. If you do the right thing and come with me, I'll give you the life you say you want."

So it was up to her whether he continued being an outlaw until a hangman's noose settled around his neck. Or maybe he was just saying what he thought she wanted to hear. Anger flushed her face.

"I never wanted you to make changes to please me. I wanted you to change your life because that's what you wanted, because what you're doing is wrong. It's not my place to make decisions for you, and you'd resent it if I did." Did he really believe that he could settle down and the law would forget about him?

He stood, looming over her. "Why the hell do you

have to make everything so difficult? We were fine until you got yourself pregnant." A finger pointed at her stomach. "That's when everything started to turn bad."

"I got myself . . . ?"

"It wouldn't surprise me if you did it to spite me."

Uneasily Annie glanced toward the window. Ione couldn't see the back of Annie's house, didn't know that Bodie was here. There wouldn't be any help this time.

"If you believe that, then why don't you just walk away? I don't understand this, Bodie. We never talked about feelings for each other, and I don't think you care about this baby. So why don't you walk away?"

"I said the right things, didn't I?" Frowning, he moved about her kitchen, pulling at the leaves of the geraniums she'd arranged on the windowsill. "You're my luck."

"But that was just lover's talk. You never envisioned anything permanent. Not really. Did you?"

She watched him trying to choose between a glib reply and honesty. "You didn't, either. At least that's what you said," he answered.

"And I meant it. I never intended to marry. I just wanted . . ." she swallowed hard with her own honesty, "to know what it was like."

"And it was damned good, wasn't it?" Turning from the sink, he raised an eyebrow, challenging her.

Since she had no experience to compare, she didn't know, but she wouldn't have answered anyway. "We never talked about love. We made no commitments." She spread her hands in genuine bewilderment. "We don't agree about much of anything. We don't want the same kind of life. I'm not your luck, Bodie. We'd be miserable together."

It made her cringe to watch him moving about her kitchen, examining her dishes and canisters. Lifting the lid off a pot simmering on the stove, he sniffed the ham and beans she was making for supper. And she kept recalling his remark about a craziness in his head.

"The sheriff's got himself a real cozy arrangement here. A nice little house, a pretty and accommodating wife, and supper waiting when he walks in the door." Bodie replaced the pot lid with a slam. "This is what I want."

Maybe he believed it, but she wasn't sure. "There are lots of women out there," she said quietly. "You can have a settled and honest life if you really want it."

"But none of those women you mention are carrying my baby."

A full minute passed before Annie could think of a response: "Do you really care that much about this baby?" Her hand rested protectively on her stomach.

"I had a notion you'd ask that question. I was going to swear that I do care. But I'm trying to be honest here. So the answer is . . . Hell, Annie, it isn't a baby yet, so how can I care about it? The important point is that the baby is mine and I don't want some bastard stamping his name on my kid!"

"This baby is just property to you?" Maybe it made sense in a twisted sort of way. He was a man who stole the property of others but couldn't abide the thought of anyone stealing something that he saw as his.

"Don't go turning words around. You and the baby are mine."

"I'm my own person. I always told you that."

"Aren't you listening? I want you to come with me. And I take what I want. Besides, I know you love me."

Standing, she faced him across the room. "Please listen. Part of me will always care for you as the father of my child. I'll think of you with fondness. But I don't love you, and I don't want to see you again. You and I could never be happy together." She drew a breath. "I didn't plan to marry Jess, but it happened. And I have a chance to be happy. Jess will be a good husband and a good father. If you ever cared for me even a little . . . then give me this chance to be happy. Leave us alone. Please."

"I'll never give that bastard what's mine."

Her heart sank. To Bodie, the unattainable would always be more desirable than what was possible.

Annie drew to her full height. "Please leave, and please don't come back." Despite the heat, a chill rippled her skin when she met his eyes.

"I'm willing to change my life to suit you." His fists opened and closed. "I'm willing to take a job I'll hate, willing to live wherever you say. That's a huge concession. Huge."

Maybe he believed what he was saying; she couldn't guess.

Striding forward, he jerked his jacket from the back of the chair and picked up his hat. "I'm warning you. Think it over, Annie."

Her legs felt as if they had turned to wood. Moving slowly, she stumbled to the kitchen door and watched him walk down the old privy path. He must have left his horse tied near the willows. It had never occurred to her that she would ever be frightened of Bodie, but twice now she had been.

By the time Jess came home, she had stopped shaking inside and believed she was calm. But the minute he walked into the kitchen carrying a bouquet of wildflowers Annie burst into tears.

"Annie?" He dropped the flowers and opened his arms as she threw herself against him. "What's happened?"

"Just hold me for a minute," she said against his neck. "I just . . . I just need you to hold me."

The moment was awkward at best, as holding a pregnant woman was not a graceful maneuver. Her stomach bumped between them, her fanny stuck out, and she felt utterly foolish, but she needed to lean on him. Needed the starchy soap scent of him and the feel of hard muscle beneath her fingertips. She needed the rumble of his voice in her ear, the warmth of his breath on her skin.

Jess shifted her to the right and then to the left, then gave up and simply wrapped an arm around her, stroking her hair and rubbing her back with his free hand. "Are you all right? Do you hurt somewhere?"

"I bought wallpaper yesterday and tried to hang it earlier, but it went on crooked, so I gave up and then the beans cooked dry and burned on the bottom, so I thought I'd take a bath, but I forgot the water was running, and water ran all over the floor and I was so tired, but I got it mopped up and then I dropped a dish and the baby has been active all day just wearing me out and I crave cabbage, but we're out and—"

His body relaxed and he rested his chin on top of her head. "But the real question is: Do you love me yet?"

She wiped her eyes on his collar. "Not yet." He pushed his handkerchief into her hand. "But thank you for the flowers."

"You're welcome." He kissed her forehead.

"Jess? Have you ever been in a situation you didn't want to be in, but there was no way out?"

Smiling, he tilted her face up. "I'm sure every pregnant woman feels the same way. But it won't be long now. Less than three more months."

In the short time that she'd known and lived with Jesse Harden, Annie had come to admire and respect him. With sudden clarity she understood that it would devastate her when he learned who Bodie Miller was, when he learned she had given herself to an outlaw wanted for murder. When he learned that he'd stood face-to-face with the man who had made love to her. He would hate her for these things.

After supper she carried a cold bottle of beer out to Jess in the yard. "What are you doing?"

"Did you have a swing when you were a little girl?"

Now she understood the holes he was drilling in a seat-sized plank of hard wood. "No," she said, tilting her neck to consider the branches of the cottonwood nearest the kitchen door. "My mother didn't think swinging was appropriate for girls."

"I didn't have a swing, either." Lifting the board, he blew off sawdust and eyed the straightness. "I decided our child will have a swing." In the evening light his eyes seemed amber rather than brown. "What else did you lack as a child?"

"Not much, actually." She thought a minute. "I wasn't allowed to play in mud."

A smile softened his expression. "Our child will be allowed."

She had to turn away. The generosity of the word *our* brought moisture to her eyes.

"And our child will always be allowed to have friends visit, agreed?"

"Agreed," she said in a choked voice, thinking of the boy who had had no friends.

Right now, she wished with all her heart that Jesse John Harden was the father of her baby. She wished her child would have his strong nose and jawline, wished that she'd see traces of Ione in her baby's smile.

She wished that Bodie Miller would ride far away and never come back.

CHAPTER 15

*B*ODIE sat hunched over a shot glass at the long bar in the Tree Stump Saloon. So far he'd done everything wrong. After two days of brooding, he'd figured that out. First, bullying Annie didn't work. Demanding that she do right by him made no impression. Trying to intimidate only drove her further away. The thing that irritated the crap out of him was that he knew better. Women responded to sweet talk. And they didn't care what a man wanted. They only cared about what they wanted. He had to convince Annie that she wanted him, and he wasn't going to succeed by frightening or threatening her.

Swearing, he gestured to the bartender to pour another round.

Second, he didn't believe Annie's explanation that she had come to his bed solely because she wanted to experience sex. Men did that, but women didn't. Did she take him for a fool? She'd come to his bed because she'd fallen in love with him. That was the only reason a respectable woman flaunted convention. Then she'd fallen out of love when he wouldn't dance to her tune. Women were fickle that way. At least that's what he'd heard. He'd never been rejected until Annie Malloy.

That's what ate at him. She had by God rejected him. And she'd been pregnant and facing ruin when she did. He refused to accept that.

And then, she had married someone else. And not just any man, no. She'd married the fricking sheriff as if to make a point. As if to say she could put his neck in a noose any damned time she wanted to. As if to say the wrong man was the better man. Well, no man worth his salt would stand for what she'd done.

Shots sounded in the street and his head jerked up. There weren't many men in the saloon at this early hour, but they all rushed to the big windows facing Main. Bodie saw traffic veering into side streets and pedestrians running into doorways before he spotted Deputy Anderson rising from a crouch to look over the top of a wagon. A shot from the far side of the street drew Bodie's attention to the park and a man using one of the benches for cover. A stray bullet shattered the window of the tack shop next to the saloon, spraying glass onto the boardwalk.

Bodie watched the exchange of shots for several minutes, enjoying someone else's fight before he spotted Jess Harden. Harden had his guns out, holding them down at his sides, and he wore an expression as hard as brown diamonds. The damned fool walked down the middle of the street like he was bulletproof, nothing but air between him and the shooter in the park. A grudging sense of admiration tightened Bodie's jaw. Harden had guts; he'd give him that.

"Anderson? Who is that son of a bitch?"

Deputy Anderson stayed in a crouch. "Wesley Slovick. Wanted for murder in Cleeve County."

The man in the park fired a couple of shots at Harden, missing by a mile. Bodie frowned. If Slovick were a better shot, everybody's problems would be solved. For an instant Bodie considered jumping into the fray, but better judgment prevailed. If it became necessary to take on Harden, he should do it with a plan and on his own terms.

Leaning against the windowsill and folding his arms across his chest, he watched Harden veer toward the park and raise his guns. In Bodie's opinion, Slovick was an idiot. If Bodie had seen a sheriff as fearless and foolhardy as Jess Harden walking toward him through a barrage of bullets, it would have scared the piss out of him. Scowling, detesting that thought, he leaned to the window.

Slovick didn't have the sense God gave an ant. He didn't do what Bodie would have done in Slovick's place. Slovick didn't surrender, and sure enough, he got himself shot in the shoulder and the thigh. Bodie had no doubt that Harden's shots were deliberate body hits or that the next shot would have been to the head. But finally Slovick stood up waving his hands in the air, bleeding all over the park bench, and shouting that he was finished.

Losing interest, Bodie returned to the bar and ordered another drink, thinking about Sheriff Jess Harden. That was the man Annie slept next to every night. He didn't know if pregnant women could have sex, but maybe they could and maybe she gave herself to the sheriff every night. Bodie couldn't have her, but Harden could. Rage choked his throat every time he thought about Annie with another man.

"I'll get her back if it's the last thing I ever do," he muttered through clenched teeth. He squared his shoulders. He'd show her who was the better man.

After Doc Willis finished digging bullets out of Slovick, Jess locked Slovick in the back cell.

"You shoulda just killed me and saved the cost of a hanging."

"Another minute, and that's what would have happened." Jess returned to his office and tossed his hat on the coat tree. "Good work," he said to John Anderson.

Anderson smiled. "He had me pinned behind the wagon. I'd still be there if you hadn't come along. You're the one who got him."

Propping their boots up on Jess's desk, they discussed the incident, then repeated the story as other deputies came in. Someone went over to Ma Golden's place to bring back coffee. Someone dispatched a telegram to the Cleeve County sheriff informing him they had Slovick, come get him.

When the noon whistle blew, Jess put on his hat and walked down to the Tree Stump Saloon, where the mayor usually took his midday meal. "Hello, Hiram," he said, taking a seat at the poker table where Meadows was eating.

"Goddamn, Jess. That was fine work this morning, mighty fine." Rising, his eyes shining, Hiram Meadows extended his hand across the table. "This town owes you a debt of gratitude. You got that son of a bitch and no residents were injured."

"That's what I came to discuss," Jess said. His smile didn't reach his eyes. "I figure you're right. This town owes me for Slovick and for keeping the peace and for staying on the job when people who should have known better messed in my private business."

A wary look flickered in the mayor's gaze as he sank back to his seat. "You angling for a raise?"

"No, something much simpler." Jess pinned Hiram Meadows with a steady stare. "I want you and Miz Meadows to invite me and my wife to dinner. It should be a large party that includes all of Marshall's prominent citizens."

The mayor blinked, then burst into laughter. "You sly dog. And you think this request is simpler than a raise? I'd rather take on the county officials than go home and tell Mrs. Meadows that she has to invite the scandalous Mrs. Harden to dinner."

"Either she does, or you can find yourself a new sheriff." Jess spoke pleasantly, but his flat voice left no room for negotiation. "Either you meant what you said about owing a debt of gratitude or you didn't. Which is it?"

Hiram pushed his fork at a pile of mashed potatoes. "Everybody in town knows you walked down the street like a hero in one of those Yellow Books, as fearless as if you were invincible." He didn't look happy. "I'll do what I can, but I'm not making any promises. There are some things a man can't order his wife to do."

Jess nodded. "The dinner invitation should arrive soon."

"Now, son, don't go setting conditions more difficult than you already have. The social season doesn't open until late September, which you'd know if you'd been married longer. I might be able to work one miracle, but not two, so you'll have to wait for that dinner party until early October."

Jess considered. He doubted Annie would choose her eighth month of pregnancy as the best moment to reemerge in society, particularly when the pregnancy had caused her downfall.

"All right," he agreed after a moment. "Tell Miz Meadows to plan the dinner party we're discussing for late November. After the baby is born."

"After the baby . . . that might, and all I'm saying is might, make the missus a fraction more agreeable."

Once Marshall's first lady opened her door to Anne Malloy Harden, the town's other ladies could not fail to do likewise. That was small-town protocol. Jess wasn't naive enough to believe the scandal attached to Annie's name would vanish. But it would fade quickly after she was welcomed by the mayor's wife. Like it or not, Marshall's society ladies would have to receive Annie.

"And Mrs. Meadows should call on Ellen Malloy."

"Well, my God." Hiram Meadows stared at him. "Why don't you ask me to raise the dead while you're demanding miracles?"

"I'm willing to wait until after the baby's born to see those miracles, but if nothing has happened by then, I'll resign and cite difficulties with you as my reason."

The mayor swore and pushed his plate away. "At least you're waiting until after the election. I suppose I should be grateful for that. And you've given me time to persuade Mrs. Meadows."

"I mean it, Hiram. Annie gets that invitation or you get my badge."

* * *

At the end of the day Jess and John Anderson shook hands and grinned, neither wanting to let go of the day's successes. "Would you like to come home with me for supper?" Jess asked. "Or would a certain Miss Morton be disappointed?"

Anderson's grin widened. "I keep saying, Miss Morton is only a friend. But I did offer to buy her a bite tonight and let her tell me how wonderful I am."

"Good. Better Miss Morton gushing all over you than my bride."

Still smiling, he swung up on the palomino and headed out of town, thinking about how his life had changed in such a short while. John Anderson had become a good friend, and Jess was moving toward friendship with a few other deputies. When he thought about opening himself to friendship, a warm sense of astonishment spread through him. He suspected friendship might always have been possible; he just hadn't accepted that he had to take the first step to make it happen, that he had to make himself accessible.

He wasn't sure how his good fortune connected to Annie, but he felt gut certain that it did. He'd taken the first steps toward friendship while he was wrestling with his feelings for her, and now he was a husband with a home and in a few months he'd be a father. Ione was healthy and happy. He was a hero again in the mayor's eyes. Slovick was behind bars. And last night, for the first time, his wife had turned to him, thrown herself into his arms, and wanted him to hold her. Life was good.

As always, Ione was waiting on her porch and he paused to visit for a minute. But after a few words she laughed and waved him toward the bunkhouse. "Go on, you. You're wearing a moonstruck look like an adolescent."

Quickly he gave her a brief account of the shoot-out with Slovick, then, eager to see Annie, smiled and waved and nudged the palomino toward the corral, glad to be home.

There were few pleasant things about August, Annie decided a few weeks later, frowning at herself in the full-length mirror in the bedroom. No holidays. Days hot enough to drive a saint mad. Dust everywhere. Flowers wilting in the garden. Never enough ice.

She wiped sweat from her brow, then examined herself in the glass. During the past month her stomach had ballooned. She could swear she was gaining at least a pound a week, if not more. Turning sideways, she studied her reflection in the lamplight.

Things were happening inside her body that she couldn't control. It was a strange helpless feeling. Pressing her hands to her stomach, she tried to remember what she had looked like before the pregnancy and wondered if she would ever look like that again.

"Shhh, baby," she said, rubbing gently. The baby was active this evening. Gone were the days of light butterfly touches. Tiny hands and feet jabbed and poked, startling her every time. It seemed impossible that she'd once had to struggle with the idea that she was truly going to have a child.

Lifting the lamp, she carried it to the nursery, looking around at the new, unfamiliar furnishings that had been delivered yesterday. Ellen and Ione had offered advice as to what would be needed. Now that almost everything was in place, a room Annie had thought was large had shrunk. She moved about, touching the cradle and the crib, a low bureau, and a child's wardrobe. There was a box for supplies and a box for the diapers that she hemmed in her spare time. A rocking chair and side table. A chest for baby toys. A rack for tiny shoes. Shelves for blankets and sheets and towels. She wouldn't have guessed that such a small creature would need so many items.

Setting the lamp on the side table, Annie sank into the rocking chair and closed her eyes. She was going to be someone's mother. For days she had been trying to understand what that meant. Could she still be herself and be someone's mother? What kind of mother would she be?

Inevitably, that question led to confusing thoughts about Ellen. They didn't think alike, didn't agree on many things. Usually Annie's thoughts stopped there, but recently she had realized she was different from Ellen because Ellen had allowed her to develop independently. Ellen had always stated her opinions, but she had permitted Annie to reject those opinions and formulate her own even when Ellen strongly disagreed. Ellen had taught Annie household tasks though there were servants to perform those chores. And it had been Ellen who encouraged Annie to read in a wide range of subjects.

Once upon a time, Ellen had sat in a nursery and dreamed a mother's dreams and gently poked back at Annie's tiny fist. Once Ellen had lovingly chosen soft blankets and had patiently cut and stitched diapers.

Moisture glistened in Annie's eyes. Resentment and hurt feelings had created a strain between them. And

Annie had to concede the possibility that Ellen and her father might never genuinely accept her baby. But she placed her hands on her stomach and listened to her heart, which told her that it was time to reach out and begin to put things right.

Her father was trying. She'd seen a plea in his eyes when he and Ellen came to dinner last week. But he couldn't find the words. And his touch was tentative, as if he, too, could not forget that he had struck her. He needed to say he was sorry and Annie needed to say she forgave him, but neither had been able to do so. Annie would have to find a way.

Rising, she walked through the darkening house, pausing in the kitchen to fetch Jess a bottle of beer from the icebox before she stepped onto the porch.

"I was just coming in," he said, sweeping wood shavings into a dustpan.

"It's cooler out here." Annie eased into a reed porch chair. "Can you tell me what you're carving now?"

"A mama duck and a duckling."

"Just one duckling?"

"For the present."

"Oh." She was glad it was too dark for him to see the blush that colored her cheeks. Any reference to their future life together always made her feel peculiar and tingly inside.

"Thank you for the beer."

Crickets and frogs sang along the old privy path. A few fireflies still flickered near the chokecherry bushes. Stars popped into view as if a lamplighter rushed about the sky touching his match to distant globes.

"Jess? Can you talk about your father?" With her

own father so strongly in mind, she suddenly became curious about his.

Jess's shadowy profile nodded once as if he'd been waiting for this question. "I don't want any secrets between us, Annie." Before she could say anything, he added, "I know. The identity of the baby's father will always be a secret. I respect your decision and I accept this exception. I know you have your reasons. But that's the only secret that should ever be between you and me. I believe we agreed to that."

Had they? Annie gripped the arms of the chair and stared toward the horizon. Guilt squeezed her chest. But if Jess knew that Bodie had been out here . . . Besides, it was over now. Bodie wouldn't return. She felt almost positive about that.

"What was your father like?" she asked quietly.

"Edward Hobarten could be charming when he wanted to be," Jess said. "And he could be a brutal son of a bitch. He was intelligent and prosperous and believed those qualities set him above the rest of the world. He was selfish enough to take whatever he wanted regardless of the ethics and morals involved. He drove his carriage at breakneck speed, drank too much, and caroused too much. He valued property above all, his holdings, his employees, his family. It enraged him that Ione didn't wish to be property and rejected his control."

No wonder Ione understood Bodie so well. "Your mother told me about the beatings," Annie said softly. "That must have been very hard for you to watch."

"I started doing odd jobs wherever we lived when I was eleven. When I was twelve, I told Hobarten I would kill him if he continued to hurt Ione. His answer was to break my arm. When I was thirteen I had saved enough to buy a gun."

"Oh, Jess." Reaching across the narrow space that separated them, she took his hand.

"One day he showed up unannounced as he always did, but this time he brought gifts. Wooden soldiers for me and a diamond pin for Ione." He shook his head. "Ione was just getting established in the honey business and we barely had money to put food on the table. But he gave her a diamond pin that she didn't want and had no good clothes to wear with and she didn't go out anyway. I'd outgrown play soldiers long ago. The gifts preceded his announcement that his wife was dying. She'd been an invalid for years. He said that soon he would be free to live openly with us. Our lives would change. There would be a big house in Chicago. Servants. The life he was accustomed to living."

Releasing Annie's hand, Jess leaned back and ran his fingers through his hair. "Ione refused him. There was an argument. He didn't hit her until after he'd finally offered marriage and Ione refused that, too." In a moment he continued. "I thought he was going to kill her this time. I believe he would have if I hadn't shot him first."

"I'm so sorry, Jess."

"Someone called the sheriff. I remember thinking I'd be hanged and thinking it was worth it. His name was Sheriff Tom Stone; I'll never forget him. Stone looked at the broken furniture and the blood. Looked at Ione's battered face and broken collarbone. Looked at Hobarten and looked at me. Then he said we needed to get Ione to a doctor and we'd deal with the accident later. I told him it was no accident, told him I'd killed the son of a bitch, had done it deliberately, and I was glad he was dead. Stone looked me in the eye and told me I had it all wrong. What happened was an accident."

"You were lucky. A different sheriff might have . . ." A shudder went down Annie's spine.

"I thought about that night and thought about Sheriff Stone for years. Because of him, my life went a different direction. Eventually I decided I couldn't do better than to pattern myself after Tom Stone. Stone knew the difference between the law and justice. They aren't always the same thing. But that's the kind of lawman I've tried to be, Annie, like Tom Stone. The law looks aside when a man beats a woman, but that night Tom Stone didn't. And the law would have hanged a boy for saving his mother, but Tom Stone didn't see it that way. It's rough justice and some would say it's an abuse of the badge. Others might see it differently."

"I'd say it depends on the man dispensing that rough justice, doesn't it?"

"There's one more part of this story I haven't told you."

Annie wet her lips and released her grip on the arms of the chair. "What?"

"Hobarten's wife died while he was traveling west to find Ione. His will left his estate to her unless she predeceased him, which she did. In that event, eighty percent of what Hobarten owned went to charity. The remaining twenty percent was bequeathed to me as his only child and heir."

"But . . ."

"But I'm the one who killed him. That's the reason I've never touched that money." Walking to the edge of the porch, he gazed up at the stars. "The Hobarten family lawyers invested my portion of the estate and they manage it. Twice a year I have to go to Chicago and sit down with a roomful of lawyers, accountants, and auditors. Over the years the amount has grown. If we use that money, we'll have a very comfortable life, and so will our children and their children."

She swallowed hard, staring at the bushes along the path to the old privy. "I'm trying to take this in, but . . ." Jess Harden was a rich man?

"Maybe twenty years of feeling guilty about not feeling guilty is long enough," he said quietly. "We'll talk about it someday. Right now you and I are still getting to know each other, but eventually we'll want to plan our future. When that time comes, maybe it will also be time to finally figure out if Hobarten's money is a punishment or a reward for killing the bastard. Or if that even matters."

The idea of great sums was difficult to grasp. Especially as right now Annie couldn't think of anyplace she'd rather be than sitting on her back porch in the dark with Jess Harden on a warm August night. Feeling his trust in her. Knowing he'd built her baby a room and a swing.

"I'd say next year we should decide where we want to live and think about building a house. In the meantime, do you mind too much living in a remodeled bunkhouse?"

"I love our little house," she said honestly. With surprise she realized she'd been happy here. The house was small enough to keep up without exhausting herself. She loved her bright sunny kitchen. The morning hours with Ione and the bees were a joy. And, she thought with a quick glance at Jess, her time with him was the high point of each day.

The only lack in her life was friends. Sometimes, in the middle of the long summer afternoons, she closed her eyes and remembered the faces of the ladies who had received her and who had come to call. Remembered the clubs she had belonged to and enjoyed. Sometimes she thought about the New Modern Woman's Association and wondered what the topic had been at the most recent meeting.

Her new life wasn't perfect, but . . . she and Jess were building a life together, establishing routines and habits, enjoying each other. She looked up with wide eyes, disturbed and confused. "I think I'll go in now."

She was at the door to the kitchen when he came up behind her and framed her shoulders between his warm square hands. When she halted abruptly, he gently eased her back against his body. Instantly a thrill of electricity flashed along Annie's spine and buttocks. She closed her eyes and sagged against him, feeling her knees tremble.

He bent his head, bringing his lips near her ear. "Talk of the future confuses you, I know. But I think about it all the time."

His hands moved slowly down her bare arms. "When the time is right, when it's our time, I want to undress you—slowly—in front of the fire. Slowly, one item at a time. I want to roll down your stockings and unlace your corset. I want to slowly take the pins out of your hair and catch the weight in my hands. Then I want to learn the feel of every inch of you."

Slowly, slowly, his hands moved up her arms again.

She felt the calluses on his palms, the shape of his fingers. And she couldn't catch her breath, couldn't wrench her mind from the images he drew. Slowly. The word reverberated in her head. Slowly. Not rushed and over almost before it began. But slowly. Savoring every heated moment.

"I want to touch you and taste you. I want to tease and torment you until you want me as much as I want you." His hands moved down her arms again, caressing her, exploring the sensation of bare skin beneath his palms. "I want to kiss you until you're wild with desire, until your mouth is swollen and you thrash beneath me. I want to see you damp with sweat in the firelight, want to see your eyes glazed with passion."

Slowly he drew his fingertips up her arms, leaving goose bumps behind, leaving her trembling against him with her mouth dry and her throat burning. No one had ever said such things to her or created such wild exotic images in her mind.

His breath near her ear ignited fire in her cheeks. His hands on her arms flashed messages through her body. A great weakness spread through her and she feared she would have slid to the floor if he hadn't pressed her against him.

"When that night comes," he said, his lips brushing her earlobe, her throat, "I am going to show you a universe you have never explored, take you to a place you have never been. I'm going to give you pleasure that you haven't dreamed. Slowly, slowly. Again and again."

What he murmured near her ear was so strange and arousing, so unnerving, that Annie couldn't remember how she got to their bedroom, managed to undress and don her nightgown, or get into bed. But for the first time, she peeked at Jess while he undressed. She saw a supple body swelling with muscle, taut thighs, and well-shaped legs. A flash of tight buttocks caught her eye before he came toward the bed and she hastily turned her head toward the window, feeling the burn on her cheeks.

Once the sheet covered him and he had picked up his book, she slid a glance in his direction. Golden lamplight played across the muscles defining his chest.

"Jess?" She wet her lips and said his name again.

"Yes?" Warm brown eyes smiled at the springy hair already finding a way out of her braid.

"You said you would take me to a place I've never been." The color in her face intensified, she could feel it, but she managed to keep her voice steady, trying to pretend they discussed something no more emotional than the moths batting against the lamp chimney. "How do you know that I've never been to that place?"

His smile widened. "Because you believe that Queen Elizabeth could sample sex to satisfy her curiosity and then walk away and never climb into a man's bed again."

"I see."

But some thought was required before she actually did. Gradually she worked it out. Jess implied that for her to believe that Queen Elizabeth could try sex once and never again meant Annie felt the same way.

Well, she supposed she did. In her opinion, the best part of sex was before it happened. Those moments when the man held her and kissed her and whispered wildly flattering compliments, those were the moments when she felt a stirring of . . . something. The sex itself was awkward and embarrassing, messy, and finished before Annie had figured out where her knees were supposed to go.

Two points occurred to her, both of which kept her awake long into the hot August night.

She hadn't enjoyed sex.

Jess was saying that she hadn't experienced all there was to experience and that when she did she was going to like it.

When the living room clock chimed twice, she found herself lying face-to-face with him. Sighing once, she gave in to impulse and jabbed a finger on his chest. His skin was firm and tight.

Instantly he sat up with a gun in his hand. Did he keep it under his pillow? Annie's mouth dropped open and she sat up, too.

"What's wrong?" he demanded after a quick look around their bedroom.

"Nothing. Nothing's wrong."

"Is it time? Has your labor begun?"

"No. I'm not due until November."

The gun vanished as mysteriously as it had appeared. He reached for her shoulders and peered through the darkness. "Then why did you wake me?"

"I just wondered . . . is slowly a good thing?"

"Is slowly . . ." His fingers relaxed and she felt rather than saw his smile. He brushed his fingertips across her lips, then sank back to his pillow. "Oh yes, Annie love. Slowly is a very good thing."

"Oh, my."

*   *   *

They had stood in the doorway, lit by the light from the kitchen. Bodie hadn't been able to see exactly what they were doing, but he'd seen Harden run his goddamn hands all over her. And Annie had leaned up against him and let him feel everything. They had stayed in the doorway for a long time, rubbing against each other and whispering. It wasn't decent. She was pregnant, for Christ's sake. And she belonged to him.

Usually they just sat on the back porch after supper, talking in low voices, not touching. Often Annie laughed, and that made him crazy inside. He hated it that Harden could make her laugh. And he hated when they leaned up against the pillows and talked in bed.

But he liked it that Annie refused to kiss the son of a bitch. After she turned out her light, she turned her back to him. Then he'd lean over and kiss her neck, which made Bodie want to kill him. Except then Harden would pause like he hoped she'd roll over and kiss him back, but Annie never did. She left him sitting up reading, and Bodie liked that. It told him that she remembered who ought to be lying next to her.

But tonight, she'd forgotten all about Bodie Miller. She had leaned back in Harden's arms and let him run his hands over her.

Never in his life had Bodie imagined that he would become the kind of low character who spied on people and looked through their windows. That's what caring about Annie had brought him to. That's what she'd done when she rejected him. Since then he'd made only bad decisions.

Grinding his teeth, he stared at the dark house. He'd never sat next to Annie while she was sleeping. She had never cooked him a supper. She had never washed his clothes or ironed his shirts or put fresh sheets on his bed. She had never looked at him the way she sometimes looked at Jess Harden, with soft shining eyes and her lips parted.

He had to fix this problem soon.

CHAPTER 16

I NEED money."

The Baylor brothers looked at each other and then swore. "It's about time. A couple more months and the bank-robbing season is over," Jimmy said, scuffing his boot in the dirt.

Hoss nodded. "Can't get away if there's snow on the ground. Too easy to track."

"Thank you for explaining the obvious," Bodie snapped.

Rocking back on his heels, he scowled at Jimmy's spread, resenting the obvious signs of prosperity. None of the other farms he'd ridden past had such a big house in good repair and freshly painted. None of the others had barns that looked brand-new, with equipment to match.

"I thought we agreed not to spend in conspicuous ways," he said, turning to stare at the Baylor boys. "What do you think your neighbors are saying about the addition to your house?"

"Hell, Bodie. What's the point of robbing banks if we can't spend the money?"

"That's right," Hoss added firmly. His place looked as spanking new as Jimmy's.

Jimmy pressed his lips together. "Maybe you're just pissy because we put our money in something solid while you spend yours on clothes, gambling, and women."

For a moment he felt like smashing Jimmy's face and riding back to Marshall. But maybe Jimmy had a point. The boys had something to show for the years of trains and banks, and Bodie didn't. Well, that was going to change.

"From now on, we don't do trains." The botched Atchison, Topeka, and Sante Fe job had proved that he needed more than three men to successfully rob a train, but he resisted complicating matters by adding others. "We'll stick to banks."

"That's fine with us." Jimmy started walking toward the house. "But let's do Kansas banks. A quick hit and then home."

"Me and Jimmy been talking about it," Hoss agreed. "Going to Missouri didn't work out too good. We were gone almost three months and got next to nothing. If we work closer to home, at least we can sleep in our own beds and see our families."

"The closer to home we hit, the bigger risk we take of being recognized."

Jimmy stopped and faced him, a challenge in his gaze. "If you're losing your nerve, me and Hoss can go it alone."

In a second he'd flattened Jimmy, laying him out on the ground with blood gushing from his nose. "I run this outfit and don't you forget it." His fists opened and closed and he wished he'd broken the son of a bitch's nose, wished Jimmy had put up a fight.

"What's gotten into you?" Hoss demanded, pulling

Jimmy to his feet. "We used to be in this together; then it turned into every man for himself. Now you're getting crazier than you used to be."

"Maybe you two didn't notice, but everything's different. We're killers now, remember?" He leaned in close to Hoss. "It's not just prison anymore; it's the end of a rope."

Jimmy rubbed his nose and inspected the blood on his hand. "You used to say if we ever killed someone, we'd quit. So, what the hell are you saying now? Do you want to quit or do you want to go out again? Which is it?"

"I'm saying we make a fast grand sweep, hit as many banks as we can, and then lay low until spring." He thought about Annie. His plan was to put on a show of going honest, then gradually resume doing things his way. He'd abandoned the thought of quitting after he killed a man. The authorities could only hang a man once. As for Annie, she'd come around.

"Well, those banks have to be in Kansas, or me and Hoss ain't going."

"All right." Bodie's eyes squeezed down to slits.

He didn't like it, but unfortunately, he didn't have time to find new men he could train and trust before the snow flew. Next spring he'd put together a better outfit. For the moment he had to placate the Baylors no matter how much that went against the grain. He needed a lot of money fast.

During the long sweltering ride back to Marshall his spirits began to improve. Since his goal was to make money for his future with Annie, his luck would turn around. He couldn't wait to tell her about the property he would buy and the big house he was planning.

*   *   *

Weeks had passed since Annie had found Bodie sitting in her kitchen. Gradually she'd recovered from half expecting to find him in her house when she returned from her morning's visit with Ione and the bees. Bodie had apparently moved on and that chapter of her life was closed. At least she hoped to heaven that it was.

But when she and Ione walked into her kitchen, Annie stopped abruptly with a sense that something wasn't right. She hadn't left a coffee cup on the table. The stew simmering on the back burner had been moved off the heat. And she smelled a faint drift of cigar smoke. Jess never smoked in the house.

"Well, that was a good morning's work," Ione said with satisfaction, heading for the stove and the coffeepot. Absently she slid the stew pot back onto the hot burner. "Thank you for your help."

The last of the season's honey had been withdrawn a week ago. Today they had finished preparing the hives for winter by removing the hives' upper stories to concentrate the frames. The reduced space would encourage the bees to cluster for warmth during the cold days and nights to come. At the end of September, they would begin feeding the bees a honey solution to see them through the winter.

"I think I've set aside enough honey to take us to spring," Ione said, pouring two cups and carrying them to the table. As casually as her shaking hands would permit, Annie removed the cup already there and placed it in the sink. "Next week we'll drape the hives with netting to keep the birds and small critters away. Once that's done, the season is officially over."

Where was he? That Bodie was in the house Annie didn't doubt. The nerves racing along the surface of her skin told her so. Tilting her head, she listened hard but heard nothing other than the usual sounds.

"Annie? You look pale. Did you sleep well last night?"

Sleep had never come as easily. At the end of the day she was so exhausted that sleep overtook her the instant she closed her eyelids.

"My legs are a bit crampy today," she admitted, walking to the dining room door as if working out the kinks. She peered inside and saw a man's hat beside the table centerpiece. Her heart turned over in her chest. The dining room table was not the usual place for a hat. He'd placed it there deliberately.

Annie's mind raced. He'd been in her kitchen and he'd seen her and Ione walking toward the house. There would have been time to put the coffee cup out of sight, but he'd left it for her to see. And then the hat. Did he guess that Ione would recognize it was not Jess's Stetson? Had Bodie left something else in the living room?

"I'll stay long enough to hem a few diapers; then you should lie down for an hour."

"I'll fetch the diapers."

Annie hurried through the dining room and skidded to a halt in the living room, her hands flying to her chest. Two chairs were overturned. Books were pulled out of the shelves, and Jess's little carved animals had been flung around the room. One was crushed as if a boot heel had come down on it hard. Gasping, Annie looked down the hallway and saw Bodie filling the doorway of the baby's room. He gave her the charming little-boy grin as if they shared a grand jest.

Heart pounding, she turned so swiftly that her skirt billowed behind her, but she paused in the dining room to collect herself.

If Ione learned that Bodie was here, she would tell Jess. That was the agreement. And then nothing Annie said would stop Jess from going after Bodie. Whatever happened to either man would be her fault.

She returned to the kitchen and held out her shaking hands. "I think I overdid it this morning," she said, trying to sound apologetic instead of frantic. "Would you think me terribly rude if we skipped coffee and diapers this morning? All I can think about is lying down."

It broke her heart to deceive Ione, but she had to get Ione out of the house, and quickly, before Bodie called attention to himself and unleashed a disaster.

Immediately Ione came to her feet with a smile. "I wouldn't think you rude at all. Frankness and honesty are traits we Hardens admire."

Honesty. Annie grimaced when Ione gave her a hug that she didn't deserve. "Thank you for understanding."

At the door Ione looked back. "Is there anything I can do to make these last weeks any easier for you?"

It was an opportunity to send a signal and for an instant Annie panicked and considered taking the chance. Then her shoulders slumped and she rubbed her eyes. Bodie was her problem. Surely she could solve this once and for all without involving Ione.

Standing at the door, she watched Ione turn the corner of the house and disappear from view. Dread settled

like a lead weight on her shoulders. She didn't move until she heard noise in the living room.

Bodie was turning the chairs upright again. "Has the
old hag gone? I wanted her to walk in here. I'd like to
have seen her face when she saw me. I'd have scared
her good."

Today he looked like a prosperous businessman. He
wore a dark suit and waistcoat and a heavily starched
collar. Although the jacket fit well, Annie saw the bulge
of a gun at his waist. He'd had a recent haircut and
wore his hair short, the way Annie had once said she
liked.

"How dare you do this?" Her voice shook.

A frown puckered his brow. "It was a joke. Nothing
got broken; I was careful." A slow smile curved his
mouth. "Except for one of the sheriff's carvings. But
that's no loss."

"I won't stand for this, Bodie. I'll tell Jess everything;
I swear I will."

"No, you won't, sweetheart." Bending he kissed the
top of her head as he moved past her into the kitchen,
picking up his hat on the way. "Coffee? Oh, I see you
already have a cup." He sat down as comfortably as if
he were in his own kitchen.

Helplessly Annie followed, pressing her back to the
sink. "I mean it. You can't keep doing this. I never
wanted to put you in danger, Bodie. But I will. I want
you to leave now, and if you ever come back I'll tell Jess
who you are and what you're doing."

"If you were going to tell him about me, you would
have done it a long time ago. You didn't tell him because you love me."

"You're the father of my baby. I didn't tell Jess before

because I didn't want you to go to prison because of me." She drew a breath, reaching for courage. "I don't love you, Bodie. I tried to tell myself that I did to justify going to your cabin. But I didn't even know what love was."

This time the boyish smile didn't reach his cool eyes. "I know you think you have to say things like that because you're married. But it pisses me off, Annie. We both know we belong together."

"You scare me with talk like that. You have to know it isn't true."

"I'm warning you, just shut up. You love me, and I love you. I came here to tell you my plans."

"Bodie, this isn't love." She didn't know what it was that tied him to her. Obsession, maybe. Fixation. A refusal to accept rejection. She felt certain it was not the baby. He didn't ask about the baby or seem interested. Desperation crept into her voice: "You don't love me."

"Sit down and listen."

Something hard and frightening roughened his tone, and Annie remembered the gun he carried. Gripping her coffee cup with both hands, she sat and made herself look at him across the table.

"I'm going to build us a big house. Bigger than this shack. Bigger even than your father's place." Watching her expression, he leaned forward. "We'll have land, and horses. And you'll have the biggest, newest brougham in the county. With your own driver. You'll have a maid, too. And a cook and someone to look after the baby so he won't be a bother."

Leaning back in his chair, he gave her a nod of satisfaction. "What do you say to that? It's a lot better than what Harden's giving you."

Annie bit her lip. "Please. I just want you to leave me alone."

"I've saved the best news for last. Me and the boys are going out for one last sweep. This time it's for you and me. And then it's over, just like you want. A few weeks of work, then I'll retire and be a gentleman farmer." One of the boyish smiles lit up his face. "You win, sweetheart. I'll be what you want me to be."

"You can be whatever you want," she said in a low voice. "What you do doesn't matter to me. It's too late."

"Not while you have my baby it isn't. You're mine." The smile vanished as if he'd wiped it off. "Are you having sex with him?"

"No!" Shock flamed on her face, followed by remorse. She should not have answered a personal question like that.

"Because if you ever do, so help me God, I won't stand for it. I've thought about this and it's all right if you stay here with him until I'm ready, but I don't want him touching you anymore."

Anymore? How did he know that Jess had touched her? A chill ran through her veins and Annie's eyes widened.

"Listen to me," she said, speaking quietly but firmly. "I don't want your big house. I don't want to be with you. I don't love you and I never said that I did. I can't state it clearer than that. I want you to leave and never come back. I don't ever want to see you again." When his eyes went stone hard, she looked away from him. "There's someone out there who will love you, but it's not me. Please, Bodie. Forget about me and find the woman who will make you happy."

"That's the trouble with you," he said in a flat voice. "You twist things around and you have to have everything your way. You get an idea in your head and you won't let it go because you can't admit you're wrong. We're going to have to change that." Standing, he stared down at her. "I came here with good news. And you can't deny I've been charming and pleasing. But you'd try the patience of a preacher and now I'm pissed off. So I'm going before you say more and make me madder." Bending, he kissed her cheek. "I'll be gone for a while, working for our future; then I'm coming to get you."

"I mean it. Don't come here again."

She waited until she heard him moving down the old privy path; then she scrubbed furiously at her cheek and burst into tears.

What was she going to do? The question kept her awake half the night even though she was bone tired.

The next day when Mr. Waters drove Ellen out to visit, Annie waited for a lull in the conversation, then bent over the oven and murmured, "Do you ever keep secrets from Papa?"

Ellen looked up from the bread dough she was kneading. "You already have secrets?" She glanced at Annie's stomach, then waved a floury hand. "Well, aside from . . ." When Annie pretended not to hear the question, Ellen pushed the heels of her hands into the bread, then flipped it over. "Every wife keeps a few secrets from her husband."

"Serious secrets?" Annie slid the first pan of bread into the oven. This evening, Ellen would take the loaves to the bake sale sponsored by her sewing circle. The sewing circle was composed of friends Ellen had known for forty years, friends who refused to punish her for her daughter's misdeeds. Annie thought of Janie and Ida Mae and wished she had them to talk to.

"Any secret between a husband and wife is a serious secret," Ellen said, testing the elasticity of the dough before she shaped the loaf and settled it into a buttered pan.

"What if the secret keeps getting worse? And what if the wife knows she ought to tell but fears that revealing the secret will cost her husband's trust, or might injure him, or might even end the marriage?"

Stating her fears aloud made Annie's throat tighten and she felt shaky inside. She'd promised Jess that he would never encounter the father of her baby, but he had. She'd agreed they wouldn't hold secrets, yet she was doing it and had even dragged Ione into keeping a secret from her son. And if Jess learned that Bodie had been in their house . . . could he forgive these things? Could he understand?

Ellen sat down and fanned her face with the hem of her apron. "Exactly what are we talking about, Anne Margaret Malloy? What have you done?"

"It's a hypothetical situation."

"I don't think so."

Annie poured tea over ice that had been delivered this morning. Ice was such a marvelous luxury and lasted such a short time. By tomorrow, a puddle would begin to form beneath the icebox.

She sat down in the seat Bodie had taken yesterday morning. "I've caused so much trouble for everyone."

Ellen's eyebrows lifted and she tidied a strand of hair that had worked loose from the bun on her neck. "We're getting through it." Given enough time, Ellen rose to meet whatever was demanded of her. "In fact, I don't know if I should mention this, but I heard the oddest rumor from Virginia. You remember Virginia; she helps Mary with the spring and fall cleanings. Well, Virginia came yesterday to start the fall cleaning."

"So soon?"

"Thursday starts the second week in September. I thought I'd get an early start this year. Never mind that. Virginia also works for Mrs. Meadows, the mayor's wife. She told Mary that Mrs. Meadows is considering calling on me!" Ellen blinked. "It can't be true, but I can't think why Virginia would say something like that if it weren't the truth."

The ramifications of a call by the mayor's wife were instantly obvious. Annie pressed her fingers to suddenly damp eyes. "That would be so wonderful." Within hours of Mrs. Meadows's visit, Ellen's sentence as a pariah would end.

"But why on earth would Mrs. Meadows make such a generous gesture? We've never liked each other. We didn't call at each other's homes even before you . . . even before."

"You always said that everything would change if I married."

"Over a period of years, not months. Small towns don't forget scandals in an eye blink. Yet Mrs. Meadows is apparently giving serious thought to ignoring our family's disgrace. I don't understand it."

Annie didn't, either. Finally, she shrugged. "All I can say is, don't look a gift horse in the mouth. If Mrs. Meadows comes to call, repay the call and resume your position in the community."

"Oh, I will," Ellen said grimly. "But certain ladies

will never be welcome in my home, and I'll never set foot in their homes. And I won't rejoin any clubs where Mrs. Morton is a member."

"Mother?" Annie contemplated the ice bobbing in her tea glass. "Will you and Papa accept this baby?"

"We've talked about it. And we'll try," Ellen said after a period of silence. "I'm trying to be involved in the preparations, and your father listens to my reports." She met Annie's eyes. "He's sorry that he hit you, you know. Some nights he can't sleep. He sits in the parlor and stares at the sofa where you were sitting that night."

"I cost him the mayoral candidacy," Annie said softly.

"Yes, you did." Ellen drew a breath. "But there will be other elections. If you can forgive him, Annie, tell him. I think he can forgive you, but he can't say the words until you do. He misses you. He's always saying the house is so quiet since you've gone."

After the loaves were baked and wrapped and tucked into a basket, Annie walked her mother out to the phaeton. She took Ellen's hands in her own.

"We haven't always agreed on everything, but you've been a good mother." To her surprise, tears leapt into Ellen's eyes. "Thank you for teaching me to think for myself even if that's led me into trouble. Thank you for letting me read whatever drew my curiosity. Thank you for trusting me when I didn't deserve it. And most of all, thank you for teaching me how to make a decent pot roast."

"Oh, Annie," Ellen said, smiling while she wiped her eyes. "I love you even though I don't always express it well."

"I know. And I love you, too, even though I don't always express it well."

"You and Ione Harden are so much alike . . ." Ellen's voice trailed. "I worry sometimes that you might . . ."

"Ione has become a good friend, and I love her," Annie said gently. "But you're my mother, and you'll always be first in my heart."

They held an embrace longer than they had in years, smiling when they broke apart. Ellen settled herself inside the phaeton, then leaned to the window. "Annie? When secrets start to unravel, and they often do, the situation always gets worse. Whatever your secret is . . . consider the consequences."

"I am," Annie whispered. "The consequences could be terrible. That's why I can't bring myself to tell him."

She watched dust spiraling after her mother's carriage, but her mind had already refocused on the problem that occupied nearly every waking thought.

That night, she closed the bedroom curtains before she climbed into bed.

Jess raised an eyebrow and smiled. "It isn't hot enough in here already?" He threw back the sheets and Annie caught a glimpse of the ridges of muscle rippling across his lower stomach.

She swallowed and fixed her gaze on the ceiling. "It's habit, I guess. I've always slept with the curtains closed." She hesitated. "If you prefer, you can open the curtains after you blow out your reading lamp."

Maybe she was doing Bodie an injustice, but she had a definite impression that he spied on them. Was he out there in the darkness, peering through the windows?

Bodie had said he'd be gone for a while, but she didn't trust anything he said.

"I think I will. If you don't mind."

Last night and tonight she'd held her breath, waiting for Jess to ask about the disappearance of the carved animal that Bodie had crushed. But the beautifully carved animals almost filled one of the bookshelves. There were enough carvings that apparently he hadn't noticed one was missing. Annie had decided if he noticed and asked she wouldn't lie. She would tell him everything. And each night that he didn't ask was a reprieve.

Reaching out, feeling shy, she took his hand, sensing his surprise. "Jess? Thank you for being a good friend to me."

"I want to be more. Have you noticed that I'm courting you?"

She smiled. "Yes."

"Is it working? Do you love me yet?"

"I admire you and like you very much."

"Progress!" he said, laughing. "I don't know what I'm going to do when the wildflowers are gone. Maybe I'll bring you pastries from Mrs. Adams's bakery. Or would you consider a snowball a courtship gift?"

"A snowball would be a fine gift." Releasing his hand, she covered a yawn, then surprised them both by saying, "I think you should kiss me good night now. It's been a long day and I'm going to be asleep in minutes."

Jess looked deep into her eyes. And this time Annie didn't hastily slide down and turn on her side. "I'll be damned," he said softly. Cupping her chin in his hand, he gazed down at her mouth, then gently brushed his lips across hers.

An electric jolt raced through Annie's body, leaving her tingling and wide-eyed. It seemed that she had waited for this moment all of her life, waited for a kiss that would awaken her to a longing for something she couldn't define. "You have gold and green flecks in your eyes," she whispered. And dark brows that curved like the wings of a hawk. And the faint beginnings of the beard he would shave in the morning. And a mouth that could be hard or tender but always was intriguing and exciting.

When she didn't pull away but continued to look at him with parted lips and a steady gaze, Jess's eyes darkened and he drew her into his arms. The heat of his chest seared through her thin nightgown and enveloped her breasts. Then his mouth came down on hers in a deep kiss that melted her breath away. His hand slipped to the back of her head, his tongue touched hers, and she felt his need as strongly as she felt her own. When they broke apart, gasping, Annie stared at him.

"My heavens," she whispered, placing a hand over her racing heart. No kiss had ever aroused such a response in her. Her body burned. All thoughts had gone up in smoke. Only gradually did she remember that she was into her seventh month of pregnancy and both Ione and Ellen had discreetly hinted that sex was unwise after the fifth month. Annie wondered if the New Modern Woman's Association would agree with what she assumed was tradition.

Jess fell back on his pillows and blinked at the ceiling.

"Annie love, right now I'm wishing my life away. I'm wishing the baby were already born and you were feeling well again and we had the whole night to enjoy each other." He reached for her hand and kissed her palm, then held her hand close to his chest.

She loved the hard, muscular look of him. Loved the way his eyes softened when he saw her. She loved it that he was even-tempered and slow to anger. She loved listening to him talk to Ione and watching his tenderness toward his mother. And to her. She loved his kindness and generosity of heart. Loved it that he could be tough and didn't shy from difficult decisions.

She, too, fell back on her pillows and stared at the ceiling. She was falling in love with this man. Feeling a desire for him that was stronger than she had imagined desire could be. And suddenly she glimpsed their future together, felt the happiness that could be theirs.

If Bodie Miller didn't destroy them. No, that wasn't correct. Annie was to blame. She'd made so many mistakes.

"Jess?"

"I love you, Annie. And someday you're going to love me." He kissed the back of her neck. "What did you want to say?"

"Nothing."

CHAPTER 17

You should have come in months ago," Doc Willis said, wiping his hands on a towel.

"I was embarrassed," Annie answered in a low voice. The shame of disgracing herself and her family hurt more when she faced a person she'd known all her life. She straightened her clothing, her face flaming as brightly as her hair.

"As well you should be," he said tartly.

Entire days passed when Annie could forget that her reputation lay in tatters, but a trip to town offered a sober reminder. Since her marriage, most tradespeople didn't make her wait but served her efficiently, if not warmly. People on the street generally looked through her and longtime acquaintances didn't nod or exchange a greeting, but few hissed or muttered hurtful comments. There would always be those who felt it their duty to remind her that her transgressions were not forgotten. Such people made their point with accusing stares or knowing smirks. Annie hated coming to town.

"But you weren't the first to buy the cart before the horse, and you won't be the last. Human nature doesn't change." Doc Willis's eyes softened.

"Is the baby doing well?"

He hesitated just a beat. "The baby's fine, but I don't like the cramps you've been having. It wouldn't surprise me if you deliver early. Aside from the cramping, how are you feeling?"

Annie sighed. "I'm thirsty all the time, which keeps me running to . . . you know." The color deepened in her cheeks. "And my hands and feet and face are swollen most days. I've been sleeping like a stone until this month. Now, the baby is often so active he or she wakes me up." She smiled. "It's nice in a way, but I wake up tired, which is distressing, because there are things I want to do while I have the energy to do them. It's getting harder to do ordinary chores like making the bed." She patted her stomach.

This morning Jess had burst into laughter as she was dressing to come to town. She couldn't blame him. She must have looked like a contortionist, rolling around on the side of the bed, trying to bend over her stomach to pull on her stockings. In the end, she'd conquered her embarrassment and allowed Jess to roll her stockings up her legs, help her into her shoes, and then lace them for her. It had been an . . . interesting . . . experience.

"Everything you've mentioned is perfectly normal," Doc Willis assured her. He squeezed her shoulder. "I want to see you the first of next month and every two weeks thereafter. If all goes according to schedule, I suspect you'll deliver the first or second week of November."

The first sweep had been successful. He and the Baylor boys had hit four banks near the Missouri border

like a whirlwind. In and out almost before anyone
knew what was happening. Then, in the midst of everything proceeding so well, the goddamned Baylor brothers had announced they were going home for a week to
sleep in their own fricking beds and see their families.
Bodie had used the week to ride around the county
looking at land for sale and brooding about losing control, considering the new outfit he would assemble
come spring.

Every night he'd ridden out to the Harden place,
crouching in the brush, smoking and staring at her
windows. She'd started closing the curtains as if she
knew he was out there in the night. He liked that. It
meant she was thinking about him. It meant she was
being considerate, knowing it enraged him to see her
with Harden. He liked knowing she was where he'd
told her to stay and that she was waiting for him.

"You want another round?"

He looked up at the bartender, then checked his
pocket watch. "No." The Baylor boys would be waiting at the Wheathill Crossing. This time he'd lead them
as far south as he could persuade them to go, hit it hard
for a week, and then they would want to go home
again. At this rate Annie's baby would be born before
he had enough money to give her everything he'd
promised.

Swearing, he tossed a coin on the bar, then went to
the stables for his horse. If Slovick had had any guts,
he would have killed Jess Harden and then Bodie would
not now be frustrated that she was still living with the
sheriff and his crazy mother. He wouldn't be worrying
that Harden was kissing and fondling her, wouldn't
have those images in his mind to infuriate him. If Harden

were dead, Bodie could keep Annie out at the cabin and start teaching her how she ought to behave.

As he rode down Main past the sheriff's office, he stared hard at the sun glancing off the window. Then, as if fate had heard his thoughts, Jess Harden stepped onto the boardwalk and paused to settle his hat and look up the street. Destiny painted a big bull's-eye on Harden's chest and dared Bodie to test his luck. A hard smile tightened his lips as he reached for the gun on his hip.

Annie came out of the doctor's office feeling euphoric. There had been that one moment, but facing Doc Willis hadn't been as uncomfortable and humiliating as she had dreaded it would be. She had survived the experience. The baby's heartbeat was strong, and she was healthy and doing fine.

A smile curved her lips and she stopped to look at the sky. It occurred to her that right now, this minute, she was as happy as she had ever been. It was a beautiful September day, not as hot as last week. Miracle of miracles, she was going to be a mother. Ione was waiting at home with iced tea and honey bread. And there was Jess. Jess loved her. It was another miracle that warmed her inside. And she was falling in love with him, feeling pretty, and on her way to meet this amazing man for lunch.

Touching gloved fingertips to her eyes, she blotted tears of gratitude, then turned eager face and steps toward his office. Her heart leapt in her chest as she saw Jess step onto the boardwalk, then turn his head in her direction. He was so handsome and confident, and looking for her. A smile lit her eyes.

What happened next was swift and horrifying. Annie heard the explosion of a gunshot and saw Jess spin violently. He struck the wall of the office and slid to the boardwalk. Annie's breath rushed out of her frozen body and she heard herself scream. A man in the street spurred his horse and rode hard, heading out of town, but not before he'd looked back at her. And she had recognized him.

Lifting her skirts, she hurried forward, unable to run and cursing her clumsiness. By the time she reached Jess, breathless and terrified, a crowd had gathered. "Please, please," she said, "let me pass."

"It's Mrs. Harden," John Anderson announced. "Step back and let her through."

Thank God; thank God. Jess was sitting, propped against the office wall, swearing at a circle of blood widening on his pants.

John Anderson watched Annie drop to her knees beside Jess, then ordered Mr. Handly to run and fetch Doc Willis.

"Never mind the doctor," Jess growled. "Go after the shooter."

Anderson swore, then shouted to the other deputies, and they ran toward the stables.

Annie flung herself on Jess's neck, sobbing uncontrollably. "It's my fault." He was alive, thank God, but the bright blood frightened her to the bone. If Bodie's aim had been better, Jess would be dead.

"I'll live, darlin'." He patted her back and shoulders. "It's just a flesh wound."

"It's all my fault!" Jess was bleeding and in pain, and she was to blame. She'd never forgive herself.

"I'll decide if it's a flesh wound," Doc Willis stated,

kneeling beside Jess. "Young lady, I'll thank you to move back and give me some room."

Gently Jess pried her arms from his neck, and Annie eased back reluctantly as Doc Willis cut open Jess's pants above his thigh. She wiped her eyes to see, but tears of guilt and fear kept spilling down her cheeks.

She had wanted to protect both Jess and Bodie from a deadly confrontation, but what she had accomplished was keeping Jess ignorant of the danger that Bodie represented. He didn't know who Bodie was or that Bodie hated him. But Bodie had known who Jess was. Annie had made her husband a sitting duck. "Oh God," she moaned.

Doc Willis glanced up at her. "The sheriff was right. It's just a flesh wound. The bullet passed through. Luckily, it didn't hit bone." He turned his head toward one of the men in the crowd. "Help me get him inside."

After Doc Willis finished cleaning and treating the entry and exit wounds, he wrapped Jess's thigh in a thick bandage. "You'll be sore as hell, son, but there won't be any permanent damage. Stay off that leg. Use a crutch for three or four days. Then put some weight on, but take it easy." He winked. "This would be a good time to take off a few days, stay home, and let Mrs. Harden fuss over you."

"I might do that," Jess said, setting aside a glass of whiskey that someone had fetched from the saloon. There was a puzzled tilt to his brows as he looked at the tears still swimming in Annie's eyes. "On your way out," he said to the doctor, "will you ask someone to bring around our wagon? It's at the stables."

"I'll drive," Annie insisted. When Jess didn't protest,

she climbed up on the seat and took the reins in her hands.

"Don't you worry none," said one of the men who helped Jess up. "The deputies will catch the bastard who shot you. Mark my words."

Fresh tears started in Annie's eyes and she blinked hard as she drove out of town. "I'm sorry the road's rough. Are you in awful pain?"

"I've felt better," Jess said between his teeth. "But I've felt worse, too. I'll be glad to get home, get out of these bloody clothes, and sit in bed." He smiled. "I'm looking forward to that fussing over that Doc Willis prescribed."

He was quiet a moment. "Mostly, I'm pissed as hell. I should have been more alert. Should have been paying attention." He made a disgusted sound. "I didn't even see who shot me."

It wouldn't have mattered if he'd seen Bodie before the shot. He wouldn't have known that Bodie posed a danger to him.

"I saw who shot you," Annie said in a low voice.

He straightened abruptly and twisted on the seat to stare. "Who was it?"

"It's not a simple answer," she said. Through the trees lining the road she glimpsed Ione's rooftop. "Let's get you settled and comfortable; then . . . Then I'll tell you the whole story."

She felt his tension as he thought about what she'd said. That his getting shot was her fault and that the identity of the shooter was not a simple answer. Jess swore softly and closed his eyes. "Annie, love, I hope what I'm thinking is dead wrong."

They didn't speak again until Annie turned the wagon into the yard and Ione came running down the porch steps. "I saw the blood on your pants from the porch. What happened?" She raised her arms to help Jess to the ground. "Lean on Annie and me."

Annie set the brake, then hurried around the horse to assist Jess into the house and down the hall to the bedroom. After Jess had told the story in a few terse statements, Ione nodded and she and Annie stepped into the hallway.

"It could have been worse," Ione said with a sigh of relief. "I'll unhitch the horse and turn him out while you get our boy settled. I think there's a crutch in the barn." Pausing, she gave Annie a long, searching look and lifted an eyebrow. "Do you think the shooter was . . . ?"

"Yes," Annie whispered; fresh tears sprang into her eyes. Both women glanced toward the bedroom where they heard Jess cussing. "I'm going to tell him everything. I should never have kept any of this a secret. Oh, Ione, I've been such a fool. I never believed that Bodie would do something like this."

"I'm sorry, Annie." Ione gave her a long tight hug. "I hope—no, I know everything will work out right. It's just that . . ." She drew back and frowned into Annie's teary eyes. "Well. Let's see what happens. Whatever he says, my boy loves you; I know that. I'll leave the crutch on the front porch."

After Ione left, Annie drew a breath and squared her shoulders before she entered the bedroom. "I'll help you take off your boots." But he'd already managed the job by himself. He'd also found a nightshirt that

Annie hadn't known he owned. Once he was in bed, his wounded leg stretched out before him, she added pillows to support his back. "Would you like some coffee? Iced tea? Whiskey?"

"Who shot me, Annie?"

"You didn't eat. Shall I bring you some of last night's stew?"

"Was he aiming for my leg, or did he miss my chest?"

Heart pounding, Annie walked to the windows. "It's hot in here. I'll open the curtains wider to let in more air."

"Will you please sit the hell down and let's get this over with."

The moment she had feared and dreaded had come. Starting to shake, she sat on her side of the bed and tilted her head toward the ceiling. Tears leaked from the corners of her eyes and trickled into the hair at her temples. She'd been crying off and on for hours. She had to look like hell. It occurred to her that the important moments in a woman's life seldom happened when she was looking good.

"Annie, if you don't—"

"Bodie Miller shot you."

She heard a long exhale; then he drew a deep breath. "Start from the beginning."

At the time, her grand affair had seemed daring and unique in the annals of the world. But telling Jess made it sound tawdry and cheap.

"So," she said when she'd finished the part about the affair, speaking in halting sentences with many teary pauses. "From the beginning there were hints that Bodie wasn't the salesman he'd originally claimed to

be." She gazed down at her hands, picked at her fingernails. "Gradually he dropped all pretense. He and two
other men robbed banks. Sometimes trains."

Jess stared incredulously. "And knowing that, you
continued to see him?"

Miserable, Annie nodded. In retrospect, her behavior
seemed incomprehensible.

"There were a handful of particular wanted
posters . . . I wondered if it could be him. A big blond,
and two shorter, dark-haired men." Jess shook his
head. His hands curled into fists against his thighs.
"Did he refuse to marry you?"

"I refused him because he wouldn't agree to take up
another profession."

"Good God, Annie. Robbing banks isn't a profession. It's a crime." He twisted on the bed to look at her
fully. "That day I found you out at the old Miller
cabin. You'd gone there to see him, hadn't you?"

"No, I knew he wasn't at the cabin. I went there to
return some money he'd given me. I didn't want dishonest money." She couldn't face the accusation in
Jess's stare.

"I didn't see a mailbox," Jess snapped. "Do you have
a secret hiding place?"

The derision in his tone brought a hot rush of shame
to her cheeks. "I didn't know if he'd get the money, because I thought he'd left Marshall for good and all." Finally, she darted a look at him, cringing from the ice in
his eyes. "I didn't lie to you, Jess. I really believed Bodie
was gone, and that you'd never run into him."

"That strikes me as astonishingly naive. You didn't
walk away from his bed when you learned he was a
criminal. Why would he believe you'd walk away for

that reason when you're pregnant and about to be ruined?"

She lifted her chin, but she didn't look at him. "Nevertheless, that's how it was. And I couldn't tell anyone who fathered my baby because then I would have had to explain why I refused to marry him. Then Bodie would have gone to prison. Please, Jess." Turning to him, she stretched out a hand, but he pulled away. "I couldn't be the person who sent the father of my baby to prison."

"You love him that much?"

"No! But it seemed that I owed him that much."

He shook his head in disbelief. "A man takes advantage of you, ruins you, then offers to marry you but only on his terms. He won't give up crime for the sake of a wife and child, so he leaves you exposed to disgrace and humiliation, your reputation destroyed. But you think *you* owe *him* consideration?"

It sounded ridiculous. "I thought that, yes."

Jess's eyes narrowed into stony slits. "I have a suspicion there's more, isn't there? Finish it, Annie."

Crying steadily, she told him about Bodie's obsession with her, about his showing up in Ione's yard that first time.

"Oh, Christ." Jess pulled a hand down his eyes and face. "Ione knows this?" The betrayal in his tone broke Annie's heart. "And she didn't tell me?"

"I begged her not to. If you knew, there'd be trouble and someone would get hurt."

Instantly he jerked upright. "You have that little faith in me? That you think some two-bit outlaw could get the better of me?"

"No, but . . ." Confusion made her stammer. "At the

time, I just . . . At the very least, I knew you'd send Bodie to prison, and I still didn't want to be responsible for . . . but Ione didn't want to agree to a secret. Finally, she did. But she said if Bodie came again, she would tell you."

"And he did come again, didn't he?"

"Ione doesn't know." Crying, hardly able to speak, she told him everything.

Jess sat up, swung his legs off the edge of the bed, and dropped his head into his hands. "That bastard has been here. In my house. Drinking coffee with my wife. Walking through every room. And you didn't tell me."

"I'm so sorry. Oh, God, Jess, I'm so sorry." Tears choked her, burned in her throat and eyes. She would have given half her life to change the decisions she'd made.

"I trusted you. I believed that phase of your life was over. I honestly believed that you and I had a chance. That we had a future together. And all the time, you were seeing him. Right here in our house."

She crawled across the bed and put her hand on his back. "I thought I could handle the problem. Each time, I thought he'd go away and never come back. Like I told him."

"How stupid do you think I am?" He shrugged off her hand. "You've just admitted that you suspect he's out there at night, watching the windows. He isn't going away and you know it; he's just biding his time. Tell me something." Turning as much as his wound allowed, he stared hard at her. "Would you have told me this at some point? If I hadn't got shot? Or would I have come home one day and just found a note on the table telling me you'd run off with him?"

"Oh, Jesse. I'd never—"

"You let me walk around out there while you knew a killer was in town, a killer who believes I stole his wife and baby. And you gave him the advantage. He knew who I was, but I didn't know anything about him. The surprise is not that he shot me, but that it took him so long to get around to it. That says he never once worried that you'd tell me about him or his background. And why would he be that confident, Annie? I'll tell you why. Because he believes you still love him."

"It's not like that!"

"The hell it isn't." His sound of disgust turned into a groan of pain as he hobbled toward the armoire.

"What are you doing?"

"I'm getting dressed. What does it look like?" Face tight and drawn, he sat on the vanity bench to pull on his pants, then flung off the nightshirt and reached for a shirt. "What did you think would happen when I found out?" he asked, pausing to look at her. "Did you think I'd sit still for you seeing him here? In our house? Did you imagine I'd say, 'Fine, you take care of the "problem," ' as you call it. 'Take your time. Of course I believe you're trying to get rid of him.' "

"Jess, I didn't know he'd try to kill you." But she should have guessed. She should have.

"Stop, Annie." He pulled on his boots. She didn't know how he bore the pain without making a sound. "I tried to do right by you," he said, standing. "I wanted to love you and make you happy. And while I was thinking of ways to do that, you were sitting in our kitchen drinking coffee and chatting about old times with your lover."

"Oh, God." She covered her face and wept.

"I can't forgive that. I can't forgive that you chose him over me every day that you wouldn't warn me a killer was looking for me."

"Oh, Jess. I didn't know he'd shoot you."

"I can't forgive you for involving Ione and asking her to keep a secret from me. And I can't forgive you for using me. You must have married me still loving him and knowing you'd see him again. Well, darlin', you can have him." He stared at her. "Unless I catch him and see him hanged first." Walking past her, he limped out the bedroom door.

"Jesse! Please!" Annie slid off the bed and hurried after him. "If you believe all that, then I didn't explain it well. Please. I beg you, please sit down and give me another chance to explain."

He threw open the front door and strode into Ione, who was coming up the steps with a crutch in her hand.

"It took longer to find the crutch than I thought," she said, anxious eyes swinging from Jess's stony expression to Annie's tear-wrecked face. "I haven't yet unhitched the wagon. You're dressed!"

"I'll be staying in town for a while," Jess said, taking the crutch. "I'll send someone back with the wagon to get my horse."

Ione put her hand on his arm. "Jesse, no marriage was ever resolved while the husband and wife slept in separate beds."

"This was never a marriage," Jess said, pulling himself up on the wagon seat. "Seems we had the wrong groom." He made a clicking sound and flapped the reins, then drove away without a backward glance.

Annie fell to her knees on the porch and sobbed.

* * *

"Annie, honey, you've got to stop crying. This isn't good for the baby." Ione cast a worried glance toward Ellen.

"And you've got to get some rest," Ellen added. "And eat something. Would you eat some pudding if I made it?"

"I'm not hungry."

Opening the door off the kitchen, Annie stepped out on the stoop and inhaled deeply. The evening air was cool and ripe with the dusty scent of early autumn. In the fading light she noticed that the leaves on the chokecherries were beginning to turn an orangy red.

She missed him so much.

Jess Harden had become the central focus of her life in the time they had been together. The rhythm of her life circled around waking up when Jess brought her coffee in the morning and then preparing his eggs exactly as he liked them: cooked in butter with the centers just beginning to set. Waiting for him to ride up to the front door and kiss her good-bye before he set off for town.

During the day she thought about what he would like for supper and how she would surprise him with a special dessert. On Mondays she washed their clothing, ironed on Tuesdays. And he always praised her when he saw fresh shirts and trousers in the armoire. He'd noticed that Friday was housecleaning day.

But the evenings were Annie's favorite part of the day. Sometimes Jess sat on the porch and carved while she cleaned up the supper dishes. Sometimes he read to her while she worked. Occasionally they walked along the road, talking about everything and nothing. He brought her gossip from town and stories about his work, carried messages between her and Janie and Ida Mae. And he listened to the small details of Annie's day as if housework and hemming diapers were subjects as interesting as the stories he brought her.

And finally, they climbed into bed together as if they'd been sharing a bed all of their lives. She knew and loved the glow of lamplight on his naked chest. Waited for the moments when he read something aloud to her from his current book. Waited especially for him to lean over and kiss her good night, then whisper about the future when they would truly be together.

Tears slipped down her cheeks. Where was he tonight? Did he think about her? Why couldn't he see that she loved him and needed him? Or did that matter anymore?

A shawl dropped around her shoulders before Ione settled her back against the porch wall. "I gave him your letter yesterday."

"How is his leg?"

"Healed now."

"I feel so helpless. I'm just waiting, dying inside," Annie said, her gaze following the sinking sun. The days were shorter now. "Do you think he'll read my letter?"

"I don't know," Ione said carefully. "He has it in his head that you love Miller. He's stubborn, my Jesse John. Gets an idea in that head of his and doesn't let go easily."

"I love him, Ione."

"I know. I probably knew before you did. It's been in your eyes and face for a while."

"I wish I'd told him." She scrubbed at her forehead and eyes. "I always make the wrong decisions."

"No, you don't. At least not always," Ellen said tartly. She handed Annie and Ione the last of the coffee from supper. "I'm not saying you haven't made some bad decisions; you have. And when you make a bad decision, it's a doozy."

Annie smiled for the first time in two weeks.

"But you make good decisions, too." Stepping off the porch, Ellen inspected a small garden she'd cleaned up for winter during her stay. "I wonder if I planted the tulips deep enough?" She waved her coffee cup. "It was a good decision to marry Jesse Harden. A good decision to start seeing Doc Willis. Everything you've planned for the baby is good. You have good instincts, Annie; it's just that you don't always follow them."

"The bad decisions are so bad." Annie pulled the shawl close around her throat. "I got pregnant out of wedlock. Ruined myself and disgraced my family. It's my fault that my husband got shot. Now I imagine the gossips are buzzing with the news that my husband has left me after only a few months." When she thought about the inevitable gossip it amazed her that she, Annie Malloy Harden, had become a source of ongoing scandal after a proper and even dull life. How had such a disaster happened? She looked at her mother and mother-in-law. "I miss him so much. Tell me what to do."

"I'm sure Mrs. Harden will agree—"

"Ellen, please call me Ione."

Ellen nodded. "There's nothing you can do except wait."

"I want him to come home." The damned tears began again. She'd cried enough to create a new ocean.

"I know," Ione said, slipping an arm around Annie's waist. Together they entered the kitchen. "I want him to come home, too. But, honey, there's nothing you can do until he works it out in his mind. All we can do is hope this turns out right."

Both women stopped abruptly, then sighed with relief as they recognized Harry Malloy walking toward them from the living room. When he saw Annie, he opened his arms.

She hesitated only a moment, then went to him, crying harder. "Oh, Papa. I've made such a mess of things."

"Shhh, Buttercup." He patted her back, smoothed her hair. "We've all made mistakes that we deeply regret." Pain made his voice scratchy. "I'm sorry, Annie."

They'd seen each other many times since that awful moment in the parlor. But tonight he'd found the words. It was a beginning. Annie knew neither of them would ever forget that he'd struck her and their relationship would never be exactly the same. But they couldn't forge whatever their new relationship would be until these words had been spoken.

"I forgive you," she said, speaking into his shirtfront. "Can you forgive me?"

"It's taken too long," he said, holding her tightly. "But of course. Yes." After a moment, he eased her back so he could look into her tear-swollen face. "Right now, I'd like to find your sheriff and beat some sense into him. Could you forgive that?"

A tremulous smile curved Annie's mouth. She couldn't imagine her balding, portly father challenging her lean, hard husband.

"I'll be back in the morning," Ellen said, kissing Annie on the cheek. To Ione she added, "I'll stay over tomorrow night."

They hadn't left Annie alone since Jess drove the wagon out of the yard. Either Ione or Ellen slept on the sofa every night and one or both stayed with her during the long, empty days.

"You don't have to tend me," she said to them. "I'll be fine alone." That wasn't true. But having one of them with her every minute didn't help, either.

On the positive side, during the last two weeks Ellen and Ione had developed the beginnings of a friendship. They were very different types of women, but they'd found commonality in Annie. She saw evidence of their new understanding in the glance they exchanged now.

"It's no bother," Ellen said briskly, pulling on her gloves.

"Your cramps worry us," Ione added, handing Ellen her hat and jacket.

The cramps concerned Annie, too. And occasionally she noticed a sharp pain in the groin when she reached toward the upper shelves. And a peculiar ache in the pelvic area. The women assured her this was normal, her body stretching and adjusting, but sometimes she wondered.

After her parents embraced her, holding her long and tightly, Ione ushered her toward the bedroom. "You've been on your feet too long. Get into bed and I'll read to you."

"I'd rather hear about the boardinghouse where Jess is staying."

What if he never came home again? That would be

the worst thing that ever happened to her. If only there was something she could do.

Frustration tightened Bodie's jaw. The women didn't leave her alone, not for one fricking minute. How was he supposed to explain why he hadn't yet come for her? Angry, he flipped a cigar into the little creek that ran through the Harden property. Tomorrow he'd leave for another bank sweep, and he fervently hoped this foray would be more successful than the last.

Everything that could go wrong had gone wrong. They'd struck one bank that, unbelievably, was in the midst of moving to another building, and there wasn't one red cent in the place. Another time, the manager was too nervous to remember the combination of the vault and a deputy had arrived before the idiot got it open. Worse, the deputy had gotten a good look at Bodie's face, because Hoss had fired a shot into the ceiling and brought down chunks of plaster and Bodie had pulled off his mask to breathe. His description and likeness would begin appearing on wanted posters if they hadn't already.

He swore, staring hard at Annie's bedroom window. She wasn't going to be lucky for him until he married her; he'd figured that out. Finally, he had enough money to buy land, but now he'd have to move out of state or risk being identified. That pissed him off because Annie wasn't going to like it and she'd give him trouble. Another thing that infuriated him was seeing Jess Harden on Main Street. He hadn't killed the bastard, had only wounded him, and from all appearances the wound had healed.

But Annie had sent Harden packing. Good girl. She

was finally seeing the light, clearing the way for him. Things would go more smoothly now.

He intended to work one more week; then no matter how successful this run was or wasn't, he was coming to get her. Wherever he decided to live, there'd be banks and he could make up any shortfall if he needed to. Annie would just have to be reasonable.

Spirits improved, he amused himself by sighting down his gun barrel, aiming at the old crazy woman's forehead. Shooting her through the window would have been a pleasure, but he sensed that Annie would be shocked and upset and that meant a headache for him. Marriage had sure made her hard to deal with. Maybe he should just live with her for a while until he found out if it was marriage to Harden that made her so pissy or if the cause was marriage in general.

When it became clear that Harden's mother would sleep on the sofa instead of going home to her own house, Bodie rode back to the cabin.

The Baylor brothers looked up when he came inside, then dealt him a hand of poker. "You're home early; what happened? Did the sheriff's wife kick you out of bed?"

They laughed, and he regretted telling them about Annie. "Shut up." Jimmy had dealt him three kings. At least he'd win the pot.

"Only you would court a sheriff's wife," Hoss marveled. "I'm out." He threw down his cards and stretched. "I'm glad this is going to be our last run for the season."

Jimmy looked up with a hard expression. "You've got our money somewhere safe, don't you?"

"I told you. It's buried on the property. After this

haul, we'll come back here and split the proceeds,"
Bodie said. Or maybe he'd just take all the money for
himself; then he could build his big house sooner. After
all their bungling, the Baylor brothers owed him.

CHAPTER 18

※※※ ※※※ ※※※

"THEY'VE been here." Bending, Jess studied fresh tracks leading to and from the corral. Grinding his teeth, he looked up at the old Miller cabin. Where Annie had opened her arms to Bodie Miller. Where she had given herself to another man whose name and face he now knew. Tormenting images wheeled through his mind. "We missed them."

"Too bad we don't have enough men to watch the place day and night." John Anderson tried the door. "Locked."

Lawmen in three counties were looking for Bodie Miller and the outlaws who rode with him. A teller in one of the banks south of Marshall had recognized Miller when he briefly removed his mask. The teller had grown up a quarter of a mile from Miller's home outside Kansas City. The identification was no mistake.

Jess had the impression that Bodie Miller's luck had gone from bad to worse. The banks he'd struck in the last month hadn't yielded much booty. He'd been recognized. And new information arrived every day, slowly tightening a noose around his neck.

The bank employee in Missouri who had heard one

of the robbers address another by name now remembered the name wasn't Jodie but Bodie. A man in Atchison had recognized a horse used in the train robbery where the robbers killed a man, because he'd sold that horse to Jimmy Baylor. Jess had asked county officials to check if Baylor's absences matched Miller's, which he'd determined aligned with outbreaks of bank robberies. And of course, Annie had recognized Miller when he shot Jess.

Walking toward his palomino, Jess stopped and turned slowly, speculating over hiding places where lovers might leave messages. He'd told himself he absolutely would not do this. But if it were him, he would have chosen a spot near the creek where tall grass and long willows could conceal any container. If John Anderson hadn't been with him, he would have taken a look. Like picking at a wound.

Once back in his office, he checked messages, then drummed his fingers on his desktop. "They'll return. It's their pattern."

"I want us to catch them before someone else does." Anderson tossed his hat toward the coat tree. "Ma Golden's for supper?"

Miller's connection to Annie would remain a secret. Jess didn't want the town to know that she was in love with a criminal any more than she wanted anyone to know. But goddamn it hurt that she'd chosen someone like Bodie Miller over him. That she'd continued seeing him.

"Jess?"

"Sorry, I wasn't paying attention."

"I've been thinking about your, ah, situation. If I were you . . ."

"You aren't." He spoke pleasantly, but his gaze warned Anderson from pushing this line of conversation any further.

Anderson shrugged, stood, and stretched. "I couldn't offer much by way of advice anyway. What I know about women wouldn't fill a thimble."

"It isn't Annie," Jess said hotly. "Annie's wonderful. She's a marvelous cook, a good housekeeper; she always looks nice and smells nice. She's smart and funny. She reads and can talk about anything."

"Well, if this separation is your fault, then you're an idiot." Anderson grinned. "Seriously, Jess. Go home. You're driving us all crazy."

"Let's get something to eat," he said, reaching for his hat. If one more person tried to give him advice, he was going to explode. Everyone from the barber to the stable boy knew Jess was staying at Mrs. Howard's boardinghouse, and they all wanted to know why and they all wanted to tell him how to fix the unfixable.

If he'd thought he could eat his supper without someone prying into his business, he'd been mistaken. His chicken and mashed potatoes had just arrived when the mayor spotted him through the window and hurried inside.

"Mind if I sit a minute?"

"Hello, Hiram. We haven't caught Miller yet, but we expect to."

"That's not what I want to talk about. First, you get the girl pregnant, then drag your feet about marrying her until her reputation is ruined and she's already showing. Now, you walk out on her and abandon her in the country, pregnant and alone. Jess, you're the best sheriff this county ever had, but my Lord, man, your personal life is a damned disgrace!"

"First, Annie didn't want to marry me; it wasn't the other way around."

"Well, maybe she suspected what kind of husband you were going to make. Leaving her alone and pregnant."

"Second, she's only a mile outside town and she isn't alone. My mother is with her, and her own mother is going out there every day."

"*You* should be going home every day." Hiram ran his hands through thinning hair. "Do you realize people have been talking about you for most of this year? Marshall hasn't had this much scandal since the librarian ran off to Kansas City with the vice president of the fricking bank. I need you to go home or catch Bodie Miller. Preferably both."

"I think I see the problem."

"Excellent!"

"But I still want Mrs. Meadows to call on Ellen Malloy, and regardless of what happens between Annie and me, I want Annie to have that dinner invitation after the baby is born."

Hiram Meadows swore loudly enough that other diners frowned in their direction. "The way the two of you are behaving is making that impossible. Mrs. Meadows will never put herself in a position where it appears that she condones this latest scandal. Do you hear what I'm saying? Never."

"I have faith in your powers of persuasion."

"Have you ever been a sheriff, boy?" Hiram asked John Anderson, who was keeping his head down, eating, and pretending the conversation didn't fascinate him. "This county could have an opening soon."

"No, sir. And frankly, I've seen enough of the job that I don't want to be a sheriff."

"Too bad." Hiram cast an unhappy look at Jess. "I had the missus all primed and ready to call on Ellen Malloy; then you showed up at Mrs. Howard's boardinghouse."

"Hiram, my personal affairs are none of your business."

"The whole damned town thinks your love life is their business. Look, pregnant women are crazy. They can't help it. That big belly drains the sanity right out of their heads, and women think strange to start with. The point is, whatever she's doing that's got you riled, whatever it is that you're fighting about, you can work it out. She's not going to be pregnant forever, although I know it seems that way right now. So you go home, son, and you tell her that she's beautiful, she's the best cook in the world, you worship her very shadow, and whatever happened is all your fault and you are sorry as hell about it."

Half the patrons in Ma Golden's place erupted in applause. "Great speech, Mayor!" "Hear, hear!" "Go home, Sheriff!"

A flush of heat stained Jess's throat. Everyone in town was discussing his private business and had an opinion about what he should do.

He put down his fork, his appetite gone. "Just for the sake of argument, what if it isn't my fault? What if the fault is Annie's?"

Hiram stared. "Well, *of course* it's her fault. She's

pregnant. Aren't you listening? Pregnant women are not normal. They don't think logically. They go all gooey and sentimental. They cry a lot. One day they hate how they look, and the next day they're charmed by the mirror. One day they hate how *you* look, and the next day you're the sainted father of their baby. Son, she's pregnant. Which means you can't win. If you agree with what she says, she's going to get mad. If you don't agree with what she says, she'd going to get mad. She can swear that her curling iron talked to her, and by God, she believes it. And you'd better believe it, too. But God help you if you tell *her* that she's only hearing talking curling irons because she's pregnant. Are you hearing what I'm saying?"

Jess walked out of Ma Golden's and headed toward the stables. Hiram, John Anderson, and all the others meant well; he knew that. But they didn't know the seriousness of the situation with Annie. She wasn't thinking crazy because she was pregnant. She was thinking about the man who'd made her pregnant.

He saddled the palomino at the stables and rode out to Ione's place, but he didn't approach her house or his own house. He put his horse in the corral, then moved quietly past the hives, circling around, pausing frequently to listen in the darkness. Annie thought it was possible that Miller spied on her at night. Jess would have loved to find the bastard peeping in his windows, but he'd seen no sign of anyone. To be fair, Miller couldn't be in two places at once. He couldn't be robbing banks in the adjoining counties and be lurking outside Jess's house. Still, Jess wasn't taking any chances that Miller had returned.

Jess looked toward the lighted window and his chest

constricted. He should have been there, in bed beside her, teasing her, loving her. In a perfect world, he would have been the man she loved, the father of her baby. And goddamn, it hurt that he wasn't.

Instead, he was doing what he'd always done, standing outside, looking in, the loneliness worse because now he'd known the joy of having someone of his own.

When her light finally went out, he slipped back to the corral and quietly led the palomino toward the gate.

"She loves you." Ione's voice floated out of the darkness.

"Not you, too," he said, dropping the reins and moving to stand beside her. Frowning, he took a cigar out of his waistcoat pocket and lit it. "People I don't even know are giving me advice."

"I'm not going to advise you. You have to make up your own mind. Maybe you can live with Annie's mistakes and maybe you can't."

"If Miller had been a better shot, I wouldn't be living with anything."

"And you think that Annie knew in advance that Miller would try to kill you?"

Silently he focused on that one point. "She might have. Certainly she should have told me it was a possibility."

"She thinks so, too. She's flogging herself mercilessly because she thinks she should have read Miller's mind. She's tearing herself apart because it never occurred to her that he might try to kill you."

Even his own mother was taking Annie's side. "She knew he was a thief and a killer."

"Did she?" Ione crossed her arms over her chest and

looked up at the stars. "Had he killed anyone during the time Annie was seeing him? That would be easy to check. Maybe she never thought of him as a killer."

He hated the way Ione could make her arguments seem so reasonable. "She didn't stop seeing him. He's still coming around. If there isn't something between them, then why does he keep coming here and why does she allow it?"

"You can interpret the situation as you have. You can believe she loves Miller and is encouraging him. You can believe they're plotting against you, can believe she used you to restore her reputation while she's waiting for Miller. I can even grasp how you might think those things."

"But?"

"Or you can believe your wife."

"Come on, Ione. Much of what she's claiming doesn't make sense."

"Since when do human beings always make sense? Did it make sense for me to take up with your father? Did it make sense that Sheriff Tom Stone didn't arrest you that night? Does it make sense that you'd marry a woman pregnant by another man? Sometimes we do things that don't make sense."

"That's a weak argument," he said finally, grinding out the cigar.

"One last thing, Son." She put her hand on his arm. "After a lifetime of being alone, you've been happy with Annie. That can be unsettling. A person can be so afraid of losing something he's always wanted that he throws it away just to get the inevitable pain over with. You think about that, Jesse John. If you need to walk away from this marriage, then do it. But be very sure you're throwing your marriage away for the right reasons."

Before he rode back to town, he embraced her. "Don't ever keep another secret from me, all right?"

"I'll try, but I'm not making any promises."

"You're a hard woman, Ione Harden."

She laughed. "And I raised a hard man. Maybe we both need a little softening."

Too much had happened for sleep to come easily. Jess sat up in the darkness of his small rented room, broke the house rules about smoking, and thought about what his mother had said.

Why was it so easy to believe his interpretation and so hard to believe Annie's explanation? Was he throwing away something too good to believe because he thought it couldn't last? Was Ione right?

Ione had also said that Annie loved him, had said it like he should know it. But Annie hadn't said the words he had waited a lifetime to hear. He wasn't sure he'd believe her if she did say she loved him. Turning his head, he glanced at the shadowy envelope on his nightstand. He hadn't read her letter and didn't want to. Why was that? Because he feared being convinced that she was telling the truth?

Smoking, brooding, he tried to figure it out, thinking about everything she had tried to explain away until his head ached. But just as he was almost ready to concede that it might—might—be the way she claimed, his mind insisted on reminding him that she had not warned him that Bodie Miller would try to kill him.

That fact couldn't be explained away, and it colored everything else. If she had cared for him even a little, she would have warned him that a killer was out there with reason to want him dead. Even Annie accepted the truth of that. From the minute the shooting happened, she'd admitted it was her fault.

And she was to blame because she loved another man. There was no other reasonable conclusion.

Stretching out his hand, he touched the side of the bed where she should have been.

Drawing a breath, Annie positioned herself in front of the full-length mirror and squared her shoulders. Damn. She looked worse than she had looked when she'd had pneumonia five years ago.

An orangy-red frizz ball surrounded her head. At the moment, she could believe that her hair was beyond hope and would never look decent again in her lifetime. Her eyes were red and puffy, her eyelashes matted together. Her face was swollen and splotchy. The wrinkled nightgown she wore pooched out as if she had strapped a bushel basket to her stomach. Lifting her hem, she stared at swollen ankles.

All right. She had her work cut out for her.

"Annie?" Ellen and Ione looked up from the kitchen table as she strode, waddled rather, into the kitchen. "You look . . ."

"I know how I look," she said grimly. "I need to change that, and I need your help. We'll start with a bath and a hair wash." Good, the stove was fired up and hot. "Ione, you know where the washtub is. Mother, would you drag out the big pot under that cabinet and fill it with water? Ione, did the iceman come yesterday? I need an ice pack for my eyes and face." She tapped her fingers on the edge of the sink. "What else? Probably some rice powder and a bit of lip rouge."

Ellen stared. "I know that look in your eyes. What are you up to?"

"I've been sitting around here for over two weeks, miserable and crying and imposing on both of you." Frowning, she reviewed the thoughts that had kept her awake most of last night. "Something happened to me almost eight months ago. I lost sight of what I thought I believed in and who I want to be. I let myself be crushed by shame and humiliation and the opinions of others. Now here I am, doing it again."

"Anne Margaret Malloy, what are you talking about?"

"I'm talking about independent thinking, Mother. I'm talking about the New Modern Woman."

Ellen groaned, but Ione's eyes sparkled.

"The New Modern Woman wouldn't sit here trapped in the misery of helplessness. She would not wait for someone to decide her future. The New Modern Woman would seize the moment and decide her own future."

"Oh Lord," Ellen said. She propped her elbows on the table and dropped her head.

"Jess is not going to come home," Annie said, steadying her voice after the wobble that appeared when she spoke his name. "The longer this separation goes on, the less likely it is that he'll change his mind. His pride and stubbornness are just going to get worse. But damn it all—"

"Annie!"

"We both promised until death do us part. So. If Jess won't come home and live with me, then I'll go to the boardinghouse and live with him."

Ellen's eyes widened in a horrified expression. "You can't do that! You can't go chasing after a man who doesn't want you. Respectable women don't do that kind of thing."

"Is there anyone left who still thinks I'm respectable? It doesn't matter anyway. I don't give a fig what they think. I've spent too much time and tears worrying about what other people think. I'm not going to lose my husband because other people wouldn't approve of me chasing after him. I only care what Jess thinks, and I can't change that if I'm here and he's there. So, I'm going to pack some clothes and go to him."

"Bravo," Ione said softly.

"If I have to, I'll keep following him and I'll keep talking until he understands that I love him and want him. I'll wear him down. I'll use every weapon I can think of to get him back. That's what the New Modern Woman would do. She wouldn't just sit here and wait while her world shatters around her."

"You're determined to do this?" Ellen said unhappily. "Even though you'll just add to the gossip and scandal."

"Mother, I came this close to getting married because I was worried about gossip and scandal."

Ellen nodded and pushed to her feet. "Point taken. I'll start some hot water for your bath."

"Where do you keep your fancy soap, the smell-good kind?" Ione asked. "And I think we should try witch hazel on your eyes before the ice."

Although she looked awful, Annie felt better than

she had felt in weeks. How could she have lost sight of herself so totally? She'd made herself miserable and helpless. But all that was going to change if she could possibly manage it.

Jess loved her and love didn't disappear overnight. And she loved him. Somehow, someway, she was going to make this right. Bodie Miller was not going to destroy her life and her happiness.

Mrs. Howard's boy found Jess at Ma Golden's having his supper with two of his deputies. The boy handed him a message, then left without a word. The boy could use a few lessons in manners. Jess wiped his hands, then opened a sheet of Mrs. Howard's stationery:

> *Dear Mr. Harden,*
> *Please come to the house at once.*
> > *Regards,*
> > *Mrs. Emily Howard*

"Is it something about Miller and his gang?" one of the deputies asked.

"No." Frowning, he folded the message into his waistcoat. If Mrs. Howard's request were based on an emergency, she would have addressed him as Sheriff Harden. Had she discovered that he'd been smoking in his room? Did she object to his habit of having supper out even though his rent included breakfast and supper? Had he left wood shavings on the floor?

Swearing under his breath, he dropped his napkin beside his plate and stood. "I need to check out something.

Later, I'll ride out to the Miller cabin. See if anything's going on."

"A bank was robbed in Atchison today, and it sounds like Miller. I doubt they've had time to return to their hideout."

Jess agreed, but he couldn't stay away from the cabin. It was like he needed a tangible thing to look at and despise, something on which to focus his pain. Angry at himself, he strode through the twilight toward Mrs. Howard's, smelling autumn in the air. He'd jailed Alfie Henderson again today for drunk and disorderly, and before he'd passed out Alfie had predicted rain for tonight. Alfie couldn't hold his liquor worth squat, but he was famed for predicting weather. According to Alfie, the autumn rains would be heavy and winter would come early this year.

Outside Mrs. Howard's boardinghouse Jess glanced up and noticed a light in the window of his room. Was that it? Had he left the lamp on all day? If so, then no wonder she'd summoned him. A fire could have resulted.

Mrs. Howard was hovering near the foyer when he walked inside. After glancing toward the staircase, she stepped close and whispered, "She's upstairs. In your room."

"She?" Puzzled, he, too, looked at the staircase. "She who?"

"Your wife. I didn't know whether to allow her . . . but she insisted."

He took the stairs two at a time, strode down the corridor, and threw open the door to his room. "What are you doing?"

But the answer was obvious. The doors to the armoire were open and he saw Annie's dresses hanging beside his trousers and shirts. Her nightgown was draped over the coverlet, and she'd set a row of shoes against the wall.

"I'm unpacking," she said, turning from the bureau where she'd set out her comb and brush and bottles of toiletries.

Good God, she looked beautiful. Glowing. She lit up the small room.

Without a word, he turned to the door.

"If you find other lodgings, I'll just follow you there," she said, reading his mind and stopping him. "We're married, Jess. For better or for worse. Until death do us part. I admit the current times are more worse than better, but we're through living apart. We have to work out our problems."

He closed the door to the corridor. "Annie, we can't put this back together."

"Not if you won't listen and believe what I tell you. If you hold to that line, we're going to have a lot of miserable years." Walking past him in a drift of verbena, she poked in her suitcase, removed a lacy shift, and shook it out before she folded it into a drawer. Next she started sorting stockings and garters.

Jess swallowed and looked away.

"I want you home, Jesse John Harden." She went on matching stockings and rolling them into balls. "You promised you'd never run out on me, that you'd always be there. I want you to come home."

He felt like a fool, standing beside the bed watching her go about unpacking intimate items like it was the most normal thing in the world. Even worse, he couldn't fully concentrate on what she was saying because the light on her wonderful carroty hair distracted him. When she looked at him, her eyes seemed greener than he remembered, her lips fuller and rosier.

"I might believe that," he said, giving his head a shake and a reminder that this was a very serious conversation, "if you hadn't let Bodie Miller shoot me. It all comes down to that."

She raised her eyebrows and stared. "I didn't 'let' Bodie Miller shoot you. That's unfair, Jess."

"You said yourself that my getting shot was your fault." If she wanted to talk about unfair, he could point out that it was unfair as hell of her to come here looking beautiful and radiant and smelling good and then wave stockings and garters practically under his nose.

"Well, I've thought about that."

"So have I."

"And I've concluded this: Yes, it's my fault that I didn't tell you about Bodie before he shot you. With all my heart, I regret that I didn't tell you. I should have. But I'm not totally to blame. The day *I* buy a gun and shoot you . . . *then* I'll be totally at fault for you getting shot. But given the facts as they stand, I am only, say, forty percent to blame."

"That is crazy."

"Is it?" Walking back and forth, she tucked the stocking balls in the drawer, then the garters; then she pulled out pantaloons adapted for pregnancy. There was lace around the legs. "Can the law arrest me for not having the sense to guess that Bodie might shoot you?"

"Of course not."

"Has it occurred to you that Bodie didn't plan to shoot you?"

Scowling, he walked to the window and looked down at the street. He could still smell the fragrance of her hair and skin. "What are you talking about?"

"He's a bank robber, Jess. That requires some forethought and planning. If he wasn't skilled at planning, he would have been apprehended long ago. Therefore, it seems to me that if he'd ridden out that day with the intention of killing you, he would have come up with a much better plan than shooting you in front of witnesses. And he would have planned a better escape than just hoping to outride your deputies. How many people recognized him?"

"At least a dozen," Jess admitted slowly. "They can't put a name to him, but they described him and they swear they'd recognize him if they saw him again."

"I think he shot you on impulse." When Jess turned, she was standing in the center of the room, looking at him. "And if you agree, then you cannot possibly imagine that I knew he was going to shoot you. I swear to you that I did not."

Everything she said made sense. So much sense, in fact, that he cursed himself for not seeing it himself. Of course it was an impulse shooting. She couldn't have known beforehand if Miller himself didn't know until opportunity presented itself.

"But you knew he wanted me dead."

"No, I knew he wanted me. In Bodie's mind, our marriage doesn't count; it doesn't exist. Our marriage is no more binding in his mind than any other law or sacrament." God help him, she kicked off her slippers and started to unbutton her shirtwaist. "Now you have to decide if our marriage is binding to you."

"What are you doing?" he asked in a hoarse voice.

"I'm going to put on my nightgown and get into bed. Then I'm going to read for a few minutes and then I'm going to sleep. It's been a long, strange day and I'm exhausted."

During the entire time they had been married she had never undressed in front of him. She'd either gone into the water closet or asked him to step into the hallway.

But tonight was going to create marriage history. She opened the front of her shirtwaist before she calmly unbuttoned her cuffs. Then, to his astonishment, she slipped out of the shirtwaist and her skirt and hung them in the armoire, walking around in front of him in her chemise and frothy petticoat. He couldn't believe his eyes.

Her breasts were full and lush, pressing against the lace and filigreed white chemise. A valley of deep inviting cleavage drew his gaze like a magnet. And my God, she had magnificent skin. Lamplight glowed on smooth cream dappled by tiny freckles. Swallowing, he stared in fascination at those intriguing freckles, wanting to touch and lick and stroke.

When he came to his senses, she was sitting on the edge of the bed, looking up at him with an expectant expression, the lamplight forming a halo around her head.

"Did you say something?" A train could have whistled through the room during the last minute and he would not have seen or heard it.

"If you'd be so kind as to help me with my stockings?"

He thought she might have blushed, but he wasn't sure because his gaze immediately dropped to her ankles. She drew up the lacy hem of her petticoat, exposing green stockings that curved over shapely legs. When the hem reached her thighs Jess spotted rose-trimmed garters. He hadn't known that she owned green stockings or fancy garters.

"Jess?"

He was frozen to the floor, paralyzed by how beautiful she was in the full glory of her pregnancy, by the wonder of her behavior tonight. Like a real wife.

Sinking to his knees before her, he gently slipped shaking fingers beneath the garter and glided it down the surface of the stockings. And then again. God. Finally, he rolled down her stockings, feeling the warm softness of her skin beneath his knuckles.

The day he'd been shot, he'd put on her stockings and garters for her, but he'd proceeded in a no-nonsense way, trying not to embarrass her, and they had both pretended it was an everyday experience. This was vastly different.

When he eased away enough to see past the swell of her belly, she was leaning back on her hands, her throat tilted, her eyes closed. At some point she had removed the pins from her hair, and wild red curls rippled toward the coverlet.

Never in his life had Jess Harden desired a woman more or wanted to make love to her like he did this minute. And she was approaching her eighth month of pregnancy.

Acutely aware of a painfully urgent erection, Jess stood and tugged his collar. "Annie?" His voice was thick, and he would have sworn it was a hundred degrees in the room. "I'm going outside for a smoke. I'll be back in about twenty minutes."

She gazed up at him from half-lidded eyes, her lashes shadowing the green to a smoky color.

"Someday we'll be ready, Jess," she spoke in a husky voice that made his groin tighten. "It will be snowing, and the whole world will be silent. There will be a fire in the fireplace, and we'll have candles and wine in tall crystal glasses. And then, slowly, you'll undress me. And, slowly, I'll undress you. Slowly. We'll kiss, and touch and explore each other. Slowly. And we will soar together into a universe we've never known."

He stared and forgot to breathe. From any other woman the words would have seemed almost innocent. But coming from Annie's lips the sentiment was the most erotic promise he had ever heard.

CHAPTER 19

※ ※ ※

WHEN Jess returned, considerably more than twenty minutes later, Annie had braided her hair and turned down the lamp and was asleep, breathing slowly and regularly.

There was no hope that he'd sleep anytime soon, so he didn't try. He stretched out beside her, inhaling her scent, listening to her soft breath, and attempted to make sense out of tonight.

She had come to him, which was a startling defiance of convention, and had moved into his room with every appearance of staying. Once he'd settled his mind and thought about it, he realized nothing she had done since arriving had been an accident. Try as he might, he could not conceive of a reason that she would set out to seduce him if she loved another man. Jess had cleared the way for her by leaving. If she wanted Bodie Miller, he had left her free to follow that direction.

Crossing his arms behind his head, he frowned at the ceiling. Had he ever really believed that Miller could mention killing him in front of Annie and Annie wouldn't warn him? Deep down, he knew her better than that. However, she must have known that Bodie Miller was capable of murder. In fact, she'd admitted to fault and begged Jess's forgiveness. What more did he want from her? He couldn't think of anything else she could do to demonstrate the sincerity of her regret.

And Annie could not have badgered Ione into keeping a secret from him unless Ione had agreed with Annie's reasoning. Was it fair to exonerate Ione but blame Annie?

As for Annie protecting Miller and not wanting to be the cause of a noose around his neck—Jess hated it, but he could grant a grudging understanding.

A long-buried memory surfaced and he remembered the night he had shot and killed Edward Everett Hobarten. Despite the pain of her injuries, Ione's only concern had been Jess's future. She'd begged Tom Stone not to arrest Jess, not to put Jess on a scaffold. She'd said over and over, "It's my fault, not the boy's." Afterward, when it became clear that Tom Stone would turn a blind eye, Ione had wept and held Jess close. "If you had died because of me, I'd never have forgiven myself."

If Annie caused Miller's arrest, Jess imagined that every time she looked at her child she'd be reminded that the child's father was in prison or dead because of her. Miller would haunt her life forever.

Finally, if Annie didn't care about him, she wouldn't be here, would she?

The possibility of happiness dangled before him like a golden carrot. And he felt his chest constrict in the darkness. What if he forgave Annie and accepted the possibility of happiness that came with her, but then at some time in the future disaster struck and she walked out of his life? Wasn't it better to take on the pain now, before there was also a child to love? While he could still almost bear losing her?

She turned then, nuzzled against him, and sighed in her sleep. He felt her heavy breasts against his chest, inhaled the warm perfumed scent of her hair. And slowly his arms came around her.

He had wanted her in this bed; now here she was. The problem was: What should he do? He almost believed he could trust her. He almost believed she hadn't been entertaining a lover in his house. But not quite.

In the morning he brought her coffee from Mrs. Howard's kitchen and a wedge of cabbage.

"I never used to like cabbage," Annie said after thanking him. "I wonder if I'll return to disliking it after the baby is born."

Shaved, dressed, and already late for work, Jess stretched out on the coverlet beside her. "We need to discuss what we're going to do about you."

"I thought we'd talk about babies' names. We need to, you know."

Sunlight lay on her cheek like a caress. She was still soft-eyed with drowsiness, her hair coming unraveled from the braid, and she smelled warm and slightly musky. At this moment Jess couldn't imagine ever not wanting her or not wanting her by his side. But having her could be as painful as not having her.

"Tell me something. You came here to seduce me, didn't you?"

"Perhaps." Lowering her head, she smiled at the cabbage leaf in her hand. A sparkling glance slid toward him.

"Well, you succeeded."

She closed her eyes and the air ran out of her. "Can you forgive me, Jess? I've made so many bad judgments."

He remembered Ione asking if he would believe his own wild speculations or his wife.

"If we go forward, Annie, we have to agree: no more secrets."

"I can't promise that."

Startled, he sat up and looked at her.

"But I will promise that any secrets will be small ones."

He sighed. "You aren't going to make this easy, are you?"

"I want us to be as honest as we can be. That means not making a promise I don't know if I can keep. Jess, are you going to come home?"

Shaking his head, he swung out of bed. "Did you drive the wagon into town? Can you drive it back?" When she nodded, he frowned at her stomach mounded beneath the sheets. "You're sure? All right then. I'll be home for supper."

Suddenly radiant, she struggled up on her knees, wobbled across the bed, and threw her arms around his waist, pressing her head to his chest. "I'm so glad!" She smiled up at him through a shine of tears.

"Wait. I'm not going to stay. We'll have supper and talk; then I'll ride back to town." Tilting her head up, he gazed into damp green eyes. "I'm struggling with some things."

"I know," she whispered.

"Give me time."

"I'll give you fifty years."

"Maybe that will be enough," he said, smiling.

"Jess?" She sat back on the bed. "There's three things you need to hear before you decide. First, I've been drifting most of this year, buffeted by confusion and the opinions of others. That's going to change. I have opinions; I'm going to stand up for them, and act on them."

"I already know you have opinions and act on them." He was still startled by the fact that she'd followed him to Mrs. Howard's with the intention of moving in whether he agreed or not.

"I want some hives of my own. If Ione will have me, I'd like to go into business with her. A woman needs her own money."

"I'll always take care of you," he said, stiffening. "No matter what happens between us."

"I know. But I'm thinking of the money Bodie gave me, and about the yellow house on the edge of town. I'd like to be able to take care of myself if I ever have to. I'll feel better about me if I know I have the freedom and the wherewithal to make my own choices."

So far she wasn't stating anything that he wasn't accustomed to living with, being Ione Harden's son. "And the last thing?"

She met his gaze squarely. "I hope Bodie Miller is caught and justice is done. But," she added softly, "I hope you're not the man who catches him."

Understanding hovered just out of reach. Jess was beginning to believe that she wanted her future to be with him. But she still felt a bond between herself and Bodie Miller. That knowledge stuck in his craw.

"I'm going to do everything I can to catch Miller and see him hanged for murder. If someone else catches him, I'm going to be disappointed as hell."

She looked down at her hands pressed against the curve of her stomach. "Is that difference of opinion enough to keep us apart?"

It stung that she didn't want him to do his job. That she didn't want him, who had so many reasons, to be the lawman who caught Miller and his gang. "I don't know," he said after a minute. "All I can tell you is that I'm going to try like hell to capture Bodie Miller and bring him to justice."

He kissed the top of her head and started toward the door, where he turned for a last word. "Every day I think about you being with Miller. But that isn't the primary reason I want Miller to hang. He's killed three men that we know about. Those men had families. They were only doing their job when Miller killed them because they stood between him and the money he wanted to steal. The world will be a better and safer place without Bodie Miller."

He arrived at his office late and out of sorts, thinking about Annie sitting on the bed holding a cabbage leaf in her hand, looking sad and vulnerable.

John Anderson rocked back in his chair and lifted an eyebrow over a grin. "Heard you had a visitor last night."

"Not a word, Anderson." He checked the cells, read the reports. The night deputies had jailed a couple of rowdy cowboys passing through Marshall on their way home to Oklahoma. Alfie was still sleeping it off. But

Alfie had been correct: it had rained before dawn, leaving an unseasonable chill in the air. "Let's get some breakfast; then we'll ride out and see if there's any activity at the old Miller cabin."

Nodding, Anderson rose to his feet. "Better check your schedule first. You're due to testify at the courthouse this morning about the robbery of the Old Town saloon. Then there's the funeral service for the head of the fire brigade."

Jess swore and flipped the pages of his notepad. "We won't get out to the Miller cabin before afternoon." He could send Deputy Morgan and Deputy Brown, but he wanted to go himself. His gut told him that Miller was coming soon.

Ione helped Annie unhitch the horse, meaning she did all the work over Annie's halfhearted protests. "Come up to the house," Ione said as they walked away from the corral. "I've got cinnamon tea and rolls that should still be hot from the oven."

"You're dying to know why I'm back so soon," Annie said.

"Only if the news is something you can comfortably share."

She told Ione what Jess had said, then squared her shoulders. "I'm not going to make it easy for him. If he goes back to town after supper like he's planning, I'll follow him."

"I'm starting to believe this is going to work out."

Annie's eyes sobered. "I think Jess wants it to, but I don't know. He has some things to think about."

"I have faith in the two of you." Ione put butter and

honey on the table. "Now if they just catch that crazy man, all will be right in the world. If Jesse's right, it shouldn't be long now."

"Bodie is crazy, isn't he?" Annie admitted slowly, lowering her teacup. "He didn't used to be. At least I never thought he was."

Bodie had been unpredictable, wild at heart, on the edge. But she'd only started thinking of him as crazy since the first time he rode into Ione's yard. A deep sadness darkened her eyes.

It shouldn't have been like this. Something had gone terribly wrong inside Bodie along the way. He possessed the charm and intelligence to have succeeded at almost anything, but he'd chosen the dark path.

"Ione . . . this is going to be a stupid question, but did you mourn for Edward Everett Hobarten after his death?"

Sympathy and understanding softened Ione's expression. "There are few people who would understand, but yes, I guess I did. I was glad the man I knew was dead, but I mourned the loss of the man he might have been. That was the man I thought of as Jesse's father. A man who never really existed. I mourned the loss of that man."

Annie nodded, then winced. "Little No-Name is active today," she said, gently rubbing her stomach. She'd been having cramps off and on since she woke. "I love Jess and I want to spend my life with him. But I wish I could turn back the clock and save Bodie. I wish I could fix whatever went wrong." Confusion clouded her brow and she shook her head. She would always struggle with conflicted emotions about Bodie Miller.

Once he had been good to her. Tender and gentle

when it was important that he be those things. And regardless how it had turned out, he had given her this baby whom she already loved with all her heart and soul. Someday, when she looked back on this period of her life, she suspected that she would think of Bodie Miller with forgiveness and perhaps fondness. Because of him, Jess had come into her life. And Ione. Because of Bodie, Annie had a suspicion that she would be a stronger woman than she would have been if this year had never happened.

"Good heavens." Lowering her head, she pressed her fingertips to her temples. In her mind, Bodie was gone. Either captured and condemned or escaped to a faraway place. Like Jess and Ione, she, too, felt a gathering tension that signaled events were coming to a head. Whatever would happen, would happen soon.

"Well," she said, summoning a smile. "Let's talk about something pleasant. We could discuss Katherine of Aragon. . . ."

Ione laughed. "I think you have something else in mind."

"Or we could talk about business." Leaning forward, Annie folded her hands on the table and tried to look like she imagined a New Modern businesswoman would look: serious, intelligent, brimming with plans. "I've been thinking about your idea that all women should learn a trade so they have a way to make money. And I've been thinking about the bees."

"You're a natural beekeeper. I've said so from the first. In fact, I saw you out at the hives recently. I suspect you're taking your troubles to the bees, like all good beekeepers do." Ione refilled their teacups. "Now, here's how I see our partnership."

"You guessed!"

Annie loved this woman and her wonderful son. And she loved the baby she would meet in about six weeks. She loved it that Jess would be coming home for supper and, if he was the man she believed he was, he'd stay at home for the next fifty years.

For that she closed her eyes and sent Bodie Miller a silent message of gratitude. Because of him, she had Jess.

At noon the temperature was still low on the mercury. For a minute the smell of wood smoke seemed appropriate and natural and escaped his notice. Then Jess's gaze sharpened on a wisp of smoke drifting above the trees nearest the cabin.

"John," he said quietly, reining in the palomino. "Go back to town and round up every deputy you can locate in fifteen minutes."

John Anderson had also spotted the chimney smoke. Without a word, he wheeled his horse and set off at a gallop.

The Miller gang had returned. Jess guided his horse off the road into a copse of cottonwoods that offered cover. Methodically he checked his pistols and the rifle in his scabbard. Then he lit a cigar, smoked, and waited.

It didn't matter how many men would be involved; this was between him and Bodie Miller. There hadn't been a doubt in Jess's mind that despite the number of lawmen searching for Miller, the final confrontation would occur here, in his county.

As he always did when he knew in advance that a

gunfight lay ahead, he ran his list of obligations through his mind. If things went bad, Ione and Annie were provided for financially. His debts were paid. His office records up-to-date. There was nothing left unsaid that should have been said.

If today was the day he died, his only regret was the uncertainty between himself and Annie. He would have liked to find out for himself if they could have made it for the long haul. He would have liked to hear her say she loved him and to believe her. But maybe that wouldn't have been in the cards anyway.

Otherwise, like he'd heard the Indians say when he was scouting for the army, today was a good day to die. But Jess didn't plan on dying. It was also a good day to live. There was that unfinished business with Annie.

"All right, men," he said, leading his horse onto the road when he heard the deputies arrive. "You two circle around back and make sure no one goes out that way. Anderson, you stay in front with me. Protect yourself, but we want to take them alive, understand? Follow my lead."

They left the horses tied to the trees lining the county road and silently filed toward the cabin. When Jess heard the signal that the deputies were in place, he shouted at the cabin.

"Bodie Miller! It's over. The cabin is surrounded. Come out with your hands up and nobody gets hurt." He counted two horses in the corral and guessed that Miller had one of the Baylor brothers with him. "Baylor, we know you're in there, too."

"They aren't responding," Anderson said, tightening his grip on his pistol.

Jess listened to another full minute of silence before he stepped into the clearing. "Come out, or we're coming in."

Glass shattered in the front windows, followed by an eruption of gunfire. Bullets pebbled the ground around Jess, struck the tree trunks. He stood where he was, considering the best way to approach the door.

Later, stories would be printed in the newspaper and the Yellow Books about Jess standing in the line of fire as if he wore an invisible shield. He'd read such reports about himself and about other men, and they always annoyed the hell out of him. There were only a few weapons on the market that aimed true, and nervous men darting in and out of windows didn't have time to aim anyway, and finally, despite legend, there were few genuine marksmen on either side of the law. He didn't consider that he was in any real peril.

When gunfire exploded from the rear of the house, Jess stepped into the trees to confer with John Anderson. "They've split their attention." From the sound of it, his deputies were firing as fast as they could, giving better than they got. "I think there's only two men inside, but we'll assume all of them are there. One man in back, two in front. You cover me while I go up to the door."

Anderson nodded and wiped his forehead. At Jess's nod, both men entered the clearing, Anderson firing steadily, Jess running for the door. When he reached the stoop, he caught his breath then kicked the door open, swinging around with both pistols in his hands.

"We give up!"

Just like that it was finished. The whole thing hadn't taken longer than five minutes. "Throw your guns out the door." Jess couldn't decide if he was happy that the fight had ended so swiftly or disappointed. Three pistols and a rifle slid across the cabin floor and spun off the stoop. "Come out with your hands up."

He moved off the stoop and to the side so he wouldn't be an easy shot if trickery was involved.

"We're coming out. Don't shoot." It was not Miller's voice.

Two men whom Jess had never seen before walked out the door. But he'd read about the Baylor brothers. A shout came from the back of the cabin: "Sheriff! We're looking in the window; there's no one left inside. We can see the whole place."

They took the Baylor brothers to the middle of the clearing, checked them for concealed weapons; then Jess said, "You're under arrest for robbery and murder."

The one named Jimmy protested, "We didn't kill nobody!"

"That's the truth," the shorter one insisted. "It wasn't us."

"Where's Miller?"

The brothers looked at each other; then the short one shrugged. "You decide," he said to Jimmy. "Makes no never mind to me. If you tell, it'll serve Bodie right for not giving us our money straightaway like he promised."

Jimmy Baylor eyed Jess. "You the sheriff?" When Jess answered with a curt nod, he grinned. "Can't you guess where he is?"

"I'm in no mood for guessing games." Jess backhanded the bastard hard enough to bloody his nose. "I'll ask you again. Where's Miller?"

Jimmy glared with glittering eyes, then spit on the

ground near Jess's boots. "He's out at your place, Sheriff. In bed with your wife."

Without another word, Jess ran for his horse. He should have known. Damn it. He'd been watching the wrong place.

After Annie returned to her own kitchen, she made herself a bowl of oatmeal for lunch but didn't eat because her stomach cramps seemed worse. Maybe bouncing around on the hard wagon seat hadn't been a good idea. Trying to walk off the cramps, she wandered through her house, but moving didn't help. Feeling a twinge of panic, she stepped outside on the front porch and looked toward Ione's house, biting her lip.

Was this what labor felt like? Should she ask Ione for help?

That thought irritated her. Where was her independence? Hadn't she just vowed to be more self-reliant? This was not labor, she told herself firmly, pressing her fingers against the front of her skirt. It was too soon. More likely the cramps were the result of having eaten a wedge of cabbage for breakfast.

"Settle down, little fellow. We're coming into the home stretch. It won't be long, but it isn't time yet."

There was a horse tied to Ione's porch railing, one that looked familiar. Probably it belonged to Charlie Hare, the man who drove Ione on her business rounds. All brown horses looked alike to Annie.

The air was too chilly to remain long on the porch, and she hurried inside to check the larder and decide what she would fix Jess for supper. So far all she'd decided on was they would eat in the dining room tonight and she'd use her best cloth and set out candles.

Bodie Miller rode a brown horse.

Remembering stopped her heart for a beat and made her hands feel suddenly colder. Spinning, she returned to the porch and peered toward Ione's. The horse was gone. Sagging with relief, Annie leaned against the post and smiled at herself for being foolish. Of course the rider had been Charlie Hare. If Bodie came out here, he wouldn't stop to say hello to Ione.

Still, this time she locked the front door behind her, then leaned against it and looked around her parlor. It had turned into a comfortable room. Not formal and stuffed with furniture and plants and fringed throws and all sorts of whatnots like her mother's. This was a room to be lived in without fear of breaking something. Her gaze touched the shelves of books and Jess's rows of carved animals, settling on the mama duck and her duckling. If Annie had her way, Jess would come home and stay home and carve more ducklings.

Daydreaming wasn't getting supper started. Checking the clock on the mantelpiece, she planned the next few hours. There was a fresh chicken in the icebox, which she would set to stewing immediately. Then she'd lie down for an hour and see if a rest might ease the cramps. That would leave enough time to make dumplings and bake apples for dessert.

Pushing back a loose tendril, she noticed her fingers were trembling. Seeing the brown horse had set her nerves on edge, and she wished she hadn't gone out to the porch.

"Stop being silly," she murmured. She was passing through the dining room when she heard his voice.

"An-nie."

Oh, God. He was in the kitchen. The hair on the

back of her neck prickled and her heart sped so heavily it made her dizzy. Gripping the back of a dining chair, she fought to steady herself. He'd come for her. What could she do? What could she do?

Shaking, trying to move silently, she backed out of the dining room, then fixed her eyes on the front door and waddled toward it, feeling as if her feet were mired in molasses.

"Damn." Her hands were shaking so violently that she dropped the key.

"That isn't funny, Annie." The tease had vanished from his tone and he sounded angry.

Whirling, she pressed her back to the locked door and swallowed. "Bodie."

"My God. You're big as a house," he said, staring. "Well, this complicates things."

"Was that your horse in front of Ione's place?"

"Don't worry about her. She won't be bothering us." Walking forward, he took her by the arm and half dragged her into the kitchen, where he pushed her onto a chair.

"What did you do?" She couldn't stand to imagine that he'd hurt Ione. Don't think about that now, she commanded herself. Think about keeping him here until Jess comes. But Jess wouldn't arrive home until supper, hours from now.

"I took all the money. The Baylor boys are going to be pissed when they figure it out, but they owe me. If it wasn't for me, they wouldn't have those big houses and barns." He shrugged. "The important thing is us." A smile curved his lips as if he'd decided to be playful again. "What do you think about going east? I was thinking Colorado, but heading west is what they'd expect, so I'm thinking Boston. There's more people in Boston than in this whole fricking state. They'll never find us. And there's plenty of banks there, too," he added with a wink.

"Bodie." She wet her lips and tried to speak louder than a whisper. "I told you. I'm not leaving here."

"Now don't start that kind of talk." Suddenly his face was ugly, his mouth twisted. "It gives me a headache. Now look, sweetheart. Me and the boys rode half the night to get here through the rain. I've only had a few hours' sleep and I'm not in the best of moods. Plus, we don't have all day. The Baylors are going to wake up and figure out where I went. Shortly afterward they'll figure out that I took the money. Now. The way I see it, we can get halfway to Kansas City by midnight."

He eyed the bulge pushing out her skirt front. "Maybe a third of the way," he amended, scowling. "Maybe three nights on the road. We'll stop in Kansas City long enough for my mother to get a look at you; then we'll take the train to Boston. See? I have it all worked out."

"I can't ride a horse."

There was no gun in the house. But even if there had been, Annie didn't know how to fire one and couldn't have shot anyone anyway. Desperately she looked around her kitchen. The knives were in a drawer, but if she managed to get one Bodie would disarm her in half a second. The water she'd boiled for the oatmeal would be tepid now.

"I've been thinking about that problem. There's a

wagon out back. We'll take that and the horse. I'll tie my horse to the back rail."

Annie released a breath, drew another. "Taking the wagon is too slow. They're looking for you, Bodie. A better plan might be for you to escape as quickly as you can and . . . and I'll meet you in Kansas City. You wait for me there."

There was something chilling in his smile. "And what if you don't come? Didn't you just say you weren't leaving here?"

"I was testing you," she said after a minute, hoping she didn't sound shrill and desperate. "Testing your commitment."

"You're a strange one," he said finally, drumming his fingertips on the top of the table. "You know I don't like teasing, but you say things to rile me. It's your own fault that I don't trust you. The only thing that saves me from having to punish you straightaway is that you never told the sheriff about me. That tells me you love me and I can trust you. But you make it hard, sweetheart."

There had to be something. "I can't travel in my condition. I'm too far along. My back aches something fierce, and I'm cramping."

"I don't want to hear about those woman things."

"Truly, I don't feel well. I should be lying down."

He placed his palms on the table and leaned forward, jutting his chin. "I'm not leaving without you, Annie, and that's how it is. I've been patient with all your crap, more patient than any woman deserves. The Baylors couldn't believe it when they heard how I've pampered you and let you have your way. Any other man would have taken you and punished you good for moving in here with the sheriff. The goddamned sheriff." He spit on her floor, then apologized when he noticed her expression. "One thing is for damned sure: the sheriff is never going to have you the way I did. You're mine. You understand that? You belong to me and no one else."

"Bodie." She didn't know what to say. He refused to hear her, or maybe he was beyond reason.

"Do you have a bag packed and ready?"

The question appeared serious. He genuinely appeared to believe that she'd been waiting for him, despite everything she had said before and now.

"No."

He shrugged. "It doesn't matter. We'll buy whatever you need along the way." Standing, he loomed over her. She'd forgotten how big he was. Tall, heavy-boned. "Get up. We're leaving."

Trembling, Annie looked up at him. "There will always be a bond between us, and I'll never forget you. But how I remember you depends on you. If you force me to leave here against my will, I'll hate you, Bodie."

Casually, like swatting a fly, he leaned forward and slapped her strongly enough to knock her off the chair. Shocked and hurting, Annie landed hard on her knees. She felt the jolt through her bones to the top of her head. The cramps bit down.

"I didn't hit you hard enough to hurt you. I don't want to do that," he said, coming around the table to help her to her feet.

This man was a total stranger. Annie gaped at him as if she had never seen him before. How could she have failed to see who he really was? Had he changed or had she been blind?

"All right, let's just see if you want to go or stay." He went to the back door and smiled. "We can leave now. Or we can sit here, have a bite to eat, talk awhile, and wait for the sheriff to come home. You can help me decide whether to pick him off his horse or wait until he's walking up the back path. Or maybe we'll let him come into the kitchen and then shoot him."

Horror dried her mouth.

"I'll go with you," she said, standing at once.

CHAPTER 20

LATHER flew from the palomino's neck as Jess galloped into the yard, leaning low over the horse's mane. The first thing he noticed was Ione's open front door. Swearing, he vaulted out of the saddle and hit the ground running. An ominous silence filled the house and she didn't respond to his shouts.

He found her in the kitchen, bound to a chair, a dish towel tied around her mouth. Bruised eyes had started to swell and turn purple; blood splattered the front of her dress. She'd put up a fight.

Grabbing a knife, he cut the dish towel and the cord tying her hands. The rope around her ankles he left for her. "Are you all right? Any broken bones?" The blood had come from her nose and a cut near her lips.

"Go!"

He ran toward the bunkhouse, swore viciously when he discovered the front door was locked, then ran around to the kitchen door, which was standing open. The chairs were pulled back from the table. Although he knew in his gut that Annie wasn't in the house, he wasted precious seconds racing from room to room to make sure.

All right. She was too pregnant to ride a horse. He

should have asked if Ione knew if Miller had brought a wagon. Damn, damn. No. There were only two horses in the cabin's corral, so Miller had ridden here. He was an opportunist; he'd steal their wagon.

Before the thought was fully formed, Jess was out the door and heading toward the barn and corral, forcing himself to slow his steps. Nice and easy, he repeated in his mind, drawing his guns and letting them drop to his sides. Feeling their comfortable weight, clearing his thoughts.

He heard Bodie calling to the wagon horse in a coaxing voice, heard Annie's soft weeping. They were still here. Thank God. The path straightened and now he saw Miller inside the corral and Annie standing on the back side of the wagon, her face in her hands.

Bodie spotted him first and jumped the corral rails, dropping down beside Annie, fumbling for the gun on his hip. When Annie raised her head, Jess saw the beginnings of a heavy bruise on her cheek. Fury exploded through his body. He would have shot Miller without a qualm, except Miller grabbed Annie and dragged her in front of him.

"Let her go," Jess ordered, hearing the snarl of hatred in his voice. "Hiding behind a woman is the work of a coward." Miller was a foot taller than Annie. Jess had a clear head shot, but it would be dangerous with Annie standing just under Miller's chin.

Bodie also realized that Jess had a clear shot. In a swift motion he placed the muzzle of his pistol against Annie's temple. "Shoot me and she dies, too."

"Is that how little you care for her and the baby?"

"I'd rather see her dead than with you. You'll never have her. She's mine and always will be."

Annie's green eyes were enormous in her white face, but she'd stopped weeping. She gazed at Jess with a calm expression.

"Do what you have to do," she said softly, resigned. Bodie's arm tightened around her throat, and she winced.

"He's not going to shoot," Bodie said. "He might hit you. And if he hits me, reflex is going to pull this trigger and kill you." His fingers moved on the butt of the gun. "If you take a shot, Harden, you kill her, too. So throw your gun in the bushes and back out of here."

Jess looked at Annie, his beautiful Annie, the only woman he had ever loved, had ever wanted to spend a life with. What the hell was he doing, questioning what she had said and done and sleeping in a boarding-house? A woman who got tears in her eyes looking at a child's swing wasn't the type of woman to welcome a lover into her kitchen. He'd been a fool.

"I won't put down my guns," he said, speaking to her. "But I'll walk away if that's what you want. It's your call."

He had to accept her decision, whatever it was, and she had to trust that he could kill Miller without killing her, too. Jess knew that she didn't want to be responsible for Bodie's death, but he saw in her expression that she understood if they were to have a future the decision had to be hers.

Moisture glistened in her eyes. "Jess? Try to save the baby and raise her well."

He had his answer. But she didn't believe she would survive and had resigned herself to dying. She accepted it.

Bodie Miller also understood Annie's decision. "Damn you," he snarled at Annie. Swearing, he bit down on his back teeth as Jess raised his right arm, slowly, taking his time so Bodie could look down the gun barrel and think about the end.

Then Jess fired, placing a bullet squarely between the bastard's eyes. Bodie Miller also fired one last shot, and Annie fell to the ground beside him.

Jess reached her in a heartbeat and dropped to his knees.

She blinked up at him with a dazed expression; then her hands flew to her temples, her throat, her breast.

Catching her up in his arms, Jess held her so tight and close that he could feel her heart thudding against his own. "You're all right; he didn't shoot you."

"My ear's ringing. I'm not dead," she said in a wondering voice. Pulling back, she stared hard at him, then flung her arms around his neck. "He said if I didn't go with him he'd wait and pick you off when you rode into the yard. Or he'd let you walk into the kitchen and ambush you in front of me. Oh, Jess." Then she shoved him away and struggled to rise. "Ione! I think he hurt Ione!"

"Not for long," Ione announced grimly, appearing beside them. She stared through bruised and swollen eyes at Bodie Miller's sprawled body. "I saw the whole thing," she said to Jess, pride lifting her expression. "You knew he wouldn't shoot Annie, didn't you?"

Jess's smile was tight. "If I'd shot fast, he might have. But no man is going to watch a gun barrel coming up and just stand there and let himself get killed. I figured if I took it slow he'd take the gun off Annie and try to shoot me first."

Annie glanced at Bodie, shuddered, then made a sound and bent forward, pressing her forehead against

Jess's chest, wrapping her arms around her stomach. When she caught her breath, she sent a desperate look toward Ione. "This is humiliating, but I think I just peed on myself."

Ione studied the widening wet patch on Annie's skirt, then bit her lip. "God help us," she whispered. "Her water's broken. She's in labor."

An hour later Annie couldn't remember how she got to the bunkhouse or into a nightgown. Only snippets of conversation remained in her memory: Ione ordering Jess to ride to town and fetch the doctor and notify the Malloys. Jess telling her that he loved her, and then gone. Ione, talking to men behind the house, telling them about Bodie Miller.

Annie dozed or was unconscious, she didn't know which, woke to a stomach pain that made her groan aloud.

"That's right, young lady," Doc Willis said, breezing into the bedroom. "Today's the day you get to moan and groan, shout and scream, all you want to. Let's have a look and see what's going on here." After he'd examined her, he sat beside the bed and took her hand, studying the bruise on her cheek. "I understand you've already had quite a day, and it appears you're not finished yet. We're going to have a baby."

Annie wet her lips. "It's too early." Fear widened her eyes.

"I'd rather have another five or six weeks," Doc Willis agreed, stroking her hand, "but you're dilated and the contractions are coming regularly." He smiled. "This is the real thing."

"Will the baby survive?" She could hardly speak the words.

"He can breathe on his own at this point. I'd say this baby is strong and is going to do just fine. He'll not only survive but thrive."

Annie tried to read Doc Willis's mind, tried to decide if he was telling her the truth or giving her doctor-speak, merely reassuring her.

"Given how far along you are now, I suspect you've been in early labor for many hours. I'd say you're moving into the second stage."

As if to make his point, the most intense contraction yet swept Annie like a tidal wave that bore down on a rush of pain. When it ended, leaving her gasping and shaken, she fell back on the pillows and flung out her arms. "I don't think I want to do this."

Ellen Malloy rushed into the room, followed by Annie's father and Jess and Ione. Heaven help her, John Anderson and another of the deputies leaned in the doorway, grinning and giving Annie thumbs-up signs.

"Every woman feels that way," Ellen said, lifting Annie forward so Ione could plump the pillows.

"What you're going through is the most helpless feeling in the world," Ione agreed.

Annie had time to stare at Ione's battered face and meet Jess's steady gaze before another contraction brought sweat to her brow and a groan to her lips. Dimly she was aware of people talking all around her while pain bore down through her body. Irritation made this contraction feel more painful than the last.

Doc Willis read her mind. "Attention, everyone. Despite what you probably think, this is not a royal birth.

Your attendance in the birthing chamber is neither required nor wanted." He smiled. "Everybody out except the father."

"What?" Ellen and Ione rounded on him like furies. "The mothers always stay. Always. The father never stays!"

"Not while I'm the doctor." Spreading his arms, he herded Ellen and Ione toward the door.

"You weren't like this for my deliveries," Ellen protested.

"This is the new modern way."

Annie heard, but her laugh was cut short by another contraction. They came fast and furious now. Her back ached like blazes. Her lower body was exploding. Her legs trembled and she thought she might throw up.

"You're sure you want me in here?" Jess asked, wetting his lips and staring as Annie flung herself back on the bed and shouted, "Goddamn!" at the ceiling.

"Yes, Sheriff, I do. It does you young fathers good to see what comes of waving that prick around." Doc Willis laughed at Jess's expression. "You'll never forget today, son. It's going to change your thinking." He patted Jess's arm. "Now take off your hat and jacket. Hang up your waistcoat and roll up your sleeves. Wash up in that basin over there. You are about to participate in a miracle."

The next two hours passed in a blur for Annie. She remembered Doc Willis telling her to raise her knees up to her armpits to give herself something to hang on to. She looked up at him incredulously. "I can't do that. In case you haven't noticed, I have an enormous stomach in the way."

"Yes, you can." Jess slammed one of her knees up, ran around the other side of the bed, and caught her dangling leg and slammed that knee up to where she had to grab them both. "Now breathe," he said, trying to look helpful.

"I *am* breathing, you idiot!"

"I mean breathe the way Doc is telling you to."

Then finally came a blissful period when the contractions stopped and Annie could catch her breath. For ten minutes she simply rested, letting her mind drift. She resented it when Doc interrupted by taking her hand.

"How are you feeling, young lady?"

"If you call me young lady just one more time, I'm going to tear your head off," she said in a dreamy voice.

"What I want you to do now is get out of bed and put your arms around your husband's neck."

"I don't want to."

"Place your feet flat on the floor about shoulder width apart and then squat. Let's go." His arm went around her and forced her to sit up. Jess swung her legs off the bed. "You hold her arms so she doesn't fall." To Annie Doc Willis said, "In a few minutes you're going to want to push. A few squats will stretch the path and hurry things along."

Jess caught her hands and brought them to his neck, placed his own hands on what used to be her waist. "You're doing fine, Annie love. I'm proud of you." His dark eyes glowed.

For the moment she felt exhausted but not in pain. Holding on to him, she gazed into his strong face. "It's going to be all right," she whispered. "I know it had to happen the way it did out there."

"Bodie chose his own road, Annie. You didn't choose

it for him. And you didn't pull the trigger. Miller's death is not your fault."

"I think I know that." Without being aware, she had slowly accepted how Bodie would inevitably end and her role in it. Right now she hated him for being willing to kill her and the baby and Jess. Someday, when the time was right, she would let herself quietly mourn for the man Bodie might have been. That day wouldn't come soon, but it would come someday.

"Squat!"

She did several squats, holding on to Jess, looking into his eyes, before she felt an uncontrollable urge to bear down. When the contraction passed, she blinked up at him. "I think . . ."

Doc Willis looked pleased. "I think we're about to get going here. Sheriff, you get on the bed and support her back. Mrs. Harden, you sit between his legs and lean against him in a sitting squat. Knees up, so you'll have something to grab to help you push."

"This is not how my mother described childbirth," Annie said. A wide smile lit her pale face. "This is the modern way, is that correct?"

"Trying to have a baby while lying on your back isn't the most efficient way to do it."

She leaned against Jess's chest and felt his arms come around her. It seemed appropriate that she had gotten this baby by behaving in a new modern mode and she would deliver it the same way. "I'm so glad you're with me," she said to Jess.

And then she went to work.

"It's a girl!" Doc Willis said forty minutes later. Annie's exhausted face broke into a smile at the sound of a thin wail. "Father, you come around here and hold this baby while Mother and I finish up." A few minutes later Doc Willis nodded. "Now show Mother what she's done here today."

Goose bumps ran down Annie's skin when she saw the tears glistening in Jess's eyes as he carefully placed the infant in her arms. Already he loved this tiny girl.

And so did she. Pushing back the blanket Jess had wrapped her in, Annie blinked through tears to see her daughter's face.

Jess sat on the bed beside her. "I counted. She has ten fingers and toes. Not too many or too few of everything else. You did a good job, Annie love."

She couldn't help herself. Wiping tears away, she tried to see Bodie in her little girl's face. But she saw nothing that reminded her of him. A knot broke in her chest, replaced by relief. But aside from a few wisps of red hair, she didn't see herself, either. This child was going to be her own person.

"What shall we call her?" Annie asked softly.

Jess smiled. "I don't think there's much choice. I believe that is Ellen Ione Harden in your arms. Haven't you heard all the fussing outside the door?"

"I didn't hear a thing!"

"If we'd listened to the suggestions and advice shouted from behind that door, you'd still be in labor." Doc Willis laughed as an eruption of pleas and knocking came from the other side of the door. "Are you ready for company?"

Reaching for Jess's hand, Annie looked up at him, her eyes soft and teary. "Thank you for staying with me. Thank you, Jess. For everything." Lost in each other's gaze, they had to be called back to earth by Doc Willis. Annie nodded and smiled.

"I won't let them stay long," Doc Willis said. "You need rest." He flung open the door. "Ladies, may I present Miss Ellen Ione Harden. Four pounds, eleven ounces, and as healthy and beautiful as her mother."

The room filled with people, all of whom wanted to kiss Annie and Ellen Ione and shake Jess's hand. Annie's father sat beside her for a long time. There was laughter and cider punch and honey cakes. Teasing and ooohing and aaahing. And love. There was love.

After Doc Willis chased everyone into the living room and kitchen, Jess extinguished the lamp and stretched out beside Annie and cradled her in his arms. Her daughter nuzzled against her breast, a precious warmth next to her body. If Annie could have frozen time, she would have chosen this moment to live in forever.

"Jess?" she murmured sleepily. "Are you home for good?"

He kissed the top of her head, and his arms tightened around her. "I'll never leave you again."

"Good." She didn't want to ever wake again and find him gone. She wanted him beside her for the rest of her life.

Before she slept, she eased back the blanket from her daughter's face and gazed at the miracle she had produced.

This day of endings and beginnings would be with Annie always. Silently she said good-bye to a man who might have been and opened her heart and soul to the man beside her.

* * *

The first heavy snow of the season began at five o'clock on the second of November. By evening, thick frost laced the windows and fat, wet flakes silently collected on the sills.

Annie had taken an hour to bathe and dress for supper in the dining room. For tonight she'd chosen a low-cut green silk dress that caught the shimmer of candlelight in the folds of whispery fabric and enhanced the green of her eyes. She'd piled masses of red hair atop her head and teased long curls down her neck. Beneath the gown she wore a new French corset, cut to accommodate her fuller breasts and slightly larger waist and hips. Her drawers were also silk, trimmed with Brussels lace. She wore black stockings and green garters. Her hair and skin were scented with jasmine and sandalwood.

Jess drew a sharp breath when he saw her, and his eyes darkened to an intense chocolate hue. He, too, had taken pains with his appearance. A crisp white shirt set off a new dark suit he'd purchased for the occasion. His dress boots were polished to a high gleam, and he'd been to the barbershop for a haircut and shave. He'd come home with the hothouse flowers that Annie had arranged in the center of the table.

"And this," he said after they abandoned any pretense of eating. He placed a box beside her china coffee cup.

"What is it?"

"A hope for tonight and a promise of other nights to come. And a token of gratitude for our daughter."

Inside the box, nested in wood shavings, was a tiny carved duckling. Annie smiled, and her mouth went dry. Tonight could be special in many ways.

"Thank you." Candlelight cast one side of his face in light, one side in shadow. He was so strong and handsome that her heart constricted and a nervous tension fluttered through her body.

His smile tightened her stomach. "Look beneath the duckling."

"Oh my heavens!" With trembling fingers she removed an emerald ring. "Jess!"

Taking the ring, he slipped it on her finger. Green fire flashed in the candlelight.

His voice roughened with emotion. "We'll add earrings and a necklace as our ducklings increase." Then, taking her by the hand, he led her into the parlor, where a fire warmed the night and flutes of wine waited on a side table. He'd spread a blanket on the floor, positioned so they could see the flames in the hearth and the snow tumbling past the windows.

But Annie had eyes only for him. "Slowly," she whispered, her voice hoarse with wanting him. They had waited so long.

"Slowly," he repeated, smiling and standing close as he removed the pins from her hair and caught the mass of curls in his hands. He brought a long coil to his cheek, then to his lips, gazing deep into her eyes.

With shaking fingers Annie removed the studs from his shirt and cuffs, letting them fall where they would, and she ran her hands inside to feel the tight warmth of his bare chest against her palms.

Jess drew her into his arms and kissed her, lightly at first, then deeper, his fingers opening the hooks running down her back.

The only lovemaking Annie had known had been fast and furious, over almost as it began, leaving her filled with frustration and a vague longing for something she couldn't define. Tonight, she sensed that everything would change forever.

Jess undressed her slowly, slowly, kissing the creamy skin he uncovered, building anticipation and a trembling tension with each teasing caress, each exploring kiss. And Annie drew off his waistcoat and shirt and his boots, unhooked his trousers, feeling heat and hardness against the backs of her fingers. A wave of dizziness sent her into his arms, and the shock of his hot chest against her bare breasts took her breath away.

When they were both naked in the firelight, Jess looked at her. "You are so incredibly beautiful," he whispered, his voice husky with desire. "I love the scent of you, and the feel of your skin and the touch of your hands on me."

Annie loved the swell of muscle down his shoulders and arms, his wide chest and narrow waist, the lean hips and hard thighs. She loved his face, glittering hard one minute, soft the next. And his woodcarver's hands, careful but sure, skilled, and knowing.

Gently he eased her to the blanket, covering her mouth with kisses that trailed down her throat to her breasts. Annie couldn't remain still; she moved and moaned beneath his lips, gasped and trembled with the pleasures he introduced. Slowly, slowly, letting their desire and their need build and build and build, Jess kissed her hips and stomach. Lightning flashed beneath Annie's skin, darted through her body from the point where his tongue tasted her, explored her. When he gently opened her thighs and kissed her there, a moment of shock paralyzed her; then a wave of heat and sensation swept her mind clear of any thought but an urgent desire for this man, this amazing, magnificent man. And then even that thought shattered on a crest of passion that erupted through her body like exploding stars.

"My heavens," she whispered when she could speak. Jess moved up beside her and she turned, shaking, into his arms. "That was . . . It was like . . ." But there were no words to describe an ecstasy she had never imagined.

He kissed her and she tasted herself on his lips. "It's a long snowy night, Annie love. We've only just begun."

And they began again, the slow building of tension, of wanting him until she ached with need, until his name was a plea, until they were both wet with perspiration and shaking with their hunger for each other.

Finally he came into her and a gasp of fulfillment lifted her breast to his lips and hands. As if they had been made for each other, they moved together, anticipated each other, discovered the rhythm that would be theirs, found a deep satisfaction in each other.

Toward morning they donned wrappers and finished the wine, holding each other before the dying fire, sated and sleepy but not wanting the night to end.

They spoke of their daughter sleeping nearby and the house they would build and the other children they hoped to have. They talked of bees and a lawman's duty and family and the dinner party they had attended at the mayor's home.

When they were in their bed, Annie curled around him and whispered in his ear, "Aren't you going to ask me?"

For a moment he didn't understand; then he turned

and kissed her, his mouth lingering on hers. "Do you love me yet?"

"I love you with all my heart and soul. I love you with every breath I take. I love you more than you can possibly ever imagine. I will love you to the end of time, Jess Harden."

They spent the remainder of their true wedding night holding each other even in sleep, their heads on the same pillow. As they would sleep every night for the next fifty years.

"Wit, style, and class. Maggie Osborne is a storyteller who consistently delivers all three."
—Nora Roberts

PRAIRIE MOON

by Maggie Osborne

Living on a rundown farm at the edge of a small Texas town, Della Ward is haunted by the bittersweet life she once lived with an adoring husband who died too soon. Then she sees a rugged stranger riding across the prairie toward her house. His presence awakens Della's heart, but she can never imagine the ways this man will forever change her life.

Lawman James Cameron believes in settling debts and living by honor. It may have taken him ten years to arrive at Della's door, but he's finally here and is determined to tell her the truth about the day her husband died. But one look at the woman whose picture he has carried with him for years and he knows that the truth may destroy them both.

Published by Ivy Books
Available wherever books are sold

Legend of The Hall

**Subscribe to the new Pillow Talk
e-newsletter—and receive all these
fabulous online features directly in
your e-mail inbox:**

♥ Exclusive essays and other features by major romance
writers like Linda Howard, Kristin Hannah,
Julie Garwood, and Suzanne Brockmann

♥ Exciting behind-the-scenes news from
our romance editors

♥ Special offers, including contests to win signed
romance books and other prizes

♥ Author tour information, and monthly announce-
ments about the newest books on sale

♥ A Pillow Talk readers forum, featuring feedback
from romance fans...like you!

Two easy ways to subscribe:
Go to **www.ballantinebooks.com/PillowTalk**
or send a blank e-mail to
join-PillowTalk@list.randomhouse.com.

Pillow Talk—
the romance e-newsletter brought to you by
Ballantine Books